AFTER THE FALL

AFTER THE FALL

THE

FALL

BRAD GRABER

ISBN: Paperback: 978-0-9976042-2-1
         eBook: 978-0-9976042-3-8

Cover design: Ronnie Seats
Interior page design: Jeff Brandenburg
Photograph: Yucel

Published by Dark Victory Press
brad@bradgraber.com
bradgraber.com

First printing: 2018

Printed in the United States of America   20180703

Dedication

To my late mother, who taught me to believe in myself.
For that, I most humbly thank her.

Just when the caterpillar thought the world was over,
it became a butterfly.
—Proverb

Acknowledgments

To Steven Bauer of Hollow Tree Literary Service who edited my book. I'm grateful for his attention to detail and guidance with storytelling. To Jeff Brandenburg who exceeded my expectations in design and layout and continues to be my friend. To Mark Woodworth for his copyediting expertise and to Ronnie Seats for the artistic cover design. Finally, to Yucel, who snapped the photograph of me on the back cover. Ah, the wonders of Photoshop.

1

Rikki braced herself as the traffic light at 73rd Avenue and Parson's Boulevard turned yellow. With one hand on the dashboard and the other gripping the door handle, she held her breath as her grandmother leaned forward and stepped on the gas. Three pigeons in the road broke into flight as the red Ford Mustang blasted through the intersection.

Rikki was furious. "Why did you do that?" she yelled. "Didn't you see those birds? You could have hurt them."

An overcast November morning in Queens, New York, and Rikki was being driven to school by her grandmother, Rita Goldenbaum. The weekend had been unusually cold, and by late Sunday afternoon, dark clouds had released the season's first snowfall. Now the temperatures were just above freezing, and the powdery white that had earlier beautified the brick and cement neighborhood had turned gray and messy in Monday morning's rush hour.

Rita let out an exuberant laugh. Her bright red hair, set in curlers and wrapped in a clear plastic kerchief, matched the chipped nail polish on her chubby hands. Rikki thought the color particularly unbecoming on a woman of Rita's age. "Honey, don't you know pigeons are just rats with wings? Filthy animals spreading disease wherever they go." A lit cigarette dangled from the corner of Rita's mouth, bobbing with each word.

Rikki rolled her eyes. "Why do you have to be so mean?" she said as she waved a hand to clear the air of cigarette smoke. "When are you going to stop that filthy habit? It's 2005 and you're still smoking."

"Mean?" Rita's voice was pure innocence as she shifted the cigarette from her mouth to her left hand. "There's not a mean bone in my body."

Never mind, Rikki thought, disgusted. She wasn't in the mood to play Rita's game.

"No, seriously," Rita said, slipping the tip of the Salem 100 out a slim opening of the driver's side window. A bit of ash flew off. "I really want to know. What did I say that was so terrible?" She looked over at Rikki. Her large brown eyes feigned concern as the car drifted from its lane.

Rikki had come to accept Rita as a complicated woman with many opinions, the chief of which was that life was unfair. A native New Yorker, born and raised in the Bronx, Rita spoke her mind. Whether her opinions were obnoxious, outrageous, or conventional, she wore them like a badge of honor. There was no filter. If it was on the brain, it came out the mouth.

"You know perfectly well what I'm talking about," Rikki said. She hated Rita's pretense almost as much as she hated her smoking.

Rita's voice rose an octave. "About vermin?"

Rikki shifted. "About everything. You're so negative."

"I'm edgy," Rita insisted, eyes focused on the road. "New Yorkers are sharp and sarcastic. That's just the way it is. I'd have thought by now, after years of living here, you'd be over all that Michigan niceness." She sniffed, as if being polite was to be avoided at all costs. "You're still not one of us. My goodness." Rita took a drag off her cigarette. "You're one stubborn young lady."

"I'll never be a New Yorker," Rikki muttered, a sadness gripping her heart as she rolled down her window to let in some fresh air.

The Mustang stopped at a red light. "Now honey, don't get all emotional on me." Rita's tone softened. "You've got to grow a thicker skin to survive in this world. Trust me. I know. I'm the expert," she boasted. "You know that I love you. Right?"

Rikki took a deep breath. Whenever they had words, Rita defaulted to pronouncements of love.

"Oh no," Rita said with a chortle as the light changed to green. "If you don't think I love you, you must really be mad. What else can I say, my darling? I keep forgetting. I have a very serious granddaughter."

Rikki barely listened as Rita rattled on. Her thoughts shifted to the upcoming day. High school had proved a hard adjustment. A junior, she was still struggling to fit in. There were so many students, and for a shy girl it was simply overwhelming. As the car approached a stop sign, Rikki grew increasingly anxious. Queens Hospital loomed ahead. They were at the halfway point. Soon she'd be in front of the school.

Rita let out a hacking cough, easing up on the gas before clearing her throat and once again accelerating. "And here I am, encouraging all your nonsense," she said, cigarette held high in the air as she took a deep breath. "You should be taking the bus like the other kids. You know your problem?" Rita lectured. "You've been raised like a fragile doll. Well, you're just like everyone else. The sooner you realize it, the better we'll all be. That imagination of yours …"

"I didn't imagine it," Rikki quickly defended herself. "It happened."

Rita waved the cigarette as if, by doing so, she could dismiss Rikki's truth. "Whatever happened, you've made too much of it … just like you always do. A big brouhaha over nothing."

Rikki pressed her eyes tightly shut. *Why did Rita have to bring it up again?* At the end of her sophomore year, walking to catch the bus in the morning, she'd been accosted by a young man. At first she thought he was going to ask for directions. He blocked her path forward. When he grabbed her by the arm, she became hysterical, dropping her schoolbooks and struggling with him until he let her go. She ran all the way home.

The encounter had only intensified her fear of strangers.

"This is such a safe neighborhood," Rita insisted as they passed a group of teenagers huddled at the corner, waiting for the light to change. "Look at them," she pointed. Two of the four were in the midst of a pushing match. The smaller one tripped and dropped to a knee, struggling to break his fall. "They're laughing and horsing around. Doing all the things kids do. Do they look afraid?"

Clearly, they were picking on the little kid. Rikki peered to see if she recognized any of the faces. No. None of them looked familiar.

"You should be over this nonsense by now," Rita griped. "I shouldn't have to drive you to school every day."

"I can't help it," Rikki answered, mindful that she was still uncomfortable negotiating the streets of Queens.

Rita repeated her familiar mantra. "There are lots of people in this world. The quicker you learn that, the better."

But Rikki couldn't help but be afraid. The borough of Queens was a giant melting pot of skin colors, religions, and ethnicities. Blacks, Hispanics, and whites. Jews, Italians, Indians, Greeks, and Vietnamese. More diversity than Rikki had ever been exposed to in suburban Detroit, where most everyone had been white.

"I know," Rikki meekly answered as they stopped for another light. Two boys ran past them, a third in close pursuit.

"You should be riding the bus," Rita repeated as they passed a bus stop where a group of children waited.

Rikki hated taking public transportation. The bus during the morning rush hour was too densely packed. If she was unable to get a seat, she dreaded touching the germ-covered metal poles, and she held her breath as strangers pushed past her, not wanting to breathe in their exhalations. As the bus bounced up and down, bags, umbrellas, and, sometimes, wandering hands rubbed up against her.

"There's no reason to be afraid," Rita insisted. The red tip of her cigarette glowed brightly as she took another drag.

But Rikki *was* afraid. Since moving in with her grandmother, she'd struggled to adjust to the world around her. Now and then, she'd have a glimpse of a happier time. But it was merely the dimmest of memories. The doctors had promised it would all come back eventually, but so far it hadn't. She had a terrible sense of a *before* and *after*, in which Queens was most definitely the *after*. And yet she did have flashes of recall about a life in Michigan. A lovely two-story brick house on a quiet, tree-lined street. A flagstone walkway that led up to a front door the color of gingerbread. Such memories contrasted sharply with the high-rise buildings that now surrounded her. The cement sidewalks that choked any bit of greenery from the landscape. When she asked Rita about what was wrong with her, Rita would become annoyed.

"Rikki, we've been through this, over and over. There's nothing wrong with you. You just need to live in the present. That's all we've got. This moment. No more."

"I want to go back to the doctor," Rikki had begged.

"That psychiatrist was a quack," Rita had insisted. "You're done with all that now. I won't have you up at night crying because you think something's wrong. You've just had an *emotional upset*. Plenty of people lose their mothers when they're young. Madonna. Rosie O'Donnell. They've gone on to have successful lives. And so will you."

Given time, the crying did eventually stop. As puberty kicked in, Rikki's body changed, and so did her focus. Looking in the mirror, she cringed at her oily skin, untamed wavy brown hair, and hopelessly oval face. The small gap between her two front teeth made her unwilling to smile. Convinced that she wasn't pretty, she'd recently gained weight, and because her breasts were still not fully developed, her figure remained awkward. She hid herself in oversized, baggy clothing. The bigger, the better. *I look like Darlene Conner from "Roseanne,"* she thought. *A cross between a tomboy and a mess.*

"I told your mother that living in that lily-white suburb was a bad idea," Rita said as the car hit a pothole and bounced. "But your mother was so set in her ways. 'Detroit isn't lily white,' she'd say. 'Maybe not,' I'd tell her. 'But Birmingham, Michigan, sure is.'"

"It wasn't *all* white," Rikki protested, eager to defend the mother she couldn't quite remember.

"It may be green in the summer," Rita snapped, "but Birmingham, Michigan, is white, white, and white. It might be a lovely place to live, I'll give you that, but it's not the real world. The real world is Queens."

"No," Rikki whispered as she rebelled at Rita's assertion. "That's *your* world."

"Don't be fresh," Rita snapped as the light ahead turned yellow. "I still have my hearing, thank you very much."

Rikki braced herself. "You better slow down."

Rita gunned it, just barely making it through as the light turned red.

"Stop telling me how to drive!" Rita complained. "My goodness. How about we listen to the radio? Maybe that'll get *your mind off of the road.*" She reached over and fumbled with the dials, ash dropping onto the leather console.

Rikki pushed her grandmother's hand away as the car drifted from its lane. "I'll do it. Pay attention to your driving."

With the turn of a knob, Rush Limbaugh's voice bathed the car in warm, somber tones as he discussed the recent election of Angela Merkel as the first female Chancellor of Germany. Rikki winced. "How can you listen to him? He gives me the creeps."

Rita took another drag on her cigarette. It was getting down to the end. "You know I love Rush. Next to Bill O'Reilly, he's the only one who can make any sense of this crazy world."

"But he's a drug addict," Rikki insisted. "All that doctor-shopping for prescriptions."

"That poor man was in pain. You don't know what it's like. When you're older, everything hurts. And when a doctor prescribes painkillers, you're supposed to take them."

"I thought you weren't old." Rikki smirked as she turned off the radio in the middle of Rush's diatribe about a new Iraqi constitution. "Maybe I should call you *Grandma* from now on?"

"Don't you dare," Rita flared, taking her eyes off the road just long enough to offer her granddaughter a sharp glare and pass her what remained of her Salem 100. "Now stop teasing me and get rid of this."

Rikki took the smoking stub from her grandmother's outstretched fingers. She rolled the passenger window down. "You promised you'd stop smoking."

"I know," Rita said.

"How about making that your 2006 New Year's resolution?"

Rita shrugged a shoulder.

"It's such a disgusting habit," Rikki said as she tossed the butt out the passenger window at the precise moment that a gust of wind spiraled the hot poker back into the car. "Oh, my God," Rikki screamed, wildly flailing, lifting herself up, arching her back, struggling against the seatbelt that was secured about her waist.

"What?" Rita yelled, as she looked over at Rikki. "Are you okay?"

The car bounced up onto the curb. Rita let out an "Oh, my God," as she struggled to straighten the wheel. Back on the road again, she overcorrected, sending the Mustang into a spin. As Rita and Rikki screamed, the car spun across two lanes, crossing the median, before coming to rest parallel to oncoming traffic.

◆

Harry Aldon was tired. He hated getting up early to walk the dog. But, living in Phoenix, Arizona, that's what he needed to do. Tender paws burnt easily on superheated pavement, and even though it was mid-November, and the intense triple-digit summer heat had long since dissipated, dogs are creatures of habit with built-in alarm clocks and a demand for consistent routine. At six a.m. Harry opened his eyes. Beetle, his wire-haired fox terrier, was wide awake and whining. The little dog's torso was pressed up against the adjacent pillow. His head rested on his two front paws as he stared into Harry's eyes.

Harry blinked.

Beetle stretched, thrusting his little body back into a downward-dog position before standing up on the bed with a brisk shake.

"Okay, okay," Harry groaned. "I'm getting up."

Harry lifted Beetle off the bed. "Good boy," Harry said as sixteen pounds of squirming energy wiggled intently in his arms. He lowered Beetle to the carpet. "No more jumping for you, old friend. We've got to keep you intact."

Grabbing a pair of black Nike gym shorts and an old gray T-shirt, Harry lumbered into the bathroom to wash his face. A nearby night-light offered the softest of illumination as he looked into the mirror. He was nearly fifty-five years old. Still vigorous. Still lean. His blue eyes clear and bright. Tiny wrinkles were just beginning to appear about his eyes and his mouth, and despite his age, he remained surprised by their presence. His dark gray curly hair, a crushed bed mess, had recently turned an interesting salt and pepper, making him, he believed, appear even older. He ran a hand through the thick curls, pushing them away from his face, only to watch as they bounced back and covered his forehead.

"Got you, buddy," he said, lifting Beetle up and carrying him off to the garage where he attached a leash to the terrier's collar. Beetle's tongue hung out of his mouth as he panted with excitement. Harry could feel the dog's rapid heartbeat in the palm of his hand.

With Beetle's collar secured, Harry pushed the button to raise the garage door. It was dark outside. The cool November air embraced Harry and Beetle as they made their way through the Arizona Biltmore neighborhood. The sweet scent of new winter grass, freshly planted and watered by early-morning automatic sprinklers, flooded Harry's senses as he strolled quickly behind Beetle, who, despite his advanced years, seemed fiercely energized by the morning hour.

As he turned a corner on the path, a distant figure loomed. Harry closed his eyes. He wished he didn't have to run into anyone at such an early hour. It was hard to be congenial when the power of conversation seemed beyond him.

"Hello!" called the figure of a woman, waving, as dawn began to break in the east.

"Hello," Harry politely said, alarmed that his tongue seemed stuck to the roof of his mouth.

It was Lil. Lil Turner. He'd run into her off and on for the last few weeks. Lil was new to the neighborhood. She'd introduced herself one morning as Harry rambled by, quite oblivious to her perky figure. Though she tended to wear her shoulder-length blonde hair tucked behind her ears, on this particular morning it was rolled tightly in a bun high atop her head. With no makeup, and in her fitted, pink yoga outfit, flat midriff fully exposed, Lil appeared much younger than her fifty years.

"It should be a beautiful day," Lil offered, examining the sky. She held a newspaper, wrapped up tightly in plastic, like a baton.

Harry nodded, hoping he might pass Lil without much interaction.

"You're awfully quiet this morning," Lil said, as Beetle sniffed her fluffy pink slippers. "Hey there, Beetle, you sweet thing. How are *you* this morning?"

Harry wondered what Beetle might do if he ever got hold of those slippers.

"I just woke up," Harry said in his own defense. "I'm not much for talk in the morning."

Lil laughed. "Oh, Harry Aldon. You're such a dud."

"Thank you, Lil," Harry said as he pushed past. "So nice of you to say."

Lil laughed again. "Honestly, *some men*," she called out.

Harry looked back and waved, hoping to signal the end of the interaction.

"Do you have plans for lunch?" Lil called, hands on her hips, newspaper tucked under her arm.

"I'm working on my novel," Harry said.

Unable to take a hint, she continued. "So, you're not going to eat?"

Harry shook his head no.

"What's a girl to do?" she asked, disappointment heavy in her voice.

Harry ignored her as Beetle humped his back, taking care of business. Harry bent down with a plastic bag as Beetle took two steps forward and kicked some loose dirt backward, catching Harry in the face. "Jesus," Harry yelled, yanking on the leash. But Beetle offered one more kick before wandering over to sniff a nearby bush.

"That's rich," Lil laughed as she strolled over to Harry. "Someday that dog is going to kick something worse than dirt in your face, Harry Aldon. And you'll deserve it." She wagged her newspaper, like an index finger, at him. "Women don't like men who play games."

Harry blushed. "I don't know what you're talking about, Lil."

"Oh, yes, you do," she insisted, turning sideways in a provocative pose.

Harry sighed. "Lil … it is six a.m. Give me a break."

And then, as if on cue, Beetle whined. He was ready to continue the walk. It was time to move on.

◆

"Are you okay?" Rita asked, clutching the steering wheel of the car.

A large city bus had stopped just short of the passenger side. The bus driver glared down at them through the bus windshield. Rikki looked away, embarrassed by the man's angry face.

"Yes," Rikki answered, her mouth dry, her nerves shaken. She reached between her legs and retrieved the cigarette butt, now extinguished, and pitched it out the window. "I have a hole in my jeans," she said, poking about with her finger. "I think I burned my leg."

Car horns blew as Rita revved into action. She shifted into reverse and slowly backed up, maneuvering the car until it was in the correct lane and facing the right direction. More horns blared as she shifted into drive. "Keep your goddamn shirts on," Rita shrieked, as if any of the other drivers could hear her. She accelerated, reaching twenty-five miles per hour before pulling her foot back off the pedal.

"You should pull over and let everyone pass," Rikki suggested, turning around to see the line of cars behind them.

"If I do, you'll never get to school," Rita said, even though she did as Rikki suggested. As the cars whizzed by, Rita held up a middle finger to the driver side window and wildly shouted, "Here's a present for you!"

Rikki blushed crimson. "If it hadn't been for that cigarette…" She decided there wasn't any point in saying any more. Her heart pounded as she relived the car's spinning. She'd never liked amusement park rides. They made her nauseous.

"I know," Rita quickly agreed.

"Then why?" Rikki blurted out, unable to contain herself. "Everyone knows cigarettes cause cancer. How can you still be smoking?"

She'd asked the same question the night before when she caught Rita sitting on the terrace, a cigarette burning brightly.

Rita opened her mouth as if she were about to speak, but nothing came out. Arching her eyebrows, she seemed to struggle to find the right words. "It's such a hard habit to break. I've been doing it for so many years."

Rikki thought she made no sense. "So, when are you going to stop?"

"I can stop anytime I want," Rita quickly answered, a lilt to her voice as the car once again entered the flow of traffic. "Stopping isn't the issue … I've stopped a thousand times. It's *quitting* that's tough."

Typical Rita, Rikki thought, irritated. *Not taking any of this seriously.*

"Trust me," Rita went on. "If I could, I would. It's so darn expensive. When I think of the money I've wasted on those cigarettes …" Rita shook her head. "It just makes my blood boil. But I'm addicted. Maybe we should look on the bright side. It could have been heroin."

Rikki was shocked. "You've tried heroin?"

"I didn't say I *tried it*," Rita said indignantly. "But if I had, I'm sure it would have been worse than these damn cigarettes."

Rikki couldn't help laughing. It was the kind of absurd remark Rita was especially adept at. And despite all of Rita's failings and Rikki's struggles with her, there were moments of levity that they shared. Rita could be entertaining. That, and the fact that Rikki had nowhere else to go. Rita was *home.*

"I hope you won't be too mad at your old grandma," Rita offered, her tone sincere and contrite even as she referred to herself in a way that Rikki couldn't.

"You only say 'grandma' when you're trying to manipulate me," Rikki pointed out.

Rita smiled. "See. You're just like me. Sharp as a tack. No one can pull the wool over your eyes."

Rikki doubted that was true. Her grandmother was just humoring her.

"I'm proud of you," Rita said, turning to give Rikki a warm smile. "You're an intelligent girl. You mark my words. Being smart will come in handy. Let the other girls be pretty and silly. Not my Rikki. You keep to your studies, and someday, you'll be a big success."

If Rita had taken a knife and stabbed Rikki, it couldn't have been more painful. Rikki was convinced that Rita thought she wasn't pretty.

"Now let's get you to school," Rita said as Queens High came into view.

◆

"Let me off over there." Rikki pointed to the corner.

"Don't be silly," Rita answered. "I'll drop you in front of the school."

"No, here," Rikki insisted. "I'll walk the rest of the way."

Rita shrugged. "Anyone would think you were embarrassed to be seen with me." She patted the plastic kerchief encasing her spoolies. "Is it my hair? Is that the problem?" She peered into the rear-view mirror.

Rikki sighed. Some truths were best conveyed with silence.

"Okay, no one has to tell me the score. Wait till you're my age," Rita said as she pulled over to the curb. "You think it's easy being Miss Queens, the reigning beauty of the neighborhood?" She barely controlled a guffaw. "You have to work hard to look this good."

"I'm sure," Rikki said as she dismissed her grandmother, who was now boldly laughing. She leaned over and gave Rita a fast peck on the cheek. "I'll see you later. Thanks for the ride." She stepped out of the car and slammed the door behind her. Looking back, she could see Rita inside, wildly waving.

As she walked through the gates and up the stairs of Queens High, Rikki merged into the rush of students. The hallways were packed. Slightly out of breath from climbing to the third floor, Rikki headed to first-period English. She was relieved to finally slip into the classroom. Among the crush of students, she'd felt intensely uncomfortable. Was she moving too slowly? Too fast? Not pretty enough? Was she taking up too much space in the hallway? Gnawing self-doubts were always with her, but nowhere as magnified, or as powerful, as in the halls of Queens High.

The class had been reading Dreiser's *An American Tragedy,* and Rikki had a well-worn used copy atop her books. Rita had taken it out of the library. "There's no point in buying a new book," Rita had scolded, "when there's a perfectly good library nearby."

Rikki had read well ahead, eager to be absorbed into the burgeoning love affair. But the book was nothing like the movie *A Place in the Sun,* with Elizabeth Taylor and Montgomery Clift, which she'd watched breathlessly with Rita on Turner Classic Movies. In the film, the characters' names were different, and Rikki didn't recognize much from the novel. *Would they ever get to the love story?* she wondered, her fingers dancing on the cover of the thick paperback.

Mr. Rosenfeld, a middle-aged man with gray hair and a matching mustache and goatee, stood at the front of the class and waited for the last of the stragglers to take their seats. He was dressed in a bright red sweater, a light blue shirt, and a black bow tie with white polka dots. The sternness of his manner contrasted wildly with the boldness of his clothing choices as he assessed the students before him.

As soon as the bell sounded, Mr. Rosenfeld began expounding on Dreiser's narrative, and though Rikki was enjoying the novel, a certain sleepiness came over her. When Mr. Rosenfeld turned his back to the class and began to write on the blackboard, Rikki was thinking about handsome Montgomery Clift. She jumped when her daydream was interrupted by a tap on the shoulder.

"Rikki, I'll meet you in the cafeteria for lunch later," Barbra whispered from behind. "I have something important to ask."

Rikki turned around.

Barbra Winer smiled, revealing a mouth full of silver. Her hair, dyed a gothic black, was piled high atop her head, knotted loosely, strands falling here and there. She wore dark red lipstick, which clashed with her olive-green blouse covered in ruffles.

Rikki thought she looked like a pirate in a beehive hairdo.

"That girl's on her way to becoming a tramp," Rita had said on more than one occasion when Barbra had visited. "That rat's nest. And those clothes. And the way she swoons over boys. Her mother needs to get that one in hand," Rita had warned Rikki, a finger in the air. "You mark my words. She's bad news."

Rikki had given up reminding Rita that Barbra's mother was long dead.

Barbra leaned forward, arms resting on the desk, stretching herself forward awkwardly. "It's a gift from my stepmother," she said defensively as Rikki's eyes fell upon one of her sleeves. "She *forced* me to wear it today." Barbra made a face as if a bad odor had come over her. "Isn't it perfectly awful? I tried to say no, but *she kept pushing.* And you know how she is. If I don't do what she wants, she talks with my father. It was just easier to wear it." Barbra shrugged as if it was all fine.

Rikki nodded that she understood, but if Rita had ever made her wear such an ugly blouse, she was certain she'd skip school altogether and spend the rest of the day in Flushing Meadows Park roaming the empty pavilions that had once hosted the 1964 New York World's Fair. Rikki loved the park with its iron spheres and weathered pavilions. So peaceful and quiet.

Mr. Rosenfeld was done at the board and called the class back to order by tapping a wooden pointer on the edge of his desk. Rikki joined the others as she spun about to full attention.

"Can anyone," Mr. Rosenfeld asked, his voice edged with excitement as he looked out at the assembled class of juniors, "tell me what Dreiser's motivation might have been for telling this particular story?" He held the hardcopy of Dreiser's book pressed to his chest.

There was silence.

"Well, it certainly is a wonderful story," he said with a big grin. "It's a classic tale of America. The hopes and dreams of a young man who struggles to better himself. So today," and Mr. Rosenfeld turned to the chalkboard where he'd written out the word *IDENTITY* in capital letters, "we're going to discuss identity—who we are as Americans, and what it means to be an American in Dreiser's world."

Rikki felt herself growing impatient. She didn't want to talk about

Dreiser's America. What was the point? How could a discussion about another time and place be instructive? She started to doodle mindlessly in her open notebook.

"So let's begin," Mr. Rosenfeld said, his voice rising to an excited pitch. "Who'd like to start? Who can tell me what is driving Clyde to leave Kansas City?"

The classroom was quiet. Rikki drew a dinosaur that looked an awful lot like Dino from *The Flintstones*. Then she heard her name being called. Startled, she looked up to find Mr. Rosenfeld standing before her, looking down.

"Rikki, let's start with you. What do you think? Why does Clyde want to leave Kansas City?"

"Well," she began, "he's unhappy."

"Yes," Mr. Rosenfeld nodded. "But a lot of people are unhappy. That doesn't necessarily make them leave home."

"But there's nothing for him there," she said somewhat indignantly, her heart beating rapidly, hoping that Mr. Rosenfeld might turn his attention elsewhere. "It all seemed so hopeless."

"Is that the only reason?" Mr. Rosenfeld asked, his blue eyes looking through her.

Rikki thought for a moment. "And he was running away from that accident. The car hit a little girl and killed her. And even though he wasn't driving, Clyde was afraid he might be prosecuted."

Mr. Rosenfeld nodded his approval.

"But he was *always* afraid ..." Rikki continued, as she realized the motivation of the character. "Afraid he'd never rise above his parents' station in life. That he'd always be the poor son of missionaries. Trapped in a life that he didn't want."

"Yes," Mr. Rosenfeld smiled, shifting his attention from Rikki to the class. "Dreiser is exploring the class system in America. And this is but one story of a young man who wants more." He raised the book high in the air. "Clyde represents everyman. He's all of us," Mr. Rosenfeld declared, just as his wrist suddenly gave way and the thick novel plummeted to the floor, landing hard on his foot.

Nervous giggles filled the classroom.

"Okay, everyone," he said as he attempted to restore order, an expression of intense pain on his face. "Start reading the assignment for tonight, and I'll be right back." And with an awkward step and hop, and then two larger hops, he left the classroom.

◆

"How's he doing?" Harry asked Dr. Newbar.

Harry held Beetle in place as the little dog squirmed on the vet's steel examining table, head hidden under Harry's arm, butt toward Newbar. Harry stroked Beetle's hindquarters in a steady motion, trying to calm him.

"Good," Newbar announced, removing the stethoscope from Beetle's underbelly and looking up. His kind hazel eyes belied his formal demeanor. The certificates on the wall indicated that he'd graduated from veterinary school with high honors and yet he was as easy to talk with as any average Joe on the street. "Everything seems normal," he said, patting Beetle on his haunch. "Of course, he still has that heart murmur."

"He's had that since he was a puppy," Harry pointed out.

Newbar nodded. "As for the coughing, I think it's just a little choking. Dogs get it as they age. It happens to people, too. We begin to forget to fully swallow. Hasn't that ever happened to you?" Newbar asked, then, without waiting for Harry to answer, added "So we cough."

Harry took in the news. "So I'm worried about nothing?"

Newbar broke into a big grin. "At least for today. Yes."

"Oh, good," Harry said, then lifted Beetle off the table and nestled him in his arms. "See, boy, it's nothing to worry about."

Harry breathed a sigh of relief. Working at home, he'd come to rely on Beetle to keep him on schedule. The life of a writer can be all-consuming; once the imagination is fired, the world melts away. But Beetle kept Harry grounded, connected. One yelp and Harry knew it was time to take Beetle out. A whine and Harry grabbed a treat stored in a blue jar embossed with the word "Cookies" that sat on his credenza.

If it weren't for Beetle ... and Richard ... Harry was certain he'd be completely isolated from the rest of the world. *Good news*, he thought, as he stood at his vet's checkout counter waiting for his credit card to clear. *Richard, we're so lucky. It was nothing at all. Just a cough.*

◆

Rikki hurried along the school corridor, pushed forward by the crowd. Everyone seemed to be speaking at once. A cacophony echoed through the building, making it impossible even to recognize the English language in the babble. It was noon and Rikki's next period was lunch. She stopped at her hall locker to drop off her books. Pressed up against the cold metal, she twisted out her locker combination, glancing over at the nearby trophy case. She was grateful for the glass display. Without its presence, she doubted she'd be able to find her locker so quickly.

"Rikki, can I have a word with you before you go to lunch?" Mr. Rosenfeld had followed her.

She glanced at her watch. "Sure," she said as she placed her books in the locker, holding onto the brown lunch bag. She turned to give him her full attention.

"I've been impressed with your work in my class. Not only do you have real insight into the literature we're reading, but you're an excellent writer," he said, his smile warm and engaging, "and I think you should consider entering the District's writing contest. It's a $1,000 prize. And it comes with a college scholarship." He winked, his blue eyes sparkling. "You should give it a shot."

Rikki was surprised. She hadn't considered entering. She hadn't thought she really had any talent. And certainly not as a writer. Rita had always stressed the importance of being able to support oneself. Rikki knew that, whatever she did in the future, it had to pay well. *You can't rely on a man*, Rita's voice echoed in her head. *Men come and go.*

Don't wind up like me, working retail... spending your days in lady's shoes. Get an education and become a professional.

Rikki wondered if being a writer paid well.

"You're talented," Mr. Rosenfeld said. "Don't waste it." He hurried off down the hall at the sound of the bell.

Rikki glanced at the trophy case. She wondered about the students whose faces were immortalized behind the glass. Where were they now? Had they achieved their dreams? How had they managed to survive all this confusion? She peered into her open locker. The cold, dark space seemed suddenly warm and inviting. If only she could climb inside, close the door, and hide.

The moment passed.

She headed to the cafeteria with the books she needed for her afternoon classes, a brown paper bag perched precariously on top, pressed to her chest. Navigating her way down the steps to the basement, she kept her eyes cast downward, only looking up when she heard the clanging of metal utensils against casserole-sized serving dishes of lasagna and meat loaf. She gagged at the funky smell: warmed-over spices—cumin, pepper, paprika—mixed with what she thought was a hint of wet dog. Students shuffled in winding lines, trays sliding along. The air squeaked with the high-pitched sound of chairs, metal tips scraping against the linoleum floor.

On the other wall of the cafeteria, she spotted a stack of trays on a conveyor belt. There were remnants of lunches half-eaten—browning apple cores, juice boxes and milk cartons, plastic wrappers entangled with empty chip bags. She swallowed hard, numbing herself to her surroundings as she walked past the cafeteria and into the noisy lunchroom. Mouths moved, bodies twisted and turned; the room was a snake pit of pulsing energy. She was desperate for an open spot in which to settle.

"Rikki," Barbra's voice called, "I'm over here."

Barbra waved Rikki over to a table at the back of the room.

Rikki experienced a terrific sense of relief. She no longer was lost in the crowd. She had escaped the middle of the room, found a place on the periphery.

"I don't see why your grandmother can't also drive *me* to school," Barbra complained. "I promise to be on time."

Rikki picked at a BLT on white toast as Barbra ate out of a plastic container. Some sort of salad which emanated a strong smell of Italian dressing. "You kept her waiting," Rikki reminded her. "She doesn't like to wait."

Barbra wiped her mouth with a napkin. "That happened once. And it was weeks ago."

Rikki shrugged. There wasn't much point in discussing it any further. Once Rita made up her mind, there was nothing she could do.

"You should see me in the morning," Barbra said as she speared a large piece of lettuce and shoved it into her mouth. She continued to talk. "I run all the way to the bus. I keep looking over my shoulder for that man. Tell me again?" she said with a great flurry of drama. "What did he look like?"

Rikki put her sandwich down. She didn't want to think about the assault.

"You should have waited for me that day and there wouldn't have been a problem," Barbra said emphatically. "I'd have kicked him right in the balls."

"Well, good," Rikki said, annoyed that Barbra seemed to view her nightmare as a form of lunchtime entertainment. "Then you should be totally safe walking by yourself in the morning."

"God, Rikki." Barbra rolled her eyes. "What's the point of being best friends if we can't ever talk? You always get mad at me when we talk about this."

Rikki shrugged as she bit into her sandwich. A stringy piece of bacon slid out and dangled from her lips. She quickly pushed the bacon into her mouth, hoping no one other than Barbra had seen her.

Barbra leaned forward, her voice lighter. "So how was homeroom? Did you see him? What was he wearing?"

Rikki pretended innocence, even though she knew darn well what he had worn. A pair of denims and a tight pink shirt, slightly open at the collar. She and Barbra were fixated on the same boy. But she didn't want to appear quite as silly. For Barbra, he wasn't any boy. He was *the boy*. Barney. The boy who made most of the girls in school ignite with excitement.

Rikki had giggled when she first learned his name. "Really? *Barney?* Is he purple? Can he sing and dance? Does he have dinosaur friends?"

Barbra hadn't laughed.

Rikki wiped her mouth. "Yes, I saw him. Tall, dark, and handsome as ever. Nothing's changed since you saw him yesterday."

Rikki and Barbra had been friends for three years ... ever since Barbra had moved from Sheepshead Bay in Brooklyn to Queens. A friendship formed less by choice and more by proximity.

"You should get to know her," Rita had suggested. "She just lives three floors below us. You're practically new here. *She's* new here. It seems that you two girls are destined to be friends!"

But Rikki hadn't wanted to befriend Barbra. Not because Rita had made the suggestion, though that alone could be grounds for resisting, but because Barbra seemed too weird. And, being keenly uncomfortable with her own lowly social status among the kids who lived in the building, Rikki had no interest in being friends with a new girl who looked even odder than she did. For Barbra had frizzy, bright orange hair, before she discovered black dye and an iron, and her clothes were desperately in need of replacement, patched here and there. Her elbows and knees appeared darker than the rest of her skin, and there were some days when Rikki picked up an unsavory scent emanating from the new neighbor. In short, Barbra was the perfect dork. A walking, talking carrot stick, in need of a good bath. But Rita was not to be put off, and in her typical boisterous way, she bullied her granddaughter into befriending Barbra. It wasn't until later that Rita changed her mind. But by then it was too late.

Barbra stopped eating, again wiping the corner of her mouth with a napkin. She focused her attention on Rikki as her voice began to rise. "Did Barney talk to you? Say hello?"

Barney Appleton rarely talked … a fact Rikki knew only too well, since she sat next to him in homeroom. She'd made a study of his poor communication skills, often wincing at the way he handled himself. He seemed to struggle with a devastating shyness, surprising in someone so good-looking. He frequently glanced down, offering one-word answers when one word was the least he could say. His favorite utterance seemed to be *yes,* delivered so softly that Rikki was certain she'd mistaken his merely taking a breath for saying the actual word.

Barney hardly spoke to anyone.

He sat quietly, brown wavy hair falling angelically about his ears, framing the angular face with its strong jaw line and high cheekbones. His blue eyes seemed to peek out into the world, oblivious to the powerful effect of his physical presence.

When Barney focused his attention on Rikki, which was rare, she became instantly uncomfortable, desperately wanting his admiration while praying he'd look away and not see the blemish on her nose, or her mismatched sweater and blouse, or an uncontrolled eye twitch, or the one-hundred-and-one flaws she imagined herself to possess every morning when she awoke. *Ugh. I should be in a freak show,* she'd think, all the while desperate to attract Barney's attention.

And though it was hard work to get Barney to talk, it was even harder to sit next to such a handsome boy and say nothing. So Rikki engaged in small talk. She asked questions. Endless questions. And though it was awkward, Rikki soldiered on.

"Isn't it a nice day?" she'd say.

He'd look over and smile.

"Did you walk to school this morning?"

He'd nod affirmatively.

"Would you like a mint?" She blushed. She didn't have any mints. She breathed a sigh of relief when he declined.

It was hopeless. Dull questions followed by uninterested head nods peppered with a *yes* every now and then, before Barney Appleton finally appeared ready to say something. Rikki's heart swooned as

Barney smiled, the corners of his mouth lifting upward to reveal the most beautiful pair of dimples as he formed his precious words. Rikki's world seemed brighter. Time stopped as she glanced at those perfect lips, watched as they parted. She held her breath.

"Aren't *you* nosey," he said, head slightly titled, before turning to look away.

Rikki winced at the memory. "We didn't talk this morning," she lied to Barbra.

"Oh, Rikki ... if he was sitting next to me—" She twirled her long black hair about her finger. "—I'd be unable to control myself. He's so freaking gorgeous. I'd probably sit in his lap."

Rikki wondered what that might be like. "No. I don't think I could ever do that," she said, somewhat disappointed in herself.

Barbra sighed, and then offered up a half-eaten powdered donut as the bell rang. It took a moment for Rikki to grab it out of Barbra's fingers. The dusty sugar coating stuck to the roof of her mouth as she gathered up the remnants of her lunch and her book pack and headed off to her next class.

◆

In Phoenix, Lil finished a second cup of green tea, seated at her kitchen counter. The warmth of the liquid calmed her as she closed the newspaper and stared out onto the patio and her small garden filled with potted plants and hanging baskets, where a gray dove perched atop a brown wicker chair. In the summer, Lil enjoyed her tea outdoors before the heat of the sun achieved its full effect. Only recently had she opted for the warmth of the house, as the mornings had grown decidedly cooler with the onset of November.

She checked her cell phone. No new messages. That was good. Her first yoga class was scheduled for eleven o'clock. She still had a few hours.

She wondered if her business partner had arrived on time to open up the studio. The summer morning when Julia had overslept, the place was blazing hot. Lil couldn't help but laugh at the memory of her middle-aged patrons, stretched out in the downward-dog pose, sweating profusely. She had to admit, it seemed like the appropriate punishment for those adults who had let their bodies go to hell. But then, that was back in August when triple-digit temperatures plagued Phoenix.

Yoga had become her second career after working as a grade school teacher in the Phoenix inner city. Eight years of standing in front of a room of seven- and eight-year-olds had proven to be more than she could handle. There had been too many moments when she felt more like a referee than an educator. She hadn't realized until her final year of teaching that she didn't particularly like children. It hit her hard one day when she was struggling to maintain order. Sweet cherubic faces, arms outstretched, vibrating little bodies with mouths constantly moving, desperate to release their pent-up energy. There was no impulse control in the room, and instead of being the person in charge, she'd grown weary of the struggle. Tired of the little hands, the little eyes, and the constant talking, she realized if she didn't do something different, she'd go completely mad.

And so she'd found yoga. And then Julia. And then the yoga studio. And that had been fifteen years ago.

She wiped down the counter as the doorbell chimed. "Who could that be?" she said aloud, tossing the sponge in the sink. She opened her front door in time to see the UPS driver pull away.

Why, she thought, *couldn't it be Ed McMahon with Publisher's Clearinghouse?* If it were, she'd be on her way to the vineyards of Italy or France. Soaking up the beauty of the countryside. Enjoying everything the world of travel had to offer: wine, food, and adventure. And men. Handsome, dark, swarthy men.

She shouted out a "Thank you!" even as the UPS truck disappeared around a turn.

She picked up the small package and pressed it close to her chest as she thought, *At least there are still available men in Phoenix. Like that delicious Harry Aldon.*

The mere thought of her sexy neighbor put a smile on her face.

◆

"We're back," Harry called out as Beetle lumbered over to his water bowl. The house was still. Harry opened the fridge and peeked inside. "Geez," he said, eyes scanning the empty shelves. *I've got to get to the* supermarket. There's nothing here."

Check the bin. There's fruit.

It was Richard's voice. Deep, warm, and reassuring. The voice in Harry's head. A voice that he'd used to comfort himself through all the years of loss.

"Oh yeah," Harry answered. He'd put on a few pounds as of late. *A healthy choice…until I get back to the gym.*

The voice. *If you don't take it off now, it'll be harder later.*

Harry had no doubt.

"Beetle's okay," Harry said as he pulled out a Gala apple from the refrigerator and inspected it. Beetle searched the kitchen floor for fallen scraps.

That's good news. It's not his time. But when it is, I'll be there.

Harry was suddenly frightened. *I don't want to think about that,* he thought emphatically, his eyes glistening as he glanced out the kitchen window and spotted a dove waddling along the flagstone around his pool. "Gosh, I love this time of year," he said, changing the subject.

Beetle looked up and cocked his head as if Harry were talking to him.

Harry washed the apple. He reached for a napkin in a large blue bowl decorated with lemons that he and Richard had purchased on a trip to Italy in 1987. Harry fingered the bowl. *We bought this in Portofino? It was a beautiful day. Afterward, we went up to the roof of the hotel and sunned ourselves. And all those European men were wearing skimpy bathing suits.* Harry smiled at the memory. "That was a lot of eye candy."

Harry reflected as he took another bite of the apple. They'd been young, invincible. Nothing could stop them. Not long before, he'd thought he'd never find anyone to share his life with. Then Richard had come along and taken hold of him.

You were innocent. I couldn't resist.

Harry leaned against the counter as he savored the last of the apple. Beetle was nearby in a sit position, staring up at him. His brown eyes seemed to search Harry's face as if waiting for a word he'd recognize, like *eat, treat,* or *play.*

Innocent, Harry thought. *You certainly brought me out of my shell.*

Hey, I didn't bring you out… I launched you out.

"You were never ashamed," Harry said. *Never wished to be anything but who you were.*

Who else could I be? It's too silly to even imagine.

Harry nodded. *You've always been a mystery to me,* he thought, as he tossed the apple core into the trash. "How did you manage to be so confident?"

It helped that I'm not crazy like you, the voice echoed.

I suppose so, Harry agreed, as he added water to Beetle's bowl. "There you go, boy. How's that?"

Beetle lapped at the bowl, splashing liquid on the floor. Harry grabbed a paper towel and wiped it up.

"Okay … come on, boy. Let's get to work. We can't stand around all day talking if we ever expect to finish that novel."

Beetle looked up, giving Harry his full attention.

"Come on," Harry repeated, and with a wave of his hand, Beetle charged down the hall and disappeared into Harry's office.

2

Rita waited impatiently for the dryer to enter its final spin cycle.

She hated laundry day.

Why an eight-story apartment building with twenty apartments per floor had a laundry room with only four washing machines and four dryers was a maddening mystery. To beat the rush, Rita arrived at six-thirty in the morning, and even at that early hour, one or two loads were already up and running. Even so, she refused, unlike many of her neighbors, to sit on the hard, wooden bench near the door, reading a novel, and waiting to move the laundry from the washing machine to the dryer and then onto the folding table. And now that she drove Rikki to school in the morning, she had to be on the road somewhere between adding the fabric softener and the final rinse. Neighbors left angry notes in her laundry basket, complaining about her inattention to the timing of the chore. Lately, she'd found wet clothes sitting in the white plastic laundry basket atop a commandeered washing machine, waiting to go into the dryer.

"Don't these people have anything better to do?" Rita had complained to Rikki as she prepared dinner. A hot rotisserie chicken from the grocery store sat on the counter, waiting to be carved.

Rikki held the offending note in her hand. "This says you left the laundry sitting for over forty-five minutes."

Rita sniffed. "You know Tuesday is my day off. I get distracted. Regis and Kelly were on."

"Well, that doesn't seem right," Rikki confessed, siding with the neighbors.

Rita snorted as she hacked at the chicken. "It's like living in China or India," she declared, though she'd never been to either place. "People on top of people."

Rikki crushed the note into a ball. "And they're all going through our laundry."

"Oh?" was all Rita could manage, her eyes wide with the sudden realization. "They are!" She held the carving knife in the air. "Examining our dainties. Touching our clean clothes with their grubby hands."

And so Rita made a decision. She would pay closer attention. Perhaps bring a magazine with her.

The next Tuesday, she was there early. *God, it's hot in here,* she thought, as she scanned a *Reader's Digest* and waited for the dryer to go into a final spin. The intense floral smell of detergent permeated the place. *This is Seymour's fault,* she groused as her eye settled on a Holland America Line advertisement to cruise the Caribbean. *We could have had a house,* she raged, still thinking of her former husband, even though they'd divorced decades ago and the poor man was long dead.

A stray voice broke her inner tirade.

"Rita?"

It was Helen Winer from 3L.

In her early forties, Helen was dressed like a teenager in tight blue jeans, sparkly red sneakers, and a high-necked top that hung loosely about her emaciated frame. *Dear God,* Rita thought. *Eat something, for Christ's sake! I'm nauseated just looking at you.* But instead she said, "Oh, Helen. I didn't see you there." Smiling to herself. *You must have slid under the door.*

"I only just came down," Helen answered, laundry basket in her veiny hands as she scanned the room. "Not one machine free? Can you believe this?"

"It's a full house," Rita intoned in her most charming voice. "I'm in dryer number two."

Helen lifted the basket and placed it atop one of the running washers. Turning to Rita, she smiled. "There, now I have a reserved spot."

Rita let out an awkward laugh, all the while wondering if it was Helen who'd been leaving her those nasty notes.

"So how's Rikki doing?" Helen asked, taking a seat next to Rita. "Are you still driving her to school?"

"Oh, she's doing just fine," Rita answered, dismissing the topic with a wave of her hand. "That happened ages ago. You know how kids are. They adjust."

"But that was *horrible*," Helen continued. "If it had been Barbra, we would have moved. Lenny would have insisted. But then Rikki doesn't have a father? Barbra told me that Rikki's mother never married. Such a shame. A girl should have a father. A man in her life."

Rita took it all in. Helen's attitude, body language, and tone. As she listened, she wondered where anyone got off judging her or her granddaughter. She was doing the best she could. She hadn't expected to be raising a teenager at this time in life. Lord knows it tested the limit of her maternal skills, which had been severely challenged raising her own kids. The plan had been that, after Seymour, she'd remarry. Preferably a rich man. She'd be off somewhere traveling, enjoying the good life, instead of passing her days with the likes of women like Helen.

"Well, if you'll excuse me, I have to get going," Rita said, standing up, desperate to get away as her dryer approached the end of the spin cycle.

"But your wash?" Helen pointed at the dryer. "You haven't taken your clothes out of the dryer yet."

Rita blinked. "Yes, well, I just remembered. I have something in the oven. I better get it out. Then I'll be right back down."

Helen shook her head in disapproval. "It's okay with me as long as I'm not waiting for that dryer."

Rita offered a curt smile. *You can drop dead for all I care,* she thought, as she left the hot room.

◆

"I can't remember her," Rikki said, dish towel in hand, drying a dinner plate.

They stood together at the sink, Rita in a pair of yellow Playtex gloves washing, Rikki drying.

"It's been years, and I still can't remember."

Rita gave Rikki a disapproving glance.

"Talk to me about El," Rikki begged, while Rita squeezed more dishwashing soap onto the sponge. "Please, Rita."

With her bright red hair slicked back, no makeup to cover her blotchy, pale skin, Rita looked every inch of her seventy-four years. Rikki wondered if she, too, might age like Rita. The mere thought gave her the shivers.

"You could never forget your mother," Rita said as she pushed the suds around in the sink, scraping off bits of charred eggplant from the broiler pan. She'd tried to prepare the vegetable without frying. It was a trick shared by a coworker. Unfortunately, she'd failed to remember to spray the pan, and the eggplant stuck.

"But *I can't remember her,*" Rikki insisted. "I don't understand. Didn't the doctor say that I'd eventually remember?"

"You were very sick, dear. Remember, you didn't talk for three months."

But Rikki didn't remember. That was the whole point. "Yes, but that was then. I'm talking now."

"But you're well now," Rita said, as she rinsed a dinner glass. "You're in school. Good grades. Why do you want to talk about a time when you were ill?"

"I want to remember," Rikki pressed. "I have to remember."

"She loved you very much," Rita stated, as if by describing Rikki's mother's affection it might fill Rikki's void.

Rikki shook her head. "It's good to hear, but that's not the same as feeling the love yourself."

Rita persisted. "Your mother used to say that nothing in the world would ever be as important to her as you. Nothing." And then she gasped, bringing a soapy glove to her mouth to stifle a cry.

"Oh, Grandma," Rikki said, a sweetness in her voice, as she put down the dishtowel. She rarely referred to Rita as Grandma, but during these moments, Rikki forgot the protocol. "Are you okay?" she asked, rubbing Rita's back. "I didn't mean to upset you."

Rita shook her head and held onto the edge of the sink, leaning forward as the hot water from the tap continued to splash onto soiled silverware. "Forgive me," she blurted out, as she struggled to pull herself together, tears flowing down her cheeks.

"Okay," Rikki sighed, an arm about Rita, comforting the older woman. "We don't have to talk about it. It's okay."

"I can't," Rita said, in an apologetic tone. She gasped for air between sobs. "It's a horrible thing to lose a child … I don't think I'll ever … ever get over it. How could this terrible thing have happened?" She offered Rikki a pitiful look. "I wasn't a perfect mother and I'm certainly not a perfect grandmother, but I didn't deserve this," she continued, shoulders slumped, chin pressed to her chest.

"No, of course not," Rikki said.

When Rita finally looked up, Rikki used her dishtowel to wipe the soapsuds from her grandmother's face.

"I'll never recover. And I just can't think about it." Rita shook her head in defiance. "Such dreadful things shouldn't ever happen."

Rikki didn't know what else to say. It had always been this way. Ever since she came to live with Rita. She couldn't remember her mother, and Rita was unable to talk about El. And because they didn't talk, Rikki feared she might never remember.

It was as if El had never been born.

Rikki removed her grandmother's gloves. "Why don't you go sit down and rest. I'll finish up."

"Are you sure?" Rita asked, eyes still glistening.

Rikki gave Rita's arm a squeeze. "Yes, now go ahead."

◆

Estelle Ida Goldenbaum had always hated her name.

Raised with girls named Susan, Lauren, Hope, and Linda, she couldn't help feeling that the name Estelle was part of a much older generation of women named Fanny, Bertha, Irma, and Gertrude. So when Estelle had turned fifteen, she made a decision. She confronted her parents during dinner, and while her father poked at the broccoli on his plate, Estelle made her announcement. "I'm changing my name to El." She glanced from one parent to the other. "El. E … L. It's short and easy to spell."

Her brother giggled.

Only two years younger, Rick was a slight, scrawny, blonde boy with thick glasses. "That's what they call the elevated train in Chicago!" he cried out in delight, his eyes seeming even smaller in the heavy black frames.

Estelle closed her eyes and tried to ignore her brother.

"I was just reading about it in the library. The first stretch was 3½ miles and opened in June 1892. At first, it was powered by a steam engine, but then in 1893, the third-rail electrical power system was introduced…"

Dear God, she thought. *Why does he have to be so darn smart?*

"…at the 1893 World's Columbian Exposition."

"Rick … we're eating. That's enough," Rita said with irritation.

When Estelle opened her eyes, her brother was looking up at her, a hurt expression plastered on his gentle face. His eyes seemed to be waiting for her response to the information he had offered. Instead, Estelle just shook her head, hoping he'd take the hint and stop talking. He did.

Her father, Seymour, offered a beleaguered look as if the difficulties of life had inflicted upon him a perpetual frown. He glanced over at Estelle's mother. "Rita, what's this all about?" The dark circles under his eyes seemed even more pronounced than usual.

Rita shrugged. She reached for a glass of water and took a sip.

"I'm serious," Estelle whined. "My name is ridiculous. All the kids tease me. They're calling me Essie. I hate it."

"Estelle was my grandmother's name," her father said, focused intently on his daughter. "You don't get to decide your name. That's something that is given to you. Offered in love. Children don't give back their names."

"I don't care what you say. It's my life!" El shrieked as she jerked herself away from the table with such force that her water glass nearly tumbled over. "I'm tired of being Estelle." She stood in defiance. "My name is El."

"Sit back down," Rita said in a firm tone, glaring at her daughter. "Where are your manners?"

Estelle defiantly stood behind her chair as if it were a shield. It all seemed so hopeless. The two adults before her would never understand. How could she ever get them to take her seriously?

"Sit down," Rita again ordered as Estelle slinked back down into her seat.

Her father wiped his mouth with a napkin as he looked over at his daughter.

It seemed to Estelle that he was seeing her for the first time.

But even as he looked at her, he directed his comments to his wife. "Rita, I've had a long day. Can't we have a quiet dinner?" His mouth settled back into its usual frown.

Rita glared across the table at her husband. "I'm sorry if this is all too much for you," she said indignantly. "Seymour, you're not the only one who works in this family. You should see the bunions on some of those women who come into the store. God. You've never seen such feet. And if you think being a mother, making dinner, and cleaning this apartment doesn't entitle me to a little peace and quiet too—well—you're wrong."

Seymour took a breath. "I'm not having an argument. It's already been a long day."

Estelle shifted nervously in her seat. She hadn't realized that her demand would bring on another family fight. All she wanted to do was change her name. Was that too much to ask?

Rita had one elbow on the table as she leaned forward. "I'm tired too, Seymour."

"Tired?" her father snapped, his head slightly tilted to the right. "*You're* tired? You drive fifteen minutes to Bayside to sell ladies' shoes. I take the New York City bus and subway system to Manhattan ... pushed and shoved through filth ... to work a ten-hour day for an accounting firm that doesn't even know my name." Her father's voice began to escalate. "They tell me I'm not up for a promotion because they want to recruit new talent." He shook his head in disgust. "New talent ... when I've given my life to that company."

"Seymour," Rita said, shaking her head, signaling that it was neither the time nor the place for his comments.

'No," Seymour answered. "It's time she learned that she's not the center of the universe. The world doesn't revolve around her little blonde head."

Rita reached for her pack of cigarettes.

"I wish you wouldn't," Seymour said. "It's like kissing an ashtray."

Rita lit up, taking a deep inhalation. She exhaled. "And since when are you interested in kissing?" she said in a dismissive manner.

Seymour pulled the napkin from his lap and tossed it on the table. "Fine," he said, hands in the air. "I give up. You smoke," he told his wife, "and you," looking at his daughter, "can call yourself anything you want. As long as you're both happy," he said getting up from the table, "God knows, I'm not."

◆

Harry stretched his neck. Why had he ever agreed to do a Microsoft *Live Meeting* with his editor?

The screen came to life as Edward Heaton flashed into view. In his mid-forties, Edward had a baby face. He'd often been mistaken for Neil Patrick Harris.

"Hey, Harry, how are you feeling?" Edward asked, a bright smile lighting up the screen.

"I'm fine," Harry winced, adjusting himself in his seat. "My back's a little stiff and I've been getting these terrific headaches."

"Have you gone to the doctor yet?" Edward asked, expressing genuine concern.

"No," Harry demurred. "You know I hate doctors. Almost as much as I hate editors."

"Nice one, Harry," Edward laughed. "After all these years of working together, I thought we were friends."

"That depends," Harry said, stroking the stubble on his chin. "Did you like the first three chapters?"

"Harry, it's just too predictable. You've got to mix it up. The plot is too similar to the last book. No one wants to pay good money to read the same story."

Harry shifted nervously. "Well, I think it's good," he said indignantly, faking an air of confidence. "I think it's my best work yet."

Edward peered into the screen, grimacing, cheeks pulled high, lips pressed tightly together. "Not quite," he said. "Not by a long shot."

"What happened to your glasses?" Harry asked.

Edward arched his brows. "I had laser surgery. I told you about it last week. I just did it yesterday."

Harry nodded. He remembered. "And you're back working so soon?"

"It didn't hurt. It was one-two-three, done," Edward said snapping his fingers.

"That's the problem with the world today," Harry muttered, mostly to himself.

Edward leaned in closer to the screen. His nose, beautifully straight and well-proportioned for his face, became a projectile as if reflected by a fun-house mirror. "What did you say? I can't hear you."

"See," Harry blasted. "You're leaning in, thinking you'll be able to hear me better. You stupid bastard. You can't hear me any better. I'm not there."

"Oh, Harry," Edward reproached him. "Is this about those chapters?"

Harry pounded on his desk with his fist. "*Everything* is about those chapters."

"Now, don't lose your temper," Edward advised. "We've done this before. Just start again. And this time, pull the reader in quicker. You write murder mysteries. That's your genre. That's what sells. And it's like I always say …"

Harry completed the sentence: "… if you write for your readers, you'll have a best-seller. I know."

"Especially when they're eagerly awaiting your next book."

Harry nodded, dejected. "Yes, I mustn't disappoint my audience. I get it."

"Good," Edward said. "I'll check back with you next week. Give Beetle a treat from me."

Harry turned to the terrier curled up in his dog bed, fast asleep. "Beetle just gave you the finger," Harry said, holding his middle finger up to the screen.

"Nice," Edward laughed. "So glad you can take constructive criticism. Why not use all that anger in your writing? It'll make those scenes jump right off the page."

◆

Rikki turned the corner and walked past the Chinese laundry, the dry cleaner, the candy store, and the barbershop. The eight-story building where she lived with Rita came into view. Terraces painted an aqua blue contrasted sharply with the red brick. Aguilar Gardens—an odd name, considering there were no flowers, just a contiguous cement walkway bordered by a chain-link fence and 3×5 *Keep Off the Grass* signs posted every twenty feet to guard a strip of greenery that bordered the building.

A raspy voice called out as Rikki approached the front steps. "Rikki, how's your grandmother feeling?"

Rikki winced.

It was Mrs. Mandelbaum from 6G. Her apartment was right across from the elevator on Rikki's floor. The old woman often popped her head out, surprising Rikki as she waited for the elevator. "That Mrs. M is such a yenta," Rita had warned Rikki. "Be careful about being too friendly. Not everyone needs to know our business."

Despite the chilly weather, Mrs. M had set up a folding chair on the sidewalk, amid the crowd of other seniors. As the old woman sat with her legs crossed, Rikki could see her pink and green housedress, paired with a blue winter peacoat. Her white hair, clipped short in a boyish cut, exposed tiny, bat-like ears. Rikki imagined those ears in a 360-degree rotation as Mrs. M clocked the arrival and departure of everyone on the sixth floor, distinguishing tenants by their footsteps. Twenty steps. The Millers in 6D. Forty steps. The Greens in 6M.

"I haven't seen her since yesterday," the yenta said, as if she was in charge of attendance at Aguilar Gardens. "Is she okay? Do I need to stop by and check on her?"

Rikki tried to keep a poker face. The mere prospect of Mrs. M entering the apartment and snooping around was abhorrent. "Oh, no. She's fine," she reassured the older woman.

Rikki hated living in the high-rise. Except in the dead of winter, seniors congregated at the front of the building to pass the time, mostly gossiping, and, according to Rita, annoying their neighbors. Some brought their own folding chairs, like Mrs. M, while others just milled about, leaning against the handrails, and in warmer weather sitting on the steps, blocking access to the front door. They seemed to know, or appeared entitled to know, everyone else's business.

And they weren't only out front.

They were in the lobby, the laundry room, and on the benches out back by the cement playground. Milling around, asking questions, prying with their eyes. Wondering how Rikki was doing in school, where she was coming from, where she was going. A million questions. Sharp tones, demanding voices, probing Rikki and Rita's personal business out on the street for everyone to hear.

"Rita's fine," she answered, knowing it was a difficult day for her grandmother, but hoping to end the questioning.

The group of adults turned their attention to Rikki. Dull eyes fired, imaginations blossomed, as Rikki sensed judgments being formed. She wanted to stab Mrs. M with her Bic pen, but then the Bic was her favorite and she saw no reason to sacrifice a perfectly good pen for the likes of Mrs. M.

The truth was that Rita had taken to her bed. It happened every year on El's birthday. Rita became inconsolable. And though Rikki, too, felt upset, her reasons were different. She didn't suffer the physical collapse that Rita endured. How could she, when she remembered nothing of her mother? Still, she was certain that she must have loved her mother very much. Hadn't she been hospitalized for three months? Didn't she have to regularly see a psychiatrist? And yet, when Rita fell apart, Rikki found herself distracted. Frightened by the intensity of the older woman's grief.

"Then why haven't I seen her?" Mrs. M continued to push.

Rikki started to make her way past. "I can't really say," she admitted, "but she's absolutely fine."

Mrs. M wasn't quite through. "Are you sure, dear? The flu is going around. How are you feeling? You don't look well."

All eyes again turned on Rikki.

"I feel very well, Mrs. Mandelbaum," she boldly answered, looking from one adult to the other. "Perhaps you shouldn't be sitting out here in the cold. *It is November.* And you're not a young woman," Rikki blurted out as she rushed up the steps, desperate to get away.

"Your grandmother has raised a very rude young lady," Mrs. M. shouted.

"Thank you, Mrs. Mandelbaum," Rikki called back. "I'll be sure to let her know."

◆

Lil struggled to concentrate, even as she reminded her students about the importance of quieting their minds while maintaining the fullness of the breath. It was the end of class. The room was dark. About her, thirty students lay on their backs, eyes closed. She sat cross-legged on the floor before them, her thoughts straying to her handsome neighbor, Harry Aldon.

It's a shame a man like that should be alone. I must invite him to dinner.

She instructed the class to take another deep breath, hold, and release.

I wonder if authors make any money. Oh, it'd be so nice to be with a man of quality. Someone who I could really trust.

She visualized the cover of Harry's latest book, which had been delivered to her front door courtesy of Amazon. The silhouette of a young man stood dangerously close to the edge of a cliff, arms extended, ready to jump. The title was displayed in bold black letters—*Death Leap*—set against a burnt-orange background.

She shifted her hips, releasing tension in her lower buttocks. *What kind of title is that? It's so dark.* She licked her lips and tried to refocus on her breath.

Her last two relationships had proven a disaster. Walter had turned out to be an on-line cheater. She'd found him trolling Internet sites. *He told me that we were exclusively dating,* she remembered with irritation. She'd trapped him by creating a bogus account on Match.com.

And then there was Peter. He'd broken her heart.

Such a lovely man, she'd thought, when they first met. Kind and affectionate, but unable to maintain an erection. *I'm too young to be celibate. I still have my needs,* she thought as Peter sat on the edge of the bed, embarrassed and apologetic. *Such a shame.* A successful lawyer. She'd so hoped Peter would be the one.

And then, the others. So many others.

Looking back, she wondered if she'd been too picky. No, she surmised. She had standards. And yet, it saddened her to think that she'd never married.

Don't focus on the negative, she berated herself. *You have a wonderful life. Not many women who are married can say that.* She suddenly felt superior. *And it's not like I chose to be single.* Though she couldn't help but wonder if her personal energy, strong and decisive, had created her current circumstance.

With a final breath she roused the class, instructing her students to open their eyes and, when ready, to sit up. Slowly, the group came to life, assuming a posture that mirrored her own. She raised her palms to her chest, pressing them together in the guise of prayer and slowly bowed at the waist. In unison, the group said, "*Namaste.*"

◆

Crossing the Aguilar Gardens lobby, Rikki spotted three adults waiting by the two elevators. She considered ducking down the hall, but it was too late. They'd seen her, turned, and smiled. So she marched forward, politely saying hello, per Rita's rules. *Always say hello when you meet people at the elevator. When the elevator doors open, stand back, and allow everyone to exit. If you're by the buttons, ask the others what floor they would like. When you arrive at your floor, say, "Goodbye." And most of all, never fart or belch in an enclosed space. People will talk.*

The two gray-haired women were in the midst of a lively conversation. Something about a sale going on at Macy's. The other woman was younger, a brunette with shoulder-length hair. She wore a black leather jacket over a pair of fitted jeans. Rikki couldn't help but notice her brown high-heeled boots. The four-inch heels were so thin, Rikki wondered how they didn't just break off.

Rikki focused on the lighted displays above each elevator as she peripherally sensed Ms. Boots staring at her. Rikki touched her face, hoping she didn't have a zit popping up. Floors eight, seven, six... the elevators were seemingly tied in a race to the lobby. Then, one elevator stopped on the fifth floor while the other continued on to the fourth floor.

"Are you El's daughter?" the younger woman finally asked.

Three, two, one. Rikki smiled.

"You look so much like her. The hair is different—but your face. It's a mirror image. I can't get over it."

The doors of the elevator opened to the lobby.

"My name is Jenny. Your mother and I went to school together. We ran into each other a few years ago when my mother moved into 5J."

Rikki nodded as all four entered the elevator. Jenny stood next to Rikki at the back. The two older women stood at the front, entering everyone's floor as it was called out and continuing to talk, but their conversation had shifted to the narrow aisles at the supermarket.

"Just last week, this dreadful woman clipped the back of my heel with her cart," Rikki overheard one say to the other. "I think she did it on purpose."

As the elevator doors closed, Rikki was struck by the intense mix of female scents: orange citrus combined with honey violet and a hint of lilac. Rikki cleared her throat, suppressing the urge to sneeze. She spied flakes of dandruff on the dark woolen coat of the woman in front of her. Oddly, it reminded Rikki of coconut. And then the woman sneezed. Rikki gasped, holding her breath as the elevator passed the first floor.

"Whatever you do," Rita had warned her, "don't touch the buttons in the elevator with the tips of your fingers. Use your knuckle. Those elevators are a breeding ground for germs. So toxic, someone should call in the CDC."

Jenny smiled as she looked at Rikki. "I haven't seen your mother in years. How's she doing?"

Rikki jerked her head from side to side as she held her breath, afraid she might be forced to take another breath before getting off the elevator.

The elevator stopped on the fifth floor—Jenny's stop. As she left the car, she turned to Rikki, placing a hand on the rubber bumper that kept the elevator doors from closing. Instead of saying goodbye, as Rikki assumed she would, Jenny said, "I'd love to see her again. Please let her know."

The other two women in the car turned to look at Rikki, who had yet to answer. Rikki finally exhaled, now gasping for breath as she said, "I can't."

"Why not?" asked Jenny, a troubled look on her face.

"Because she's *dead!*" Rikki blurted out, exasperated by having to explain. As soon as the words left her mouth, she felt a deep shame, as if El had somehow abandoned her because she was unlovable.

Jenny's face went pale. "Oh, my God." She stepped back from the elevator, her face registering a pained expression, confirming to Rikki that her personal tragedy was just as awful as she believed it to be.

◆

Harry shielded his eyes from the bright Phoenix sun as he hurried along the walkway past five identical, three-story white buildings in search of building A.

There must be a sign somewhere, he thought, as he crossed a maze of pathways, spying one door and then another. He imagined old people wandering aimlessly, constantly lost in their own housing development. *This is really impossible,* he decided as a woman above called out "Yoo-hoo!" Harry looked up. He spotted a large letter A plastered high on the corner of the building.

"Damn," he said. *I was supposed to look up. Why didn't I look up?*

"Yoo-hoo!" she called again, hand waving from the terrace. It was a sunny eighty-five degrees, and she was dressed in a bright yellow sweater. "Are you my ride?"

Harry smiled. "I'm your guy," he said loudly, just in case she was hard of hearing.

"I'll be right down. Don't go anywhere."

It was Tuesday, the day Harry drove seniors to their doctors' appointments. He'd been doing it for three years, ever since he'd decided that writing full-time had become too isolating. Today, he was picking up Mrs. Adeline Jones.

"You can take someone grocery shopping or drive them to their doctor's office," Sue, the volunteer coordinator from Duet, had informed him at the volunteer orientation session.

Harry hated the idea of going supermarket shopping. Not being much of a cook, he found supermarkets overwhelming. Carts darting in and out of the aisles and those long check-out lines. "I'll take the medical appointments," he answered, worried that he might not be up to the task. Small talk had never been his thing. But fortunately, most of his riders were eager to chat. They often talked from the moment his car left the curb until he dropped them back home. They reminisced about relatives, friends, and the places where they had lived; childhoods, marriages, and children. They provided an oral history of a vanishing generation. The Great Depression. World War II. The McCarthy years. Harry listened intently, mesmerized by their stories, pleasantly distracted from his own concerns.

"Let me get that door," he said as Mrs. Jones approached the passenger side of his Ford Escape. Her posture was perfect. Probably no taller than five feet, the little lady bent forward at the waist, placing a large wicker purse with a mother-of-pearl clutch on the car floor. "Oh my, this is a big car," she said sweetly as she hoisted herself in with a firm pull.

"Watch your head," Harry warned out of habit, though her head was nowhere near the car's roofline.

"Aren't you a nice young man?" Mrs. Jones cooed as Harry settled into the driver's seat. "And so polite."

Harry smiled and nodded. "Ah, thank you. But I'm not young."

"That all depends," Mrs. Jones said. "How old are you?"

"Fifty-five come January."

"Hmm," she hummed. "Well, I'm eighty-five." Her tone was boastful.

"No," Harry said, turning to inspect the lovely lady next to him. "I don't believe it."

"Well, it's true," she said, giving him a sideways glance. The twinkle in her eyes was coy. Almost seductive. He could sense her examining his face even as the car pulled forward.

"You know, when I look at you," she started, "I'm reminded of my third husband, Edgar."

"Third husband?" Harry said, bemused, as the Ford left the parking lot heading west on Camelback.

"Yes," she said, head held high. "You wouldn't know it, but I was once a pretty hot number. I worked as a stewardess in 1946 for United Airlines."

"Oh," Harry said, looking at the still very pretty woman. He imagined her young. It wasn't difficult.

"A lot of people don't know it, but back then, we had something called lap time."

Harry made a right on 32nd Street as he listened.

"Newbies had to sit on the pilot's lap. It was kind of a rite of passage."

"Really?" Harry said. "That doesn't seem appropriate."

"Oh, we didn't mind. It was fun. You know, back in those days, they weighed you every week. And you couldn't hold the job if you were over the age of thirty-two."

Harry was appalled. "That seems so wrong. Didn't that bother you?"

"Oh, no." Mrs. Jones smiled as they pulled into the parking lot of the medical office building. "That's the way it was and I just loved it."

◆

Rikki sat on the bed, an open diary across her lap.

Her room, painted a bright yellow, was anything but cheery. It had once been a den, but with Rikki's arrival, Rita had removed the coffee table and added a single bed, which now faced a canvas sofa. Her desk, a wooden folding table Rita had swiped from the storage room, sat at the head of the bed. The walls, covered in posters of matadors, red capes high in the air poised to face the charge of the bull, had been collected during Rita's many trips to Mexico. Small clay pots sat on shelves above the tan sofa. A tall black warrior sporting a sword and red, white, and blue feathers stood on a side table guarding the only picture of Rikki's mother in the house. A 3 × 5 photograph encased in a silver frame.

Rikki held the frame in her hand as she stared at the picture. The photo was of El's high school graduation, a carefully posed, static moment in cap and gown that seemed to obscure any real sense of El's personality. Rikki had spent hours staring at the photograph. Studying it. Trying to animate the smile. Wondering how her mother might have moved her head when she spoke. Raised her eyebrows as she asked a question. Smiled when she expressed love. And how did her voice sound? Rikki was certain that if she could only hear her mother's voice, the memories would flood back. But now, as she looked at the photograph, she felt frustrated. The face seemed familiar. But was it because it was the last thing she looked at before closing her eyes at night? She just couldn't be sure.

"Great traumas can result in a loss of memory. It's the way the brain protects us," Dr. Gillian, the psychiatrist at Sun Haven, had explained. A grandfatherly man with wispy white hair and a long, prominent nose, Gillian generated a kindness that had captured Rikki's trust at the start. "You mustn't be too hard on yourself. When you're ready, you'll remember. It'll come back in bits and pieces. Slowly. Very slowly."

But that had been so long ago, and still, Rikki struggled.

Maybe if I focus, Rikki thought as she stared at the photo. And though she wanted to once again ask Rita about El, she decided against it. *What was the point?* she thought, running a hand across the picture. It was abundantly clear that Rita couldn't talk about El without becoming upset.

Rikki had only recently begun to keep the diary, a long-ago gift from Dr. Gillian. It was the only thing that had remained as proof of her time in Sun Haven. Rita had made certain of that. "Write, my child," Dr. Gillian had said. "Your ability to remember is wrapped up in your unconscious. Tap that source and it will all become clearer."

"You're absolutely fine," Rita had pronounced upon first seeing her granddaughter in the dayroom at the psychiatric hospital. "There is nothing wrong with you," she had said with such conviction that Rikki was certain she was lying. "You're as sane as anyone here," Rita whispered, nervously looking about the room at the other in-patients.

But Rikki knew everyone there was crazy.

She was able to recall snippets of her life in Michigan. The house where she was raised. The neighbors. Old schoolmates and friends. It was just the specifics about El that seemed to be displaced. As if her mind had selectively deleted any memory of her mother. And even with the little she did remember of her life before, she was afraid it too would eventually slip away, lost to the darkest corners of her mind. That fear was exacerbated by her disappointment at losing touch with friends and neighbors from her old Michigan neighborhood. Rikki had written letter after letter. Sent holiday cards. And yet there had been no response.

"Some people just don't know how to behave," Rita had offered as one explanation. "They never really cared about you. They certainly didn't offer to help when you needed it. No. That was my job. Oh, but advice. Now *that* they had plenty of to spread around. Well, don't you give them another thought," she'd said, waving a hand in the air. "*Elitist snobs.* Every last one of them. You don't need those people in your life. They're not interested in you. They're all surface. Focused on themselves. Besides, you now live in Queens. You can't expect people from Michigan to stay in touch. Everyone has moved on. They have their own lives and you have *yours.* It's absurd to think that you can maintain friendships at such a great distance."

Perhaps they have all forgotten me, Rikki thought. *Perhaps Rita's right.*

◆

When El Goldenbaum had turned seventeen, she left Queens for Michigan and the Cranbook Academy of Art. Her parents, who had waited until her graduation from high school, separated that year, much to El's relief. They had fought continuously through El's junior and senior year of high school, and when the split finally came that June, El was all too happy to get away.

"But why not go to Queens College?" her mother implored, disappointed that El had opted to attend school so far from home.

El didn't bother to look up as she knelt on the floor packing a duffel bag with her clothes, rolling her jeans and blouses so that everything would arrive wrinkle-free. "Because," she explained, exasperated by Rita's petulance, "it's time to move on. I'm becoming an adult." El said this proudly, though deep down, she wasn't quite certain.

"That packing can wait. Come here," Rita commanded, arms outstretched.

"Mom, please," El implored. "I have to get this done."

"Why is it that whenever I ask you to do something you give me a hard time? Is it so much for a mother to ask her daughter to return her affection?"

The last thing El wanted was another scene. Rita had become almost impossible to live with as the day approached for her to leave. "Okay," she finally agreed, doing as her mother asked and standing to allow Rita to wrap her arms about her.

"You know how I feel about you. You're my special girl." Rita pressed El tightly to her. "It's so hard to let go. You'll see. One day, when you have a daughter, you'll discover how difficult it is to see her grow up and leave." Rita tucked a stray tress of El's blonde hair behind her daughter's ear as El started to pull away.

"Really, Mother. You're holding on too tight," El protested.

"Promise me," Rita said firmly, "that you won't do any late-night partying or go walking alone. And no drugs or sex."

El glared back. "Mother!"

"Now promise," Rita said, crossing her arms, her face set in a determined gaze. "I need to hear you say it."

El exhaled. "It's the '70s. Drugs are everywhere," she answered breezily. "I won't make a promise that I may not keep. I have no idea what's out there."

Rita clasped a hand to her mouth, weighing her daughter's words. El turned her back to finish packing. "Okay," Rita acquiesced, her hands now on her hips. "Marijuana. But no heroin or cocaine. Nothing you snort or inject. Promise."

El crossed her fingers. "Sure," she said, doubtful that she'd ever try those drugs but covering her bases just in case.

"And no sex."

El grabbed a sweater and started to roll it. "Are you serious? I'm going to college, not a convent."

Rita took a breath. "The least you could do is lie."

El took her mother's hand and pulled her over to the bed where the two sat down side-by-side. "Really, mother. It's time for me to live my own life. Now that Daddy and you have split," El continued, "you have to get on with your own life. I wouldn't dream of telling you what to do. That would be silly. You go and find yourself and maybe," and El smiled despite Rita's awful frown, "you too will find a new life."

But Rita's expression didn't change. "I'm over men. I won't remarry. I'm going to be alone for the rest of my life."

El resisted Rita's obvious attempt at manipulation. "Now don't be silly. Besides, you still have Rick. He won't be going to college for another two years."

Rita shook her head in defiance. "He's a boy. It's different."

"I know." El hugged her mother tightly. "But it's time for me to leave."

"I suppose," Rita acknowledged as she wiped a tear away with the back of her hand. "We've always been so close. Your brother keeps to himself. He's distant, quiet. I could never crack that shell."

"Don't be so hard on him," El said. "He's just off in his own world. A lot of boys are like that. Be glad he's so darn smart."

Rita huffed. "Mensa. That's too smart for me."

El laughed. "He's gifted."

"A real genius," Rita said sarcastically. "With a personality to match."

El had heard her mother's objections before. And though there was truth to the fact that Rick was difficult to communicate with at times, El had always known that she was the favored child. That awareness made her feel sorry for Rick, altering her view of her little brother. Between bouts of obnoxious know-it-all behavior, Rick often sat quietly, seemingly dejected, as if observing the family from afar. Once, on a trip to the Amish country, they'd actually left him behind at a rest stop.

"Where's your brother?" Rita had asked El with alarm, who was busy reading in *Teen Beat* about David Cassidy, her favorite pop star, before noticing Rick wasn't in the car. They had all laughed nervously, even joked that being with Rick was like being alone.

"A lot of great company he'll be," Rita mourned as she blew her nose into a tissue. "At least if he had friends … he'd seem normal."

El hated it when Rita picked on Rick. "Mother, he can't help being different."

"Different, all right," Rita agreed.

El covered her ears. "Stop it. I don't want to hear another word about Rick. He's unique. Special. And I love him."

3

It had taken Harry an hour before he stopped wandering about the house and seriously sat down to face the edits recommended by Edward. "Dear Lord," he grumbled as he scanned the pages.

Beetle, nestled in a dog bed by Harry's desk, looked up. Harry continued to mutter even as he spotted Beetle's sudden interest.

"Am I talking to *you*?" Harry asked in a sing-song voice as Beetle sat up, his body vibrating with enthusiasm. "No, I'm not. I didn't once say *eat*."

Beetle let out a long, whine.

"For an old guy, you still got a lot of spunk." Harry playfully grabbed Beetle's snout as the terrier rolled onto his back and gently swiped at Harry's hand. "You're such a good boy," Harry sang, getting down on his hands and knees and crouching next to Beetle, mesmerized by the sparkle in the dog's brown eyes. As Harry got to his feet, Beetle growled. Someone was approaching the front door. "Oh damn," he said to Beetle. "We're not alone."

The bell rang and Beetle lurched into action. His body violently shook with each high-pitched bark. Harry covered his ears as he hurried to the door. "Coming," he shouted as Beetle followed by his side, his body erect, on full alert.

It was Lil.

"Yes?" Harry said, peeking out from behind the door.

Lil stood with her hands firmly planted on her hips. Her eyes seemed to glow as she broke into a big smile. "Harry, I just had to tell you," and then Harry noticed what was tucked under her arm. It was a copy of his first book, *Tensions in Paradise*. "This book is amazing.

I really enjoyed every line, Harry. And now I'm reading *Death Leap*. I had no idea that you were such a great writer. I just thought you were"—she seemed to search for the right word—"unfriendly. But now I know why. Harry, you're really a well of deep emotion."

Harry blushed. "Lil, I'd love to let you in, but I'm writing right now. I never have visitors when I'm writing," Harry said, though he hadn't exactly been interrupted. Still, it was the principle of the thing.

"Oh, Harry," Lil admonished him as she pushed open the door. Spotting Beetle, she kneeled in the entryway as the pitch of her voice escalated. "Oh baby, there you are. How can you live with this mean old man? He's such a stick in the mud."

"I assure you, Lil, he thinks I'm fabulous."

She looked up and laughed. "Oh, I'm sure he does, Harry. And you know, when a dog loves you, well, you just can't be all bad."

"Lil," Harry said briskly, "is there something you need? This is my time to write. And you're interrupting. I wish you'd call before you just stop by."

Lil cocked her head as she stood up. "But Harry, I wanted to ask you to go to Happy Hour so we can discuss your book. I want to know all about those marvelous characters."

"It's fiction, Lil. There's nothing to tell."

"Harry, I won't take no for an answer," she firmly said. "You simply must. I spent twenty-five dollars on this book, including tax and shipping, and I want to talk with you."

Harry realized there was no other option. "All right," he said, surrendering. "I'll meet you in front at four o'clock."

"Be there or be square," she called as she headed down the pathway, waving Harry's book.

◆

So you've got a date? Richard's voice intoned.

Harry had just stepped out the shower and started to dry himself off. "I wouldn't call it a date …" *Just company.*

She's a very attractive woman. Does she know?

Harry caught his reflection in the mirror. *What's there to know?*

Oh, Harry, sometimes you're such a child.

Harry ignored the comment as he applied his shaving cream.

Too bad. You really should be honest with her. She has the hots for you.

Harry examined his face in the mirror. "And why not?" he said as he ran a finger across his thick brow. *I'm still an attractive man.*

But she's not for you.

"Of course not," he said as the razor glided over his cheek. *Of course not.*

◆

Living in Aguilar Gardens is like being in prison, Rikki thought as she looked out the sixth-floor bedroom window to the cement playground below. Children ran about, enclosed by a tall chain-link fence, playing hide and seek among large concrete barrels placed on their sides, the openings large enough for a tricycle to pass through. Some climbed atop the barrels, kicking at the others while precariously balancing themselves. The abutting courtyard, a large, rectangular area bordered by green benches, hosted a group of boys playing stickball. A group of girls were hopping among boxes etched in white chalk on the nearby walkway.

The noise carried through the courtyard, beyond the playground, and up to Rikki's ears.

The vibrant colors of Michigan trees popped into her head. Come late September, early October, the trees transitioned from a verdant green to a lush orange-brown, and as the leaves dropped, they created a wonderful crunch on the sidewalks and pathways. She closed her eyes and could see the majestic beauty. Feel the chill in the air. Smell the wonderful scent of grass, mixed with the decaying leaves, a feast for the senses.

"A penny for your thoughts," Rita said as she entered the room with a plate of Oreos and a glass of milk.

"What's that?" Rikki asked, despite being very sure what her grandmother was holding.

"A snack. I thought you and I might talk."

Rikki offered a jaundiced look. "You know I'm not eating those cookies."

"Honey, a little cookie couldn't hurt."

"I don't think so," Rikki said as Rita put the plate and glass down on the card table desk.

Rita acquiesced. "Okay. We'll leave it for later. So," she said sitting down and leaning forward, eyes searching her granddaughter. "What's up?"

Rikki hated these intrusions. Rita periodically seemed intent on having a heart-to-heart talk. It had gotten so bad that Rikki found herself making up things just to get Rita off her back.

"You seem blue. Tell me about it."

"There's nothing to tell," Rikki said, popping up and grabbing a cookie. Anything to stop herself from talking.

"Is it your mom?" Rita asked sympathetically.

Rikki didn't want to have another El scene with Rita. What was the point? Rita would only clam up, as she'd done so many times before, crying, leaving Rikki frustrated.

"Is it living in Queens?"

Rikki shook her head, no. They'd been through that discussion before, too.

"You must tell me," Rita insisted. "I want to know."

Rikki mustered her courage. The small voice in her head said, *here we go again.*

"I hate it here," she finally admitted, cookie crumbs sticking to the corner of her mouth. "It's dirty and crowded. There's no nature. None. Michigan had beautiful trees and lovely parks. Not a playground that looks like a parking lot. I know this is your home ... but it will never be mine." She closed her eyes, pressing back tears. "I miss my life.

Why couldn't you have moved to Michigan? I'd have been in the same school with friends, not in some awful place where I don't fit in."

Rita shook her head in agreement as she listened. "I'm sorry," she said, "that you're so unhappy. But this is the way it had to be. I'm an adult, so I don't have to explain my reasons. Let's just say that we were not going to be able to stay in Michigan. And that is that."

"Then what's the point of even talking to you?" Rikki snapped, her irritation growing.

Rita folded her hands in her lap. "Look," she said, the tone in her voice changing from sympathetic to defensive. "This isn't my idea of heaven on earth, either. Do you think I wanted to live in Queens my whole life? But it's *what we can afford.*"

"But why not Michigan? We had a perfectly nice house."

"I told you," Rita repeated. "We couldn't afford it."

Rikki clasped her hands to her face. "I've lost everything. And you refuse to help me."

"How can you say that?" Rita answered, a shocked expression on her face.

"Because you've made this whole thing about you. You're the hurt party. You're the one who has suffered a loss. I have to comfort you. Well, I'm tired of it," Rikki said, rising to her feet. "Stop asking me what's wrong if you don't intend to help."

"It's been four years, Rikki. Four years of my feeling bad about you being sad. I think four years is long enough. You need to get over this."

Rikki seized the moment. "Maybe I should talk with Adam."

"Adam?"

"Yes. Adam Burtock."

"Burtock?" Rita remembered. "I don't think that's such a good idea."

Rikki had spent six months as a patient of Adam Burtock after moving to Queens. Twice a week, she'd visited the social worker in apartment 8B. The second bedroom was set up as an office with a desk and sofa. A television sat on a built-in countertop by the window. Tall and lanky, barely any weight on his lean frame, Adam resembled a skeleton. His bony hands reached out to make a point as Rikki sat and listened to him lecture her on being kind to her grandmother. Rikki imagined Burtock watching *Family Feud* in between counseling sessions.

"At least he listened to me," Rikki said.

"Sure, he listened," Rita said indignantly. "I paid him. Good money, too. Do you think anyone wants to voluntarily listen to you go on and on about how unhappy you are? I wish someone would pay *me*."

Rikki had no answer.

"I'm tired, Rikki. You're wearing me out. I'm not a young woman. I don't have the tolerance for all your *teenage angst*."

The two sat and stared at each other.

"I didn't ask for this," Rikki finally said, her defiance unmistakable. "This isn't my choice to live with you."

Rita's face went pale, and without another word she stood up and left.

◆

Lil left a phone message while Harry was in the shower, asking him to meet her at Seasons 52 at Biltmore Fashion at five o'clock instead of meeting out front at four, which they had earlier agreed to. Two more messages followed in rapid order, changing the time once again.

"I can pick you up," Harry suggested when he called her back.

"I don't know," she answered. "I'm going to be late, but I'm not sure how late."

"How about we do it another time?" Harry suggested, leaning back in his chair, eyes fixated on his computer screen. There was nothing worse than growing bored with the editing process, believing there was a golden kernel buried in every sentence, and being unable to unearth it. He was definitely done for the day. "No big deal," he assured her, wondering why he always returned to his office, no matter the time of day, no matter what his plans, to sit in front of his computer.

"I'm just conflicted," she said, apologetically.

"Okay, then let's not," Harry offered, losing interest in the back-and-forth over such a simple matter. "This whole thing was your idea anyway."

"No. Meet me at 5:30," she said before once again adjusting the time. "Better make it 6:30. The reservation will be in your name."

Harry shook his head as he hung up, oblivious to the fact that the casual Happy Hour had morphed into dinner. He was just grateful she'd finally made up her mind.

What's wrong with that woman? Everything is such a big deal!

◆

"Aldon," Harry said, as he approached the Season 52 hostess. "For two."

The tanned young woman checked her list and flashed a smile. Harry had never seen such white teeth. "This way," she motioned as Harry followed her slim figure in a tight white mini skirt and spiked black heels into a dimly lit room of stone and warm wood tones. *How handsome,* he thought as he slid into the secluded booth. Lit votive candles and a tiny pussy willow in a miniature vase decorated the table. It had been a long time since he'd last seen a pussy willow. He touched the gray velvety tip and thought *lovely.*

He ordered a glass of merlot as he patiently waited. Lil was late. *It was nice to be out of the house,* he thought, noticing the many couples gathered about in the cozy, romantic setting. Picking up the votive, he scanned the menu. Lil's voice broke his concentration just as he was deciding between the caramelized grilled sea scallops and the seafood paella.

"Harry," she cooed, her voice warm and inviting.

He looked up. She was wearing a figure-hugging black dress and black pumps. A gold belt, cinched at the waist, matched her bracelet and pendant earrings. Her skin looked iridescent by candlelight. Her blonde hair had been pulled back and tucked behind her ears, and she was beautifully made up to highlight her eyes and full lips.

Harry drew a breath. "You look amazing."

"Of course," she said with a girlish laugh as she spun about, offering Harry a full view before sliding into the booth.

"You did all that just for Happy Hour?" he asked innocently.

She gave him a coy look. "You're pretty reclusive, aren't you?"

"I try to be," Harry answered seriously. "It's not easy working from home. There are interruptions all day long."

She tilted her head and smiled. "You shouldn't be such a loner."

He nodded, not so much agreeing, but uncomfortable talking about it. He was out now. He'd prefer to just enjoy his wine and the company. He had no other expectations.

"You know, Harry," she started as she glanced at the menu, "You're a very attractive man. Why are you still single?"

The question immediately put Harry off. It was too personal, coming from someone he hardly knew. Harry needed more time to get to know the other person before discussing intimate topics. Harry doubted Lil would ever be a person he'd confide in. "I like to live alone," he lied, sidestepping her question. "It's my world—my life."

She smiled. "That's not why," she said as if she had access to Harry's secret world. "You're shy, aren't you?" She reached over and grabbed his hand.

Harry didn't want to appear rude. But he wanted his hand back.

"You've been living alone too long, Harry Aldon. Men aren't meant to be alone. No one is. You're just awkward. Sweet—but awkward. I could tell immediately. I bet you think that you don't even like people. Am I right?"

Harry couldn't disagree. He was terribly uncomfortable with most people. Always had been. It was a weakness that few people discerned. Instead, they interpreted Harry's quiet nature as being rude. Nothing could have been further from the truth.

As Lil searched his face for confirmation, Harry became anxious. Aware that Lil was flirting in a very direct and uninhibited manner, he slowly withdrew his hand.

"You don't need to be shy with me," Lil assured him, reaching for his wine glass and taking a sip.

"Would you like a glass?" Harry asked, his heart wildly racing, wondering how to make a graceful exit. "I'll get the waitress," he said as he waved at a young lady who passed by and failed to notice him.

Lil laughed. "Oh, Harry," she said, in a tone not much different from the one he'd heard from his mother when he was a boy and had done something silly. "You're not much for adult relationships, are you?"

Harry, speechless, stared at her.

"Well, it's time that changed, Harry. There's a whole world out there. And I'm here to show it to you," she said with such insistence that Harry worried his life *was* about to change—whether he liked it or not.

◆

Rikki was barely able to sit still in homeroom. It was her time of the month and the bloating was excruciating. She fidgeted, wishing the day was already over. Barney had not shown up for class, and she was relieved. With Barney's chair empty, she could relax and be herself. Doodle in her notebook, daydream about being anyone other than Rikki—a tall, gorgeous model—a woman of mystery and importance—a temptress—instead of the swollen adolescent with a pimple coming up on the tip of her nose.

Come lunchtime, she found her way to the table that Barbra already occupied.

"Where have you been?" Barbra asked.

"In the bathroom," Rikki whispered.

"Oh, God." Barbra reacted to Rikki's face and low energy. "Well, come sit down," she said, already hacking her way through some sort of salad in a green Tupperware container. "You tell me your problems, I'll tell you mine."

Rikki wasn't in the mood for drama. But at least Barbra could be distracting. "What's the matter?" she asked as the scent of Italian dressing reached her nose.

"What's the matter?" Barbra mocked her words. "What *isn't* the matter? That awful woman has decided that I should go away for Christmas. She wants me to go visit my uncle in Toledo while she and my father take a cruise in the Bahamas."

"Toledo?" Rikki burst out with excitement. "Toledo, Ohio?"

"Have you ever been there?" Barbra answered, scanning Rikki's face. "It's not a place to get excited about. There is no there there."

Rikki clasped her hands and held them to her chest. "I can't believe it."

Barbra's face registered confusion. "Believe what? This is terrible news. Who wants to go to Ohio and freeze your ass off when you could be in the Bahamas? If my mother were alive," Barbra took a breath, "I'd be with them on that trip. But that miserable bitch—she couldn't possibly let me go." Barbra pulled a carrot stick out of a small plastic bag and pointed it at Rikki. "I hate her."

Rikki just smiled.

"Well," Barbra said indignantly, "if that's how you're going to react to my news, maybe we're not the friends that I thought we were."

"Oh, no," Rikki said, one hand on Barbra's arm. "I'm sorry…truly I am. But do you think," she said in a begging manner, "that there is any way I might be able to go along with you?"

"To Toledo?" Barbra asked, staring at Rikki as if she'd just lost her mind.

◆

Christmas 1974

Hey El,

Rita's upset that you decided to spend the weekend with your friends in Miami instead of coming back to

Queens. You're practically all she can talk about. How the holidays will never be the same.

If only I could escape and be with you.

I found out yesterday that I received the Merit Scholarship to attend Cornell a year early. Rita is convinced it's the best news possible. She can't wait till I'm gone. She says I'm like living with the Sphinx. We don't talk any more. What's the point?

She's never liked having me around. As she said yesterday, I just mean more work. Though I don't quite understand how that can be, since she insists that I do the laundry—and I've learned how to cook—so I prepare dinner three or four times a week. She says it's good training for my eventually being on my own.

Yeah—right.

I may be a member of Mensa, but Rita is beyond my comprehension.

Oh El, I really miss you. I wish you were here. It's no fun without you.

Please don't forget to call on New Year's Eve. I know Rita will be anxious to hear your voice—and so will I.

A big hug.

Love,

Your brother

◆

When Harry opened his eyes, he was naked in bed, lying face down. His head felt like a giant water balloon, and when he tried to raise it, pain shot clear to the back of his skull. He moaned, sitting up, aware Beetle was nowhere to be found.

"Beetle, here, boy," he whispered, a hand on the side of his head, hating the vibrations that his voice was making between his ears. "Where are you? Beetle?"

He wandered into the kitchen, nude. There he found Beetle. Parked intently beside his food bowl, waiting. "Beetle, why didn't you wake me?" Harry said, noticing the time on the microwave oven. "Christ, it's ten o'clock."

Used to getting up at six, Harry felt that ten o'clock meant half the day was already over.

"Okay, buddy," Harry said as he leaned down to pick up the metallic bowl. "Dear God," he cried out as the fluid in the balloon shifted, pressing his brain against his eyeballs. He scooped wet dog food out of the can and placed it in the bowl, and with all the enthusiasm he could muster said, "Oh boy, Beetle. There you go." He tried not to gag.

You really tied one on last night, Richard's voice said, a bit too loudly for Harry's comfort.

"I did," Harry weakly answered, bent over the counter, leaning on both elbows, his head between the palms of his hands.

You better get to that puddle Beetle left in the dining room.

Harry had spotted it when he passed by.

You can't expect him to hold it all night and through the morning too.

Harry felt guilty. *I suppose not.*

Did you tell her?

Tell her what?

Don't be such a child.

Harry ran a hand through his curls as he stared into the sink. Was he going to pitch? Shouldn't he do that in the bathroom? "She must already know."

So you said nothing.

I've never been very good at that kind of thing. You know that.

You mean being yourself?

Harry took a deep breath. It was true. He'd never quite gotten over his fear of rejection.

You're still ashamed, Richard corrected him. *An adult man and you're still ashamed of who you are?*

Harry nodded as he measured out with a teaspoon the correct amount of coffee and added it to the auto-drip basket. "I suppose."

Beetle happily ate his breakfast while Harry dropped a slice of bread into the toaster and pressed down. He admired the simplicity of the mechanism as the filament turned a bright orange. He was grateful that there were no complicated instructions or keypads to touch. Just a gentle pressure downward and the toast was under way.

You're really ridiculous. Still afraid of your own shadow.

Harry bit his lower lip. *I never had your courage. You were always fearless.*

I always knew who I was.

Harry nodded. *How did you manage that trick?*

Richard's voice was calm and reassuring. *There never was another choice. I was always 100%. A gold-star gay.*

Harry remembered. Richard had never slept with a woman.

And you never could drink. Why did you do it?

Harry had no clue.

Because you were scared?

Fear had been the driving motivation in Harry's life. Fear of intimacy. Fear of not being published. Fear of not writing anything worthwhile. But mostly fear of judgment. The judgment of others.

Just then, Beetle growled as Lil appeared, coming around the corner from the guest bedroom. She wore one of Harry's white dress shirts, crumpled, and too large for her tiny body. She was bare-legged and bare-footed.

"What are *you* doing here?" Harry asked, flabbergasted, reaching for a nearby dishtowel to cover his parts.

"What do you think?" she said. "God, you snore. It sounded like a freight train." She pulled out a stool tucked under the kitchen counter.

"I had to sleep in the guest room. So, who were you talking to?" she asked looking about.

"No one," Harry said.

She changed the subject. "I don't think that towel is big enough to cover everything," she laughed. "So, what's for breakfast?"

The blood rushed to Harry's face, miraculously curing his aching head. "Cereal?"

"Do you have any Greek yogurt?" she asked, despite Harry's bewildered look. "I really don't eat carbs."

◆

Harry waited for the water in the shower to heat up.

So she's finally gone, Richard's voice pressed. *Disgusting.*

"It was kind of nice," Harry said, shaking his head in disbelief as he stepped into the shower, the hot water hitting his face, cascading down his body. *But I did have too much to drink.*

It takes more than liquor to do what you did.

Not when you're lonely, Harry thought.

Couldn't you see what she was up to? Little Miss Yoga Pants. How can you be so innocent at your age?

Harry burst into laughter. "Innocent?" he said, opening his mouth too wide and catching a stream of hot water. He spit the water out. *I'm not innocent.*

You should have known.

Maybe. She did surprise me. But I rose to the occasion, he thought with a smirk.

It was Richard's voice again. *When I met you, I thought you were such a closet case. And then I figured you were confused. A gay man who thought he was bisexual. That's how you coped. Not really straight, but someone who could pass. And so you proved it to yourself again last night. Three drinks and she had her way.*

I was never a gold-star like you. You never slept with a woman.

And I'm proud of it.

Harry turned off the shower. Beetle was lying on the rug in front of Richard's sink, stretched out, paws supporting his head, his eyes studying Harry.

"Hey, boy," Harry said. "What are you doing there?"

Beetle closed his eyes.

"I know." Harry leaned down and stroked Beetle's back. "You just want to be close. I know. Everyone needs someone to love."

◆

Rita washed her hands in the kitchen sink. "Did I ever tell you about your mother's name change?"

Rikki looked up from her homework assignment. *Isosceles triangles. What a waste of time. Who would ever need to know such nonsense?*

Rita had been out grocery shopping. In lieu of her housecoat, she wore a simple white blouse and a blue skirt. Her hair and makeup were impeccable. Whenever she left the apartment, unless it was to drive Rikki to school, she'd dress up. "You never know who you might run into," she'd say as she checked the mirror before walking out the door. "Mr. Right might be just around the corner," she'd announce, winking at her granddaughter.

She's so odd, Rikki would think. Rita clearly wasn't interested in men. And certainly not dating. Besides, she was much too old. And as for getting dressed up, Rikki was certain that her grandmother did it for the other women in the building, always trying to look her best when running into the neighbors.

Rita wiped her hands on her apron. A seasoned chicken sat on the counter in front of her. "I can still see it all as clear as day. She'd be sitting at the same table you are, reading the latest issue of *Life Magazine.*"

Rita's voice changed. It took on an indignant tone as she channeled El. "*'How could you ever name me Estelle?'*" Rita sighed dramatically.

Rikki had heard the story before.

"Estelle is a perfectly lovely name," Rita continued, playing her part as if her daughter was in the room. "It rolls right off the tongue. So elegant."

Rikki watched Rita's performance. It beat working on mathematics.

"Then your mother let out a laugh. *'Really, mother!'* she said. *'I wasn't born during the Great Depression.'*"

Rita stood back and admired her seasoned chicken.

"I don't care what you say," she said defiantly to her ghost of a daughter. "It's a perfectly lovely name. Lovely. And very befitting such a pretty girl."

Rita wiped her eye with the back of her hand. "She always wanted one of those modern names. Something simple." Rita slipped the chicken into the preheated oven. "But we're not simple people. Everything comes to us the hard way," she said sarcastically, as if finally giving into her daughter's point of view. "Do you know the first thing I said when I saw your mother?"

Rikki knew the answer—but she didn't want to interrupt—grateful for any discussion about El. Even if it was repetition.

"She was such a beautiful baby. All round and pink...oh, and those tiny fingers and toes. They had her tightly wrapped in this lovely pink blanket covered with tiny bunny rabbits. It was so adorable. And I held her close; her head, so warm, touched my cheek." Rita closed her eyes as she brought a red potholder to her face. "The world stopped at that moment." Rita's voice was gentle and loving. "It was heaven on earth. Absolutely heaven on earth."

"And then you ruined her life with that awful name," Rikki wise-cracked, unable to contain herself.

"Yes, that's right," Rita acquiesced, hands on her hips. "It was all part of my greater plan. You see, when I held your mother, I thought, how can I ruin this child's life? I hadn't yet divorced her father. It would take years before that idea would come to me." An index finger pressed to her temple. "So the next best thing was to name her Estelle. And by doing so, that dear woman's soul might forever hover over and protect my precious daughter." Rita had a far-off look in her eye. "And totally screw up her life."

Rikki couldn't help but laugh. Her grandmother had a natural way of turning a story mid-sentence from sweet and warm to falsely mean-spirited, regardless of the circumstance. "Oh, Rita," was all Rikki could manage as they both chortled. Rita, at having told it well, and Rikki, at the absurdity of her grandmother.

4

Barney Appleton had a secret.

Every now and then when Rikki raised her hand in class, she noticed Barney would flinch. She'd caught sight of the subtle jerking of his head, almost a nervous tic, out of the corner of her eye. At first, she'd thought it nothing. And then it started to bother her.

He's so arrogant, he's probably afraid I'll accidentally hit that hand-some face. The notion that he thought her an awkward klutz enraged her. *He's no better than me,* she thought, looking over at her desk mate defiantly. And though the fixed glare partially melted away when Barney glanced back, she remained essentially defensive.

"What?" he asked, leaning in close. He squeezed his nostrils together with his thumb and index finger. "Is it a booger?"

She recoiled in horror. "No. Absolutely not."

Standing by her locker, exchanging her books for a brown lunch bag, Barney stepped out of the passing crowd and leaned up against the adjacent locker. Just shy of six feet, he towered over her. A lock of brown hair fell across his eye as he slouched down, one shoulder pressed up against the metal locker. "Just tell me why you are always looking at me."

Rikki felt the blood rush to her face in a mix of embarrassment and instant desire. "Like you're too good for me to even look at," Rikki said in her iciest tone.

Barney's eyes searched her face. "What does *that* mean?"

"You think you're better than me, don't you?" she said, horrified even as the words left her mouth.

"Not at all," Barney answered, blinking hard, his lanky frame bending toward her.

This was the longest conversation they'd ever had.

"Then why don't you ever talk to me?" she asked. "I've been sitting next to you for weeks and you've barely said a word."

Barney looked away. "I like to keep to myself."

"Now there's a ridiculous answer," she snapped, instantly hearing the sound of Rita's voice echoing in her words.

"It's true," he said, turning back to look at her, his blue eyes piercing her soul.

"But why?"

Barney swallowed hard. "I shouldn't say."

Sensing his vulnerability, Rikki instinctively reached for his arm, blushing as she touched him. Instantly, he pulled back.

"Excuse me," she bristled, shutting her locker door, angry at his rejection.

He stepped closer, now leaning on her locker as he whispered into her ear. She felt the tension in her body ease as his breath caressed the side of her face. "It's not you," he said. "I'm sorry. I just don't like to be touched."

"But why?" she said, as if he'd offered a hint to a great riddle that she needed to solve.

He gazed into her eyes, as if considering what to do and say next. He then slowly rolled up the sleeve of his shirt.

She gasped. Along his arm were a series of deep scars.

"What happened?"

"My father," he answered sheepishly. "He beat the crap out of me as a kid. Always punching me in the stomach, and if I didn't block my face, he'd land one on my jaw. These," he emphasized with a movement of his arm, "are the cigarette burns he gave out when he couldn't find an ashtray."

Rikki had no idea. "Oh, my God. That's horrible."

Barney's tone changed. "Miss Nosy Body ... I didn't tell you because

I wanted your sympathy. I told you because you never stop asking questions."

Rikki ignored his comment. "I don't understand. How does this happen?"

"When you're me, you don't ask those questions," he muttered. "My father has been beating the crap out of me for years. I'm just lucky Social Services finally pulled me out when I was nine. If they hadn't, I'd probably be dead."

"But why would he do that to you?"

Barney looked at her and she could see him turn inside out as if there might be a reasonable explanation for the abuse. "My dad was an alcoholic. It's a sickness. When he drank, he was mean."

"And your mother?" Rikki wanted to know. "What possible excuse could *she* have?"

"She died when I was young. She was killed in a traffic accident."

Rikki covered her mouth with her hand. "Oh, I'm so sorry. I had no idea."

"How could you?" Barney said, the sadness in his eyes revealing a painful truth that he was used to keeping to himself.

◆

"Can anyone tell me why they think Dreiser named the book *An American Tragedy*?"

Rikki rolled her eyes. She'd finished the lengthy tome two weeks before and was eager to move on to another book. But for some reason, Mr. Rosenfeld appeared stuck on Dreiser. Out of sheer boredom, she'd swiped a copy of Rita's *Valley of the Dolls* by Jacqueline Suzanne. *Trash*, she thought with an air of superiority, even though she couldn't help but race through it with all the enthusiasm of a voyeur.

The class was quiet as Mr. Rosenfeld looked about for someone to answer his question.

"Barbra Winer," he called out. "We haven't yet heard from you. Can you help shed some light on Dreiser?"

Rikki turned about and caught Barbra's frightened look. *Had she even read the book?* Rikki wondered.

"Well," Barbra tentatively began, a nervous tremor in her voice. "It's such a sad story. And it takes place in America. So, the title totally makes sense."

Tittering broke out among the students and Mr. Rosenfeld insisted everyone quiet down. "We don't do that here," he said, most indignantly. "When we discuss great writers, we all learn something valuable. I'd suggest," he said, looking about, "that everyone here listen up. You never know what pearls of wisdom are about to be presented."

The room was once again quiet.

"And do you feel," Mr. Rosenfeld directed the question to Barbra, "that it's a story that resonates today?"

Barbra nervously twirled a jet-black curl, seemingly lost in thought. Mr. Rosenfeld slid down to sit on the edge of his desk as he waited.

"Yes," she finally blurted out, to Rikki's immense relief. "The desire to succeed, to be better than your parents, is still a powerful story. But I think," and as she said the words her eyes brightened, "if Dreiser were telling the story today, it might be about an undocumented immigrant. That seems to be the modern story of struggle and injustice," she announced, head held high.

"Very good, Barbra," Mr. Rosenfeld was up on his feet. "Bravo. I think you're right."

◆

"That was impressive," Rikki said as she and Barbra pushed their way through the crowd of students heading into the cafeteria. "You really pulled that one out."

Barbra laughed. "I did have a moment there."

"Did you even read the book?" Rikki quietly asked, conspiratorially.

"Of course," Barbra snapped back.

Rikki gave her a sideways glance that left little doubt that she didn't believe her.

"I *did*," Barbra insisted before offering a short giggle. "But that question! Who expects that kind of question?"

Rikki nodded in agreement. "I just wish he'd get off Dreiser. You'd think they were lovers," she said off-handedly.

Barbra quickly turned to her friend, grabbing her arm. "Oh, my God. Do you think Mr. Rosenfeld is gay?"

Rikki had never given it a thought. As far as she was concerned, Mr. Rosenfeld had no existence outside of the classroom. And certainly no sexuality. None of the adults with whom she interacted seemed in any way sexual. "I have no idea," she innocently answered. "How would *I* know?"

"Oh, Rikki," Barbra said in a shrill voice. "I think you hit on something. I think he is!" she said, with the wonder of having discovered the meaning of life.

"Don't be so silly," Rikki answered, increasingly uncomfortable with the discussion. "How could anyone know that? And what does it matter?"

Barbra's eyes bulged as she leaned forward and whispered in Rikki's ear. "You know how parents are. They wouldn't like knowing that their child is being taught by a gay teacher."

Rikki sneered. "It's not a disease, Barbra. You can't catch it."

"Maybe not," Barbra answered, pretending to be aloof to Rikki's admonition. "But it's nice to have something on him."

Rikki was shocked by Barbra's suggestion. "Barbra, what are you talking about? You wouldn't dare do anything to hurt him. He's such a nice man. And he hasn't bothered us."

"So you do believe *he's gay*," Barbra said, jabbing a finger in Rikki's direction.

Rikki shrugged.

"He keeps calling on us in class."

"He does that with everyone," Rikki answered.

"Well, I don't like it," Barbra said as she opened her Tupperware bowl and began to mix her salad with a white plastic fork.

"You're just lucky you had such a great answer in class," Rikki told her friend.

"No," Barbra said ominously. "*He's* lucky."

◆

"But you can be an artist in New York City," her mother said during one of their many Sunday evening long distance phone calls. El closed her eyes in disbelief.

It was April 1977 and college graduation was just around the corner.

"Mom, forget it," El said, exasperated after discussing the same subject every Sunday. "I'm not coming back to Queens."

There was an awkward silence. El held her tongue and waited. She knew that if she spoke first, Rita would think she'd have to get in the last word. The moments seemed to pass slowly as mother and daughter reached a stalemate.

Rita was the first to break. "I just don't know what I did to make you turn against me."

Unable to control herself, El let out a deep laugh. The more Rita tried to paint herself as the victim, the more confident El was in her decision. "Okay, Mom," she said, cutting off the conversation, happy she'd won out. "I'll speak to you next week. I've got to run."

"But wait, El," Rita begged, unwilling to let the conversation end. "What about graduation? We haven't spoken about graduation. Should I come up for the day? I only ask because your brother will come up from Cornell and then I'd have to stay overnight with him in a motel and you know how I feel about that."

El hated it when Rita talked about Richard. She could be so mean.

"If I have to stay in the same room with him, I'm going to make him wear a muzzle. Last time he was home he told me, 'You're one crazy bitch.' Nice, huh, talking to your mother that way?"

El's heart went out to her little brother. He'd written her letters regularly since she'd left for college—filled with things Rita had said, or worse, did. "She says I'm the smartest moron she ever met," Richard complained. "I just placed in the top ten in my class and she thinks I'm a moron."

It had been rough since El had left. She was relieved when Richard headed off to Cornell through an early-admissions program on a full scholarship. But distance didn't seem to solve the problem between mother and son. El couldn't help but wonder what caused Rita to treat Richard so poorly.

"He thinks he's better than all of us," Rita would complain. "All smartass and fresh."

El sighed. It seemed, from as far back as she could remember, Rita had disliked him. And then amid one of Rita's rants, El had simply posed the question. "Mom, tell me. What is it about Richard that you don't like?"

Rita had seemed taken aback by the question. "What do you mean?" she had said indignantly. "I love both my children."

El had only to give her mother a knowing tilt of the head before Rita confessed.

"I don't know," she lamented. "A mother should love her children. I know that intuitively. But what do you do when you don't? There's no book to consult on that one. Trust me," Rita said, an index finger wagging at El. "Dr. Spock never wrote about that."

"But when did you first know?" El pressed.

"Know what?" Rita asked, feigning ignorance.

El's jaw jutted forward. "That you didn't like him."

Rita thought for a moment. "It was one of the times when your father walked out on me."

"What? You two had split before?"

"Yes," Rita admitted. "This was the first time. And, of course, Richard was sick again. There I was. At my wit's end, and Richard demanded my attention. He was throwing up and he had diarrhea. It was disgusting. I spent the night cleaning up after him and doing the laundry. It was as if he knew all I wanted to do was be left alone—but he had to have my attention."

The mere memory produced a sour look on Rita's face.

"How old was he?" El wanted to know.

"Two," she said quickly.

El could hardly believe her ears. "*Two?* When he was two, you decided you didn't like him?"

Rita simply nodded. "That's right. Two."

◆

"I've had it with that bitch," Barbra hissed. The background noise of the crowded cafeteria was deafening. "I should hire a hitman to kill her."

Rikki had heard it all before. Barbra hated her stepmother. There seemed nothing the woman could do that was ever right. "What happened now?" Rikki asked, more out of exasperation than sympathy.

"*She thinks I should consider applying to ROTC. Me!*" Barbra said most emphatically, a finger nervously twirling a lock of black hair into a tight knot.

Rikki listened, intent on saying nothing until Barbra had gotten it all out of her system.

"Jews don't do ROTC," Barbra squealed. "Our parents pay for our college education." She spat the statement out as if it had been written in the Talmud.

Rikki nodded her head, not so much because she agreed, but because she couldn't imagine Barbra in military garb. How could she ever get that beehive hairdo under a helmet?

"She wants me gone," Barbra said, sliding her uneaten salad aside. "Killed in action. Dead. Out of here."

Rikki had no idea what to say. Instead, she moved closer to her friend, rubbing Barbra's back in a circular motion.

A female voice asked, "What's going on?"

Rikki turned and locked eyes with Janet, a tall, red-headed girl, with fierce green eyes and a striking figure, wearing a sweater dress so tight that Rikki wondered how she didn't blush just walking through the hallways. Her long hair was slicked back into a ponytail, and even though she was very beautiful, it was hard for Rikki to truly see her. Meanness clouded any external effect that Janet attempted to create.

Janet leaned down, too close, the glint in her eye threatening. "What are you two lesbos up to?" she said with a nasty smirk on her face.

"What?" Rikki pretended as if she hadn't heard her.

"Deaf too?" Janet said it so loud that Rikki blushed.

"Go away," Rikki pleaded, still rubbing Barbra's back. "Can't you see Barbra's upset?"

"All I can see," Janet said, "is that you and your little missus are in love."

Rikki paled. "We're not scared of you."

"Really?" Janet pulled hard on Rikki's chair, momentarily shifting Rikki off balance.

"Everything all right here?" Mr. Rosenfeld said, appearing out of nowhere.

Janet backed away.

Barbra wiped her eyes.

Rikki smiled awkwardly.

"Good," he said, looking intently at Janet. He nodded his head in the direction of where Janet's friends were sitting. The table of seven girls was looking over. "Then we should all be eating our lunches." Janet abruptly turned and left. "You girls okay?" he asked again, this time taking notice of Barbra's red eyes.

Rikki and Barbra meekly nodded, and Rikki offered a weak smile.

"Rikki, have you thought any more about that essay contest?"

Rikki had put it completely out of her mind.

"Don't make a mistake and lose an opportunity," he warned. "When you get to be my age, you'll learn that opportunities are few and far between. If you want something, you've got to grab for it."

Rikki listened, but she had no idea what he was talking about. *It was just an essay contest.*

"You should enter it," Barbra agreed.

Rikki wondered if she was saying that since Mr. Rosenfeld had ushered Janet away.

"Take my advice," Mr. Rosenfeld said as he scanned the lunch-room, his attention slowly drifting away. "Grab the first lifeline that's offered." A loud clatter and laughter drifted from across the room, the sound of a tray dropping to the floor, and Mr. Rosenfeld was gone.

"Did you see that shirt he was wearing?" Barbra remarked to Rikki.

Mr. Rosenfeld had been dressed in a white shirt with pink stripes topped by a bow tie of bright blue that matched the color of his eyes.

"What a fag," Barbra snickered.

◆

"I should never have come back here," El sighed as she lowered the volume on the portable black-and-white television Rita kept atop the kitchen counter. Walter Cronkite had just announced that David Berkowitz, the Son of Sam killer, had received twenty years to life. "Who does such a thing, running around the city, shooting innocent kids in their cars?"

"It can happen anywhere," Rita assured her as she cleared the dishes from the table. "Now, don't forget. Put the gloves on first."

El gave her mother a dismissive glance. "Like suddenly I don't know how to do this," she snapped back as she opened the Revlon box and removed the plastic bottle before opening the packet of Playtex gloves. "God, I hate these things," she said as she pulled on the yellow rubber gloves, wiggling her fingers as they slipped into place. Holding her hands up in the air she announced, "I'm ready. Where's that dime they're always talking about?"

"Oh, don't be ridiculous," Rita sniffed, as she dried the last plate with a red kitchen towel and put it away. "How you do go on."

El examined the plastic bottle now mixed with the solution and gave it another shake. "When was the last time we did this?"

"Who remembers?" Rita answered, now seated in front of the kitchen sink wearing a plastic poncho. She flattened down the front of her hair to show El the gray roots. "I'm just glad you're home. It's a big world out there. But you have only one home. And that, my darling, is here with me."

"Now that's depressing," El countered. "You know, this is only short-term."

El sighed. She hated the whole affair. Mixing the henna. The smell. Slipping on the rubber gloves. Parting her mother's hair in strategic spots to apply the dye. And the mess. It always seemed the dye got everywhere.

"Mom, I don't understand. Why can't you go to a hairdresser like everyone else?"

Rita shifted, sliding the chair closer to the sink. "Of course I can. Have you looked around lately?" she said, waving her hand about the small galley kitchen. "This isn't a mere two-bedroom apartment—it's an estate on Long Island. My name isn't Rita Goldenbaum. I'm Lady Astor. Come to think of it, I'll be wearing those lovely yellow gloves tonight with my ball gown when the Prince picks me up."

"Prince Spaghetti?" El added.

"Oh well, yes. I like all my beaus to be made of semolina."

El just shook her head. "Sometimes I think this is the only reason you wanted me to move back to Queens. So you could save money by having me do your hair."

Rita laughed. "I love having you here," she admitted, her voice uncharacteristically tender. "I can't help it if I like being with my daughter," she said turning to look at El as she grabbed a rubber-gloved hand. "I can't help how I feel."

El smiled. She loved Rita. Absolutely. And yet, she also knew that she had to get out of Queens.

"I know this is not for you," Rita admitted, leaning forward as El searched for the first spot to apply the dye. "I know you aspire to bigger and better things in life."

"I'm going to be a famous artist, Ma. You'll see. One day, my work will hang in the New York City galleries."

"Oh, El," Rita moaned. "Why not use your talent to make real money? You've been to college. You're a smart girl. Apply yourself and maybe *you* could live in Manhattan."

El applied the cold, wet dye to her mother's scalp.

Rita held a paper towel to catch any stray liquid that might drip onto her face. "I know how you feel about painting, but wouldn't it be more practical to start a career with a chance of success? Something within reach. As an interior decorator?"

El had heard it all before. Rita had nagged for years that the idea of being an artist was absurd. "Jewish girls from Queens don't live to hang in the Louvre," she was fond of saying. "They live to carry Louis Vuitton."

"Mother," El repeated, irritated by rehashing the same point. "I want to paint. I want to do faces. It's thrilling to capture the essence of a person in oil. Can you understand what I'm saying?"

Rita leaned forward as El added more dye to the back of her crown. "Darling," she answered, her voice low, "the only oil I've ever been interested in comes from Texas. The rest is Crisco to me."

El rolled her eyes. There was no point arguing. Not unless she wanted to hear more of her mother's sass. And she'd already heard enough.

"Hon," Rita's voice had softened. "How do you think I'd look in that Dorothy Hamill haircut?"

5

Rikki pleaded with Rita. "I want to go. Please ..." An uneaten plate of spaghetti sat before her. Despite Rikki's request, Rita had not stopped serving pasta. Rikki had read in *Cosmo* that pasta was her enemy. "I'll be with Barbra's family," she said. She held her hands before her in entreaty.

"No way," Rita said as she began to twirl pasta about her fork. She leaned forward and popped the ball of gluten into her mouth.

"But why not?" Rikki demanded to know.

Rita finished chewing. She dabbed each corner of her mouth with a tip of the napkin. "I don't like the idea of two young girls traveling alone on Amtrak. God only knows what can happen."

"Are you kidding?" Rikki could hardly believe her ears. "We live in Queens. Since when is this neighborhood so safe? Just last week, someone was mugged around the corner. And the Chinese laundry was robbed two months ago. And you drive me to school every day. It seems to me that Amtrak couldn't be much worse."

Rita twirled another forkful. "It's not just that. Amtrak is unreliable. And they've have a lot of accidents," she said shaking her head defiantly. "We just can't risk it. You're too precious. And far too young."

Rikki clenched her fists. When Rita's mind was made up, it was impossible to change it. "Then I'll go without your approval."

Rita offered a sharp glare. "You better think twice before you make that decision," Rita warned, her jaw firmly set. "You leave here without my permission and you won't be welcomed back. You know I love you," she said, "but this is not a democracy and you're still fifteen years old. In this house, you do as I say."

Rikki bit her lower lip. Rita could be scary when she got angry, and Rikki had already pushed her to the edge. "Fine," Rikki said, surrendering to the inevitability of Christmas in Queens. "Fine." She jerked herself hard away from the table, the pasta still untouched. "I'm done eating."

"That's fine and dandy with me," Rita said as she spun her fork into the pile of Ronzoni. "The pasta will keep. Maybe you need some time to be alone," she suggested, as if Rikki's stomping off was actually *her* idea.

◆

"She won't let me go," Rikki told Barbra at school the next day. Together they sat in the cafeteria, their lunches untouched.

Barbra's eyes popped. "But why?"

Rikki shook her head, unwilling to go into the specifics. "What does it matter? A no is a no."

"I can't believe it," Barbra said, exasperated. "It could have been so much fun. Now I'll have to go without you. I counted on you going," she whined dramatically, hands buried in her hair.

"It won't be so bad," Rikki offered, trying to cheer her friend.

"Oh, yes, it will," Barbra grumbled, popping open a green Tupperware. The intense smell of Good Seasons filled the air. "Have you ever been to Toledo?"

Rikki hadn't.

"It's a horror," Barbra assured her. "There's more going on in a cemetery."

Rikki giggled. "Now you're exaggerating."

"I'm not," Barbra said as she attacked a piece of wilted lettuce with a fork.

"How can you eat that?" Rikki asked.

"What else can I do? *She made it.* I've told her not to put dressing on it. That I can get dressing at school. But no." Barbra held up the fork to which the soggy lettuce clung. "She has to ruin everything. Even lunch. She makes me want to scream."

Rikki removed her sandwich, wrapped in aluminum foil, from the brown paper bag. She smelled it. "At least you don't have to eat peanut butter."

"Oh, I love peanut butter. I'd eat that in a heartbeat. What's wrong with peanut butter?"

"Do you know how many calories are in one tablespoon? 190." Rikki unwrapped the sandwich and lifted it to eye level. "How much would you say she slathered on this?"

"Don't forget the bread and the jam."

"Right. She wants me fat," Rikki announced. "If I'm fat, I'll never leave. If I'm fat, I'll be forced to spend the rest of my life with her. Lonely, depressed," and then Rikki broke into a mischievous smile, "drowning in adolescent angst."

Barbra burst out laughing, spitting up bits of chewed tomato, and snorting so loudly that those sitting nearby turned to see what was going on.

"Shh," Rikki said, an index finger to her mouth as she joined in the laughter.

◆

"What are you doing?" Rita asked as she put on her coat, ready to go grocery shopping. "I thought you said you were coming with me."

Rikki sat at the kitchen table. "I'm almost done." She scribbled out a final sentence, as a look of pleasure swept across her face.

"That must be some letter," Rita huffed. "Who are you writing to?"

Rikki held up the legal pad. "This isn't a letter. It's a short story."

"Well, excuse *me*," Rita snapped sarcastically, hands on her hips, winter coat wide open. "My mistake. So, are we going or not?"

"Yes," Rikki said as she marched off in her slippers to the bedroom. "I need to change my shoes. I'll just be a moment."

When Rikki returned, coat in hand, Rita was sitting at the kitchen table reading. She looked up as her granddaughter approached. Rikki was suddenly unnerved. There was a look in Rita's eyes she hadn't seen before. A look she didn't understand. She readied herself for the criticism. To be mocked. Her adrenaline surged as she prepared to defend herself.

Rita smiled as she held the yellow pad. "This is good. Where'd you come up with the idea?"

Rikki rushed forward and grabbed the pad. "It's not done yet."

"Oh, but it's very good. I'd like to read more."

Rikki suddenly felt ill. "It's only a first draft."

"I didn't know you could write." Rita opened her purse and searched through it. "Why didn't I know this?"

Rikki shrugged her shoulders. "There's really nothing to know. It's a writing contest. The winner gets a scholarship. No big deal. I probably won't win."

Rita pulled out a Salem 100 and gently tapped it on the table.

"Please don't light that. Please," Rikki begged.

Rita tried to squeeze the cigarette back into the pack. "Damn," she said as the cigarette broke in half. "Rikki, these are expensive. Now look what you made me do."

"One less nail in the coffin," Rikki muttered.

"Why didn't you tell me about this short story?" Rita asked. "Am I that older woman?"

"It's not about you," Rikki clarified.

"Well, that isn't very flattering. I'm thinking I'd make an interesting character." Rita slid out of her coat and let it drop to the back of the chair. "So, what's it about?"

"A journey," Rikki offered. "A young girl goes off to find herself."

Rita broke into a broad smile. "Oh, well, that makes sense."

Rikki pulled out a chair and sat down. "She travels to a place she's never been before and all sorts of wonderful things happen to her."

"Like *Alice in Wonderland*? *The Wizard of Oz*?"

"Kind of …"

And despite Rikki's request, Rita took out another cigarette and this time she lit it, inhaling deeply before exhaling up toward the ceiling. "Honey, it's been done before and by far better writers."

"I suppose," Rikki said as she clutched the short story to her chest.

"You know, you remind me of your mother right now." Rita took another drag as she eyed her granddaughter. "She thought she had this great talent. She attended Music and Art High School in Manhattan. I didn't want her to go. It was so silly. No one can earn a living as a painter, unless of course they're painting the outside of your house. And then she got that scholarship to Cranbrook's Academy of Art. Spending her day dreaming impossible dreams. I think of that and wonder what might have happened if she'd been an administrative assistant or a bookkeeper. Something practical. Logical. She might still be alive." Rita shifted her focus to her right index finger and a chipped nail.

"At least she was happy," Rikki said, bringing her back to the conversation.

"Happy? You think she was happy?" Rita shook her head to the contrary. "She wanted to live in Europe. Study in Paris. She'd often say. *'If I had studied overseas, I'm certain I could have become a marvelous portrait painter.'*"

"Why didn't she go to Paris?"

Rita put her cigarette out, smashing it into the ashtray with a twist. "Because people like us don't go to Paris. We don't do anything extraordinary. That isn't who we are. So she didn't study in Paris. Instead, my walls were lined with still lifes; fruit baskets overflowing with apples, oranges, bananas; vases upon vases of Gerbera daisies; loaves of bread laid out on white, silken tablecloths. Paintings hung one atop the other, rising from the floor to the ceiling. An odd, densely packed wallpaper of her 'little darlings' that she either couldn't sell or refused to sell. No space to spare. No wall left uncovered."

Rikki looked about. "Where?"

"Here," Rita waved a hand about. "Right here."

Rikki was astonished. The walls in the apartment were bare. White everywhere. "What happened to all of her work?"

Rita gathered herself up, ignoring the question. "We better get going. I don't want to miss out on the specials."

"But what about my mother's art?" Rikki demanded to know. "Where is it?"

"I donated it," Rita said, somewhat indignantly. "I brought it to Goodwill and said, 'Here, something wonderful to cheer up the needy. Some wonderful artwork from my dead daughter.'" Rita gasped, covering her mouth as she choked back tears. "A still life from a stilled life."

◆

"And then she told me that she'd given away all of my mother's artwork," Rikki shared with Barbra. "Can you believe her? Who would do such a thing?"

Barbra listened as she tore through her salad, enraptured as if it was the latest segment of *Grey's Anatomy*.

Rikki held a Gala apple in her hand. Two bites missing. "I don't think I'll ever get over it," she said waving the apple. "That was rightfully mine. She destroyed my personal property." Rikki was filled with righteous indignation.

Barbra leaned forward. "Did you ask where she donated it? The store might still have a few pieces left."

"What good would that do? It was over four years ago. I'm sure it's all gone by now. It must be."

"Oh, Rikki, I'm so sorry. I can only imagine how you must feel."

Rikki took another bite of her apple, satisfied that she'd won Barbra's sympathy.

"It seems to me that your grandmother is one selfish lady. It would serve her right if you just took off and went with me to Toledo anyway. It would teach her a lesson."

Rikki took another bite of her apple as Barbra popped the lid back on the Tupperware dish.

"You should do it," Barbra coaxed.

"Do what?" Barney asked as he slid into the seat next to Barbra and across from Rikki. A small, lunch-size carton of milk was in his hand.

Barbra's mouth dropped as Barney swiveled sideways, one elbow on the table, his head resting in the palm of his hand.

Rikki tried to act casually. "Take a trip."

"Where?" Barney asked, his bright blue eyes fixed on Rikki. "Where are you going?"

"Nowhere," Rikki admitted. "At least not at the moment."

"Too bad." Barney opened the milk and took a swig. "Sounds like fun."

"She's afraid," Barbra announced. "She's afraid to come with me to Toledo."

"Spain?" Barney asked.

"Ohio," Barbra quickly clarified.

Barney pointed at the unopened bag of Fritos by Rikki. She nodded. He took the bag and opened it. "Why are you afraid?"

"I'm not afraid," Rikki answered.

Barbra shifted about in her seat to face Barney. "Her grandmother won't let her go. It's Christmas and she wants to keep her close. She wants to poison her mind against her mother."

Rikki rolled her eyes as Barbra continued.

"She doesn't want Rikki to be a writer, because her mother was a painter."

"Oh Barbra, stop it. That isn't true," Rikki insisted.

"Yes, it is," she assured Barney. "She's trying to break her spirit. Just like she did with her mother. Breaking her like a rancher does a wild stallion."

Barbra had Barney's full attention. A strand of hair fell near his left eye. He pushed it back, tucking it behind an ear. "You can't let her do that," he opined to Rikki. "You have to be free."

Rikki had no clue what he was talking about. And the more Barbra went on, the more scared she became. "Okay," she finally said. "Conversation over. This is ridiculous. To listen to you two, you'd think I was being kept captive against my will. I love my grandmother. I'd never want to hurt her."

"Then you'll never have a life," Barbra warned. "Take it from me. Hurt them now before they hurt you. You're nothing more than an obligation. Someone who she has to look after. You've told me how mean she is."

"You're wrong," Rikki protested as she looked at Barney for support.

"Hey, I don't know anything about family," he admitted. "I'm strictly room and board. The State pays for my housing. The people I live with, they don't know me. I'm just—there."

Barbra gave Barney a wistful look. "That's so sad."

"Hey," he snapped, offering her a disparaging glance. "I'm just stating a fact."

Rikki looked from Barney to Barbra and then back again. *Maybe they're right*, she thought. Maybe they knew more about her situation than she was willing to admit. Maybe she needed to rethink Ohio.

◆

Harry was lost in his own world when Beetle started to rouse. It was noon and they'd been in Harry's office since eight o'clock. Beetle shifted, stretching his front paws forward and yawning. Harry tried to ignore him, frantically working to finish a paragraph. The words that had been flying out of his fingertips all morning had suddenly stopped.

Beetle let out a low growl.

Harry sighed as he leaned back and waited for Beetle to go off. It was inevitable. Either UPS or FedEx was delivering a package. Or a neighbor, enjoying the sunny day, oblivious to the two occupants inside, was strolling past the office window. Or the next door neighbor's cat, Marley, was out on the patio, digging in the potted plants, an action that had driven Harry's gardener to distraction.

Beetle looked at Harry. His brown eyes telegraphed concern. "Don't ask *me*," Harry said. "My hearing was never all that good. I wouldn't know if someone was in the next room."

Beetle stepped out of his bed and stretched.

Convinced that it was nothing, Harry refocused just as the bell rang and Beetle, barking loudly, took off for the front door. Shaken by the sudden outburst, Harry laughed at his own foolishness. *I knew he was going to do that.*

It was Lil standing in the open doorway, holding a plate covered in tin foil. "Why haven't you returned my calls?"

"Lil, I told you," Harry reminded her. "I don't like to be disturbed when I'm writing."

"Oh, Harry Aldon," Lil laughed as she pushed her way in. "You're really too much. What's a girl supposed to do? I call, you don't answer. If you're such a great writer, you could at least drop me a note."

Harry followed her into the kitchen, where she placed the dish on the counter. "Now when was the last time you had a decent lunch?" she asked, giving his tummy a gentle poke.

Harry defended himself. "Lil, I eat when I'm hungry."

"But not regularly," she admonished him.

"Lil, I don't need a mother. I'm too old to be mothered."

"Mother?" she snapped, hands on her hips. "Do I look like your mother?"

Harry smiled. With her trim figure and beautiful skin, Lil didn't look like anyone's mother. "Of course not."

"So let's eat," she said, turning to open the utensil drawer. "Now, where do you keep your forks and knives?"

"I'll do it." Harry came around and bent over to retrieve two place mats out of a drawer. Lil took them out of his hand and set them next to each other on the counter. Harry added the napkins and glasses. Lil removed the tin foil from the plate, to reveal two stacked sandwiches. Harry pulled down another plate from the cabinet. "There you go," he said as Lil separated the sandwiches, cutting each in half.

"See, it isn't so terrible to eat lunch with a friend."

Harry lifted the sandwich. "BLT on toast? I thought you avoided carbs. And bacon …" He took a bite.

"Oh, Harry. I know what men like. I wasn't going to bring you my Tofurkey."

Beetle let out a low-pitched whine. Lil looked down. "Oh, honey," she cooed, "I didn't forget about you." She retrieved a doggy bone out of her pocket. "May I?" she asked Harry. He nodded and she reached down. Beetle grabbed the bone and wandered away.

◆

Mr. Rosenfeld stood at the front of the room in a dark purple shirt topped by a lime-green bow tie. His blue corduroy pants, held up by bright orange suspenders, gave the impression that he'd stolen the outfit from Barnum & Bailey. He was in the midst of discussing Hardy's *Tess of the D'Urbervilles*, the next book on the class's reading list. He was practically giddy with excitement, his hands flailing about as he talked about the novel and its importance.

Rikki stifled a yawn as a tight wad of balled-up paper suddenly landed on her desk. Mr. Rosenfeld was now behind her, walking through the aisles as he tended to do when lecturing. Rikki unrumpled the note. It was Barbra's handwriting. In bold letters it read: WHAT A FAG!

Rikki immediately crumpled the paper as Mr. Rosenfeld approached her desk.

"Is that something you'd like to share with everyone?" he said in an imperious tone.

Rikki's lips went dry.

"Let me see that," Mr. Rosenfeld said putting out his hand.

Rikki passed the note over. She suddenly felt ill.

It seemed to take forever before Mr. Rosenfeld opened the ball of paper. Rikki watched his eyes as he scanned the message. She opened her mouth as if to say something but couldn't manage to get a word out. He looked at her, his face bright red, and she could sense the disappointment in his eyes. It was that look that scarred her. The intense hurt of someone who'd been so kind to her. She wanted to cry out, to deny ownership of the paper, to disavow any knowledge of it.

Mr. Rosenfeld slowly nodded his head. His expression shifted. His lower lip all but disappeared as he bit down. "I'll see you after class," he told Rikki as he slipped the ball of paper into his pocket and continued on about the writings of Hardy, though far less animated than before.

◆

Rikki slowly approached Mr. Rosenfeld's desk as the rest of the class streamed out the door. She waited, eyes glued to the floor, as Mr. Rosenfeld closed the door behind the last student.

"I'm surprised at you," Mr. Rosenfeld said as he crossed back to where Rikki was standing and sat on the edge of his desk.

Rikki nervously pursed her lips. She wanted to deny that she'd written the note, but then, she'd have to give up Barbra. And she didn't want to get her in trouble.

"I'm terribly sorry," she offered, her face burning as she made eye contact with her teacher. "It will never happen again. Never."

Mr. Rosenfeld sighed. "I want to be your friend, Rikki. I want to help you. I see that you stick to yourself for the most part. You're not like the others. There's a depth. It comes through in your creative writing. But there's no place for name-calling and put-downs. Accusations can be very dangerous things."

Rikki nodded as her stomach lurched.

"I don't want to have to talk to you again about this," he warned. "I've never been so disappointed in a student."

A tear escaped Rikki's eye.

"And I know you didn't write the note," he said, standing. "I know everyone's handwriting in class. That," he assured her, "is not yours."

Rikki was confused. If he knew she hadn't written the note, then why had she stayed behind?

"You should be careful who you choose to befriend," he went on. "Not everyone is worthy of your time."

So Mr. Rosenfeld knew it was Barbra.

"When someone is mean to others, they're telling you very clearly who they are. You should listen to them and be warned. You never know when they might turn on you."

Rikki shrugged. Barbra was her friend. She had no idea what Mr. Rosenfeld was talking about. "May I go now?" she asked.

"Yes," he said as she rushed from the room.

◆

"It's Barbra," Rita said as she held the phone in her hand. "Why does she call during dinner?"

Rikki took the receiver. "We're eating," she said, slightly exasperated. "I told you before, I don't want to talk about it."

Rita gave Rikki a sour face as she wiped up what remained of the gravy on her plate with a piece of challah.

"I'll call you later," Rikki said before finally hanging up.

"What's wrong with her?" Rita wanted to know.

"Oh, nothing. Just something about homework," Rikki lied.

"Well, she should do her own work," Rita huffed.

Rikki nodded. "Would you excuse me? I'm done."

"You are not," Rita admonished, checking out Rikki's dinner plate. "You've hardly touched my pot roast."

"I can't," Rikki explained, hands in the air. "It's delicious, but I can't."

Astonished, Rita asked, "Are you feeling all right?"

"No," Rikki lied again. "I think I'll lie down," she said, leaving the table.

"Yes," Rita surmised. "It must be easier to talk to Barbra from the other room lying on your bed."

Rikki smiled as she slinked away.

"I'm going to save your dinner," Rita called out. "Come back and eat when you're done. My word, you'll grow up to be skin and bones with a friend like Barbra."

◆

Dr. Newbar slid a hand up and down Beetle's tummy as the wire fox terrier struggled.

"Take it easy, boy," Harry said, holding Beetle by the collar as Beetle's back legs continued to kick and slide on the metal examining table. "He's not going to hurt you," Harry assured him.

Newbar smiled, letting go of Beetle. The dog practically launched himself into Harry's arms.

"It's just a sore tummy. Nothing to be concerned about," Newbar said in such a loud voice that Harry was startled.

"Do you have anything for the diarrhea? It's kind of nasty."

"Sure." Newbar stroked Beetle's back. Beetle clung ever closer to Harry with each touch.

"What do you think caused it?" Harry wondered, lifting Beetle off the table and out of Newbar's reach.

"Hard to say. He could've picked something up off the ground. Has he been getting into the garbage?"

Harry shook his head no.

"Hey, it's no big deal. Give him some boiled chicken and white rice—and then slowly shift it over to his regular food. I'm sure he'll be fine."

Back at home, Harry filled a soup pot with water.

What did the doctor say? Richard wanted to know.

"Nothing," Harry said as he turned on the flame.

That was a lot of upset stomach for nothing.

Beetle sat at Harry's feet as if waiting for a treat.

"He probably got into something." *No big deal. It happens.*

Not the way you watch him. That dog is never out of your sight.

Harry agreed. He was exceptionally attentive with Beetle. The diarrhea had been an odd occurrence.

Maybe it was your girlfriend. She's been giving him treats. Maybe she's poisoning him.

Harry burst into laughter. "Lil?" *She adores him. She'd never hurt him. And besides, she isn't my girlfriend.*

She's here all the time. Is that good for your writing? Has Edward seen the next set of pages? Aren't you running late?

Harry dropped the skinless breast into the simmering water. He watched as the fat from the breast created a foamy white film on top.

She's going to get in the way of your writing.

Harry had no doubt that was true.

Get rid of her, Richard's voice pressed. *You don't need a woman to be happy.*

◆

"I'm not telling you," Rikki told Barbra for what seemed like the billionth time. She held the receiver tightly to her ear as she curled the cord in one hand. "That was a private conversation between Mr. Rosenfeld and me." There was silence on the other end of the line. "Are you still there?" Rikki asked.

"Yes." Barbra's voice was dour. She was clearly disappointed. "I don't see why you won't tell me. A friend would tell."

"Barbra, I *am* your friend. But even between friends, certain things are private."

"I don't see why," Barbra huffed.

"They just are." Rikki held her ground.

"Maybe we really aren't friends after all," Barbra said.

"Barbra, you'll always be my friend," Rikki calmly said. "Now I have to go. You've tired me out." It was one of Rita's favorite expressions.

◆

Rikki wondered if it were true that her mother's artwork had been donated to Goodwill, where it would have been available to anyone for next to nothing. It didn't seem reasonable that Rita would have given it away. But then, what else might Rita have done with the artwork?

Perhaps it's in the building's storage room, Rikki considered as she tossed and turned, unable to sleep. *I bet that's where it is,* she thought with excitement at potentially solving the mystery.

Getting up at five o'clock in the morning, she grabbed Rita's keys off the counter, left the apartment, and headed down the elevator to the lobby.

Rikki froze when the doors opened. Willy, the building superintendent, was dealing with Aguilar Gardens' bug infestation. Despite being in his fifties, Willy retained the powerful physique of a high-school athlete. His close-cropped Afro was stained with patches of gray. Recently the building's owner had removed the incinerator and replaced it with a trash compactor. Since Willy could no longer burn the garbage, there had been a growing infestation as the roaches had discovered the rotting food. In the early morning hours, the bugs seemed to be the most active, crawling over the lobby walls and ceiling, and sometimes falling on the heads of unsuspecting tenants. Using a broom, Willy knocked the bugs to the floor and then quickly swept them up into a vibrating brown pile.

Rikki ran past Willy, covering her head.

"Good morning, sweetie," he called as Rikki raced by. Her goal, the storage room. A large locked area where tenants stored possessions for safekeeping.

With a turn of the key, the door opened and Rikki stepped into a damp, musty odor.

She twisted the electric timer by the door, illuminating the tight space. Bare pipes ran across the ceiling and up and down the walls. Fine cobwebs had formed here and there. Rikki swiped at them as she made her way through the dank, narrow room, passing by clusters of furniture, large black trunks, rows of bicycles, and large and small boxes of every shape and size. Each grouping was gathered under a name prominently displayed on a piece of board that hung from an overhead pipe—along with an apartment number.

Rikki searched for Goldenbaum. She passed by Sardell, Stein, Spiegel, Hoffman, Morgenroth, Blance, and Tucker. The dust was so thick she thought she'd choke as she made her way to the back of the storage area.

And then she spotted it.

A black trunk in the back corner near an old wooden dresser. Goldenbaum.

It was a miracle. She knelt down and examined the trunk's lock. Holding Rita's keys in her hand, she searched for a key that might fit. And then the room went pitch black. Terrified, she leapt to her feet and rushed ahead toward where she thought the door was, only to collide blindly with what seemed to be a stack of boxes. She screamed and dropped the keys. The noise reverberated off the ceiling.

◆

"Are you okay?" Willy asked as he helped her to her feet.

Her jeans and shirt were covered in a film of dust. "What happened?" she asked as she brushed herself off.

Willy looked over at the toppled boxes. "It looks like you were 'Dancing in the Dark,'" he cheerily sang.

Rikki offered a blank stare.

"Bruce Springsteen," Willy clarified. "*This gun's for hire… even if we're just dancing in the dark.*"

Rikki shook her head, not recognizing the tune.

"Young lady, your musical education is woefully lacking," Willy laughed. "And next time you come in here. I'd recommend you give that timer a full rotation if you plan on staying longer than a few minutes."

"Oh."

Willy eyed her suspiciously. "People don't usually spend a lot of time in here. They come in, get what they want, and leave. They sometimes forget to turn off the lights. So I installed that timer."

Rikki nodded as she looked about.

He stroked the stubble on his chin. "So, what are you doing up so early and what exactly are you looking for?"

"I dropped my grandmother's keys. I've got to find them." She was becoming increasingly frantic.

"No need to panic," Willy advised.

This was the longest conversation Rikki had ever had with Willy. She hadn't realized how very kind he was and wondered why she didn't already know that. After all, he always seemed to be about, fixing this or that.

Together they searched.

"I don't see them over here," he said, scanning under a table with a small flashlight that he retrieved from his tool belt. "So you didn't answer my question. What *are* you doing in here?"

"Nothing," she replied innocently, crouched down to look behind a mirror leaning up against three stacked boxes.

Willy was poking around a washing machine. His tone became conspiratorial. "Now, come on. You can tell me what you're up to. It'll be our secret. Promise," and he crossed his heart before holding up two fingers just as she looked his way. "Scout's honor."

Rikki took a breath. "I'm looking for my mother's artwork. She died when I was eleven. I thought Rita might have stored it here."

"Here?" Willy looked about. "Now I'm not an art critic, but this is the last place you'd store artwork. It's too damp."

Rikki was not about to give up. "Yes, but I found a trunk. Maybe it's in the trunk."

"Could be," Willy confirmed.

Rikki felt a sudden glimmer of hope. "But I can't open it," she said, focused on the missing keys. "Oh, my God. I've lost Rita's keys," she cried. "I can't get back into the apartment without those keys."

◆

"Here they are. Right over here," Willy called as he bent down and reached between a standing lamp and something covered by a white sheet. He offered the keys up in the palm of his hand.

"Oh, thank goodness," Rikki said with delight. "Now which key do you think will open the trunk?"

Willy rifled through the set of keys anchored by a gold R before selecting a small silver key. "I'd bet on this one."

Kneeling down next to the trunk, Rikki looked up at Willy just as the key slipped in. She broke into a big grin.

"Now, before you do this," Willy said, a troubled look on his face, "don't you think you really ought to talk with your grandmother?"

Kneeling by the trunk, the center latch opened, Rikki worked to unsnap the metal clasps on either end. "There's nothing to talk about."

"Maybe your grandmother has her reasons."

Rikki barely took a moment to respond. "Now, why would she want to keep anything of my mother's from me?"

Willy paused, kneeling down so that they met at eye level. "People have all sorts of odd reasons for doing what they do."

Rikki offered a puzzled look.

Willy grimaced and stood up, rubbing his thighs. "I guess I'm not as young as I used to be. Gosh, that hurts."

Rikki ignored his complaint. "What did you mean?"

Willy's brown eyes locked onto Rikki's. "Honey, sometimes the things we adults lock away in trunks are the things we can't bear to part with ... even if we don't want to look at them any longer."

Rikki lifted the top of the trunk. A layer of dust caught her by surprise, forcing a sneeze. There before her eyes was a photo album perched atop nothing more than a few old blankets and pillows.

Rikki flipped open to the first page. Black-and-white photographs held in place by white triangular edges. Rikki immediately recognized her mother. El must have been about fifteen at the time, the same age as Rikki. Standing next to a tree, she had pulled her long blonde hair into a ponytail and her lovely figure was already clearly in view. She wore a simple white shirt with plaid bell-bottom pants. "She's practically a girl," Rikki told Willy as he glanced over her shoulder and smiled.

"She's pretty," Willy said.

"Uh-huh," Rikki agreed.

"Just like you," Willy continued.

"Oh, no. We're nothing alike. My mother was tall with blonde hair and hazel eyes. Flawless skin," Rikki said instinctively as she brought a hand to her face. "She was positively lovely. Lovely."

"How old was she …?" Willy asked as his voice trailed off.

"When she died? Forty-five. She was only forty-five."

Willy sighed. "That's heartbreaking."

"I know," Rikki quickly agreed. "But the saddest thing is," and she looked up at the big man with his tender expression and suddenly felt safe in sharing her secret, "I can't remember her at all."

"How old were you when it happened?"

"It was four years ago," Rikki admitted, a tremble in her voice. "How can you forget your own mother? It just doesn't seem possible."

Willy tilted his head as he looked down at her. "It *is* strange."

"I know," Rikki agreed. "But it's true."

Willy checked his watch. "I better get going. Do you want to take that book with you and lock up the trunk or should I just leave you be and come back later?"

Suddenly panicked, Rikki's eyes opened wide and her mouth descended into a frown. "What time is it?"

"It's 6:15."

"Oh no," Rikki gasped. "Rita will be getting up. I have to get back." And without another word, she lifted the book out of the trunk, slid it under her arm, and slammed the trunk shut, pushing in the lock and turning down each clasp.

Together, they left the storage area. But before Rikki stepped on the waiting elevator, she turned. "Please don't say anything," she begged Willy, who had already taken up his regular post with the broom.

He winked. "Don't worry, sweetie. Your secret is safe with me," he said as the elevator doors closed.

6

Mr. Rosenfeld stopped Rikki in the hall.

"I liked it," he offered without bothering to specify what he was talking about. "I think you have a really strong chance."

Rikki nodded, realizing he was discussing her short story. "Thank you," she said, still not sure if writing a short story was much of a big deal. After all, she'd just strung some words together. And yet, she couldn't help but feel nervous about others reading it. As if strangers were about to tap into her most private thoughts.

"You're really talented," Mr. Rosenfeld continued.

Rikki didn't know what to say.

Mr. Rosenfeld looked about the hallway as the other students passed on their way to class. "You think you're just like everyone else. As if anyone can write like you."

Rikki felt a blush creep up her face. "It's no big deal," she answered, desperate to make an escape.

"But you see ..." His yellow and blue polka dot bow tie wiggled with each glide of his Adam's apple. "Not everyone can. You see things as they are. You see people for *who* they are. You're sensitive," he said, as he nodded his head in confirmation, before turning to walk away, his black corduroys creating a swooshing sound.

Rikki watched as he headed down the hall. The last thing she ever wanted was to be sensitive. She wanted to be strong. Invincible. Impervious to those around her.

Rita too had often told her that she was different. Not like anyone from Queens. It wasn't meant to be a compliment. And even though Rikki relished being from the Midwest, she didn't want to be perceived as someone from the Midwest. *It makes no sense,* she'd say to herself. And yet, it remained true. She didn't want to be anyone's rube.

"I saw you talking with her," Barbra whispered at lunch.

"Her?" Rikki had no clue who Barbra was talking about.

"You know. *Mr. Rosenfeld.*" Barbra smiled as if they shared a secret. Before Rikki could ask anything further, Barney came into view. "He's coming over," Barbra squealed, her neck turned about in Barney's direction. "I can't believe it."

Her foolishness rubbed Rikki the wrong way. "Stop it. You'd think you'd never seen a boy."

Barbra's smile shifted to a plaintive look. "Not a boy who looks like him."

Barney slid his tray next to Barbra and sat down. She dropped her shoulders, appearing smaller than her actual size. "Hey, Barney," Barbra said, all aglow.

"Hey," Barney acknowledged with a shake of the head.

"What are you doing after school?"

Rikki blushed. Barbra was so brazen. She acted as if Rikki wasn't even at the table.

"Nothing," Barney answered as he lifted a burger to his lips, registering a sour expression as he sniffed it. "God, what kind of meat do they put in these things?"

Barbra leaned up against him. "It would be fun to hang out together."

Barney nodded without making eye contact.

"Great," Barbra exclaimed. "Then we're all set."

Barney took a swig from his cola. "Are you gonna be there?" he asked Rikki.

The girls exchanged quick glances.

"I need to go straight home today," Rikki lied.

"Yeah," Barbra agreed, her eyes wide and focused on Rikki. "Rikki hasn't been feeling well."

Barney jerked his head back, giving Rikki the once-over. "You seem fine to me."

Barbra interjected. "Well, that's just the thing. She seems okay—but she has a doctor's appointment."

"Where?" Barney asked.

Rikki felt the heat rise in her face. She was never much for lying.

"Dr. Jacobi," Barbra offered. "He's all the way over on Union Turnpike."

"That's a long walk," Barney said. "You shouldn't walk over there alone."

A look of panic crossed Barbra's face.

"I'll walk you," Barney offered, much to Rikki's shock. "Just to make sure you get there in one piece."

◆

Barefoot, Lil walked across the wooden floor, stopping now and then to help a client in a particularly awkward pose find a more balanced stance. With a gentle touch to the back, a client might relax and ease the curvature of the spine. A hand to the shoulder ... the shoulder drops. "That's it," she'd say in her melodic voice. "This is yoga. There's no competition. It's all about being one with your body. Allow yourself to ease into the pose."

With each reminder, the group released a collective sigh. She was used to such sounds. Belching and farting were not uncommon—and happily welcome as a natural part of the human condition. When an especially loud fart sounded as she moved the class into a downward dog, she reminded everyone, "We store tension in our nerves, muscles, and most certainly, within our digestive tract. This is your time to let it all go. Here, together. This is a safe space."

She moved through the dimly lit room. The class members now lay on their backs in silent meditation. Assuming her spot at the front, she slipped to the floor into a cross-legged position. And though she'd actively led the session, mindful of her students' gentle breaths, she was unable to get Harry out of her mind. It had been a while since she'd met a man so special. Someone who seemed genuinely kind without being needy. She'd been surprised by his reluctance to engage sexually, but in her own indomitable way, she'd been undeterred.

He's so sensitive and intelligent. Almost gentle, she thought, as she tried to reconcile her perceptions of a mystery writer with that of the man she'd come to know. And as she glanced about the room, trying to determine if she was ready to conclude the session, a stray thought crossed her mind. *Perhaps he's shy sexually. Or maybe he's one of those celibate types who prefers conversation to sex. A chaste man who I've pushed against his will?*

The thought at once seemed absurd, and yet, there was something that bothered her. She sensed his reluctance to connect. She wondered if she was projecting her own feelings onto him. After all, she was still single. She'd been reluctant to engage in a serious relationship, coming to the conclusion early on that love and marriage were really not *her thing.* But even though she was committed to daily yoga practice, she still sneaked a candy bar and a cigarette every now and then.

The snore of an older man in the front row grabbed her attention.

"Okay everyone, on the count of three, I want you to slowly awake. One ... two ... three! There. You should be feeling fresh and alert," she said as the man up front struggled to sit up on one elbow. "It's going to be a wonderful day, full of energy and life," she softly said as the group mirrored her cross-legged position. She bent slightly forward at the waist and offered a *"Namaste."*

◆

When the final bell rang, Rikki rushed along the hallway with the rest of the class, hoping to make it out before running into Barbra or Barney. She had no intention of spending more time with Barney, struggling to talk with him. And she certainly wanted no part in hurting Barbra's feelings. If Barbra was determined to make a fool of herself with Barney, Rikki was only too happy to step aside.

"Hey, wait up," Barney called from behind.

Rikki pretended she didn't hear him.

"Hey," he said jogging up to her side and tugging on her arm. "Wait up."

She turned, and though she wanted to tell Barney that she was fine managing on her own, one look at him and the thought was gone.

"I told you that I'd walk with you," he said, catching his breath. He wore a black leather jacket and a red and white scarf wrapped about his neck. He pulled on the knot of the scarf, seemingly self-conscious of the bold fashion choice. "It's cold for the beginning of December."

She nodded, lost in the sparkle of his eyes.

"Let's go," he said, breaking the awkward moment as they headed down the steps and out the doors. "Which way do you usually walk?" He looked about.

"This way," she said, pointing in the direction she took home, forgetting about the lie, too consumed by his sudden interest and flattered by the attention.

They walked along together, not saying anything for two blocks. Rikki racked her brain to come up with a suitable topic. As they stood on the sidewalk waiting for the light to turn green, panic gripped her heart. She had to say something. They couldn't continue to walk together in silence.

As they crossed the street, she heard a woman's voice. *When you don't know what to say, ask the other person about themselves. Everyone loves to talk about themselves.*

Rikki let out a gasp. She hadn't been able to conjure a single memory of El in four years and yet, in the middle of 73rd Avenue, for one brief moment, El had come back to her, her voice vibrant and very much alive.

"Are you okay?" Barney asked as he pulled her across the intersection and back up on the sidewalk.

Rikki covered her mouth with the palm of her hand as she looked up at the sky. "That was the most amazing thing. I can't believe it."

Barney looked at her as if she was crazy. "What gives?"

"I lost my mother four years ago and I haven't been able to remember anything about her. Nothing."

"What?"

"It's true," she said, wiping a tear. "Not a thing… until now. I just heard her voice. Clear as if she was standing next to me. My mother," she said, grabbing both his arms and giving him a shake, "just spoke to me. I heard her."

Barney bit his lower lip. "I knew it," he said pulling back and pointing a finger at her. "When we first started talking, I thought you were a little nuts. Now, I know you're completely nuts."

She offered a frown. "Don't say that. It's an awful thing to say."

"Okay, okay." He surrendered to her request as they continued walking. "So you really don't remember your mother at all?" he asked in a serious tone.

"Nothing," Rikki admitted. "The doctors said that I had some sort of shock. That I'd eventually remember. But I haven't. Not until now."

Barney's eyes brightened. "Well, maybe that's because of me. I must be good luck."

"Maybe," she said looking at him askance. "Or maybe it's that photo album that I found," Rikki said, partly to herself. "I've been looking at it every morning while my grandmother sleeps."

He sighed. "I can tell you one thing. I wish I could forget *my* family."

She shifted the focus. "Tell me about your foster family. Who are they? Where do you live?"

Barney visibly recoiled. "There's really nothing to say." He looked straight ahead as she struggled to keep pace with his long strides. "I'm there until I'm eighteen. There are rules that I abide by, but come my eighteenth birthday, I'm on my own."

Rikki couldn't imagine it. No matter how challenging her relationship was with Rita, she had no doubt that she had a safe place with her grandmother. "What will you do then?"

"Go to college. I'm going to need a scholarship to make it through. It won't be easy, but," he said with the maturity of an adult, "I have no choice."

His words echoed in her head. *No choice.* He seemed, despite his challenging family circumstances, to have figured out how to move forward. He'd owned his situation and decided to rise above it. "I wish I was more like you," she admitted.

"Me?" He sounded surprised. "You don't want to be like me."

She stopped walking and turned to him. "Oh, I think you're wrong. You know who you are and where you're going."

He let out a laugh. "It only seems that way. Those are words. That's all. Words I've heard from social workers and counselors. I'm not even sure I believe any of it."

"But you *must*," she said with such powerful conviction that she surprised herself. "You must believe that things will get better. And that one day, you'll have a family. And you'll be there for your children. Protect them. Give them what you didn't have."

He looked down. "I'm not sure how anyone can give what they've never known."

She reached for his arm and pulled him close. He looked down at her as she stood on her tiptoes and offered him a gentle kiss on the lips.

The borough of Queens disappeared as the two teenagers stood on the corner.

"You will," she said confidently, suddenly feeling every inch a woman. "And they will be lucky to have you as a dad."

◆

Booth Memorial Hospital was bustling with activity as father and daughter walked through the hallways hand in hand. Seymour Goldenbaum had stopped at the flower shop and purchased a huge bouquet of red roses. Little Estelle, barely two, grasped a small brown teddy bear sporting a red bow tie. She dropped the bear twice on the ride up in the elevator to the maternity floor before Seymour slipped the bear under his arm.

Rita was dozing as they entered the room. Seymour placed the bouquet on a chair tucked in the corner and slipped Estelle out of her red winter coat. He thought his daughter was pretty as a picture before he noticed that the child's Mary Janes were slightly scuffed from the walk through the parking lot. Estelle had fallen, as children tend to do when first learning to walk, and had inverted the black shoe on the gravel.

I hope Rita doesn't notice her shoes, he thought as he removed a hanky from his pocket and, with a little spit, tried to recapture the luster. As he wiped, Rita opened her eyes. "Guess who's here?" he gently sang out, standing up, still holding Estelle's little hand as if he was presenting their daughter as a gift. "It's your little darling."

Rita's weary expression shifted to spontaneous joy. "Oh, sweetie," she called, arms outstretched. "Come to Mommy."

Little Estelle let out a joyful squeal as she wobbled over to the bed. Seymour grabbed her under the arms from behind and lifted her high in the air before bringing her slowly down to sit on the edge of the bed close to her mother. Estelle let out a cry of sheer ecstasy.

"Who's Mommy's love?" Rita cooed, running her palm over her daughter's soft cheek. "Look how pretty you are," she said, kissing her child as Estelle leaned in to her mother.

"How are you feeling?" Seymour asked, lifting the flowers to move the chair closer to the bed.

"What's that in your hand?" Rita asked.

"Roses for you, my darling," he said gleefully as he leaned over and kissed his wife on the cheek.

"Sy, how many times have I told you about roses?" Rita scolded, a sharp edge to her tone. "I'm allergic. You know that."

"Oh, my God." Seymour slapped a hand to his forehead. "In all the excitement, I completely forgot. I wasn't thinking. Okay. Not to worry. I'll give them to the nurses. Someone should enjoy them."

Rita made a face. "I hate to give them a gift when they never answer the damn buzzer. This morning alone, I waited fifteen minutes before someone showed up to help me to the bathroom. They don't deserve flowers."

"Oh, come on, honey. This is an amazing day. Let's be happy."

"Amazing for *you*," Rita groused. "I've been up since three in the morning pushing that baby out. I hurt everywhere. And you show up with *roses*." And then, as if on cue, she let out a roaring sneeze. So loud that little Estelle jumped.

Seymour slid a box of tissues closer to his wife. "I better get these flowers out of here," he said, stepping out of the room momentarily and then rushing back in. "Oh, you should have seen their happy faces," he said.

Rita didn't appear to be listening. She was fiddling with Estelle's top. "What's this on her blouse?" She pulled on the white top. There was a minor discoloration.

Seymour glanced over. He'd put on Estelle's bib and carefully fed her, and still, a spot of chocolate ice cream stared back at him. "Nothing," he answered, raising the teddy bear up in the hope of distracting Rita. "Look. Isn't it sweet?"

Rita was having none of it. Her expression turned dark. "Did your father feed you ice cream this morning for breakfast?" she asked her daughter.

Estelle broke into tears.

"Did you give her ice cream?" she asked Seymour.

Seymour lifted Estelle into his arms to soothe her. He used the little teddy bear to refocus the child's attention. "It's a special day."

"She's already too chubby."

Seymour waved a hand at his wife. "She's only two. What are you talking about? She's a perfectly lovely child. There's nothing wrong with her weight."

"And that stain? Who is going to get that stain out?"

Seymour sidestepped the question. "Have you seen the baby this morning?"

"Yes," Rita answered. "I'm going to have to go to a bottle." She rubbed her right breast. "It was so uncomfortable."

Seymour blushed. He didn't like discussing such matters. "But you had no trouble with Estelle."

"So does that mean I have to breast feed every baby? Why don't you try it—if you're such a big fan?"

Seymour rolled his eyes. "I guess there's no pleasing you this morning."

Little Estelle started to fidget so he sat down and placed her on his lap.

"I wish we hadn't done this," Rita admitted. "I think this is a mistake."

Seymour's heart sank. Rita had been miserable throughout the pregnancy. He'd just assumed that once the child was born, her spirits would lift. "We both agreed to have another child," he reminded her.

"But a boy," she said. "I don't know."

Seymour kissed Estelle on the forehead. "You thought all along it might be a boy."

"Yes," Rita agreed, "but thinking it and knowing it are two very different things."

Seymour bit his lip. He wasn't sure what to say. Or how to deal with Rita.

"I know it's been a rough morning. It's just the drugs talking." He caught Estelle's eyes and repeatedly smacked his lips, much to the baby's delight. "Honey, maybe I should take you home. Mommy still isn't feeling well," he pretended to explain to Estelle, who had managed to get a paw of the teddy bear into her mouth and was happily sucking on it.

◆

Alone in her bedroom, Rikki pored over the photo album that she'd swiped from Rita's trunk. Each morning, she'd awake early, and make her bed. Then she'd retrieve the album, and while Rita slept, study the photographs, carefully cleaning up any black specks that might spill from the disintegrating construction paper as she flipped through the black-and-white photographs.

She marveled at the change in Rita. She'd once been a stylish brunette with wavy hair, and a lot trimmer. *A lovely figure*, Rikki thought, on closer inspection.

And there were other pictures, too. A man she'd never met, holding two babies up for the camera. One, a towheaded little girl, the other, an infant wrapped in a blanket. Rikki explored the man's face as if the picture might reveal something about his character.

So Rita did have a husband, she thought, fully aware that a man had to be in the picture to conceive children. She wondered what had happened to him and the marriage. And as she turned the pages of the album, she became keenly aware of the second child. A little boy. Younger than the little girl.

El had a brother. I have an uncle.

Rikki racked her memory. Rita had never mentioned another child.

Rikki stared into the past, mesmerized by El. An extremely photogenic girl with blonde hair, blue eyes, and a huge smile. *Everyone has a childhood,* Rikki thought, and yet, as page after page unfolded, it was a revelation to see her mother as a toddler, tween, and adolescent. She'd never thought of El as being any one particular age, and yet here, in this photo album, El was all ages.

The boy, too, was in a number of photos, but not nearly as many as El. Rikki studied his face in a Little League photo. He didn't look happy. Actually, as she turned through the pages she realized that he rarely smiled.

Rikki longed to ask Rita why she'd locked the album away. Who the other child was, and why the album stopped at El's high school graduation. There were still blank pages. Surely there must have been opportunities to take more pictures, and yet, there were none.

"Rikki," Rita called out, gently knocking on the door. "Are you up?"

Startled, Rikki slammed the photo album shut and slid it under the bed. "Yes, I'm awake."

Rita opened the bedroom door. "What are you doing?" she asked, noticing the bed was already made. "When did you get up?"

"Me?" Rikki answered, stalling for time.

Rita stood, hands on her hips, giving Rikki an odd look.

"I've just been lying here thinking about how much I've come to love Queens."

Rita's face broke into a smile. "Really? Oh, I'm so glad. I knew we'd eventually win you over." She pulled out Rikki's desk chair and sat down. "It's such a relief," she continued, giving her neck a twist. "Everyone told me, *just give her time. She'll adjust.* But I have to say, waiting for you to come around hasn't been easy."

Rikki shifted her position, sitting up and pulling her knees into her chest, wrapping her arms about her legs. "So, what about breakfast?" She wanted Rita out of her bedroom so that she might hide the album in the back of the closet. Somewhere Rita would never look.

"You seem so jumpy," Rita said, narrowing her eyes and inspecting Rikki. "What's going on? Is it school?"

"Oh, course not," Rikki answered, her patience running short. "I'm just hungry," she said matter-of-factly.

"No, it's more than that." Rita looked about. "Everything seems in place. Nothing's wrong?"

"Of course not. Let's eat," Rikki said, leaping to her feet as black specks from the pages of the album fell from her lap.

"What's this?" Rita asked, suddenly alarmed. "Oh, my God. It's snowing ash."

Rikki wiped her lap. "It's nothing. Just some dirt."

Rita fell to her knees to examine the carpet by the bed. Her fingers lifted some of the black specks. "What is it?" she asked again, looking at her granddaughter. "I've never seen anything like it."

Rikki's heart raced. How to escape Rita's intense inspection? "It's nothing," she repeated, this time standing in the doorway. But before she could say another word, Rita lifted up the bed skirt and ran a hand under the bed.

◆

"How did you get this?" Rita asked. Her stony face seemed impervious to emotion. Rikki had seen her mad before, but this was different. "I asked you a question."

Rikki wasn't sure what to say. She just stood in the doorway and, for the moment, felt as if she were holding it up.

"You went through my things, didn't you?"

The answer seemed obvious. Rikki saw no need to confirm Rita's conclusion.

"Well, I just don't know what to do with you." Rita held her head high. Her eyes were cold. "I do everything I can and you go behind my back. Now tell me exactly what you're trying to find out."

Rikki had no answer.

"It must be something," Rita shouted, now up on her feet. "A young girl doesn't sneak around for no reason."

Perhaps it was the accusatory tone of Rita's voice, Rikki wasn't sure, but suddenly Rikki's lips were moving and her voice was rising to meet Rita's pitch. Fear had morphed into resentment, and then anger. There was no holding back as the words spewed forth. "Why did you get rid of my mother's artwork? Why have you tried to obliterate her memory? Why can't I ever mention her name without you changing the subject? And why," Rikki asked, wildly gesturing, "are there no pictures of my mother in this apartment?"

Rita jumped up and pulled Rikki back into the bedroom. She closed the bedroom door. "Lower your voice. Do you want everyone in the building to know our business?"

"I don't care who hears me!" Rikki shrieked "I don't care!"

Rita gave her granddaughter's shoulder a shake. "I won't be spoken to like this. You lower your voice and talk to me plainly or we aren't going to talk."

"But that's the problem," Rikki said. "You don't talk. You don't tell me anything. You want me to forget my mother, don't you? You never loved her. Never. And you don't love *me*."

Rita's eyes flashed. "How can you say that? Do you know what it's like to lose a child? Can you ever know what kind of pain a mother goes through? You're too young. God willing, you'll never experience it."

Rikki had heard it all before. The twist of the screw. How Rita was able to turn a conversation and make it all about herself. She was a pro when it came to manipulation. "I'm not listening to you," Rikki yelled, covering her ears. "I don't want to hear how this is all about you. Your daughter. Your loss. I've heard all I'm going to hear."

"You're ungrateful," Rita said, opening the bedroom door. "An ungrateful, spoiled, little girl. I deserve better than you," she announced as she gave Rikki the harshest glare yet. "I'm going out. You can manage on your own to get to school. You won't be bothered by my company. And when you're ready to apologize, I'll be waiting."

◆

"I caught him limping this morning," Harry explained. "I have a deadline coming up, but I thought I'd better bring him in."

Dr. Newbar watched Beetle walk, the left rear leg held up in the air as he hopped along. "Okay, I see. Let's get him on the table," he instructed Harry. "Now hold him below the belly and lift him up slightly off the table."

Harry did as he was told. He could feel Beetle's heart beating intensely, the terrier's chest expanding broadly with each breath as Newbar manipulated each of the rear legs. Harry looked away, unable to bear the thought that Newbar might be hurting the dog.

"Yup. Here it is," Newbar said. Harry turned his attention to the leg. "Right here," Newbar declared. "He's got a torn anterior cruciate ligament."

Harry thought he'd faint.

"Okay," the vet said as he released Beetle to Harry, who whisked the frightened animal into his arms, gently rocking him. "It's age. Wear and tear."

"But what should I do?" Harry asked, his heart already in his throat. "He loves to walk and play ball. How can he do that now?"

The vet was writing a note in the medical record. "Well, he *can't* do that now. For the time being, he's going to need to rest. No jumping, no running. You've got to keep him quiet. With luck, the joint will calcify and repair itself to some degree. But that will take months. Until then, he's going to have to take it easy."

"What about surgery?" Harry asked.

Newbar shook his head. "Not with congestive heart disease. It's out of the question."

"Congestive heart disease? What are you talking about?"

Newbar stopped his scribbling. "Harry, that heart murmur is the beginning of congestive heart disease."

"But you never told me that," Harry said indignantly.

"Well, it doesn't always happen ... I didn't want to worry you. But the signs are all there. He's at the very earliest stages of it." Newbar offered Harry a sympathetic face. "I'm so sorry, Harry."

"And now he'll be limping?"

"Dogs under thirty pounds can do quite well, given time. My advice is, let him be thirteen. That's his age; that's how you need to be caring for him."

Harry didn't like the vet's implication.

"You're a great doggy dad, Harry, but Beetle is a senior dog."

In front of the vet, with Beetle in his arms, Harry completely lost it, breaking into a loud wail.

◆

"Oh, Harry, how awful," Lil said upon hearing the news.

A pizza box from Babbo's Italian Restaurant lay open on Harry's kitchen counter. She'd brought it over after hearing Harry's voice on the phone.

"Now, you've got to eat something," she implored as she lifted a slice and placed it on a plate. She set the plate down on the coffee table in front of Harry.

"I don't know," he said, pushing the plate away. "I just can't. To some people it might seem ridiculous, but I love Beetle more than I love myself. I just can't imagine my life without him."

"I understand," Lil cooed, coming over to the sofa and sliding in next to Harry. She gently glided her hand over Harry's lower back and up to his shoulder blade. She gave him three good squeezes.

"That feels good," he said as he started to relax.

"Now, you just sit back," she said, moving her hand away so that Harry could sink down into the sofa. "There you go," she said, giving him a pat on the inner thigh as she pivoted to offer his forehead a gentle rub. "You're so tense. No wonder you're all upset. You're holding all that negative energy. You have to release those toxins," she said, "or it'll damage your organs."

Beetle, lying in his bed nearby, whined, causing Harry to sit right up.

"What is it, boy?" he asked, sliding off the sofa and onto the floor to be next to Beetle. "Does it hurt?"

"Oh, Harry," Lil said. "Don't be ridiculous. He just wants your attention."

Harry pressed his head next to Beetle's. The terrier's eyes closed as Harry rubbed up against him. "He's the most important thing in my life. I love this dog."

Lil stood up. "I've got to go."

"Don't leave, Lil. We still have the pizza to eat."

"What's the point, Harry Aldon?" she said, hands in the air. "What does a girl have to do to get your attention?"

Harry sighed, oblivious to Lil as he continued to pet Beetle.

"I'm out of here," she announced in an exasperated tone as she headed for the door.

◆

I thought she'd never leave. Richard's voice was back. *Boy, she's pushy. Pizza? Like that's supposed to cheer you up.*

"It was nice," Harry said. *She's nice.*

But does she know about you? What you're like? That you have a voice in your head? That you've been with men?

"That's *my* business," Harry said to no one other than Beetle.

You're gonna ruin your life for that yoga yahoo. She might be able to touch her toes with her nose—but she's not good enough. You deserve a sweet guy who will look after you.

Harry made a face. "I'm a successful author. I don't need anyone to take care of me." *I'm perfectly capable … I've lived alone all these years without you.*

You've had Beetle.

"Yes," Harry agreed.

You're really a child. A sixty-year-old child.

I'm fifty-four and a half, Harry defended himself.

What are you, in kindergarten? Adults don't describe themselves in half-years.

"I do," Harry said, giving Beetle another kiss on the head. *Now, if you don't mind, Beetle and I have work to do. I need to wrap up a few scenes before I finish the next chapter.*

Come on, now, Richard said. *I'm following that story of yours and it makes no sense. Face it, you've lost yourself in that convoluted plot.*

Harry rose to his feet. "Don't you worry. I'll figure it out. You know my books come to me as I write them." He reached down and lifted Beetle into his arms.

You'll never write your way out of that mess if you marry Lil.

"Marry?" Harry let out a laugh. *How did you get there? I barely know the woman.*

She has designs on you, Harry. Any fool can see that.

◆

That evening at dinner, Rita remained aloof. No matter how Rikki tried, she couldn't engage her grandmother. *Yes, no, maybe* had been the limit of Rita's contributions to the dinner conversation. Frustrated, Rikki found herself unable to finish the baked chicken on her plate. She slumped in her seat as she watched Rita bite into a tater tot. "Okay, I give up," Rikki acquiesced. "I'm not doing this anymore. I'm not going to sit here and try to make conversation. What's the point?"

Rita took a sip of water. "I'll have you know that I returned that album to where it belonged."

Rikki clenched her fists, trying to control her intense frustration. "I don't understand," she finally said, unable to silence the voice inside her head. "Why are my mother's things stored away? And why would you give away her paintings?" And before she knew it was coming, Rikki blurted out, "And who was that little boy in those family pictures? Do I have an uncle?"

"That's none of your business," Rita snapped.

Incredulous, Rikki pushed back from the table and stood up. "Why? What are you keeping from me?"

"This conversation is over," Rita declared as she picked up her plate and walked over to the sink.

"No," Rikki said boldly. "It's over when I say it's over."

Rita's eyes flashed. "You've turned into quite the teenager. Sneaking around and lying."

"I never lied," Rikki insisted. "But *you* have. You won't discuss my mother and now you won't talk about that boy in the pictures."

"I don't owe you an explanation!" Rita shrieked so loudly that Rikki was certain her voice must have carried at least two floors below. "I'm the adult. I decide what you need to know."

Rikki suppressed the hot flash of tears. *I'm not going to cry,* she told herself. *You can't win if you cry.*

"Now if you're done with your dinner, you can go to your room," Rita stated flatly.

Rikki sat on her bed clutching her pillow. The confrontation with Rita played over and over in her mind. It all seemed so senseless, so unreasonable.

What can possibly be going on? What had happened to her mother and uncle? She struggled to understand how her relationship with Rita had so quickly fallen apart. And then there was a knock on her bedroom door. Rita came into the room, appearing to have calmed herself since their last interaction. Rikki noticed the dark lines under her grandmother's eyes. She looked tired.

Rita sat on the canvas sofa. A bullfighter's sweeping red cape hung on the wall within inches of her head.

"I've given it some thought—and I think we need a time out."

Rikki stared at Rita. "What do you mean?"

"I think we need some time apart," she simply stated. "You're beginning to wear on my nerves. I'd like to take a break."

Rikki's heart lurched as she considered the implication of Rita's words.

"After all," Rita began, "we haven't been getting along, so maybe we need some distance."

Rikki struggled to catch her breath. "But how?" she stammered.

"You want to go with Barbra to Toledo. I think you should go."

Rikki could hardly believe her ears.

7

El Goldenbaum hated her job at Macy's. Working nine to five at the perfume counter was a soul-crushing schedule for an artist who, against her better judgment, had followed her mother's advice and graduated with a Master of Fine Arts in interior design from Pratt Institute in New York City. Sharing a two-bedroom flat in an East Village walk-up with five other girls had become too much for El. The mess and filth of six human beings stuffed into such a tight space wore on her nerves. And though she prided herself on being an independent adult, she often returned to Aguilar Gardens to settle back into her old room, allowing Rita to baby her. It was during one of those hiatuses from the East Village that El shared the news about Haney & Lewis Interior Designs. She'd been recommended by Lee Rator, one of the celebrated professors at Pratt, to interview for an intern position. H&L, located in the heart of lower Manhattan at 7th Avenue and Broadway, was one of New York City's most exclusive interior design firms, with a roster of high-end commercial and residential clients.

"I *knew* it." Rita clapped with glee. "I knew this day would come," she said after El explained the opportunity with H&L. "This is just what we always wanted."

El eyed her mother suspiciously. Rita was overwhelmed with joy, bouncing about the kitchen as she prepared Sunday brunch. She'd never understood El's passion for painting. Even at this moment, with the internship at her fingertips, El couldn't muster the enthusiasm to match Rita's excitement. As El sat at the kitchen table watching Rita pull a tray of corn muffins from the oven, she felt as if she'd given up on her dreams. Surrendered to the inevitable.

"Will there be a lot of money involved?" Rita asked, as El sipped her coffee. Rita stood in front of an open refrigerator.

"A stipend comes with the internship. But it's *not much*. Lee says I really should be paying them for this chance."

"Lee?" Rita asked. "Is that a man or a woman?"

"A man, mother," El answered, amused that anyone would ever consider a six-foot-three former high school quarterback a woman.

"Well, it *could* be a woman's name," Rita defended herself, retrieving the butter dish and placing it on the table. "Lee Remick. Lee Grant."

"Or Lee Marvin. Lee Majors … *The Six Million Dollar Man*," El said.

"Talk about *confusing a child*," Rita said. "It reminds me of that Johnny Cash song, 'A Boy Named Sue.'"

"Mother, really, you should read a magazine every now and then. There are lots of names that are interchangeable. Sandy. Leslie. Dana. No one but you seems confused."

Rita took a seat. "Now, don't get fresh," she said as she sliced a muffin in half and covered it in butter. "I read. Do you think I live in a hole in the ground?"

El looked about. "No. Last I checked this is the sixth floor."

"Don't be funny," Rita answered, clearly not amused.

And then El took a chance. It was a blind shot. "Have you spoken to Richard?"

"Why are you asking me that?" Rita asked defensively.

"Just wondering."

"You know we don't talk." Rita leaned in and bit into the muffin. Crumbs cascaded across the plate.

El had not interfered in months. She thought it hopeless to try to get her mother to reconcile with her younger brother. *Besides,* she thought, *that isn't my job*. Yet she couldn't help but be disappointed in Rita.

"You should bury the hatchet. How long do you plan on punishing him?"

Rita bristled. "I'm not punishing him. He's punishing me."

"Okay, okay," El responded, hands in the air. "Keep your cool."

"God, I hate when you do that," Rita barked. "You bring it up and then you tell me to keep my cool. Maybe you should mind your own business."

"Oh, Mother," El sighed. "Really! You should give it a rest. He didn't do anything to you. Being homosexual had nothing to do with you."

Rita straightened her back. "I know what everyone thinks. I was the one who *did it to him*. It was my fault. Of course it's always the mother's fault," she sniffed.

"Did you ever think maybe he was born that way?"

Rita laughed indignantly. "Born that way? No one is born that way. I've never met a *homosexual baby*."

"Well, maybe you did," El said as she sipped her coffee, "but just didn't know it. Clearly, it happened."

"I don't want to talk about this anymore," Rita warned. "I want nothing more to do with him," she said, though El thought she spotted a glimmer of remorse. "I've wasted enough time thinking about your brother."

"Then why not read a book or go to a support group? You're not the only one in the world with a gay child."

"I don't see why you're defending him." Rita offered a withering glance. "I'm still your mother. You should be taking my side in this."

El shook her head. "What?"

"You heard me," Rita said indignantly. "You should be on my side."

"What side?" El asked, growing increasingly agitated. "There *is* no side."

"Yes, there is. There is *my* side. And if you want to stay in my good graces, I'd suggest that you remember that."

El reached for a corn muffin. "I swear to God. Sometimes you make no sense."

"I don't want to talk about it any further," Rita warned. "As far as I'm concerned, the subject is closed."

El shook her head. It was sad. Terribly sad for Richard to have such a mother, and sad for El, too. She now knew that there were limits to her mother's love. It had proven very conditional in her brother's case.

◆

Lil's voice boomed across the phone line. "Harry Aldon, I don't see why you can't come over tonight for dinner."

Harry paced in his office. "Lil, I just can't," Harry pleaded. "I'm struggling with the end of the novel and I can't be interrupted. And why do you insist on using my last name when you're pissed?"

Beetle lay nearby in his dog bed, fast asleep.

"But you have to eat, Harry."

Harry closed his eyes. What had once been a welcome respite from his work was becoming an annoying interruption. He'd tried to meet Lil halfway, but despite his best intentions, he was unable to continue to perform sexually. He didn't wish to hurt her, and yet he couldn't bring himself to reveal that he was conflicted sexually. Embarrassment turned to annoyance. "Lil," he quickly unloaded. "I can't help it if you're lonely, but I told you at the very start that if you needed a lot of attention, I was the wrong guy. Lil, my work comes first. It always has. And I can't be pressured into doing what you want. I'm already too old and set in my ways to accommodate you. I'm sorry if that's a problem, but you've been warned."

There was silence on the line. Beetle shifted positions. Harry peeked out the window. The morning sun was intensely bright. Another Phoenix day with unrelenting cheer.

"Now, I have to go," Harry said lacking any force behind the words. "Lil? Lil? Are you still there?"

He could hear breathing.

"I'm hanging up now!" he said, shouting into the receiver. "This is the sound of me hanging up." He placed the receiver in the cradle. "Damn woman," he muttered, his thoughts now all clouded by Lil's demands. "Gosh, she's smothering me," he told Beetle as he settled at his desk. Chapter Ten lay before him. Nine chapters done and the tenth still blank. "Damn," he said again as he slid back into the chair. "I have to be free to write. I can't be screwing around with Lil."

You mean you shouldn't be screwing around with Lil.

Harry smiled. *I wondered when you'd show up.*

Harry, Harry, Harry… don't you know that I'm never far away?

"That's comforting," Harry said, his voice ringing with sarcasm.

She's ruining your concentration.

Yes, Harry admitted. *I must have been nuts to let her in.*

Or lonely, Harry. Maybe just lonely.

"But what am I going to do?" Harry asked as he ran his hand through his hair. Beetle sat up in his bed and tilted his head. Harry waved a hand and Beetle settled back down. *It's not like she's evil. She's a good person. I like her company. And now, I'm hurting her.*

Ah, the problems of reluctant bisexuals.

Don't make fun. I don't want to be involved. I can barely handle Beetle.

In all our years together, Harry, you never strayed with a woman. A man? Yes.

Harry remembered.

"I don't know what I want," he sighed as he leaned back in his chair. "I'm attracted to both sexes."

Is there a preference?

I think it depends more on the person than the genitals.

Harry, you shouldn't be alone. You were a wonderful partner. You took care of me, loved me, and put up with my family when things got tough. You deserved better, Harry. You did.

"I remember it all," Harry softly said. *And I'd do it again. I loved you, Richard. I truly loved you.*

◆

Rikki was grateful Rita had changed her mind about letting her go to Ohio for the Christmas holiday, but unfortunately, Barbra didn't seem quite as eager to have her friend trail along. There had been a change in Barbra's attitude. They no longer ate lunch together. It had been less of a falling out than a falling apart. One day, Barbra was simply not where Rikki expected to see her. Instead, she'd joined another table of girls on the other side of the cafeteria. Rikki took it in stride. There was nothing she could do if Barney preferred her company to Barbra's. She certainly didn't think that was her fault.

"What happened to your friend?" Barney asked, a glint in his eyes as he pulled up a chair across from her. His brown lunch bag had a grease stain on the bottom.

"What are you eating?" Rikki asked as she pushed a half-eaten peanut butter sandwich aside. "Sludge?"

Barney laughed. "I guess my tuna sandwich leaked. It must have too much mayo."

Rikki made a face. "That's disgusting."

"Do you want me to move?" Barney asked, a serious expression on his face. "You know, I can," he said as he started to stand.

"No, don't," she gushed and started to giggle.

He was partly standing up, looking about. "I see an empty seat across the way."

"No," she said emphatically, eyes wide open, head nodding for him to sit. "Don't be so silly."

"But you'll have to look at my disgusting lunch..." He was now standing up.

"Oh, Barney." Her face lit up in a huge smile. "Have my peanut butter." And she slid her sandwich over to him as he slipped back down into the chair. In seconds it was half-eaten.

Over the few weeks that they'd been together, she'd discovered Barney's playful side. From the serious boy who said few words, he'd morphed into a sweet chatterbox. Always talking to her about the future.

"And one day," he admitted, "I want to be an actor. Maybe even a movie star." As soon as the words had left his mouth, he blushed crimson.

"Wow," Rikki had answered, proud that he'd confided in her.

"Why not?" he said, as if she'd questioned his choice. "I have the looks—don't you think?"

She only had to nod once.

"All you have to do is recite lines and look good." His dream rushed forth as if it could no longer be contained. "I know it's not a traditional kind of career. But I think I can do it," he said with surprising confidence.

She wondered if such a career was even possible. The best she'd hoped for was grade school teacher.

"That's an amazing profession," he'd told her. "You should be proud to be a teacher. Kids need someone to look up to. Someone who cares about them."

That's true, she'd thought. And yet, she couldn't help but feel sad. She was certain that Barney's good looks doomed any future they might have together. She had to be honest with herself. Barney was much better looking than she was. The dimples... the angular jaw and cheekbones. Eventually, he'd realize that and turn his attention to other girls. Prettier girls. With shapelier figures, brighter smiles, and better hair. It was inevitable, she supposed. And yet, that very thought tugged at her heart.

He finished her sandwich, motioning to his to ask if she wanted it. When she declined, he unwrapped the tuna fish and ate it with gusto as Rikki looked on.

"So, when are you leaving for Ohio?" he said between bites, offering her his open bag of Fritos.

She took a corn chip. "There's no school on the Friday before Christmas so we're leaving that afternoon... the 23rd. The plan is for Barbra's dad to drop us off at Penn Station to catch the 3:40 train."

"Sounds like fun," Barney said, wiping tuna fish from his lips with a napkin.

Rikki caught the far-off look in his eyes. "What's the matter?"

"Nothing," he answered, his voice sullen.

"Come on, out with it," she said as she reached for the Fritos, extracting two more chips and popping them in her mouth.

"I'm going to miss you, that's all."

The look in his eyes bore a hole through her heart. At that moment, she felt closer to him than anyone she'd ever known. And though she was certain that she loved him, she was afraid that he was going to hurt her. That his infatuation with whatever they had was transient, impermanent.

"I'll miss you, too," she said, placing a hand on his. "I will."

"And what about Barbra?" he asked, looking across the way in the direction where Barbra was seated. "Is she even talking to you?"

"We're still friends," Rikki assured him. "I know she wants me to go."

"So she's staying away at lunch because of me?"

Rikki was uncertain how to answer. "She'll come around. By the time I get on the train, she'll have forgotten all about whatever is bugging her. Barbra and I will always be friends. Always."

◆

"Harry, I'm coming out there," Edward said, concern in his voice as he peered into the Microsoft *Live Meeting* screen, causing Harry to laugh. "I know something must be wrong. In all the years we've worked together, you've never been this unfocused. Are you sick?"

Harry made a clicking sound with his tongue. "Don't be ridiculous. Nothing is wrong. I've just hit a speed bump. I need time."

Edward offered a suspicious look. "Would it help if we talked through the challenges facing your protagonist?"

Harry thought about it for a moment. Would Edward be able to be impartial? This new book was so very different. And though they'd known each other for twenty years, could Edward really understand? After all, they'd slept together a few times, mostly when Harry had been in New York on business. In the beginning, Harry had even wondered if Edward might be his next long-term partner, but the timing never seemed right between them. When they had met, Edward, younger by some fifteen years, was just getting settled into New York City after moving from Saint Louis. And Harry, who had spent years in the city, had to leave.

"It's the bisexual thing," Harry admitted. "I'm kind of stuck on that."

"Oh God, no," Edward intoned, a hand on his forehead. "You're going to totally alienate your audience, Harry. No one believes in bisexuals. Not as the protagonist in a murder mystery. Give the ladies what they want—a strong, virile male figure."

"Someone must," Harry insisted. "Otherwise they wouldn't have that *B in LGBT.*"

Edward shook his head. "But those people are not your target audience," he said most emphatically. "They don't read."

"How could you possibly know that?" Harry argued as he slumped backward into his chair. "And exactly who *is* my target audience?" He knew full well what Edward was about to say.

"Women. Lots of straight women. Thirty-five and older. Fifty-year-olds are the sweet spot. They buy and read books. They're the reason you're a money-maker, Harry. You know we don't continue to carry authors who don't make money. And if you want to keep us happy, Harry, you'll do what I ask."

Harry arched his brows. "I don't know. Next you're going to insist that my book has one of those erotic covers. Half-naked men. Jesus. Maybe if you added a few male nudes, we could sell even more books."

"Don't be crass," Edward answered. "Leave the porn to the amateurs. You create art."

Harry sighed. "Well, I can't help it. I have to write about what interests me. What I want to read. What's wrong with that?"

"Okay," Edward said. "Do what you must, but in the end," and he leaned forward and into the screen, "make him straight."

Harry bit his lip. "I'll think about it."

◆

Rikki had been told to report to her guidance counselor, Mrs. Cole, only to find Mr. Rosenfeld sitting in one of the two chairs in front of Mrs. Cole's desk.

All students were required to meet with their guidance counselors during the school year. Rikki had already met that obligation, though she hadn't really seen any good reason to do so. Mrs. Cole, who was approaching retirement, had always seemed rushed and overwhelmed. The pinched indentations on her nose were deep, even though her eyeglasses mostly hung about her neck from a gold chain. Her gray hair, in a loose bun off-center atop her head, made Rikki wonder if Mrs. Cole needed to hold her head at a certain angle to keep the bun upright.

Mr. Rosenfeld smiled. "And how is my favorite writer doing today?" he asked.

"Fine," she answered, unclear why Mr. Rosenfeld was joining her for the appointment.

"Come in, come in," Mrs. Cole called as Rikki stood in the doorway. "Please take a seat and close the door."

Rikki did as she was told, though she had an overwhelming desire to excuse herself and run off to the bathroom.

"I've got great news for you," Mr. Rosenfeld said as she settled in. He patted the arm of the chair where she sat, his voice tight with excitement. Rikki thought she might need to cover her ears. "You did it. You won third place."

"Really?" was all Rikki could manage to get out.

"This is such terrific news," Mr. Rosenfeld gushed. "Do you know that in all my years of teaching, you're the first student who has placed in the competition?"

Rikki didn't know what to say.

"Now the prize is $500—which is okay—but the scholarship is $1,500 per year, with stipulations that you maintain a 3.0 grade-point average."

Rikki shook her head as she took it all in.

"Now we're going to have to get your mother to come in and accept the check."

Mrs. Cole loudly cleared her throat, signaling Mr. Rosenfeld to stop.

"Oh God," he said, apologetically. "In all the excitement I forgot."

Rikki shrugged. She was used to people forgetting.

"Well, your *grandmother* will have to come by," Mrs. Cole said, holding the check in her hand.

"Why not just give it to her?" Mr. Rosenfeld suggested. "She's a good girl. What harm can come to it?"

Mrs. Cole crinkled her nose. "Five hundred dollars is a lot of money. I'm not about to give this child a $500 check. That'd be irresponsible."

Mr. Rosenfeld sighed. "I guess that makes sense."

"Besides," Mrs. Cole said, "an adult needs to sign for the receipt of the check."

Rikki had a thought.

"Mr. Rosenfeld, why don't you sign for it, and then I can take it home."

"I don't think so." Mr. Rosenfeld said, smiling. "But how about if, instead, I go home with you today, meet your grandmother, and get her signature?"

Rikki wondered how Rita would respond. She'd been so angry lately. They'd barely spoken a word to each other.

"I think that's fine," Mrs. Cole agreed. "The quicker the money gets into the proper hands, the better."

"Then we're all set," Mr. Rosenfeld said, as Mrs. Cole handed him the check. "Rikki, I'll meet you after your last class."

◆

"That's a very strange man," Rita said, once the door closed and Mr. Rosenfeld had left. "I've never seen such bright colors. A red bow tie, black shirt and purple corduroys. I almost expected him to be wearing an orange wig and a bright red nose."

Rikki held the check in her hand.

"He teaches English?" Rita asked as she opened the refrigerator and peeked inside.

"Yes," Rikki answered.

"Thank goodness it's not sex education." Rita placed a head of iceberg lettuce on the counter. "God only knows what he'd be teaching."

Rikki folded the check and slipped it into her pocket. There'd be time enough for depositing the check into her bank account tomorrow.

As Rita unwrapped the plastic from the lettuce, she changed the subject. "Maybe you should give me that check. You don't want to lose it." She slammed the core of the head against the counter, then twisted it loose.

"I won't," Rikki answered, patting her pocket. "It's safe with me."

"I hope so," she said, obviously questioning her own judgment. "So," she continued as she sliced up a cucumber to go along with the lettuce in the bowl. "Are all the English teachers fruity like that?"

Rikki tried to ignore her. "I guess," she answered, hoping to end the conversation.

"Are there a lot of other teachers who are queer?"

"Rita," she admonished. "Do you mean is he *gay*? I don't know if he's gay."

"My dear," Rita said with confidence. "Trust me. He is."

Rikki couldn't care less whether Mr. Rosenfeld was gay. It seemed odd that Barbra and Rita shared something in common. Rikki had caught the negative implications, the judgments, but it had not affected her one way or another. She thought it was no one's business.

"So what?" she said to Rita defiantly, exhibiting a rebellious nature reserved exclusively for the older woman. "Who cares?"

"Well, I do," Rita announced as she tossed the salad with olive oil and vinegar. "And I think a lot of other parents would."

"It's 2005, Rita. No one cares."

"President Bush cares," Rita argued. "Last year he called for a constitutional amendment banning same-sex marriage. So, even in 2005, nothing has changed," Rita said confidently. "Americans don't approve of homosexuals. You mark my words. People like that," and she pointed a paring knife in Rikki's direction, "will get their comeuppance if they don't mind their p's and q's."

Rikki rolled her eyes. *What were "p"s and "q"s?*

◆

"It's okay, Harry," Lil said as she gathered up her clothes. "You're just not in the mood. I get it. It happens to everyone now and then."

Harry remained in bed, turned on his side away from Lil.

"I have this strange effect on men," she admitted. "In the beginning, it's always terrific, and then, I guess, I just wear on them." She slipped on her jeans.

Harry turned onto his back.

Lil searched for her Danskin. It was on the floor by the dresser. "You can't help the way you feel. We're both old enough to know that it's just the way it is."

Harry sat up and slid backward, leaning against the headboard. "Lil, you can't take it so personally."

Lil wiggled into her athletic top. "I'm not," she said.

He was unconvinced. "It's me, not you."

Lil laughed. "Oh, Harry, if I had a dollar for every time I've heard that one ..." She slipped into her pink Nikes. "You men are all alike. Doesn't anyone have an original line?" She turned to look in the mirror that hung above Harry's dresser. "Dear God, I'm a mess," she said as she pulled her hair back from her face. "A mess."

"No, you're not," Harry said. "You're beautiful, Lil. Really beautiful."

"Am I?" she asked, turning to him. "Do you really think so?"

"Oh, yes," Harry said. His voice was warm and loving. "You truly are."

"Then tell me one thing, Harry." She sat on the edge of the bed, near him. "Why is it that a smart lady like me is unable to take a hint? Why is it that when I see what I want, I just push forward?"

Harry took Lil's hand. "It's not such a bad quality."

Lil's eyes filled with tears. "It must be, because I'm still alone after all these years," she stammered, a hand to her forehead. "Still a very single lady."

Harry pulled her close. "Oh, Lil," was all he managed to say before she kissed him with a depth of intensity that eliminated all resistance.

8

"Has he been coughing a lot?" Dr. Newbar asked as Beetle squirmed on the table.

"The same," Harry answered, worried that Beetle's heart had enlarged even more.

Newbar listened intently with a stethoscope. "Good strong beat. I'd say the medication is working. Have you been counting breaths?"

"Twenty-two," Harry answered.

"That's good," Newbar affirmed. "As long as he's not in congestive heart *failure*, I'd say we're managing him well. And when things begin to change, we've got some other medications to try."

Harry nodded as Newbar went into the minutiae of the diagnosis. All the medications that Beetle might take, the ups and downs, reasons to hold off on any change. Harry listened patiently as Newbar lectured, finally lifting Beetle off the exam table. Beetle calmed down in his arms.

"I don't think I'll need to see you for another two months," Newbar said as he left the exam room.

Harry hoped Newbar was right.

◆

Rita was lying down on the canvas sofa as Rikki finished packing for Christmas break. It'd be cold in Ohio in December, not much different than the weather in Queens, and still Rikki wondered if the sweaters she'd included might be too heavy. Finished, she placed the roller bag by the front door of the apartment, along with a knapsack that she'd stuffed with reading material for the train ride.

Rita lifted her head. "All set, then?" she asked.

"Yes," Rikki answered. "How's your headache?"

Rita raised herself up on one elbow. "It hurts."

Rikki checked her watch. "I better get going. I told Mr. Winer that I'd meet him downstairs. We're going to need plenty of time to get into Manhattan."

Rita sat up. "I'm not sure this is such a good idea. Hanukah is the same day as Christmas this year. That's two holidays we'll miss spending together."

"Hanukah!" Rikki said with surprise. "Since when do we celebrate that?"

"Well, we could," Rita added. "If it's important to you."

Rikki smiled. Rita was nothing if not consistent.

"You're going to have to sit up all night in coach. That'll be a rough trip. And the train will be packed. Christmas Eve is tomorrow."

Rikki ignored her. "Maybe I should wait downstairs? Mr. Winer said he'd buzz on the intercom, but since I'm ready, I'll just go downstairs."

"Rikki, I'm sorry," Rita said softly. "I'm sorry if I've made you feel uncomfortable. I only wanted," and tears began to flow down Rita's cheeks, "to protect you."

"From what?" Rikki asked, aware she had the upper hand.

"You're so young. I just didn't want you to suffer through the trauma of the loss all over again."

Rikki's anger flared. "So you tried to erase the memory of my mother?"

"It's more than that," she struggled to explain. "There are things you don't know."

Rikki bit her bottom lip. The intercom buzzer interrupted them. "I've got to go. It's time," she said as she grabbed her luggage and rushed from the room. Rita followed closely behind. Pressing the button on the wall unit that allowed her to speak, Rikki called out. "I'll be right down."

"Don't go like this," Rita pleaded. "Not mad."

"Rita, I've *got* to go. My ride is here. I'll be back a week from tomorrow just in time for New Year's Eve. Enjoy your week," she said, before hurrying out the door.

◆

"I'm still working on those pages," Harry said, as he fiddled with the pencil on his desk. Years ago, he'd written everything in long hand. Those days seemed a million years away.

"What? I can't hear you." Edward leaned into the screen.

"Geez," Harry called out. "Back up. I don't need to see every one of your nose hairs."

Edward chuckled as he straightened up. "Sorry about that, Harry. But I think I'm having some trouble with my laptop. For some reason I'm catching a lot of interference."

Harry broke into a smile. "That isn't interference. Beetle's asleep. He's snoring."

"Are you telling me your dog is making that racket?"

Harry laughed. "That, and more. I'm kind of used to it. Can't work without it."

"Then why are you short those pages?"

Lil had occupied an increasing amount of Harry's time. Under her influence, he'd started hiking in the morning, going to the top of Squaw Peak, which offered a thrilling view of the valley.

"I'll get it done," Harry said. "I just need some more time."

Edward frowned. "It's not like you, Harry, to be so consistently late. You know there are other writers who'd be glad for my time. Maybe we should hold off for another two months until you're ready."

"But I'm in the middle of the project," Harry complained. "If we stop now, I'll never get this damn book done."

Edward rubbed his eye. "Well, then, maybe it's not the right time to do the project. Here we are, coming up on the holidays, and you're so unfocused."

"No," Harry insisted. "I'm going to get it together. I'm sorry, Edward. I promise. You'll get the pages in the next few days."

"So you'll be in Phoenix for Christmas?"

"Where else would I be?"

Edward sat back in his chair. "You're not spending the holidays alone, are you?"

"Of course not," Harry answered. "I have Beetle."

"But you do have plans, Harry. Dinner with friends. Holiday parties."

Harry sighed.

"Oh Harry, you shouldn't be alone. Really. It isn't healthy."

"As long as I have Beetle, I'll be just fine."

◆

Pennsylvania Station on the Friday afternoon of Christmas weekend was packed with people as Rikki trailed behind Barbra and her father. The distinctive, sooty smell of the place clung to the top of Rikki's palate as she waited patiently with the luggage while Barbra's father purchased the tickets. After a sweet goodbye, she and Barbra were finally alone as they made their way to the platform.

"He's awfully nice," Rikki said about Barbra's dad.

"He's nothing of the sort," Barbra complained. "If he was nice, I'd be going with him on that cruise."

"I guess it's an adult thing," Rikki innocently said, not giving much thought to her words.

Barbra's temper flared. "Are you going to defend him, Rikki? Is that the kind of friend you've turned out to be?"

Rikki was flabbergasted. "What did I say?"

"You know what? I'm not so sure that you're a very nice person."

Rikki stopped dead in her tracks as the girls faced each other. Yes, Barbra had been aloof at school. But now they were alone in Manhattan at Pennsylvania Station, waiting to board a train to stay with

Barbra's relatives. Surely, this was not the best time to get into a fight. "I'm sorry. Whatever upset you, I take it back."

But Barbra was not about to let Rikki off that easy. "You stole my boyfriend," Barbra said, accusingly.

Rikki took a breath. "I know how you feel about Barney, but honestly, I didn't do anything."

Barbra raised an eyebrow. "You mean to stand here and tell me that you didn't work behind my back to get him to like you?"

Rikki shrugged her shoulders. "Is that even possible?"

A vein popped in Barbra's forehead. "You know darn well it is."

"Barbra, I don't know what to say or how to make it up to you," Rikki admitted as they boarded the Amtrak coach.

"You can stay away from him," Barbra suggested.

Rikki took a breath. How could she? Over the last few weeks Barney had become too important to her.

"This is ridiculous," Rikki insisted as they made their way down the aisle in search of seats. "Barbra, it's not like I've ever said anything to Barney, one way or another. Really. I don't know why he has chosen me over you. Honestly. I have no idea."

The train lurched forward as Rikki grabbed for the handle atop a nearby seat. Unable to maintain her grip, she fell forward into Barbra, as Barbra reached for and grabbed the arm of a middle-aged man seated nearby who was holding an infant in his arms. "Hey," the man yelled, as he struggled to hold the baby. He glared at Barbra. "What the hell is wrong with you?"

Barbra turned to Rikki. "You did that on purpose, didn't you?"

Rikki was flabbergasted. "Of course not."

"You've told Barney terrible things about me, haven't you?" Barbra's voice escalated.

"Absolutely not," Rikki defended herself. "You're my best friend, Barbra. I'd never do that."

"I don't believe you," Barbra said. "Real friends don't betray each other's trust."

"Well, it's true," Rikki insisted. "What can I do to make you understand?"

Barbra's eyes flashed. "You can begin by getting the hell away from me."

Rikki panicked. The train was picking up speed. "What do you mean?" she asked as Barbra took a window seat, placing her bag on the aisle seat. "We're going to be together for a week."

"No, we're not," Barbra answered emphatically. "You're not coming with me."

Rikki could hardly believe her ears. She held tight to the top of the aisle seat as the train accelerated. "Well, I'm on the train. I must be going somewhere."

"Maybe," Barbra sarcastically answered. "But not with me. I don't want to spend one more moment with you."

"But your aunt and uncle will be expecting me for Christmas," Rikki said, trying to reason with her as the floor beneath her feet vibrated with a steady rhythm. "You can't just decide at the last minute that I'm uninvited."

Barbra glared at Rikki. "I'll just tell them that you got sick and were unable to come, after all."

Rikki could hardly believe her ears. "Oh, Barbra, you wouldn't." The car lurched forward and sideways. The motion was becoming too much. She needed to sit down, "And what will you tell your father?"

Barbra offered a callous smile. "They don't care about me ... I truly doubt they'll be concerned about you."

"But they'll surely ask questions."

"I'll just tell them that you got homesick and took the next train back. You already have a return ticket. Just tell them at the station that you want to use it now. Problem solved."

Rikki's stomach rolled from the motion. "Oh, Barbra, you should have told me all this before. You're not being fair."

Barbra didn't answer. She just turned her head to look out the window.

◆

Two cars away from Barbra, Rikki finally settled into an empty coach seat. Barbra's words echoed in her head as she tried to figure out what to do next. The whistle of the train signaled a tunnel up ahead as the interior lights suddenly came on and the outside world turned black. All Rikki could see was her reflection in the glass. The troubled look of a young girl.

As the train emerged from the darkness, Rikki took account of her situation. She had $300 in cash, courtesy of her prize winnings. Rita had insisted that the other $200 go into her savings account. She slipped a finger in her right jean pocket to confirm it was still there, nicely folded. Rita had provided a Visa card in case of emergencies. Rikki felt confident that the cash and the credit card would carry the day.

She checked her watch. It was 4:30 p.m. In approximately sixteen hours she'd arrive in Toledo. It would be early morning. She'd then have to figure out how to get back to Queens. It crossed her mind that she might still be able to work it out with Barbra. That was worth a try. But she couldn't imagine how she could persuade Barbra to change her mind. *No,* she thought, remembering Barbra's angry face. *I think I'm going to just have to go back to Queens.*

She unzipped her backpack and pulled out a sandwich Rita had made for the trip. BLT—her favorite. The first bite eased her mind as she savored the salty bacon. The sights of New Jersey's plants with their plumes of smoke shooting high in the air passed by as she realized that this was the first time she'd ever been on her own. She felt a sudden inner confidence growing. The first taste of adulthood. It was exciting. She could do as she pleased. Whatever decision she made, it would be her choice.

As the factories faded and the New Jersey suburbs came into view, a heavy-set man with a cane tottered up the aisle. His face ashen, his movements unsteady from the train's motion, he appeared to struggle with every step. His mouth, crooked, evidenced a slight droop. Rikki looked away when he smiled at her.

"Is this seat taken?" he asked, his speech slurred as he poked his cane at the seat.

Rikki removed her backpack and placed it by her feet. The man sat down as Rikki returned to the passing view of rolling fields and red barns.

"Lovely, isn't it?" the man said, pulling her attention away from the scenery.

"Yes," she agreed.

"I was raised on one of those dairy farms."

She said nothing as she examined the man's face. His eyes, slightly bloodshot, seemed kind.

"Of course, that was back in Iowa. Many years ago."

Rikki smiled politely and then looked away again.

"Are you alone?" the man asked.

Rikki thought to lie as she continued to look out the window. "No. I just thought I'd sit by myself. My family is in the other car."

The man nodded. "You know, it's interesting what you can learn living on a farm."

Rikki was beginning to feel nervous. She didn't want to talk to the man. She couldn't help but wonder why he'd opted to sit next to her. As she looked about, there were other seats. Perhaps he was lonely.

"The closest I've ever come to a farm," she admitted, "was when I lived in Michigan."

"Yes," the man said as he suddenly, and most inexplicably, placed the palm of his hand on Rikki's knee. "There are quite a few out that way."

Rikki froze.

The man straightened up. His hand slowly began to slide up the inside of her thigh. "I especially like the cows. Have you ever tasted cow's milk fresh from the udder?"

Rikki was horrified. She started to stand but the man pulled her back down.

"Now, young lady, I think you might be in need of some company. Perhaps some adult supervision."

"Get away from me," she said, "before I start to scream."

"You're not going to scream," he said, as he leaned in close. "If you were going to scream, you would have already."

"Hey, creep," a voice called out as a hand grabbed the older man by the back of his jacket. "What are you doing?"

It was Barney. Barney was standing in the aisle, pulling the man right out of the seat.

The old man stumbled, landing hard in the aisle.

"I wasn't doing anything," he said as he struggled to his feet and scrambled away.

◆

"Oh, my God, Barney!" Rikki said as she broke into tears. "What are you doing here?"

Barney put his arm around her shoulder as she pressed her face into his neck.

"I was thinking it might be fun to go to the Midwest for Christmas," he said. "And I remembered which train you were taking and boy, am I glad I did. I didn't know you liked older men," he gently teased, eliciting a smile from her. "Besides, I didn't want to spend the holidays alone. It's a good thing I made that decision."

"But what about your foster family?"

Barney sighed. "They think I'm going to visit a cousin. They even gave me money to buy the ticket. I told them that I'd check in with them every day. But to be honest ... I think they were kind of relieved to see the back of my head."

She suddenly pulled away, realizing the situation. "But where will you stay in Ohio?"

"I have no idea," he admitted. "I just sort of decided to do this at the very last minute. Packed a bag, bought a ticket, and here I am. I guess I can crash on Barbra's uncle's couch. I'm sure they'll find room for an adorable runaway."

"Barney," she said warmly, slipping her arm into his as she nestled close, "Barbra's no longer talking to me."

"Why?"

"We had a fight. Something silly. She said I wasn't a friend and I couldn't spend the week with her."

"Oh," he waved a hand. "She'll forget all about that when we get to Ohio. She probably just needs some time alone. I bet, wherever she is now, she's regretting every word."

"Do you think so?"

"Sure. Absolutely."

Rikki wondered if he was right.

◆

As the train approached Toledo, Rikki had already been up for an hour. It was 6:15 in the morning. Barney had disappeared some twenty minutes earlier, saying he was off to the restroom. As Rikki checked around the seat for her belongings, she worried that Barney would miss the stop entirely.

Where can he be?

She pulled down her travel bag from the overhead rack, dropping it onto Barney's seat. She'd spent a long night worrying. They'd both tried to talk to Barbra but with no luck. She was being bratty and had no intention of taking them along with her, even though, for a moment, Barney had said he thought he'd broken through. "But when she heard you had to come along too, all bets were off. If it was only me, I definitely could have convinced her. She kept saying. '*You have a roundtrip ticket... just go home.*'" He laughed at the absurdity of their predicament. "All these hours on a train to Ohio, sitting up, and we have no place to go for Christmas Eve. So much for the well-planned journey. It kind of reminds me of Mary and Joseph."

Rikki wished it was funny. All she felt was irritation. And after this, she knew her friendship with Barbra was over. No matter what their history, she had no intention of ever talking to Barbra again. That was certain.

"Over here," waved Barney as he came up the aisle. "Man, the crowds are intense. Are you hungry?"

She nodded.

He miraculously produced a banana from his pocket. "Pretty cool, hey? Someone left it on a table in the dining car."

"Is that where you were?"

"Well," he said smiling, "this banana didn't come from the men's room."

She laughed, for the moment forgetting their dilemma. It was easy to do when staring into Barney's blue eyes. All troubles seemed to fade in his presence.

"Well, I guess we'd better get a move on," he suggested as he slipped into his leather coat. I bet it's plenty cold out."

He buttoned the top of her jacket, knotting the long red and white scarf he'd worn earlier about her.

"But where should we go?" she said. "Back to Queens?"

"Hell, no," Barney said, linking his arm in hers. "We're on an adventure. It's too early to turn around now. The world is ours. We can go anywhere. Do anything."

Rikki smiled. He was joking. Being lighthearted, unaware that she had $300 in her pocket.

Barney's voice assumed an air of confidence. "So where would you like to go?" he asked, pulling her into a hug.

Rikki gave the request genuine consideration. "Well," she began, "I wouldn't mind going back to Michigan. That's where I was raised."

"Michigan, huh?"

"Sure," Rikki said with growing excitement. "To my old neighborhood. I'd love to see my old house."

"Do you remember the address?"

"Why, sure."

"But I thought you had no memory."

"It's the strangest thing," Rikki admitted. "I remember Michigan. Going to school, the house, and my old neighborhood. It's my mother who I can't remember."

"That's weird."

"I know," Rikki said, her expression slipping from sheer joy to sorrow.

"Oh, no," Barney said, lifting her chin. "Don't be sad. We'll figure it out. You'll see."

Rikki pressed her face to his chest and once again heard the voice. *Don't be sad, honey. I'm always with you.* It was El.

◆

Barney rubbed his hands together. "How much money do you have?"

"Where are your gloves?" Rikki asked. "It's freezing out here."

Barney shoved his hands in his pocket. "How much money?"

"Enough," Rikki answered, unwilling to reveal the exact amount of cash. "Why?"

"I looked up the schedule, and we can take a later train to Dearborn."

Rikki offered a blank stare. She'd never heard of Dearborn. "Where's that?"

"In Michigan," Barney said. "Near Detroit. You miss Michigan. You wonder what happened to your mother's friends. Your friends. I say, let's go. Let's go visit where you used to live. We have a week before we need to be back. Visit the neighbors—find those old friends. Find out why you haven't heard from anyone since your mom died."

Rikki felt both excited and afraid. "What if they don't want to see me? What if they're all away for Christmas? I don't know," she whispered.

"Now come on," Barney answered. "This is the moment. Look at us. We're in Toledo with no place to go. Barbra's long gone. That little bitch barely gave us a backward glance. We're on our own, and I think," he said, eyes squinting in the morning sun, "we should make the most of this."

Rikki grabbed his hand and warmed it in hers. This was the ideal opportunity. Rita was hundreds of miles away. She couldn't stop her. Besides, Rita thought she was with the Winer family. "Okay," she agreed. "Let's do it."

"All right!" Barney shouted. "That's my girl. Being all brave. That's the Rikki that I like."

Rikki laughed. "But the doors to the train depot are locked." A red sign hung on the door, sporting the face of a clock. The little hand on the nine. "We can't wait out here for hours. We'll freeze to death."

Barney pulled Rikki into an embrace as a yellow taxi cab pulled up. A dark-skinned man sporting a black ski hat and a dark beard and mustache leaned over the seat and called from the open passenger window, "Hey, you two. Need a ride?"

Rikki and Barney looked at each other. Barney spoke. "Is there someplace open for breakfast nearby?"

"Sure," the cabbie said. "Not far at all."

Rikki nodded.

The cabbie hopped out and rushed to the rear of the taxi, loading their bags into the trunk. "Nice and cold," he said, his words creating a white cloud. "Where are you two from?" he asked as the cab pulled away from the curb.

"New York City," they answered in unison.

He turned to look at them. "Ah, the Big Apple. I'm from Bangladesh. Almost as crowded."

Rikki and Barney looked at each other.

"You haven't heard of it?"

Barney nodded. "Sure, but we don't know anything about it."

"Why should you?" the cabbie said as he eyed them in the rearview mirror. "You don't live there. Visiting family here for the holidays?"

"It's kind of a lark," Rikki explained. "We're catching another train in two hours."

The cabbie nodded his head. "Detroit."

"Why, yes," Rikki said, surprised.

"I know all trains passing through. You need to if you drive a cab."

"Your English is great," Barney observed.

"Oh, thank you. In Bangladesh, we all want to come to America. You can do anything here." He cleared his throat. "Even at your age, we all want to come."

As they turned a corner, Rikki could see the blinking lights of the restaurant. It was nothing more than a white wooden structure with a door in the center flanked by a window on either side. The neon sign flashed red: *Good Eats*.

"This is it," the cabbie said, his hand extended as he pulled the taxi over.

Barney looked at Rikki and then back to the cabbie. "Isn't there a McDonald's nearby?"

"McDonald's?" the man shouted, his hand still pointing at the front door. "Why would anyone want a McDonald's when you have this wonderful place?"

"Are you sure?" Barney asked.

"Absolutely," the cabbie said, before giving Barney and Rikki an odd look. "Have you two done something wrong? Are you running away?"

"Oh, we're not running away," Rikki said somewhat amused. "Not at all."

"Okay," the man said, his dark brown eyes projecting concern. "You go in and get some breakfast and I will come back later for you."

"That's not necessary," Barney said. "I'm sure we can grab another cab."

"This is Toledo," the cabbie explained. "You can't just grab a cab. You need to call for one. So, I will come back."

Barney leaned forward. "Okay, well, what do we owe you for the ride?"

"Nothing," the man said waving a hand. "It's nothing."

Rikki scooted forward. "Oh, but that isn't right."

"Okay, then. You can pay me after you eat breakfast," the man said.

"We'll make it a round trip fare of five dollars. Does that seem all right?"

Both teens nodded.

"You know, when I first arrived in Toledo, I had no idea where I was. I wasn't much older than you two. Only eighteen when I left my family. I had an uncle who had a grocery store here. I worked and stayed with him. Then, he suddenly died. The grocery store closed. Kind people helped me. So, now I will help you. Go inside, have breakfast, rest, and when I return, I will take you back to the station."

◆

At the age of twenty-three, El found herself as an intern at Haney & Lewis, one of New York's hippest design firms. It offered much more than home décor. With a cadre of talented artists, architects, designers, and project managers, the firm understood how to transform texture, color, lighting, and architectural symmetry into a lifestyle brand. Located in a former sweatshop, H&L retained the exposed pipes, high ceilings, and industrial windows so fashionable in Manhattan's burgeoning loft market. The massive brick interior, carved up by movable faux walls, was a showcase to dazzle the high-end tastes of its elite clientele.

"I think we're going to need to work on that last name of yours," said Bill Allington, Chief Operating Officer and Founding Partner of H&L.

Together he and El sat in his plush office, he behind a gorgeous mahogany desk and she in an antique Victorian side chair. Allington radiated a youthful, yet sophisticated *joie de vivre*, even as he admitted to being in his late forties. His voice and manner so reminded El of Tony Randall that at first she thought he was putting her on with an imitation.

"Oh," was all that El could manage to say. "But that's my *name*."

"Yes," Mr. Allington acknowledged as he rubbed his chin. "Perhaps to your family," he said with certainty, "but to our clientele…

that name … is far too ethnic." He rolled a black, shiny Mount Blanc pen between his index finger and thumb. "I know. How about Lisa Richards?"

El was speechless.

"Yes," he said, "Lisa Richards. It has a solid ring to it."

"Mr. Allington, Richard is my brother's name. It would be too strange."

"No," he said with self-satisfaction. "It's perfect. You'll never forget it."

"Couldn't I at least keep my first name?" El asked.

Mr. Allington paused and then began to search his desk, finally retrieving El's resume. After a moment he looked up with a flash of what El could only think he believed was creative inspiration. "How about we spell your name E-l-l-e, like the magazine. Oh yes, that's very elegant."

El pondered the change. "Well, I guess that will work."

"There's no guessing about it. Young lady," Mr. Allington said boldly and with all the dramatic flair he could muster, "you're about to be reborn."

Elle's stomach lurched. If this was her rebirth, she'd hoped it might come with a bit more money than an intern's stipend.

◆

After breakfast, Rikki and Barney found the cabbie had been true to his word; he'd returned and was waiting outside of the restaurant. "Did you like the food?" he asked as they settled into the back seat. He turned around and flashed a bright smile as he accepted the five dollars that Barney offered.

"Yes," Rikki answered, mesmerized by the man's beautiful white teeth. "Very much."

"Oh, I'm glad," he said, shifting his attention to Barney.

"Yes, yes," Barney stuttered. "Yes, it was very nice."

Rikki couldn't believe the man's smile could get any wider and yet with Barney's affirmation, Rikki could now see a gold molar in the rear of the cabbie's mouth.

"That is so important. You see, I own that restaurant." The pride in his voice was unmistakable.

"You do?" Rikki said. "How can you be a cabbie and own a restaurant?"

"I can do both," the man answered matter-of-factly. With an index finger held up, he emphasized his point. "You can do whatever you want in America. Work two jobs. Work three. My cousin, who came over three years ago, manages it for me. His wife was your waitress."

Rikki nodded, suddenly realizing that the husband and wife were similarly ethnic. "Well, they are very good at what they do," she offered.

"Family is so important," the cabbie declared as he shook his head back and forth. "We must take care of our own. Now, it is still early. Do you want to go back and wait for the train? Or, maybe, I can drive you to Detroit. It isn't that far."

"Drive us?" Rikki lurched forward. "Oh, no. We can't afford that." Rikki looked over at Barney.

"How much would you charge?" Barney asked, taking ownership of the situation.

The man rubbed his chin. "Just a bit more than the price of two train tickets," the man haggled. "You won't have to wait for the train, and I'll make sure that you get to your destination."

"No," Barney wavered. "I'm not sure …"

"You leave it to me," the cabbie said. "I will only charge you one hundred dollars. That's less than those two train tickets. And I'll take you directly to your destination."

Rikki considered the terms. "But why would you do that?" she asked suspiciously.

"Do what?" the man said, confused. "This is something that I must do. I can't let two young people wander alone. No," he confirmed, wiping away any doubt with the wave of a hand, "Samir will see you safely there. It will be my honor. And please, call me Sammy."

Rikki exchanged worried looks with Barney. That was one-third of the cash she had on hand. Though she still had Rita's credit card, she was reluctant to use it. "Barney," she whispered, "do you have any money?"

He leaned close to her. "I have my return Amtrak ticket and the fifty dollars that I earned last summer cutting grass."

Rikki couldn't imagine anywhere in Queens with enough grass to even merit such a job.

"I know you're good kids," Sammy continued. "I can tell. So, you will do me this honor. It's my way of *playing with it forward*."

Barney laughed. "You mean *paying it forward*."

"Of course," Sammy jovially answered. "That's what I said."

9

Lil examined her figure in the studio mirror as she stretched in preparation for the 6:00 a.m. Christmas Eve class. Though things had certainly shifted, she'd maintained her lean shape. *I couldn't very well be a pudgy yoga instructor,* she thought as her eyes strayed to her feet, the one part of her body that had suffered the most wear and tear over the years.

There had been a time when she'd had beautiful feet.

Toes well-shaped and nesting together like a lovely fan in the closed position. But as a child, her mother wanted her to study ballet. Five years of en pointe had taken the soft skin and hardened it. Thick calluses had formed as a protective layer. And when she was fifteen, enrolled in ballet class, she began to bleed as the nails shredded under the weight of her adolescent growth spurt. The blood seeped out of the lining of her toe shoes and onto the highly polished floor, causing her to lose balance as she performed a chassé, sending her tumbling onto her rump and breaking her right ankle.

Though she never danced again, her feet had been hopelessly marred. Going for a pedicure caused intense anxiety. She thought of her feet as claws, eagle talons that, in her professional life as an instructor, she needed to expose, all the while being ever mindful and self-conscious of what others must think.

She'd been grateful that for the longest time Harry had not noticed her feet. She'd worked hard to make sure they were always covered up. Even in bed, while other women might keep their bras on due to insecurities about the shape or size of their breasts, Lil was focused on her feet. The mere sight of them dangling on the end of her graceful legs killed the mood.

"Do you always wear socks in bed?" Harry had finally asked one night, which had almost caused her heart to stop.

"My feet are always cold," she muttered, hoping to quickly change the subject.

"Really?" he said, sitting up in bed and pulling her closer to him. "Maybe I should rub them. It could be poor circulation."

Instead of giving into the moment, she pulled away. "I really should be going," she'd said, feet now on the floor as she gave her hair a quick shake. "I've got an early morning class tomorrow."

"You know you can stay," Harry had offered, though it sounded to Lil half-hearted.

She let out a sharp laugh. "Oh Harry—you don't want me here when you wake up. When I stayed in the guest room, I saw the look on your face that next morning. You nearly had a heart attack." She slipped on her panties. "And besides, how would Beetle feel about that?" she teased. She looked over at Beetle, who was tucked into a tight crescent, fast asleep in his crate by the bed.

"I guess you're right," Harry admitted. "Beetle wouldn't like it."

"That's what happens when you sleep with your dog," she said, grateful to be on her way. "They become very protective."

Harry nodded. "That's right."

"It's hard to let others in." She pulled on a pair of jeans and slipped into a simple white T-shirt. "But that's okay. We're independent people. We're used to being on our own."

Harry watched as she checked herself in the mirror.

"I'll see you later," she said, one of her many throw-away lines that had no particular meaning and offered no promises.

"Later," Harry had said as she walked out of the bedroom and through the living room and onto the street. There was a beautiful orange and pink sky.

How lovely, she'd thought as she'd wandered back to her house, doubtful that life could ever be happier than at that precise moment.

Give a man a little space… and see how his attitude changes. Oh, Harry.
You're not so hard to figure out, she decided, planning her next step in
the pursuit.

◆

It was about an hour's drive from Toledo to the outskirts of Detroit,
but, caught in the backseat of Sammy's cab, Rikki discovered that
the trip was indeed a lot longer. Driving at sixty miles per hour, well
under the seventy-five-mile speed limit, Rikki and Barney suffered
as the cab's shoddy shocks encountered endless miles of potholes on
Interstate 75. Sammy, unfazed by the teens bouncing about in the
back seat, was eager to talk about his life.

"Oh, yes, my mother died when I was a teenager. But I was lucky. I
told you that I had an uncle in the United States. He was a good man.
Hardworking. Caring. Not everyone has that blessing."

"And your father?" asked Barney. "Where is he?" His finger caught
in a small tear on the back seat. Rikki swatted his hand away.

"I don't know," Sammy announced sadly. "He left my mother when
I was very young."

"Oh," Rikki said, giving him her full attention. "I never knew my
father."

"Ah. You see. Your destiny is the same as mine. To discover on your
own the meaning of life. You are a *seeker.*"

"Yes, I suppose," Rikki answered, despite being unsure what Sammy
meant.

"That's a funny thing to say," Barney added as he looked at Rikki.
"Maybe that's the bond that we share."

Rikki looked at him askance. "You think?" A draft was blowing on
her legs. The windows of the cab were closed. She wondered, *Where
is the breeze coming from?*

Barney ran his hand through his thick hair. "Sure. It's got to be."

"Are you an orphan, too?" asked Sammy, seemingly surprised to
have two kindred souls in the back seat of his cab.

Barney nodded.

Sammy looked in the rearview at the pair. "I knew you two were special. I could feel it. Sammy is very spiritual," he said, talking about himself in the third person. "You will see. I will take care of you like you're my very own. We'll get you safely to Michigan."

Rikki had no doubt. Just then, the cab hit another pothole. "When did they last fix this highway?" Rikki asked as she held onto the cab's door handle, steadying herself.

"They pave every year," Sammy explained. "But the winters undo most of their good work. The roads in Bangladesh can be far worse."

Rikki realized that Sammy had an endless bounty of good feeling for his adopted country. No matter what had happened in his life, once he was in America, he had been determined to make the best of it. She had a mix of admiration and disbelief that any human being could hold such a magnanimous outlook about the goodness of other people.

"I love America!" he shouted as they passed the sign that read *Welcome to Michigan.* "The best day of my life was the day I moved to Toledo."

Rikki wondered whether anyone born in the United States had ever said that about Toledo, Ohio.

◆

"This is so beautiful," Sammy called out as they rumbled past the small shops of Birmingham, Michigan, windows dressed for the holidays in red, white, and green trimmings. A Santa stood on the corner of Maple and Old Woodward Avenue, ringing a bell for the Salvation Army. People rushed about, some holding Starbucks cups—most with shopping bags filled to the brim with the morning's bounty.

"Isn't it lovely?" Rikki said, steeped in wonder.

Sammy slowed the cab, parking across the street from the Townsend Hotel. He turned to look over his shoulder.

"Does any of it look familiar?" Barney asked Rikki.

"Oh, yes. I remember being here."

"Do you remember your mother now?" Sammy wanted to know as Barney unfolded the map they'd picked up at a rest stop on Interstate 75.

Rikki shook her head. "No," she admitted, her eyes following a young couple dressed in blue matching down jackets and walking a basset hound wearing reindeer antlers. "But it feels so wonderful to be here," she said, suddenly choked with tears.

"Yes," Sammy agreed. "Christmas is a wonderful thing when you're wealthy. Everyone enjoys spending money. But for those of us who have to work for a living, it seems wasteful."

"No," Rikki said, correcting him. "That's not it at all. It isn't just the season. It just feels so right. So clean. So very ... safe."

Sammy turned to look at Rikki. "You think a wealthy neighborhood is safe?" His brown eyes sparkled as if it was a riddle.

Rikki wasn't sure how to answer. She wanted to say *yes*.

"Perhaps you are right," he agreed, turning back around to face the steering wheel. "But I think people are people. Poor neighborhoods look out for their own. Just because you're poor doesn't make you a criminal."

Rikki supposed that was right, as a toddler in a pink snow suit, grasping the string of a red balloon, ran by, letting out a squeal of sheer delight. The woman who chased closely behind quickly caught up, lifting the child in her arms. Child and mother laughed, reveling in each other's company as Rikki had a mental flash. The face of a pretty woman, her blonde hair cut in a short bob, her blue eyes glowing with a radiant intensity. "Oh, my God," Rikki said.

"Are you okay?" Barney asked, looking up from the map.

"Yes," Rikki answered, in gleeful reverie. Not a photograph ... a flat, two-dimensional image ... but a genuine sense of El's radiant life force.

"She's just enjoying all the Christmas hoopla," Sammy laughed as he again turned about. "All the childlike wonderment."

"But she's Jewish," Barney said, as he lifted the map closer to his face and squinted, running a finger along a route. "I remember you telling me that," he said, without bothering to look at her.

Rikki admonished him. "Jewish, Muslim, Christian—Christmas isn't about religion—it's the wonder of everyone coming together in the spirit of good will."

Sammy smiled and Rikki recognized immediately that he thought she was just being naïve.

"I'm glad for Christmas if that's what it takes for everyone to just get along," he said, resolving the discussion amicably. "But I think Christians would think it was very much about religion."

"I got it," Barney said, staring down at the map. "Your old house isn't far from here."

◆

Edward's voice came through loud and clear. "I'm arriving on American #2055. I should be there about 2:00 p.m. Got it?"

"Got it," Harry said, as he wiped the sleep from his eyes, the phone receiver pressed to his ear. "I'll pick you up."

"No, Harry. I think I'd better rent a car."

"Now, why would you do that?" Harry asked. "You know I have a spare bedroom."

"I'm not sure we should be staying together," Edward said. "You know, the blurring of work and play isn't ideal."

Harry sighed. "That's ridiculous. Now, I don't want to hear another word about it. I'll pick you up and you're staying with me."

"Only if you insist," Edward finally agreed.

"Of course I do. Beetle will be happy to see you. Remember when he was just a pup?"

"Yeah."

"Well, he's a lot older now." Harry smirked as he looked over at Beetle, fast asleep, curled up in the blanket. "He sleeps a lot now."

"Lucky dog," Edward answered. "I wish I could."

Harry nodded. "I know what you mean."

There was silence on the line.

Harry cleared his throat. "So how long will you be staying?"

"Only one night. It was practically impossible to get a seat. With Christmas and all, I could only fly Christmas Eve and return Christmas Day. And first-class at that, Harry ... these tickets are costing a fortune. We're lucky the company was willing to cover it. I'll need to be back in New York to prepare for our January meeting to discuss the 2006 publication list. I'll have to be able to tell the team the status of your book."

"The book!"

◆

Harry examined his face in the mirror. The three-day-old stubble was all gray. It had once been dark, giving his face an irresistibly sexy allure. Now, the stubble just made him look like an old, weathered codger. Someone's grandpappy. And though Lil didn't seem to mind, he knew better than to let Edward really see him, close-up, looking so scruffy. *No,* he thought, running fingers through his hair; he needed to clean up.

"Come on, Chris," Harry begged when the scheduler at Mane Attraction passed him through by phone to the owner. "If I get there by nine, that'll be plenty of time before you need to close the shop for your Christmas party. I'll even bring a bottle of champagne. Please. Please. You've got to squeeze me in."

Later that morning, Harry sat in a chair at Mane Attraction with the last of the holiday customers who were being colored, cut, teased, and brushed out.

"Whoa, Harry. I haven't seen you in a long time," Chris said, examining his scalp. "This is some mop you've got going."

"It's not like I see anyone," Harry said, his gray curls falling about his face. "Any chance you can do something special?"

Chris's brows arched. "'Special?' What does *that* mean?"

"I don't know," Harry admitted.

"Color?"

"No." Harry's body lurched forward.

"Should I cut it short?"

Harry had no clue.

"Leave it long?"

Harry closed his eyes. This is why he hated getting a haircut. He wanted to look good, but he had no idea how to answer all these questions. "I really don't know," he answered, a sinking feeling in his gut as if he'd failed some important test.

"Hey, don't sweat it," Chris said, a hand on Harry's shoulder. "Just leave it to me. You'll look great when I'm done."

Harry hoped so. Edward could be very critical.

◆

Rikki focused as the cab turned east down Fourteen Mile Road. She now occupied the passenger seat next to Sammy. "That's it," she cried. "Up ahead. Shipman Boulevard. Make a left."

Sammy did as he was told, slowing the cab as they entered the street. "Which house?"

Rikki glanced ahead. All the tiny cottages appeared to have been built from the same spec blueprint, with modest changes. Some had front porches with elaborate lattice work, others carports, and still others attached garages.

"The fourth house on the left," Rikki called out.

Sammy stopped in front of the brick cottage with a carport.

"We're here!" she shouted to Barney. "This is it."

"Wow," Barney said, admiring the tall trees on the street. "This certainly isn't Queens. It must be amazing in the summer when the leaves are out. Did it always look like this?"

"The houses aren't very big," Sammy seemed compelled to point out. "But that's America for you. Everyone has a house."

Rikki started to cry. Sammy and Barney waited for her to regain her composure. "I haven't been here since I was eleven years old," she explained, wiping her tears. "I wonder if the neighbors are still the same."

"There's only one way to find out," Barney suggested. "Ring a doorbell."

Like a flash, Rikki darted out of the cab, leaving Sammy and Barney on their own as she raced up to the Shermans' front door. She'd explained on the way up from Toledo that the Shermans were like her second family. When El had worked late, it was the Shermans who took Rikki in and fed her. And since they had no children of their own, Rikki had been a welcome guest.

"Oh, my God!" Evelyn Sherman screamed when she opened the front door. "Look what Santa brought me for Christmas! Oh, my God! Rikki. I can't believe it's you." She practically vibrated with delight as she pulled Rikki into her arms for a warm hug. "How many years has it been?" she asked, stepping back and taking a long look at Rikki.

"A long time," was all that Rikki could manage as she remembered the afternoons spent doing homework at the Shermans' kitchen table while Evelyn fiddled about, sometimes rolling out a pie crust or preparing a roast or addressing fundraising letters at her counter for Cancer Care.

"How beautiful you are," Evelyn said as she pulled Rikki along through the front door and into the living room.

The house was exactly as Rikki remembered. The living room fireplace, a white painted brick, dominated the cozy room. Two high-backed white sofas sat perpendicular to the fireplace, facing each other, separated by a glass coffee table with a metallic base. The accent colors in the room were a pale blue, reflected in the pillows, window curtains, and Asian pottery. And there was a six-foot Christmas tree nestled in the corner. The green branches were beautifully decorated with colorful ornaments and silver jingle-bell garlands.

"So, what are you doing here? Is Rita with you?"

Rikki hesitated.

Evelyn smiled. "Talk to me. What's going on?" she said as she offered the teenager a seat on the sofa and slid in next to her. "I haven't seen you in years," she said placing a hand on Rikki's knee and giving it a loving shake. "Why did you never answer my letters? Herbie told me that was because you were going through"—and her eyes opened wide as her voice deepened to imitate her husband—"'a *rebellious teen adolescence. You can't expect a young girl to sit down and write you a letter just because you miss her,*' he'd tell me." She offered Rikki a sad, wistful look.

"I never received any letters," Rikki said with alarm.

"You didn't?" An odd expression crossed Evelyn's face.

"No."

"Then you don't know about Herbie, do you?"

Rikki covered her mouth as she stared at Evelyn.

Evelyn clenched her jaw. The muscles in her cheeks flexed. Then she sighed. "I lost him last year. He got up that morning and said he wasn't feeling well. When he stepped out of bed, he just keeled over. Dead."

Rikki gasped. "I didn't know."

"Of course not," Evelyn whispered, stroking Rikki's arm. "If you had, I'm sure you'd have been in touch."

"I never saw a letter," Rikki said emphatically. "Never."

Evelyn just shook her head. "Oh Rikki, you must have thought that we'd forgotten all about you."

Rikki jumped to her feet. Her temper flared. "All this time Rita told me that no one in Michigan cared about me. Why would she do that? Why would she want me to feel so terrible?"

Evelyn looked down at her hands. "I also called quite a few times that first year to check on you, but she'd never let me talk with you. There was always a reason. Always an excuse. So I stopped calling and wrote letters instead."

"Why was Rita so intent on separating us?" Rikki asked angrily as the doorbell rang.

Rikki suddenly remembered Barney was waiting outside and she still needed to pay Sammy.

◆

Evelyn set the table for lunch. Three place mats, three plates, three glasses. Barney, already seated, waited patiently as Rikki answered Evelyn's questions.

"So Rita has no idea where you are?" Evelyn placed a bowl of potato chips on the table.

"None," Rikki answered, taking a seat.

Evelyn stopped and assumed a parental tone. "This is not good. I should call her."

"Oh, please don't," Rikki begged. "This is my one chance to finally understand what is going on."

"You mean with Rita?" Evelyn asked, as she handed Barney a cola. He nodded in appreciation.

"Yes. She'll never talk about El. And when I try to bring her up, she cries. It's as if she's the only one who suffered a loss. I was the one who lost my mother. And living in New York," Rikki sighed dramatically, "Evelyn, you just can't imagine what that's like."

"Don't exaggerate," Barney interjected as he reached for the bowl of chips and piled some on his plate.

Evelyn had prepared a platter of turkey sandwiches. She brought over mayo, ketchup, mustard, and relish, placing the condiments in the center. "There. That should do it," she said as she pulled out a chair and sat down. "Does anyone need anything else?" she asked, looking at Barney. He'd already reached for a sandwich and was busy eating, signaling his approval with his eyes and with grunts of satisfaction.

"So, how are you doing in school?" Evelyn asked Rikki. "Good grades, I hope."

"Oh, yes," Rikki said, dismissing the question. She reached for the bowl of chips.

"Then you're doing fine," Evelyn confirmed.

Rikki merely looked at the chips before placing them back down on the table. And then Rikki tossed out the name she'd seen in the family album. "Evelyn, who is Richard?"

"Richard?" Evelyn repeated.

"Yes, who is Richard?"

"Did your mother ever tell you about a Richard?"

Rikki offered Evelyn a withering glance. How could she possibly know if she couldn't remember El?

Evelyn waved her hands as if to erase the question. "I'm so sorry, sweetie. You just seem so unchanged. Just as I remember you. It's such an odd thing."

"Well, we seem to be the kind of family that likes to keep secrets."

"Oh," Evelyn balked. "That's not fair, Rikki. I was one of your mother's closest friends. She wasn't like that at all." Evelyn glanced over at Barney. "How are you doing, dear? Can I get you anything else?"

"Evelyn, please," Rikki interrupted. "If there's something I should know, I'd like to hear it. Please."

Evelyn took a deep breath. "It's hard to know where to start," she said. "When I first met your mother, she was a *very* single young woman. I once tried to ask about your father, but she brushed me off. I'd assumed they'd only been together a few months before she moved to Michigan, so I never bothered to ask again. It wasn't any of my business. And I didn't want to put her off. She'd just accepted a new job with Jacobson's in Birmingham," Evelyn explained, "a high-end store where she was able to use all of her artistic talents working as an interior decorator. Of course, Jacobson's was in trouble financially in the late '90s. It went out of business soon after your mother died. She'd worried about losing her job for so long—that's why she was interviewing the week she died."

Evelyn sighed.

"But I'm getting ahead of myself," she apologized, as she looked at the faces across the table. "So, Elle rented the house next door. My neighbors had bought a property in Traverse City . . . oh, but you don't care about that," she self-corrected.

"I was nervous when I heard there was going to be a renter. But the day the moving truck showed up," Evelyn said, a wistful look on her face, "there was your mom. She was so pretty, with her blonde hair pulled back in a ponytail, dressed in these scruffy jeans, all set to direct the unloading." She smiled at the memory. "And then I saw you," she said, her eyes focused on Rikki. "The most beautiful little girl. You couldn't have been more than three, just a toddler. With your brown hair pulled up high in the cutest little pigtails. Your mother was so proud of you. We were formally introduced right on my front steps. I still remember that moment."

Rikki filled in the rest of the story for Barney. "I lived here until I was eleven. When my mother died, I moved, but I don't remember much about that. It seems like I was suddenly living with Rita in Queens."

"Not all that suddenly," Evelyn pointed out.

"Yes," Rikki replied, unwilling to discuss the months of hospitalization.

"After your mother died, your grandmother flew out here. I picked her up at the airport."

"I know nothing about this part," she told Barney. "This is all new to me."

"Your grandmother was very angry. At first I thought—*well, that's natural.* Any parent would be upset after losing their only child. Especially a daughter."

"But I thought you said," Barney interrupted, directing the question to Rikki, "that you had an uncle."

"I did," Rikki confirmed.

"Not that *I* knew," Evelyn answered. "There was no one else but your mother. I would have known if Elle had a brother. Most certainly."

Rikki thought for a moment. "Are you sure?"

◆

Harry honked his car horn. He could see Edward off in the distance, standing near the taxi stand.

Edward still looked remarkably fit. His short wavy hair, close-cropped, added a surprising youthfulness to his presence. Dressed in a blue sport jacket over black jeans, Edward stood expectantly, his flair for style on full display. Except for the designer eyeglasses, in a startlingly bright red frame, he looked every inch the hip college professor.

Edward waved as the white Ford Explorer pulled up. "New car?" he asked, placing his bag in the back seat.

"Are you kidding?" Harry said, as he pulled away from the curb. "This is a 1999."

"Well," Edward defended himself. "You know I'm car-blind."

"That's what comes from living in Manhattan," Harry offered, merging into traffic. "No one drives."

"Not much, at least. Except in the summers. I still get out to Fire Island."

"You don't take the bus to the ferry?"

Edward looked askance at Harry. "No … friends drive. I'm too old for the party bus."

"No, you're not," Harry said, sneaking a glance at Edward.

Edward smiled. "You can still be charming when you try. I guess you haven't changed much."

Harry let out a belly laugh. "Are you kidding me? I got all dolled up for you," he admitted. "I didn't want you to see me looking like a bum."

"You mean *the real Harry?* The guy from Microsoft *Live Meeting.*"

"Say what you will … I just didn't want to be judged. Especially on Christmas Eve."

"Oh, *Christmas Eve.*"

"That's why you're here, isn't it? Couldn't stand to be away from me for the holidays?"

Edward laughed. "Oh yes, that must be it," he said sarcastically. "Who can resist Christmas in the desert?"

Harry followed the signs to AZ-51. "It *is* beautiful this time of year."

Edward nodded as if he understood. "Well, I'm not going to ask why you're still living out here, if that's what you're worried about." Edward turned to look out the passenger window. "Or why you continue to live alone. Richard's been gone a long time. What's the sense in isolating yourself?"

"I'm not isolated," Harry answered as he pulled onto the highway. "There are a lot of amazing people living in Arizona."

"Tell it to the Republicans."

Harry bellowed, "I'm not a Republican!"

"Living out here," Edward snapped, "you might as well be."

◆

"You look good," Edward said as Harry showed off the backyard. Both men had changed into shorts. "Love the red bougainvilleas."

"Every day is amazing." Harry gestured for Edward to take a seat on a red lounger. "Try it. It's very comfortable."

Edward paused a moment, touching the cushion. "Is it clean?"

"Of course," Harry answered.

"Do I have to kick off my shoes if I do?"

Harry laughed. "No. I get that would be too much to ask of a New Yorker to completely chill. No—by all means, keep those shoes on. Maintain control. I know how important that is."

Edward kicked off his Gucci loafers. "See?" he said, holding the shoes up for Harry's inspection. "I can do it." He sat on the edge of the lounger. "So why, Harry? What's going on with the book? Why so late?"

Harry sighed. "What's the temperature in New York City right now?" He glanced up at the sky. "The high in Phoenix today is 83."

Edward rolled his eyes. "Hmm. Fascinating. A weather report. Perhaps you might squeeze in a prediction on when I might see the next two chapters."

Harry stretched out on the adjacent lounge chair. He waved a hand, signaling for Edward to do the same. "There, isn't that better?"

For the moment Edward seemed to relax into it. He closed his eyes

as Harry sneaked a peek at him. Even though it was the early afternoon, stubble was beginning to show on Edward's baby face. Harry
thought it wonderfully sexy.

Edward tilted his head toward Harry. "I haven't forgotten why I'm
here. And may I remind you, I have other projects to oversee, Harry.
You're not my only focus. I really can't afford to take this kind of time
to babysit."

Harry laughed. "There we go. Right to work. Not even a moment to
appreciate how blue the sky is. The warmth of a winter sun."

Edward shielded his eyes with the palm of his hand as he sank back
into the lounger. "It's so damn bright here. How can you stand it? I
hope you're using sun protection."

Harry smiled. Edward was already looking for what was wrong.
"Maybe in the summer, but not in the winter. I think I'm fine."

"I wouldn't trust that, Harry. Melanoma can be a killer. How old
are you now? Fifty-one?"

"Somewhere in that vicinity," Harry answered, refusing to be
pinned down.

Edward yawned, raised his arms, and slipped his hands behind his
head. Eyes closed, he tilted his face up to engage the warmth of the
sun.

Harry shifted onto his side as he admired Edward's profile. He'd
nearly forgotten Edward was so handsome after seeing his face dis-
torted on Microsoft *Live Meeting* for so many months.

"You still have that great, aquiline nose," Harry offered.

"Sephardic Jews from Turkey. The nose runs in the bloodline."

"Right," Harry remembered. "A Sephardic Jew from Saint Louis,
Missouri, named Edward Heaton. Now how did *that* happen?"

"No one wanted an agent named Shlomo Carasso," Edward said
with gusto. "I'm just lucky my nose can carry the new name."

"Literary agent. That sure didn't work out."

Edward sat up in the lounger. "Now, that wasn't my fault."

"Right." Harry raised his eyebrows. "The world wasn't ready for
you."

"No," Edward admitted. "I wasn't ready for it. I'm a better editor than an agent. Besides, I like a steady paycheck. Working for a publishing house beats freelance."

"Hmm," Harry said, stretching his neck left and then right. "Smell that?"

"What?" Edward asked.

"Barbeque."

"I don't smell anything."

"I do," Harry jumped to his feet. "*I want me some barbeque.* How about we go to Don & Charlie's for a late lunch. A Christmas Eve celebration."

Edward suddenly brightened. "Friends of yours?"

Harry smirked. "It's a restaurant. The best barbequed ribs. Ever heard of Carson's?"

"In Chicago," Edward confirmed. "I've had dinner meetings there."

"Right. This is the same owner as Carson's."

"Okay," Edward agreed. "But I don't really eat barbeque."

Harry chuckled. "A Midwesterner who doesn't eat barbeque? Who *are* you?"

"A New Yorker, Harry. I'm a New Yorker."

10

"Are you sure we shouldn't be calling Barney's family to let them know where he is?" Evelyn asked Rikki as she made up the guest bed after settling Barney on the sofa in the living room. "They might be worried about him," she continued as Rikki stuffed a pillow into a fresh pillowcase.

"You better talk to Barney about that," Rikki advised, unwilling to discuss Barney's circumstances.

"And as for *you*," Evelyn said, sitting down on the edge of the bed, "what shall I do about you?"

Rikki stood wide-eyed, unsure what to say.

"Come sit." Evelyn patted the spot next to her. "I know all about your grandmother. Believe me, I do. But she doesn't deserve to worry. That really isn't fair."

Rikki sighed. "I know that she'd be upset if she knew I was in Michigan and not with Barbra—but there is no way for her to know. And if I had told her, well, I'd be right back in Queens, and I'd never have had the chance to visit with you."

Evelyn smiled. "You know, you have that same look in your eyes that your mother had."

"Really?" Rikki said.

"Whenever your mother wanted me to do something for her, all she had to do was look at me. She had these beautiful blue eyes. The shade of a robin's egg, I used to tell her. It's an unusual color."

Rikki leaned in.

"And I always promised your mother, no matter what, I would be there to help her out. You know, it's not easy for a single mother to raise a daughter."

Rikki listened.

"And so, I'm about to do something I hope I don't regret."

Rikki waited.

"I *do* know about Richard."

Rikki gasped. "You do?"

"Yes. I do," Evelyn confessed.

"But why the secrecy? Why didn't you come out and tell me right away?"

"I guess I needed to see that look in your eyes. I had always thought it was the color that set your mother's eyes apart. But your eyes are brown, and still ..." Evelyn stopped talking as if she was lost in thought. "It wasn't the color at all. It was something deeper. Something I can't quite explain." Evelyn shook her head as if coming out of a dream. "It made me realize that I had no business helping Rita alter the past. As we discovered, she's already cut me out of your life. So what harm can any of this do now?"

◆

Harry slipped out of bed, searching for his underwear. Beetle looked up at him from his locked crate.

"Where are you going?" Edward asked, suddenly roused as he rolled over.

"I need something for my indigestion," Harry admitted. "I love barbeque, but it doesn't love me."

Edward laughed. "Maybe we should have waited until you'd had more time to digest."

"I thought we did," Harry said.

"Lightweight."

"Hey," Harry answered. "When you get to be my age, you'll see." Harry spotted his black shorts by the side of the bed. He bent over and picked them up.

"Oh, Harry. You're not so old."

"Older than you," Harry snapped, stepping into his Calvin Klein's. "Nothing really fits well any more," he complained, tugging on his underwear, slipping a hand down the front to adjust himself before disappearing into the master bath.

"You still look great," Edward called out, rolling onto his side.

Was that smart? Harry wondered as he searched for a bottle of Gaviscon. *Should I really be sleeping with everyone who walks through the front door?* He located the Gaviscon in the back of a drawer, shook out two white tablets, and popped them into his mouth. The chalky, minty flavor sent chills up his spine. *Disgusting,* he thought as he chewed, breaking out into goose bumps up and down his arms. And then he remembered. Richard had taken tons of Gaviscon during the last year of his life. His stomach always seemed upset. It had been nearly impossible for him to eat.

"Are you still alive?" Edward called from the bed.

Harry leaned on the vanity. He looked in the mirror. He'd maintained his physique. Eating most meals alone will do that. Lifting weights had helped retain his musculature. Even his abdomen had cooperated, remaining mostly flat. "Maybe it isn't all so bad," he whispered. "Maybe there's still a chance."

"What's that?" Edward called from the bedroom. "What did you say?"

"Nothing," Harry answered as he returned to bed.

◆

Evelyn took Rikki's hand in hers. "So, before I say anything more, we need to make a pact."

Rikki was growing tired of Evelyn's buildup. In so many ways, Evelyn was beginning to remind her of Rita. Everything seemed to be a negotiation. Nothing could ever be told straight out. It all had to come with conditions, wrapped in mystery. Rikki wondered if that's how adults communicated. It all seemed so tiresome.

"I'll tell you, but you won't tell your grandmother."

Rikki was confused. "What does it matter? You said yourself that she had cut you off."

"Yes," Evelyn acknowledged, "but now you're back. I don't want to lose our connection. You're still a minor. Your grandmother can make it very difficult going forward."

Rikki quickly agreed. "Okay. Fine. Now tell me."

Evelyn took a breath. "Well, I don't know all that much. But I know your mother loved him."

"Then why don't I know about him?" Rikki asked. "Why is he such a big secret?"

"I only know why your mother never discussed him," Evelyn explained. "She promised your grandmother that she wouldn't. And you were so young, she didn't want you to slip and accidentally tell your grandmother. But I'm sure she'd planned on telling you when you were older. When she was sure you might understand. Older. Perhaps your age now."

◆

When Harry returned to the bedroom, Edward was sitting up against the headboard, the sheet covering his groin. Without clothes, Edward looked even younger.

This is a mistake, Harry thought, a depression settling in.

Edward seemed to sense the change in Harry. Calm shifted to concern. "What's wrong? Is it more than your stomach?"

Harry sat on the edge of the bed, his shoulders hunched. "What are we doing?" he asked.

Edward came behind him, a leg on either side of Harry. Harry's back rested against Edward's chest. "What do you *think* we're doing?" Edward whispered in his ear, then softly bit the lobe.

Harry sat straight up as Edward's fingers caressed his chest, pulling gently on his chest hair, teasing one nipple. "I don't know."

Edward pulled Harry into a tight embrace, burying his face in

Harry's neck. "Then we're doing nothing. Nothing at all," Edward said. "It doesn't have to mean anything or *be* anything. It can be whatever you want."

Harry leaned forward, pulling out of Edward's embrace. "But what does it mean to you?"

Edward ran a finger down Harry's back. "The truth is, I love you, Harry. I think I've loved you from the moment I laid eyes on you. But you never believed me. I was either too young or I lived in New York City. You always had an excuse."

"Well, you *are* too young," Harry answered. "Much too young for an old man like me."

Edward slipped off the bed. He stood naked before Harry. "Take a good look, Harry, because I'm not a kid any more. I'm forty. I just had a birthday, not that you remembered. There are only three ages for a gay man: 18 to 29 when you're young, 30 to 39 when you still *think* you're young, and over 40, when you're invisible. We're now old together. I've crossed 39 and it's like crossing the Jordon. That means we're both standing on the same bank of the river."

Harry laughed. "Nice metaphor."

Edward took a bow.

"But you're still too young."

Edward sneered. "You haven't changed. You still won't let anyone in, will you? I'll always be standing outside your door trying to get in."

"But you *did* get in," Harry reminded him. "Most definitely … in."

"Not the way I hoped," Edward answered, biting his lower lip. "I had thought that maybe there was still hope for us. Maybe one last time … you might reconsider."

Harry took Edward's hand and brought it up to his lips. He gently kissed it. "I'm sorry. I've disappointed you. You believe that life is like the ending of one of my novels. Where everything ties up nicely."

"No," Edward said, as he withdrew his hand. "That's not true, Harry. Life is not like one of your novels. There is no *audience*. You only need to satisfy yourself. No one else really matters. You can have a happy ending."

"Life doesn't work that way," Harry assured him. "Nothing ever really ends well. It's all about mess."

Edward shook his head. "Dear God, Harry. Whatever you do, don't put that in your next book. It's such a downer."

◆

Evelyn took a breath. "Do you know you're named after him?"

Of course! Rikki thought. *Why hadn't she realized that?* "So he's dead," Rikki stated the obvious.

Evelyn nodded. "Yes. He died before you were born."

Rikki had hoped that perhaps her uncle might still be alive. That he might be someone to whom she could talk about her mother. At once, a dark cloud descended, blocking her view of Evelyn. She was alone in the bedroom. Alone in the world.

Evelyn seemed to notice the change in Rikki's demeanor, rushing ahead with details to salve the wound. "He was very bright," she said. "I remember your mother telling me that he excelled in everything he did."

"But what was he like as a person?" Rikki still wanted to know. "And why is it that Rita never mentions him?"

"I can't really tell you all that," Evelyn admitted. "I know he left home to go to college when he was sixteen. I remember your mother talking about that. He had a scholarship to Cornell. A full ride, your mother said."

"Those are facts," Rikki said, somewhat disappointed. "Like telling me his height and weight." And then she realized she didn't even know those details.

"I'm sorry, sweetie," Evelyn offered. "I really don't know much more. Your mother did talk to me about him, but to be honest, it's hard to remember any details about someone you've never met. If there is anything to tell … well, you should try talking to his *friend.*"

"*Friend?*" Of course, Rikki thought. *He must have had friends.*

"Yes. He's a writer. I think he lives in Phoenix, Arizona."

◆

Edward stepped out of the shower, a white towel wrapped about his waist as Beetle started barking wildly.

"Whoa, boy," Harry said, hopping off the bed and opening Beetle's crate. The terrier was out in a flash. "Who the hell is ringing the doorbell at this time of night?"

"Expecting a booty call?" Edward asked, peeking out from the master bath as the excited terrier lunged at the bedroom door.

Harry caught the scent of Irish Spring. "Don't be ridiculous," he shouted over the noise, suddenly aroused again by the sight of Edward, all fresh and clean.

"Well, you'd better answer the door before Beetle tears his other ACL."

"Oh, my God, you're right about that," he said as he rushed over, still in his underwear, and opened the bedroom door. "Beetle, chill!" he ordered, but the terrier took off down the hall with Harry in close pursuit. "No, Beetle!" he shouted, hoping to slow the dog down.

It didn't work.

Flipping on the hall light, Harry jumped with fright. A face peering into the side panel of glass stared back at him.

What the hell? he thought, partially opening the door. "What are *you* doing here?" His tone was sharp.

Lil smiled apologetically. "I thought you might like some company," she said, eyebrows arched. "It *is* Christmas Eve."

"Not tonight, Lil," Harry answered, speaking through a two-inch crack in the door, not wanting to hurt her feelings and yet annoyed that she'd shown up without calling. "You know I sometimes work at night," he lied. "Haven't we agreed you need to call first before showing up?"

"Oh, Harry Aldon," she said, pushing the door open and stepping inside. "Like I've never seen you before in your underwear. When did you get so shy?" She knelt down and rubbed Beetle's head. "You're really too much. Such a stick-in-the-mud. Hey, Beetle, baby. How are you?" she intoned, practically singing. "I brought you something wonderful." Beetle eagerly sniffed the package in her hand.

"Lil, this isn't a good time," Harry repeated, feeling foolish standing in the hallway in only his briefs as he lectured Lil. "I'm going to have to ask you to leave."

"Why?" Lil asked, looking up at Harry. "What's the big deal?" She eyed him. "I've seen you in less."

Harry felt a blush rising on his cheeks. "Lil, please," he practically begged.

"Okay, okay, I can take a hint," she said, assuming her full height of five-foot-three. "But let me just put this in the kitchen for Beetle." She walked on through to the kitchen with Harry and Beetle in close pursuit. "I met some friends tonight at Wally's on Camelback and 44th. Six very single ladies, all on their own. The most depressing thing you've ever seen. Eggnog and men. That's what we talked about. I had some prime rib left over. It's perfect for Beetle."

"Lil, that's kind of you, but this is not a good time for a visit."

Together they stood in front of the open refrigerator.

"Really, Harry, you should go shopping every now and then," she scolded as she placed the container on the top shelf. "There's nothing here to eat."

"I'm doing just fine," Harry answered, stepping back from the cold.

"Hello." Edward's voice rang out as he entered the kitchen. The white towel was still tightly wrapped about his waist.

"Oh, hello," Lil answered, eyeing the stranger suspiciously. "Harry, why didn't you tell me you had company?" She pushed past Harry. "And you are …?" she asked, extending a hand.

"Edward. I'm Harry's editor."

"Oh!" Lil said. She looked from Harry to Edward and back again as if there was another explanation for why an attractive stranger, dressed in only a towel, was in the kitchen of the man she adored. "Did you fly in to work on Harry's new novel?"

Edward glanced over at Harry. "That was the reason," he said in a confident voice.

"And here I am interrupting," she continued. "I'm so sorry."

"We were just getting ready to go to bed," Harry said. "Edward flew in from New York and needed a shower."

"Oh. Yes." Lil eyed Edward once more. "I can see that. Well, I'd better be getting home," she said as she knelt down to rub Beetle's head. "And as for *you*," she said to Harry, up on her tiptoes to offer him a peck on the lips, "I'll see you tomorrow."

◆

"Really?" Edward asked.

Harry shoved his tongue into his cheek.

"Oh, this is rich." Edward laughed. "You're sleeping with her, aren't you?"

Harry didn't answer.

"And here I've been feeling so sorry for you. Poor Harry. Living alone. Only his dog to keep him company. And you're screwing the next-door neighbor."

"She isn't the next-door neighbor," Harry objected. "She lives down the street."

"Who cares?" Edward offered. "Next door, down the street. These are minor details."

Harry crossed his arms. "What can I tell you?"

"Nothing," Edward said, laughing. "It would be funny if it wasn't so sad. Does she know?"

"There's nothing to tell," Harry defended himself. "Nothing."

Edward placed his hands on his hips. "Not exactly true," he said. "There's an awful lot to tell."

Harry headed back to the bedroom. "I really don't want to talk about this."

"Oh Harry, don't shut me down now," Edward called after him. "I may want to use this in my debut novel."

"You're not writing a novel," Harry said, certain that, if Edward had been, he himself would have known about it.

"Not now," Edward admitted. "But the future looms brightly," he said, close on Harry's heels. "And with this kind of material, hell, I think I might have a best-seller."

Harry leaned against the wall in the hall. "She overwhelmed me," he admitted.

Edward nodded. "I can see that. She *is* about five-foot-three," he said. "A big guy like you had no chance against her mighty ways."

"She doesn't take no for an answer," Harry burst out. "And she pushes and pushes until there's no getting away from her."

"Ah." Edward bowed his head. "Now it's getting clearer. She forced you into bed and against your wishes you had an orgasm. Oh, Harry, how do you manage?"

"I know it sounds ridiculous. I know," he admitted.

"So, you're bisexual?" Edward waited for an answer as Harry ran a hand through his hair.

"I don't know what I am."

"Well, you have to be something," Edward insisted.

"Do I?" Harry asked. "Can't I just be a human being?"

◆

Rikki awoke early on Christmas Day. She slipped into a pair of blue sweatpants and her favorite red cashmere sweater, and wandered into the kitchen. Evelyn was dressed in a pink bathrobe, her brown hair pulled away from her face, and was placing dough from an opened Pillsbury pop-and-bake container onto a greased pan.

"Oh, my God," Evelyn cried, a hand to her chest as she spotted Rikki. "You just took two years off my life. I hadn't expected you to be up so early."

"I had trouble sleeping," Rikki admitted, as she took a seat at the kitchen table. "Merry Christmas," she said, as she rubbed her face with both hands. "I didn't mean to scare you."

"Oh honey, I'm just so used to living alone. Well, never mind. It's wonderful to have you here. You've made my Christmas so special.

And I thought, since we're together, I'd make my famous homemade cinnamon rolls." Evelyn lifted the empty tube. "I sold the recipe to Pillsbury, you know."

Rikki smiled.

"There's nothing like hot cinnamon rolls in the morning. Unless you're diabetic." Evelyn arched a brow. "Thank goodness that doesn't run in my family," she said in a sing-song voice. "How about some orange juice?"

Rikki shook her head. "I don't think so. I'm trying to watch my weight."

"Oh honey, not on Christmas day. You can't. It's practically un-American," Evelyn said as she passed Rikki a cold glass of orange juice. "Do you think Barney might enjoy a big breakfast?"

Rikki ran her fingers though her long wavy hair. "Oh, I'm sure he would. Barney likes to eat."

"Oh, good," Evelyn said rubbing her hands together. "It's been a while since I've cooked for a man. I think this morning, I'm going to pull out all the stops."

"Hey, good morning," Barney called out over the clatter as Evelyn sorted through the pots and pans. He wore jeans and a white T-shirt. A cowlick stood up from the back of his head. His feet were bare. "What did I miss?"

"Nothing yet," Evelyn assured him as she lifted a pan and placed it on the stove. "Aren't your feet cold?" she asked, pointing.

Rikki giggled as she spotted Barney's bare feet. To her, even Barney's feet were beautiful.

◆

At breakfast, Rikki watched as Barney wolfed down scrambled eggs and pancakes while she picked at a bowl of oatmeal. She couldn't muster an appetite.

"Are you okay?" Evelyn asked as she slid into the chair next to Rikki's, a mug of coffee in her hand.

"'Okay?'" Rikki said dramatically. "I thought I'd discovered a relative, only to learn that my mother's brother died before I was born."

"Oh, honey." Evelyn offered a sympathetic look.

But Rikki was not comforted. "My whole family is dead. I'm an orphan on the end of a dead limb of a tree. I'm it. The last stop. Finito."

Barney stopped eating. "I know how you feel." He placed his fork down on the plate. Two half-eaten pancakes drenched in syrup awaited. "But the good news is, you still have your grandmother," he said, his mouth stuffed with scrambled eggs.

Grossed out, Rikki passed Barney a napkin. He wiped his mouth.

Evelyn offered a sympathetic nod. "I know it's not easy. But you're young. One day, you'll have a family of your own. Then, you'll feel different."

"I don't want to be like Rita," Rikki said, tears running down her face. "She's just awful. Sometimes I don't think she even likes me." Rikki covered her eyes with her hands.

"Sure she does," Evelyn said, passing Rikki a clean napkin. "Of course. She's your grandmother. She loves you."

"Then, why is it every time I talk about my mother, she shuts me down? And why is it I've never heard about Richard?"

Evelyn looked at Barney as if searching for help in answering the questions. "All I know is," she began, "when some people are hurt in life, they react strangely. They get angry, and instead of holding on dearly to those they love, they push them away. They make it impossible for anyone to get close and hurt them again."

Rikki stopped crying.

"Your grandmother," Evelyn continued, "is a difficult personality. Your mother had issues with her. But then who *doesn't* have problems with their parents? I had problems with *my* mother."

"Sure," Barney agreed as he stuck a fork into the pancakes. "Still, no one has the right to hurt a young girl who has lost her mother."

Evelyn's eyes scolded Barney as she worked to change the subject. "So, what are you going to do now? Do you want to stay with me until it's time to go back to Rita? We'd have the entire week. We'll be spending Christmas Day together. Or Hanukah," Evelyn laughingly corrected herself. "Whichever one makes you happy."

"No," Rikki said emphatically. "I want to go find my Uncle Richard's friends. You said there was a writer who lived in Phoenix. I want to find out what happened in the family."

Barney smiled. "Good for you."

"Brave girl," Evelyn said, twisting her napkin into a knot.

◆

"You're such a little thing," Bill Allington remarked as he appraised Elle's new outfit.

Seated at his mahogany desk, he looked positively regal.

"Now turn," he ordered, an index finger spinning. "Knockoff Dior," he said with derision.

Elle could hear the *tsk, tsk, tsk* in his voice.

"I thought after we promoted you, you'd be able to afford something a bit more becoming," he said emphatically.

Elle was aghast. How could he be so rude?

"And those shoes." Bill rubbed his chin and nodded. "Well, there is nothing designer about those shoes. Are you trying to put Jimmy Choo in an early grave?"

Elle had no idea who Jimmy Choo was or why he might be dying.

"Where are you shopping?" Bill demanded to know.

Elle gathered her wits. "Loehmann's."

"Well," Bill said in an exasperated tone. "That explains it. You can't be wearing discount clothes here. You need to be shopping at Saks or Neiman Marcus. Our clients expect the best."

Elle's heart sank. Did her clothes really matter? Didn't the work stand for itself?

"Now, you turn around this very moment and head over to Saks," he insisted. "Give them my name. I have an account. Shop and buy what you need."

"I can't go now," Elle explained. "I have a meeting with the client in three hours and I wanted to go over the plans with you one more time."

Bill clicked his tongue. "There's nothing more to discuss. Those plans are wonderful. Why do you think we offered you the job? Talent is what we're all about at H&L." He swiveled about in his chair and then stood up. "And you're exquisitely talented." He bowed his head.

Elle blushed. "But I still need your initials." She pulled out the design boards tucked under her arm.

"Of course." Bill laughed, stepping slightly back and eyeing her. "My God, those boards actually improve the look of that dreadful suit."

"Bill!" Elle said, exasperated. "You're really hurting my feelings. How can you expect me to work here when you belittle my taste in clothes?"

"It's not your *taste*," Bill said as he leaned over the boards on his desk and scribbled his initials. "It's your price point."

◆

"Maybe you should first ask your grandmother about your Uncle Richard," Evelyn advised. There was a gentle quiver in her voice.

"Do you think your grandmother will tell you anything?" Barney asked, perking up at the challenge before Rikki.

Rikki shook her head. "There's no way," she said with certainty. "Whatever happened, Rita would never tell me."

"But now that you know," Barney added, "surely she'd have to. What's the point in keeping a secret that you've already figured out?"

"But I haven't," Rikki answered. "I still know essentially nothing," she said as she looked over at Evelyn.

Evelyn raised two fingers in the air. "Girl Scout's honor. I've told you everything I know."

"But there's got to be more information," Barney insisted. "It's a big country. You just can't search for someone without knowing anything about them."

Two faces turned to Evelyn.

"Honestly, I don't know anything else," she said. "But maybe," and it seemed as if a thought was percolating, "maybe someone *else* would."

Rikki leapt at the chance. "Who? Who else is there?"

"The people at H&L," Evelyn offered. "Elle made some very close friends there. If anyone would know—they might."

Rikki was heartsick. "But that's all the way back in New York City. I don't want to go back to New York," she blurted out, to Evelyn's astonishment.

"Oh, honey, you're going to have to go back. Your grandmother has legal custody."

Rikki quickly corrected herself. "I'm not looking to run away. I just don't want to go back *now*."

Evelyn nodded as if she understood.

"Evelyn?" Barney asked, "May I use your computer?"

◆

Minutes later, Barney returned from the den. He directed the question to Evelyn. "What does H&L stand for?"

"I'm terrible," Evelyn admitted. "I really don't remember. It was always H&L. That's all Elle ever said. But it was a high-end interior design firm."

"Haney & Lewis?" Barney asked.

"Why, yes," Evelyn said with astonishment. "That's it."

"I've got their phone number, right here," he said, showing a piece of paper to Rikki. "We can call them. Ask to speak to the president of the company."

"Yes," Evelyn agreed. "But not until Tuesday. So today, we have Christmas together, and tomorrow, Monday, everyone is off. So, you're going to have to wait until Tuesday morning. We can do it Tuesday morning."

◆

Edward sat at the kitchen counter, paging through the special holiday edition of the *Arizona Republic*. "Wow. Look at all these amazing places for Christmas dinner. My God. Who knew Phoenix was such a gastronomic hub? I should have booked a later flight and stayed for dinner."

"Typical New Yorker," Harry said as he poured himself another cup of coffee.

"New York by way of Missouri."

Harry laughed. "So now you're a Midwesterner."

Edward smiled. "It's Christmas. Excuse me for being sentimental."

"Oh, no," Harry offered. "You should embrace it. We're all products of our upbringing. The good and bad. You'd never be the person you are today without it."

"I suppose," Edward agreed, looking up from the paper. "But the Midwest is not a place for gay people."

"There are plenty of gay people there. Living ordinary lives. Mixing in with the community. Going to church. Indistinguishable from anyone else."

"How the hell would *you* know, Harry? Living your quiet life locked up in this house? Phoenix is not exactly a slice of Americana."

"I disagree," Harry said, holding up his coffee cup. "Phoenicians come from all over. Many from Illinois, Michigan, Indiana, and Iowa. Some of the nicest people you'll ever meet."

"Oh," Edward said as he turned to the Op Ed section of the paper. "And a very opinionated bunch, I see."

"Hey, that paper is often accused of being too liberal."

"This is still a red state. That governor of yours—and the *sheriff*. And why does anyone have a sheriff in 2005? Where are we? The wild, wild West?"

Harry stretched his neck. "I know," he agreed. "It seems odd. But trust me. Phoenix is an amazing place."

Edward didn't miss a beat. "So, where are your gay friends? I'd like to meet them."

Harry sipped his coffee before answering. "You know me. I've never been great at making friends."

"But you *do* have friends," Edward pressed.

"A few, yes, but not anyone special."

"Oh. So you've talked about Richard to these friends."

Harry bit his lip. "What do you mean?"

"I think that was pretty clear, Harry."

"Well, there's no need to bring that up."

"The man you loved isn't worth mentioning? You've never told anyone that your first partner died of AIDS?"

Harry shook his head. "It was so long ago."

"What does *that* mean?" Edward asked, a tone of outrage in his voice. "Harry, you don't get to conceal the facts of your life because they're inconvenient. You should honor that relationship. You took care of him. You loved him. He's still a part of you. You can try to bury all of that deep inside, but he's still there."

Harry put his cup down on the counter. "How about if we change the subject."

"Would you rather talk about what's going on with Lil? What the hell is *that* all about?"

Harry pointed an index finger. "I don't need to explain anything to you."

"Oh, Harry," Edward said in a disheartened tone as he rose to his feet. "Okay. I'll let it go. But it's too sad for words."

Harry reacted without thinking. "I thought you were here to work on the manuscript, not critique my life."

Edward nodded. "Right," he said, as the sparkle in his eyes transformed to a dull stare. "Last night, after you drifted off, I reread the last chapters of that novel of yours. You still have work to do, Harry. A lot of work. The story is still not flowing properly. I left my notes on your desk. I'd suggest you read through it. Now, I'd better shower and get dressed if I expect to catch that noon flight."

Harry dropped his head to his chest. "I'm sorry, Edward. I didn't mean what I said. At least have something to eat. Let me fix you some breakfast."

Edward frowned. "Oh, yes, you did. You meant every word of it. Harry needs to be alone. Harry is a victim, unable to make decisions, unless, of course, you're a character in one of his novels. Then Harry can write it anyway he sees it."

Harry felt awful. "Edward, really..."

Edward crossed the kitchen. "You know, Harry, being lost and confused in your twenties and thirties is understandable. But a man of your age should have a better sense of himself. It's a damn shame," he said, before disappearing down the hall.

◆

"Are you ready?" Harry called out. "You'd better get a move on or you'll miss the flight."

Beetle scampered about, excited by Harry's voice. Harry side-stepped the terrier, almost tripping over him. Edward emerged from the guest room, pants on, shirt noticeably missing. "Can't wait to get rid of me, can you?"

"You know how I am," Harry apologized. "I hate being late. Besides, you need to eat before you go."

"You mean you hate my being late and possibly missing the flight. Well, don't worry. When you make me sleep in the guestroom...hey, I know it's time to go," Edward said disappearing back through the doorway.

"I can't help it," Harry called out. "I can't sleep with anyone in my bed."

"You mean you won't," Edward shot back.

Harry decided to let the matter rest. He was tired of explaining his proclivities to Edward. All he ever did was explain himself, which was odd since Edward had read everything Harry had ever written. *If he doesn't know me by now, what's the point?* Harry thought. *It's hopeless.*

With breakfast on the table, Edward took a seat. "This must be a real day of celebration. Pancakes? You made these for me?"

"Well, it *is* Christmas day," Harry said as he sat down, coffee cup in hand. "I know you like pancakes."

"Is there any syrup?" Edward asked, looking about.

Harry slapped a palm to his forehead. "Syrup. Damn, I forgot all about it. I don't have any."

Edward sighed as he used his fork to cut his way through the stack. "Isn't it just like you? Halfway Harry. Give a little, hold back a little."

"Now," Harry objected, "that's not fair."

"Isn't it, though?" Edward said eyeing him. "Isn't it just a little true?"

Rikki was eager to get outside after being in the house all of Christmas Day. With Christmas falling on a Sunday, Monday was the observed business holiday, and so many of the stores remained closed. "We can go to a movie," Evelyn suggested as the three sat at the breakfast table deciding on the day's activities. "Or, we can always take a drive."

"I wouldn't mind seeing some of the city while we're here," Barney said, his mouth full of toast.

Evelyn obliged, suggesting a tour of the Detroit suburbs. Loaded into Evelyn's Honda Accord, Rikki in the backseat, Barney upfront with Evelyn, the three traveled south along Woodward Avenue, turning east onto Eleven Mile Road as they made their way into the suburb of Royal Oak.

Rikki stared out the window. Everything seemed oddly familiar, as if she'd seen it all before but through the lens of a camera. Distant and yet very real.

"Oh my," Rikki said as Evelyn headed south on Washington Avenue, passing a number of the small shops, the windows covered in tinsel and glitter. "I remember that store."

"No wonder," Evelyn laughed. "That's Gayle's Chocolates. Your mother loved that place. Chocolate-covered Oreos and graham crackers were her favorite."

"Evelyn, can we come back when the store is open?"

"Well, honey," Evelyn said, "they'll be open tomorrow. Tuesday is a working day. We'll come back then."

"Okay," Rikki said, now leaning forward, a hand on Barney's

headrest as she scooched further up. "But tomorrow, we have to call H&L and find out about Phoenix."

Evelyn hit the brakes, sending Barney's head jerking forward. "Hey," he called out, seemingly alarmed by the hard stop.

With the car in the middle of the street, Evelyn turned to face Rikki. "You're not going to leave . . . are you?"

Rikki blinked. "Evelyn, that depends on what we learn. I'm going to try to find my uncle's friends. And we only have a few days left to find them."

"But that only gives us today," Evelyn complained as she looked from Rikki to Barney.

Barney chimed in. "We're here to learn about Rikki's family. She wants to know what happened to her uncle. I think we owe it to her to help."

Evelyn sighed. "But they might live anywhere. Even in New York City. You're not going to hurry back to New York?"

Rikki thought about it for a moment. "No, I guess not. If they're in New York, it can wait till we get home."

◆

Rikki struggled to sleep Monday night. All she could think about was that slip of paper with the H&L phone number. Eventually, she drifted off, only to awake at ten o'clock, later than she had planned. She jumped out of bed and rushed into the kitchen where Barney and Evelyn were already up and talking. "I overslept," Rikki cried as she searched for the slip of paper with the H&L phone number. "I thought we left it by the phone," she moaned as she eyed the perfectly clean counter.

"I slipped it into the top drawer," Evelyn said.

Rikki rummaged through the drawer until Evelyn came over and finally found the slip of paper. "Here," she said, handing it to Rikki. "Calm down, young lady."

Rikki held her breath at the sound of the first ring. Would anyone be able to help her? Even remember her mother?

"Haney & Lewis," the voice rang out after the fifth ring. "How may I help you?"

Rikki searched for her voice. She wasn't quite sure what to say while Barney and Evelyn sat around the table, their eyes glued on her.

"Hello," the voice called out. "Is anyone there?"

Rikki held the phone away from her ear as she spoke into the mouthpiece. "Yes," Rikki gasped. "I'm right here."

"May I help you?"

"I'm looking for someone who might have known my mother," she said, certain that she sounded like a complete fool. "I mean … my mother used to work for your company. She's dead now," she muttered, shaken as the words left her mouth, as if a scar, poorly healed, had once again been ripped open.

There was silence on the other end of the line. And then a concerned voice said loudly. "I can direct you to Human Resources."

Rikki looked at Evelyn, who nodded her head in the affirmative.

"Yes, thank you," she said.

◆

The office of Hanley & Lewis was abuzz with activity when a secretary from Human Resources rushed through the showroom to knock on the closed door of the boardroom. "Mr. Allington," she said demurely, "there's an important call for you, sir."

Surrounded by his top three designers, the old gentleman showed his displeasure at being interrupted. "I can't be taking any calls now, Greta. Please take a message and I'll get back to them," he said, redirecting his attention to the boards spread before him. "Are you sure lime green is the color palate you want to use?" he asked one of the designers. "It just seems too bright."

"Mr. Allington," Greta intoned with importance. "The call is from Elle's daughter, Rikki."

Allington looked up, his expression full of surprise. "Well," he said, as Greta chased after him. "Can I take that call in my office?"

"Yes, sir," she affirmed. "She's waiting on hold."

◆

Rikki was startled by the boom of the voice on the other end. "Rikki? Can it be you? Rikki Richards?"

Rikki had no idea who she was talking to or why the man had changed her last name. "This is Rikki Goldenbaum," she answered, more amused than confused as she mugged to the two around the kitchen table.

"Ask who you're speaking with," Evelyn whispered.

"This is Bill Allington," the voice replied, without Rikki needing to say another word.

Evelyn gestured for Rikki to pass the phone, which she did.

"Hello, sir," she said, and introduced herself. "I'm a family friend of Elle's and her daughter, Rikki, and Rikki would like to learn more about her mother. She'd also like to find out about her mother's brother, where he lived, and maybe anyone who might have known anything about her uncle."

The voice steadied. "Well, then, she's come to the right place. I was her mother's mentor. I adored Elle. She was like a daughter to me," he said with genuine emotion. "I've tried to reach out and communicate with Rikki, but that horrible woman blocked my path at every turn. I finally gave up. But I'm so glad that Rikki's contacted me. That little girl is a beneficiary in my will."

Evelyn registered a surprised look.

"So, how is Rikki doing?" the voice asked.

"Oh, here, let me put her on and she can tell you herself." Evelyn passed the phone to Rikki.

"Hello," Rikki tentatively said.

"Rikki, is that you? Rikki, I'd love to see you. Are you in Manhattan?"

"No," Rikki answered. "I'm visiting with Evelyn in Michigan."

"Oh," the voice answered. "Well, you probably don't remember this, but I helped change your diapers."

◆

December 1981

Dear Richard,

I'm finally settling into my life. After a year, I'm beginning to believe that perhaps interior design is an acceptable way for an artist to earn a living. With the bonus I got from working on the Revlon offices, I've been able to find an apartment in Turtle Bay. So I'll be moving next month. The United Nations is just a few steps away. Imagine! Please say you'll come visit. I'm dying to show off my wardrobe. You won't recognize your big sister. And even though I'll miss the East Village, I won't miss the roaches. We just had the place fumigated again. The restaurant downstairs is a regular breeding ground. I pray the roaches don't get ahold of my uptown address.

How are your studies going? I bet you're acing all your classes without even breaking a sweat. Let me know.

I miss you, my darling brother. Don't be a stranger.

Write soon.

Love Elle

◆

"Evelyn, I don't know how to thank you," Rikki said as the Honda Accord made its way in the dark along Interstate 94 to the Detroit Metropolitan Airport that Wednesday morning after Christmas.

"I should have my head examined," Evelyn chided. "Putting two kids on a plane to Phoenix on a wild goose chase. And at such an early hour! Did I tell you that you're stopping in Chicago and changing planes?"

"Yes," Rikki answered, excited about the trip but feeling guilty about taking advantage of Evelyn's generosity. "I'm sorry," she blurted out. More of a statement of fact than a genuine sentiment.

"Well, here we are," Evelyn said as she took the exit to Merriman Road. The terminals slowly came into view. "With the time change, you should be in Phoenix by ten." Evelyn called to the back seat. "Barney, are you still alive?"

Rikki turned about to see Barney dozing. "He's fast asleep," she said.

"*Great,*" Evelyn blurted out as Rikki spotted the sign for Northwest Airlines.

"I'm going to drop you by the doors," Evelyn said as the car slowed. "Now, remember what I told you. If you need anything, ask the flight attendants. And when you get to Phoenix, call me." She turned to look at Barney, who was starting to rouse. "Promise me."

"Oh," was all Rikki could manage as her eyes grew moist.

"You better get a move on," Evelyn added as airport security approached the car. "They won't let us sit here too long."

Together, the three gathered on the curb as Barney retrieved the luggage from the trunk. Evelyn embraced Barney and then Rikki.

"Be sure to call me from Phoenix," Evelyn said, as she tucked a stray lock of Rikki's hair behind her ear. "I need to know that you're okay."

"I will," Rikki said. "And thank you so much for buying my airline ticket. I know it must have been a fortune."

Evelyn smiled. "There are those rare times in life that we get to do something special for someone we truly love. I'm glad I was able to do it for you."

"And thank you for *my* ticket, too," Barney added.

Evelyn smiled, pulling Barney into an embrace. "Now, make sure you take good care of our girl."

Barney nodded as the security guard approached. "You'll have to move that car."

Evelyn released Barney and offered Rikki a final kiss on the cheek.

As Rikki passed through the sliding glass doors, she glanced back as Evelyn pulled away from the curb. Her mother's voice echoed in her head. *Good people show up when you need them. Always try to be a good person.*

◆

Rikki waited in the passenger lounge for Barney to return from the restroom. The gate was packed with holiday travelers on their way home, some sporting red Santa hats, many with small children. A young woman with blonde hair, a toddler in tow, passed by. She had on a distinctive perfume. A scent that Rikki recognized as her memory triggered.

She closed her eyes as the present moment faded. She was a small child traveling from Michigan to New York to visit Rita. She and her mother made the trip twice a year, during the Christmas holiday season and in summer when school was out.

"Honey," she heard her mother call to her as they waited for their flight, "please come back over here and sit down."

"But Mommy, there's a puppy in that lady's travel bag. A white poodle."

"Yes," Elle said, all smiles as Rikki obeyed. "Very sweet, my darling. Maybe we can get a dog, too. Is that something you'd like?"

"I'd love it," Rikki gushed.

"Oh, I nearly forgot. Uncle Bill bought something for you," she muttered as she searched through her work bag, filled to the brim with papers.

Rikki giggled. Her mother never seemed able to find anything in the oversized black bag.

Elle looked up and laughed along with her daughter. "I'm impossible," she said. "I seem to lose everything in this darn bag." Her eyes shimmered.

Rikki leaned in for a hug. "It's okay, Mom."

Elle refused to give up. "I know it's here somewhere," she said as she returned her attention to the overstuffed bag. "Aha. Here it is." She pulled out a book titled A Case of Bad Stripes. "Hmm," she said, giving her daughter a conspiratorial look as she tugged on Rikki's chin. "Perhaps I should read this instead of reviewing the floor plans for Marsh and McClennan's redesign."

The memory flooded back with such clarity that Rikki was afraid to move. She closed her eyes and savored the moment. She could still smell Elle's perfume, feel her mother's touch upon her face. It was as if Elle were still alive. A moment of pure ecstasy.

And then Rikki opened her eyes. A West Highland terrier let out a yip as it scurried through the crowd. The spell was broken.

◆

Lil didn't think much about meeting Edward until that Wednesday morning yoga class. As the students entered their final pose, the image of the two men in different stages of undress flashed before her. Lights dimmed, participants on their backs, Lil ran through the scene from days before. The awkward look on Harry's face. The strange stare from Edward. She'd somehow interrupted. That was clear. But interrupted what?

If I waited for Harry to call, I'd wait forever, she thought as she calmly instructed the class. "Breathe in, breathe out. Feel the relaxation flowing through your very being. Release the tension you've been holding."

Sitting, with her legs crossed, she was unable to quiet her own mind.

Harry is such a beautiful man. And so attentive in bed. Almost gentle, she thought, remembering how he had held her after achieving orgasm. Most men she'd known would have rolled away, disengaging once their needs had been met. But not Harry. He'd been—and she took a deep breath as she searched for the exact word to describe him—*tender. Yes, that's it,* she thought as she once again addressed the class.

"And as I count to three, you'll come back to the present, refreshed and awake and ready to start the day."

Edward appeared, his sinewy musculature emblazoned in her mind.

"And open your eyes," she said, though her eyes remained closed, lingering on the memory of Edward's slender body.

"And sit up," she murmured in a low, almost indecipherable voice.

She took one final deep breath, opening her eyes and pressing the palms of her hands together as she gently leaned forward, imagining Edward and Harry kissing, before saying *"Namaste."*

◆

With little time to spare at O'Hare, Rikki and Barney rushed along to their connecting gate, arriving just as the flight to Phoenix was finishing the boarding process. "It's a good thing I picked up that cheese Danish at that Starbucks back in Detroit," Barney said as he stashed their carry-on luggage in the overhead compartment, before taking the aisle seat next to Rikki. "Are you okay?"

Rikki nodded. "Just a little out of breath."

"No wonder. Can you believe how far we had to go from gate F15 to G21? It sure doesn't sound that far."

Rikki agreed as she buckled her seatbelt. The woman in the window seat, reading a book, barely looked up as Rikki turned to offer a quiet "hello."

Barney rubbed his palms together. "Well, now we're on our way to Phoenix."

"I was just thinking of Evelyn. She's so alone."

Barney pulled out a packet of cinnamon Dentyne from his pocket. "Evelyn must have friends. She doesn't strike me as someone who'd be lonely."

"Yes," Rikki agreed. "But she *is* alone."

"Aren't we all?" Barney answered. "In one way or another?"

Rikki wondered if that was true. "I guess," Rikki agreed. "But it scares me," she said, slipping her hand into Barney's palm. "I hadn't realized that adults can be alone. I thought once your life was under way, there were always people around."

"Maybe some people just like to be alone," Barney countered. "I know some deserve to be alone."

"Not me," Rikki said with certainty. "I want a family. And one day, I'm going to have one. And I'm going to love them. I don't want to wind up like Rita. Bitter and angry."

"Then I wish that for you," Barney said with a wide grin. "But in the meantime, until that first baby arrives," he teased, "what are you hoping to find out in Phoenix?" Barney unwrapped a piece of gum and popped it into his mouth. He held out the pack to Rikki. "You want some?"

She took a piece of Dentyne, rolling it between her fingers. "I'm not sure," she started, uncertain how to explain. "I don't really know. But whatever I learn has to be better than knowing nothing. Why is everything such a damn mystery?"

Barney stretched his arms, reaching overhead and playing with the on/off switch for the reading light. "I guess that's how old people roll. Maybe they don't want to face their mistakes. They don't want you to know how they messed up. That allows them to be the victim or the hero of their own story."

Rikki wondered if he had a point. "Okay. But there *is* no victim or hero. I have no information at all. Remember Dreiser's *An American Tragedy*?"

Barney nodded.

"Clyde was ashamed of his parents. The poverty, lack of education … the religious fervor. Well, I don't know anything about my family. I don't remember my mother. I know nothing about her life. But I do remember Evelyn crying."

"That's new. When did you start remembering?"

"It's beginning to come back to me," she acknowledged. "Slowly."

"That's a good sign."

"But I never went to my mom's funeral," she stated clearly. "It's as if my mom never existed. She just suddenly disappeared. Now how can that be? How can she be there one day and gone the next?"

Barney rubbed his face. "How old were you when your mom died?"

"Eleven."

"And you don't remember anything?"

"I remember the pained look on Evelyn's face that morning," Rikki admitted. "I knew something terrible had happened. The rest of it all seems a blur."

Barney slipped an arm about her shoulder.

"I don't know," Rikki admitted, thinking about the trip ahead. "It's just a feeling. If I was named after my uncle, my mom must have had a close relationship with her brother."

Barney spit out the gum into a leftover wrapper. "Boy, that's intense," he said. "Practically burns your tongue. So who is this guy we're looking for?"

Rikki retrieved the slip of paper from her pocket on which she'd written the name given to her by Bill Allington of H&L.

"Harry Aldon. His name is Harry Aldon," Rikki said just as the pilot announced over the loudspeaker that they had completed the boarding process, requesting that the flight attendants prepare the cabin doors for departure.

◆

Elle bit her bottom lip. Before her was a cup of coffee and a slice of Entenmann's cheese Danish. Both untouched. "I'm sorry, Mother. I know this isn't what you expected."

"How *could* you?" Rita said, exasperated. "I never thought a daughter of mine would be having a baby out of wedlock."

Elle folded her hands. "Well, Mother, it really wasn't the plan, but it happened.'

"Things like this don't just happen," Rita said adamantly. "You're not a child."

Elle had no interest in the back and forth. "I'm not here to ask your permission," Elle clarified. "What's done is done."

"And what about the man who did this to you?" Rita asked. "Where's his responsibility in all this?"

Elle sighed. She had no intention of discussing the father with Rita any more than she did her sex life. *Why is it,* she'd thought, *when an unmarried woman becomes pregnant, it means she's promiscuous? But when she's married, it's a celebration of new life?* "He doesn't matter," she explained to her mother. "He's not interested."

Rita's voice registered revulsion. "Oh, Elle." She shook her head in dismay.

"No!" Elle shouted. "No more! I support myself, live on my own. It isn't what I planned, but I'm certainly not going to sit here and let you make me feel bad about it," she said, pointing an angry finger at her mother.

"But will they let you keep working?" Rita asked. "And how will you take care of the child once it comes?"

"Mom, I'm not going into all these details with you. Those are my issues to solve. Bill Allington has assured me that the firm will be there. He's been so good to me. Like a father."

Rita offered her daughter a jaundiced look. "Really?"

"Yes," Elle emphasized.

"Maybe *too* good," Rita said. "And maybe not good enough."

Elle shook her head. She was not going to engage in her mother's nonsense.

"What about an abortion?" Rita asked. "Will Mr. Allington allow that?"

Elle stood up. "Mother, this conversation is now over."

12

As the plane taxied to the Phoenix gate, Rikki ran a brush through her hair. It had been a long morning. After take-off from Chicago, Barney had slipped off to sleep, leaving Rikki to worry alone about Phoenix. She tried to distract herself with the Inflight magazine, but was too anxious to concentrate. Instead, she scribbled in her diary—filling the pages with questions. Questions about the future and how her life might turn out.

"You're nervous, aren't you?" Barney asked, after letting out a yawn.

"A little," Rikki admitted, though it was more than just that. It was as if she was standing on the precipice of a great discovery, one that Rita had worked hard to conceal. She hoped to soon learn all the secrets that Rita seemed intent on hiding. But what exactly *were* those secrets? Could they be so terrible that perhaps she was better off not knowing? And what if this Harry Aldon didn't want to even talk with her?

The pilot's voice came over the loudspeaker. "Ladies and gentleman, welcome to Phoenix, Arizona, where the sun always shines. We'd appreciate it if you'd pull down your window shades so that we might maintain the temperature on the plane while we're on the ground. Thank you."

Barney shifted about in his seat while Rikki remained lost in thought. Perhaps they should have stayed in Michigan until she'd been able to make phone contact. But time was running out on the Christmas holiday. It was already Wednesday and she'd have to be back in Queens soon. *He has to be here. Please, God. Let him be here. Don't let this trip be a wild goose chase.*

"Cheer up," Barney said as they shuffled off the plane in single file, Rikki ahead of him. "It'll be fine. Imagine. First Toledo, then Michigan, and now Arizona. I don't know about you," he said enthusiastically as she turned about to see his dimples flashing. "I'm having a great time. This has been a lot of fun."

Rikki wasn't so sure she agreed. Visiting Evelyn had been one thing. She'd been a next-door neighbor, someone who Rikki had actually known. But Harry Aldon was a complete stranger. She didn't even know what he looked like.

Her courage started to falter. "I don't know," she said, grabbing Barney's arm in the terminal, stopping amid a sea of people. "This just doesn't feel right."

"What are you talking about?" Barney said, arching a brow. "You're about to meet someone who knew your uncle. An uncle you've never met. Now, that is really cool."

"Yes," Rikki agreed, "but what if he doesn't want to talk with me. What if he hates my family? Hated my mother?"

"You mean hated your grandmother."

Rikki nodded.

"Well, you're not them," Barney said pulling her into an embrace.

"But why should he help me? I'm a total stranger."

Barney gently rocked her as she started to cry. A little boy dressed in an elf outfit passed by and slapped her leg. The boy's mother tugged on his arm and apologized as the little boy looked up at Barney and Rikki and let out a mischievous giggle. Both Barney and Rikki laughed at the little boy's impish joy at his misdeed.

"Feeling better?" Barney asked, running a thumb down her cheek. "I bet you needed that cry."

She wiped her eyes. "A little."

"Good. Now let's get out of here," he said.

Dutifully she followed Barney as he led her out through security, down the escalator and through the sliding glass doors, into the fresh air where a taxi waited.

◆

When the phone rang, Rita was making the bed. Trudging back and forth, she straightened the sheets and blanket. *Such foolishness,* she thought. *Every day I make this bed, only to mess it up again.* But she couldn't help herself. She liked the way the bedroom looked with the spread on. It was welcoming. Ready for company. Even though, with Rikki gone, no one beside Rita had set foot in the apartment. Still, it mattered. *I'm just a solitary soul,* she thought as she reached for the receiver, the blue satin spread still requiring a tuck about at the corners. *Who needs other people? They just wear you out.*

"Hello," she said, slightly out of breath and annoyed by the interruption.

"Hello," the female voice answered. "Is this Rita Goldenbaum?"

"I'm not interested in buying anything," she warned, ready to hang up.

"Rita, this is Evelyn. I'm not sure if you remember me. I was a friend of your daughter's."

Rita remembered. "Why are you calling me?" she asked, her tone snappish.

"I want to talk with you," Evelyn said.

"After all these years, there's nothing to say. Absolutely nothing."

The voice on the other end sighed. "I think there is, and I think what I have to say you'll want to hear."

Rita plunked herself down on the edge of the bed as she listened in disbelief to Evelyn's explanation of her granddaughter's journey to the Midwest. "I don't understand," she kept repeating, even as it was intensely clear exactly what had happened. "But I was certain Barbra's family was expecting her ..." She muttered on as if that had anything to do with the present circumstance.

"I should have called earlier," Evelyn said.

"Yes, you should have," Rita agreed. "Your behavior is simply irresponsible. I should call the police and have you arrested for child endangerment," she said, not quite certain if that even applied.

The phone went silent as Rita weighed her options. She had to know where Rikki was. There was no point in shutting down her only source of information. With her free hand, she clutched the front of her housecoat tightly into a fist and softened her tone. "Well, no harm has been done, and you've called me. I guess the only option is to go after her and bring her back."

"Yes," Evelyn agreed.

"And to do that, I will need to know exactly where she is."

Evelyn sighed. "That was the whole point of my calling."

◆

Harry sipped his coffee as he tried to refocus on his novel. Edward's visit had proven a distraction. With Edward's notes by his side, he was at loss on how to fix any of the issues. Harry struggled to concentrate. Monday and Tuesday had been a complete washout. With Edward gone, he'd been unable to write. Intention didn't translate to accomplishment. *If only…*

He leaned back in his swivel chair and stared out the window. A dull emptiness filled the space left by Edward. Increasingly frustrated by his inability to engage with his work, he slid down to the floor to stroke Beetle, resting his head against his dog's. The sleepy terrier looked up and offered a lick to Harry's nose before dropping back down into a tight curl. Harry continued to provide long, loving strokes, strokes that calmed him.

The phone rang but he didn't pick it up, preferring to screen the caller. It was Lil. Could she stop by?

Hell, no, he thought. *I'm writing.*

Another call. "I have to see you."

Harry clenched his teeth. He was in no mood for company. He had a lot to do and no intention of being upset by mindless interruptions.

Another message. "I'm on my way over."

◆

Rikki huddled up against Barney as the cab pulled away from the airport curb. "It's pretty here," she said as she spotted the mountain peaks surrounding the Valley of the Sun.

"Still nervous?" Barney asked as the meter clicked away.

"Not so much," Rikki admitted, comforted by his attentive presence.

Barney looked at her and smiled. "I'm glad. Really. What's the worst thing that could happen?"

Rikki tilted her head and gave it a moment's thought. "He doesn't open the door."

Barney grinned. "Yup. That would be bad."

Rikki shifted, sitting perfectly straight. "He tells us to leave."

"If he's home," Barney pointed out.

She ran her fingers through her dark mane, pulling it tightly behind her head into a knot. Her lip curled up into a shy, awkward smile. "He calls the police."

"Well, that would be pretty bad," Barney agreed. "I think that's the worst thing that could happen."

"Or," and Rikki paused before she spoke, "he hugs me and says he's heard all about me and is so grateful I came to visit."

Barney coughed. "Very unlikely."

"Perhaps," Rikki said, reconsidering. "But really, anything is possible. Anything. It's like an adventure. You never know what someone's going to say or do."

"Sounds more like a nightmare to me."

"That's because you don't have faith in people."

Barney conceded. "I don't. After the experience with my parents and two foster families, I'd say faith is something I'm sorely lacking."

"Well, don't you worry," she said as the cab hit a bump, sending her practically bouncing off the seat. "I have enough faith for both of us."

◆

When the bell rang, Harry was all set. Beetle was firmly in his arms so that the terrier, torn ACL and all, wouldn't make a mad dash for the front door. As Beetle squirmed, Harry held on tight. "Now, take it easy," he told Beetle as he got to the door. "No getting yourself excited." And though he tried to get Beetle to remain calm, the second time the bell sounded, Beetle nearly leapt out of Harry's arms, requiring Harry to put the dog down as he opened the door.

Beetle held his rear left leg high as he barked fiercely.

Lil stood in the open doorway. "Oh, Beetle, look at you," she called out in such a high-pitched voice that Beetle attempted to jump up but failed.

"Please," was all Harry could muster at the sight of the blonde. "Keep your voice calm. We're trying to keep Beetle quiet."

Lil stepped inside and immediately knelt to the floor. "Oh, Beetle," she cried out. "Are you still not feeling well?"

"Lil, it's an ACL tear," Harry reminded her, completely irritated.

Beetle again attempted to leap at Lil.

"Poor darling," Lil cooed as Harry reached down and lifted Beetle off the ground.

"Christ, Lil, don't you ever listen?"

Lil blinked hard. "What do you mean?"

"Here I am trying to tell you to quiet down, and all you can do is keep revving Beetle up. You know it's not good for the leg."

Lil crossed her arms and locked eyes with him. "Harry Aldon, you're a bully. I mean it. A real bully. I wasn't trying to get Beetle all excited. It's just my way. I have that effect on animals, and even on some men I've known."

"Undoubtedly," Harry answered, wishing she'd make herself scarce. "Well, I've got to get back to work," he said dismissively.

Lil uncrossed her arms. "But Harry, I just got here and there's something I want to discuss."

"Not this morning, Lil. You can come over and ring the bell—but that doesn't mean you're coming in. I have things to do and I have to get back to them. You *know* I work in the morning."

"But Harry," Lil called out as Harry backed her up in the doorway and started to push the door closed.

"Sorry," replied Harry, though there was no note in his voice of genuine regret.

"Oh, Harry," Lil blurted out as she turned to go. "Did anyone ever tell you that you're a real asshole?"

"Sounds familiar," Harry said as he slammed the door and locked it.

◆

When Harry Aldon's bell rang less than ten minutes later, he went off like a firecracker.

"Goddamn that woman," he bristled as Beetle escaped his grasp and rushed down the hallway, left paw held high as he hopped along, yapping wildly. It was all too much for Harry as he turned the corner and reached the front door. *Two interruptions in one morning. Lil, I swear. I'm going to kill you!*

Reaching down, he lifted Beetle up with the sweep of an arm before pulling the door open and locking eyes with two strangers. "Yes?" he said, brows arched, certain they were at the wrong door. "Can I help you?"

The young girl wore a blue Old Navy sweatshirt. Her thick brown hair was pulled back into a ponytail. She had an oval face with a good, strong nose. Instead of being just pretty, she looked intelligent with a sharp gleam in her eyes. She gave Harry the once-over. Perhaps she expected to see someone else? The young man next to her looked just as smart. Taller than the girl, he practically stood at the same height as Harry. His hair, parted in the middle, fell carelessly over one eye, almost hiding a remarkable shade of blue.

"Wrong address?" Harry asked as Beetle calmed down. He placed the dog on the ground.

"I don't think so," the young girl said holding up a piece of paper. "You are Harry Aldon?"

Harry sighed. *What could this be? Was his name on a fundraising list? Were these two kids from the Mormon Church? Did they even let boys and girls do mission together?* He took a breath. *Patience,* he thought.

"What can I do for you? If this is a political thing, I'm not interested. I hate the GOP as much as the Democrats. And I'm not buying raffle tickets to help you with a school project. And I don't eat Girl Scout cookies. Too many calories."

"Oh," the girl said, seemingly surprised by his answer.

"So, I'm not interested in anything you're selling." And just as he was about to shut the door, Beetle charged past him and rushed up to the girl, who knelt down to pet him.

Harry rolled his eyes. Leave it to Beetle to check out the ladies.

"We're not selling anything," the young man said. "We're here to meet Harry Aldon."

Oh, shit, Harry thought as he checked out their serious expressions. *Fans. Coming to my front door. Geez. How do I get out of this?* "Are you sure you want Harry Aldon?" His voice signaled that he was somewhat resigned to the interruption.

"Most definitely," the young man answered. His presence seemed to grow stronger by the minute.

And then a thought popped into Harry's head. *Is this one of those "You're my Dad!" interventions?* His mind raced. He'd had unprotected sex in his youth. Even an affair or two with women that had lasted two or three months. Could one of these two kids be the result? It could be possible. Could he be someone's dad?

"I'm sorry," Harry tried to beg off. "But I don't have time for visitors. Not today," he said as he began to close the door.

"But you have to see us." The boy pushed back on the door as it was closing. "We came all the way from Michigan to see you."

Harry pulled the door open again. "Michigan?"

"And we have no place to stay," the girl added.

I don't have time for this, Harry thought as he reluctantly welcomed the two into his home. *We'll just make it quick.*

◆

"Okay, for starters, how old are you?" Harry asked, looking at the boy and then the girl as the two youngsters sank down in one of the overstuffed sofas in Harry's family room. Beetle rested calmly between their feet. Harry took a seat across from them on the matching sofa.

"Fifteen," the girl answered, one hand reaching down to stroke the top of Beetle's head. "I'm Rikki," she said introducing herself, "and this is Barney."

"Sixteen next month," Barney replied.

So young, Harry thought as he eyed the two fresh faces. "How did you get here?"

Rikki was the first to respond. "Evelyn. She bought us two plane tickets."

Harry searched his memory. "Evelyn? I don't remember an Evelyn."

Rikki giggled. "Why *would* you?"

Harry jerked his head sharply to the left. "Wait a minute. How did you get my name?"

"Uncle Bill," Rikki naively stated. "He remembered that you were a writer. We Googled you."

Harry nodded with some pride. He, too, had Googled his own name from time to time and was reassured to see a list of his novels.

"But I don't know a Bill in Michigan. And how did you get my address?"

"No," Rikki corrected him. "He's from New York City. My mom used to work with him. He found an address in an old file—and guessed it might be yours—but we couldn't get your phone number."

"That's because I'm not listed," Harry quickly answered. "'Mom'? Who is your mom?"

This time Barney answered. "Elle Goldenbaum."

Harry's heart practically stopped. "Richard," he said, suddenly aware of the connection. "You're Richard's niece?"

"Why, yes," Rikki repeated. "My name is Rikki Goldenbaum and this is my friend Barney. That's what we've been *trying to tell you.*"

"Oh, my God," Harry said, a hand covering his mouth.

Beetle sat up and looked about.

"This is unbelievable. How did you get here?" Harry asked again, more a comment than an actual question.

"He's doesn't listen very well," Barney said to Rikki. "Didn't you just tell him?"

◆

As Rikki and Barney filled Harry in on their journey, Harry's mind drifted back to the day he'd met Richard. He remembered arriving at a cocktail party alone. It was a fundraiser held in a private home where he found himself immersed in a roomful of strangers, wine glass in hand. Amid a general murmur of background chatter, he had skated past the crowd in a desperate attempt to find a safe corner, to gain his bearings.

What was the charity? He struggled to remember. *How did I know about the event?* It was his first time in a room of self-identified gay men. *Someone must have told me about it. Or did I read about it?*

It was an odd time in his life. After being with women, he'd decided to explore the other side of his sexuality. The side he'd kept clandestine. And this, because his relationships with women had not worked out. The sexual attraction seemed transitory. The emotional connection, uncomfortable. He'd repressed his attraction to other men for years, acting out in those dark, hidden places where gay men of a certain generation congregated. He'd heard the term *latent homosexual* and wondered if that applied to him. It seemed a derisive term. An unpleasant label. Something he was unwilling to embrace.

Barney's voice jolted him back to the present. "And then, this guy Sammy drove us all the way to Birmingham, Michigan."

"He emigrated from Bangladesh," Rikki explained. "He's only in his twenties and he owns a taxi cab and a restaurant."

Harry was impressed. "Wow."

"And he's kind," Rikki added, looking over at Barney. "He really looked out for us."

"Sounds like you were lucky to meet him."

Both teenagers nodded as Harry realized the two might be hungry. "Have you had anything to eat?"

Beetle squirmed with excitement and whimpered. Harry laughed. "Chill out," he said, trying to soothe the dog. "*Eat* is his favorite word."

"He's adorable," Rikki offered.

Harry reached between them and lifted Beetle off the ground. "I'm afraid he's an old boy," and with that, Beetle let out a long deep cough as Harry gently lowered him back down to the floor. "Congestive heart disease," Harry explained as Beetle continued to cough. "It's nothing to worry about," Harry assured them. "He'll be fine in another moment." And sure enough, Beetle eventually looked up, the hacking stopped, and his tail wagged at the three concerned faces.

Harry lifted Beetle again in his arms and sat back down, cradling the animal. "There you go," he said as he stroked the terrier's face, starting from the brow and running his palm over Beetle's head and down the length of his body. "You're okay."

Rikki came about the coffee table and sat next to Harry, intently watching Beetle. Harry spotted a familiar expression. A certain curl in her lips, a gentle rise in her cheek. It was one of Richard's expressions, unnerving as it was instantly recognizable. Harry studied her face. She looked up, offering a sweetly disarming glance; the sparkle in her brown eyes hinted at an inner vitality touched by kindness, a warmth that eradicated any resistance he might have normally felt to strangers. It was a moment that seemed familiar. As if it was part of his destiny to have met her, though for what purpose he didn't yet quite understand.

"Food," Harry said, remembering his offer. "And I guess you two need a place to stay. Am I right?"

They both nodded.

"Okay. Well, you're staying with me. But," Harry said with his firm adult voice, "separate rooms."

Rikki blushed deep red. "Of course," she answered, not looking at Barney.

Barney smiled. "Absolutely," he confirmed, as Harry stood, content to leave Beetle in Rikki's care as he headed off to the kitchen.

◆

Evelyn grabbed the phone on the second ring.

"He's so nice," Rikki gushed. "Thank you so much for doing this."

Evelyn exhaled a sigh of relief. "Oh, thank God." Rikki's words were music to her ears. "Well, it's Bill you should be thanking. He's the one who made the connection."

"But I would have never found Bill without you."

Evelyn knew it was true, and still, she felt no pride in having helped Rikki. She'd worried terribly about the wisdom of two teenagers traveling across the country and showing up at a stranger's door. As soon as she had pulled away from the curb at the airport, she'd instantly regretted the decision. *I wish I knew what that man is going to tell her*, Evelyn thought. *What if he tells her something hurtful? Something about her mother?*

Rikki's voice interrupted. "Evelyn, are you still there?"

"Yes, I'm right here," she reassured Rikki. Hearing the excitement in Rikki's voice, she now regretted the call to Rita. She'd helped Rikki and Barney get to Phoenix, but she hadn't trusted her heart. She'd been afraid for them. "Has he told you anything about your mother or Richard?"

"We haven't talked about all that yet. We really just got here."

"Oh," Evelyn answered, surprisingly relieved.

"He ordered lunch. Pizza. He doesn't cook."

"Oh, my," Evelyn said. "I hope he knows he has two hungry teenagers under his roof."

Rikki chuckled. "We're going to the supermarket this afternoon. I can make dinner," she boldly added.

Evelyn had not seen any sign of that skill. "He must have been surprised that you were able to find him."

"He seemed more surprised when I mentioned Uncle Richard's name."

"I bet," Evelyn answered, suddenly nervous about what Rikki might discover. "Have you told him why you wanted to meet him?" Even as she asked the question, she realized it was all too complicated.

"Not really," Rikki answered.

"Well, I hope he gives you the answers you're looking for," she said, concerned by what Rikki was bound to discover.

"He will. I'm certain," Rikki said. "I bet you'd really like him too."

Evelyn had no doubt.

◆

Gathered about an open box of Domino's Pizza at the kitchen table, half the pie gone, Rikki wondered how to begin the conversation and whether Harry would be forthcoming. Beetle, curled into a crescent on a nearby dog bed, gently snored as Harry offered each teen a refill on their colas. Barney wiped his mouth with a napkin and Rikki picked at the cheese on what remained of her second slice as she thought about what to say. When she looked at Harry, he seemed to intuitively understand.

"So, you want to know all about your uncle. Is that it?" Harry asked, clearing his throat as if he were preparing to go into a long speech.

Rikki hesitated answering, hoping to clarify. "Not just about Uncle Richard, but about my family. My mother, Rita ... anything that might help me understand what happened."

"'Happened?'" Harry asked, a surprised look on his face. "Didn't your mother tell you?"

"I'm having trouble remembering my mother," Rikki admitted. "You see, she died a few years ago." Rikki folded her hands in front of her, uncertain how to explain. "I was hospitalized. I don't know all the details," she admitted. "Rita won't tell me anything about what happened." Tears escaped her eyes as she brushed them away with the back of her hand. "And so, I'm not sure what actually happened. And then I discovered that I once had an uncle, too."

Harry offered Rikki a napkin. "You mean to tell me Rita never talked about Richard?"

Barney took another slice of pizza, taking a bite as Harry continued to speak.

"... and your grandmother ..." Harry exhaled, not finishing the sentence. "Well, I don't know what to say about her."

"She's tough," Rikki offered, thinking that was what Harry was referring to.

"You mean difficult?" Harry answered, his tone revealing that there was more to his feelings.

Rikki sipped her cola as Harry seemed to search for the right words.

"Look, kid, I don't want to say anything unkind about your grandmother. I don't know your relationship with her. And I have no interest in telling you things that might reflect badly on her."

Barney jumped in. "Oh, man, you have to."

Harry shifted his focus. "No ... I don't think so," he said rather emphatically.

"Oh, yes," Barney insisted, now referring to Rikki. "Her grandmother won't tell her anything. Nothing. Nada. Zippo. You've got to help her out."

Harry relaxed back into his chair. "I'm probably the wrong person to talk to."

"Why?" Rikki asked as she pressed her palms flat on the table and raised herself up, slipping one leg beneath her as she sat back down, looking taller, more mature, and capable of hearing anything Harry might offer.

"Well," Harry started, "to begin with ... your grandmother's a total bitch. There," he waved a hand in the air, "I said it. A real bitch. She made your uncle's life unbearable."

Rikki sat captivated. Barney continued eating.

"She forced him out of the family as soon as she learned he was gay."

"Gay?" It was the first time Rikki had heard her uncle was gay.

Barney jerked his head. "Her uncle was a homo?"

"Hey." Harry pointed a finger of warning at Barney.

Barney tilted his head in a gesture of apology. "Sorry."

"How could you not know he was gay?" Harry asked as he looked over at Rikki.

"Is that something that would make a mother disown her son?" Rikki asked, as she absorbed the news. "It doesn't seem like a big deal."

"Back in 1977 it was a very big deal," Harry assured her. "A big fucking deal."

◆

"Why did you have to tell her?" Elle asked her brother as they sat together at Serendipity in Manhattan, a specialty dessert restaurant, in front of two frozen hot chocolates. "Did she really need to know?" Elle plunged a straw into the center of the chocolaty frost.

Richard's voice was defensive. "Hey, it's who I am. I'm not lying. She'll just have to get over it."

Elle doubted Rita would ever get over it. It wasn't in her nature. Holding grudges, being angry—that was the mother Elle knew. "Don't you see that she's going to dig in her heels and make life impossible?"

"For whom?" Richard asked between sips of his drink.

"For you ... for me. For everyone," Elle answered.

Richard tilted his head as he examined his sister's expression of panic. "Really? That's what this is about? How she's going to be treating *you*?"

Elle lifted her chin in defiance. "We're a family. What happens to you, happens to me. Remember that."

Richard laughed. "Elle, we're both too old for these games," he said, using a long spoon to lift the whipped cream from the top of his drink. The spoon disappeared into his mouth as she waited for him. He licked his lips. "Let's face it. She never liked me. You were always her favorite. I was just an annoyance. It was bound to come to this."

Elle refused to accept his explanation. "There had to be another way."

Richard curled his lips and then his cheeks rose, creating a sardonic smile. It was Richard's signature expression. A signal that there was no point in arguing with him. "Did you ever notice that everything that happens in our family is *about her*? Your success...is her success. Your looks came from her. When I ask questions or require anything...I'm bothering her. It's really insane, Elle. She can drain the life right out of you."

Elle knew only too well. "So, how did you leave it with her?"

"The way we've always left everything. Badly."

"So what will you do now?"

"Nothing," Richard said, his eyes focused on Elle.

"Please, Richard. Promise me you'll call and tell her you were only joking. You're not gay. Tell her anything, but call."

Richard weighed her suggestion as two young girls, giggling, squeezed into the adjacent table, nearly knocking over the water glasses.

"I can't," he answered. "I can't, Elle. Not even for you."

◆

Rikki listened intently as Harry explained about his early life.

"It was so different back in the early 1970s," Harry began. "The American Psychiatric Association hadn't yet declassified homosexuality as a mental illness. That didn't happen until 1973. It was a terrible stigma. Making connections with other men was impossible unless you were willing to risk being caught in a very public place. Parks, back rooms, adult movie houses, baths. It was this parallel world created by need. And sometimes, very scary. You were a pariah."

Rikki couldn't quite imagine an alternative world where men

hid about the edges. But the way Harry spoke, lowering his voice in secrecy, she was intrigued. "It sounds so exciting," she said as she looked over at Barney, who was scratching Beetle under the chin.

Harry's voice quickly changed. "Exciting?"

"Yes, with all that sneaking around. And having to pretend to be someone else. I've always wanted to be someone else," she said.

"No," Harry waved his hands. "You don't understand. You couldn't be yourself. Those who could pass—passed. The rest... Well, there were few choices for them but to keep their heads down and say nothing."

Rikki leaned forward, ignoring his explanation. "So, he had never been with a woman?"

Harry raised an eyebrow.

Barney glanced over at Rikki, offering an expression that Rikki interrupted as meaning that she might have crossed a line.

Harry ran a hand through his curls. "That's a little personal."

Rikki didn't miss a beat. "But isn't that what you're saying?"

"Yes, I guess so," Harry muttered. "But he had a life."

"But aren't you trying to tell me that his life was ruined because he was gay? And that's why he lost touch with his family?"

"Well, not exactly," Harry sighed. "His life wasn't ruined. He had this inner strength. A real confidence. A genuine need to be himself. He didn't believe he'd done anything wrong. And then, later on ..."

"But my uncle *is dead*. He died before I was born. And you"—Rikki looked about at the darkened house—"seem to live here all alone. It must be a lonely existence."

Harry gasped. "Well, not exactly lonely."

"But you don't have any family. You've never married or had any kids? And you're living here by yourself. Right?"

Harry covered his mouth. "Wow," he said in a low voice, unsure how his explanation had gotten so off-track.

"That's terrible," she said, looking at Barney, whose eyes had closed. She struggled to conceal a yawn.

Barney opened his eyes. "I'm beat."

"I'm sorry," Harry answered, seemingly taken aback. "But I thought you wanted to hear this."

"We do. But when are you going to get to the part about her uncle?" Barney asked, looking over at Rikki, who also looked exhausted.

"Oh no, it's my fault," Rikki said, stopping Barney. "I want to hear everything, but," she said blinking, "I can barely keep my eyes open."

◆

"So how did he die?" Barney asked Harry, as he stretched his arms overhead and Rikki slid down, eyes closed, head resting against the back of the sofa.

Harry was transported back to the hospital room with its dingy yellow lighting, institutional smell, and cold tile floors.

Richard had yet to be placed on the ventilator. His frightened eyes searched for an escape from the terrible struggle to breathe. The memory was frozen in Harry's mind. "I'm sorry," the young doctor had said upon introducing himself to Richard. He ignored Harry. "The test results are conclusive. You're HIV positive, which explains the pneumocystis."

Harry refocused. "How does anyone die?" he finally answered, eluding the question.

Barney rolled his eyes. "Either you tell us too much or nothing at all. We're here to learn the truth. What's *your* deal?"

Harry laughed to cover his sudden discomfort at Barney's keen observation. *Smart kid,* he thought, *calling me out on my shit.* Harry rubbed his face. "The truth is," he said, struggling to get out the rest of the sentence, "I wasn't there when he actually died," again sidestepping the real answer.

Barney's eyes explored Harry's face as if searching for the information that Harry didn't want to share. "How old was he?"

"Thirty-three," Harry answered. "Only thirty-three."

"That doesn't seem so very young," Barney said.

"That's because you're fifteen going on sixteen," Harry assured him. "When you get to be thirty-three, you'll see how young that is."

"Did he know he was going to die?"

Harry felt a horrid depression settling in. It was as if he was disappearing ... slowly dissolving into the furniture. "It was AIDS," he finally admitted. "Full-blown AIDS."

Harry massaged a numb face with his hand. Was his blood still flowing? Was his heart still beating? This is why he didn't want to remember. Why he refused to write anything about that time in his life. It had all become too real again. Too painful. Hearing Richard's voice in his head had saved him from the abyss. He'd kept Richard alive. The best part of Richard. Not the sickness. Not the dying. But the loving voice of a man who had adored him. It had been Harry's means of survival.

"Rikki doesn't know anything about this," Barney said as Rikki gently snored next to him.

"I know," Harry answered. "Do you think she'll care?"

Barney didn't respond and, for the moment, Harry sensed judgment in Barney's manner. About what, he wasn't sure. Maybe it had nothing to do with Richard and AIDS. Perhaps it was a discomfort with all things gay. Or maybe it was something else.

"Do you think she cares that her uncle was gay?" Harry asked.

"Oh, no," Barney answered. "We know there are gay people in the world."

"Then it's the AIDS?"

Barney offered a suspicious look. "Why would she care about that?"

Harry shook his head. "So, then what is it? What's the problem?"

Barney sat up. "You two were together, weren't you?"

"I thought you already knew that," Harry said nonchalantly. "Wasn't that immediately clear?"

"No. Why would it be?" Barney answered.

Harry smiled. *What a generation. I'm still hiding, and they don't care.* "Yes, we were partners."

"Dude," Barney said slicing the air with a wave of his palm," you've got to stop using that term *partners*. It sounds like you were in business together."

"Right." Harry smiled, acknowledging the confusion. "I suppose it does."

Barney squinted. "If you two were together, how is it that you never got sick? How can that be possible?"

Harry exhaled. "I don't know. I've asked myself the same thing over the years. But I never did get infected. Call it luck—call it natural immunity. I don't know the answer. No one does."

◆

Harry held the telephone receiver to his ear with one hand and wiped the sleep away from his eyes with the other. "Mr. Aldon?" the voice had asked.

"Yes," Harry groggily answered. "Who is this?"

"This is Covington Hospital calling."

Harry shot straight up in bed, his heart racing as he glanced over at the alarm clock and noticed the time. Did he oversleep? He was supposed to be taking Richard home. He'd promised to be there by 8:00 a.m. It had all been planned. Harry had even arranged for a home care nurse to start that very afternoon.

"I'm afraid we have some bad news. Mr. Goldenbaum passed away this morning at five-thirty."

Harry heard the words, but the meaning eluded him.

"Mr. Aldon, did you hear me?" the voice said.

Harry blinked twice. "Did you just tell me Richard Goldenbaum died?"

"Yes. I'm very sorry to have to tell you."

When did you say he died?"

"Early this morning."

"But how?" he had asked, as if he was completely unaware of Richard's precarious health.

"Heart, Mr. Aldon. He suffered a massive heart attack."

◆

Barney waved a hand wildly. "Boy, you really go in and out ... don't you?"

Harry forced a smile, though he was reeling as if he'd just received the phone call about Richard's death. Thinking about the past had always seemed a waste of time. All that sorrow. He didn't want to go back. It had been the worst time of his life.

Barney offered a dimpled smile. "So, what about Rikki? Does she look like him at all?"

Harry studied her sleeping face. "She has some of his facial expressions," Harry acknowledged.

"Was he a nice guy?"

"*I* thought so," Harry answered, again eluding the specifics.

Barney leaned forward. "You're going to have to do better than that," he warned Harry. "She didn't come all this way to hear platitudes. She wants to know who he was. How he lived. The relationship he had with her mother and grandmother. She may seem like she has her shit together," Barney added in a whisper, "but she's fragile. You need to help her."

"And you?" Harry asked, impressed by the forthrightness of the young man before him. "What's your story? How did you and Rikki meet?"

Barney glared at Harry. "Oh, no. This isn't about me. We're here to help her. She's the focus. So let's keep it real. I have nothing to do with this."

Harry wondered how that could be true. "You came all this way just for Rikki?"

"I don't have a family. Maybe this is my way of helping someone else figure it all out."

Yes, Harry thought. *A remarkable kid.*

13

Rita's voice boomed. "Are you enjoying Toledo?"

Rikki pulled the receiver away from her ear. "Yes," she lied. "How are you?"

"Not so well," Rita announced. "It's snowing and I'm staying in. Did I ever tell you I have terrible arthritis in my left thumb?"

Rikki rolled her eyes. "A million times." How Rita's thumb seemed connected to the snow eluded Rikki.

"Well, it's worse than ever. And it's been very lonely here without you. I miss you. But I know being with your friend Barbra is important. I remember what it was like to be your age."

Rikki found it difficult to imagine Rita being any other age than old.

"So, tell me about Barbra's family," Rita asked. "Who else is there?"

Rikki ran her finger over the counter, collecting a crumb. *Harry needs to clean the house*, she thought as she examined her finger under the bright overhead lights. Thank God she was on the phone. Lying caused her to blush. "You know. Her uncle and aunt. Some cousins," she said, hoping to keep it short and sweet. The less said, the better.

"And what are their names?"

Rikki felt her heart thump. "What?" She pretended as if she hadn't heard the question as her mind raced.

"Their names. What are their names?"

Rikki stalled. "That's a strange question, Rita. So, tell me more about your thumb. Are you going to the doctor to have that looked at?"

But Rita didn't seem to be buying the ploy. "Let me speak to Barbra's aunt. I'd like to thank her."

Rikki looked about. "She's not here."

"Okay. Then her uncle."

"He went with her."

"All right, then. How about Barbra? Let me speak to her."

Rikki's face was on fire. "She also went with them."

Rita sounded incredulous. "And left you all alone?"

Rikki reached for an excuse. "Oh, I don't mind," she said. "It's nice to spend time alone."

The jig was up.

"Rikki … I know you're not in Toledo."

Rikki rubbed her forehead. "No, I'm not."

In a stern voice, Rita asked the next question. "Then, why are you lying to me?"

"Because you're lying to *me*," Rikki defended herself.

"Rikki, I've never lied to you."

"Yes, you have," Rikki shouted into the receiver, highly upset. "You've been lying to me all along. What happened to my mother? And why is it that I never knew I had an Uncle Richard?"

"I'm not here to answer your questions," Rita scolded. "Your job is to do *as I say*."

"Well, Rita," Rikki boldly announced, "that isn't really working for me." And she hung up.

◆

Angered by the phone call, Rikki clenched her fists as Rita's words echoed in her ears. *I'm not here to answer your questions.* Rita had been stonewalling all along. Deliberately avoiding telling Rikki anything about the family.

But why? Rikki wondered. *Had Rikki herself done something wrong? Was she responsible in some way for her mother's death?*

A cold dread gripped her heart. She had to understand. Why was Rita being so secretive? Why was Rita unwilling to share anything with her?

If only I could remember, she thought. There had to be a reason why she'd blocked it all from her memory. *I must have done something awful to my mother,* Rikki surmised. *I must have.*

◆

Beetle rushed the door as soon as the bell rang. It was past eleven o'clock and the kids had retired, Rikki to the guest room and Barney to a blow-up mattress in Harry's office. Harry tried to suppress his irritation as he opened the door.

He leaned against the jamb. "It's late," he said.

Lil was holding a bottle of red. "I was feeling a little lonely and thought maybe we could talk."

"Lil, how many times have I said that you need to call first?"

Lil pursed her lips as she gave Harry a seductive glance. "Harry, it's just as easy for me to walk over. If you don't want me to visit, just tell me so. I can handle the truth."

Harry shrugged and opened the door. "Maybe just one drink. And that's it. I have some guests staying with me—and I don't want them disturbed."

"I didn't see a car out front," Lil said as she glanced about, as if she expected to see the reported guests sitting in the living room.

"Come this way." Harry waved to her as he headed to the kitchen, switching on the light.

Two empty pizza boxes sat on the counter. "Oh, Harry," Lil pressed, lifting the boxes up, "you better dump these in the trash unless you want ants. Now go on," she nudged him as he lifted the boxes and left the room.

When Harry returned, Lil was nowhere in sight. Heading down the hallway, he came up to his office. The door was open, and Lil was sitting in his desk chair talking with Barney, who was sitting up on the blow-up mattress. "Look who I met," Lil said, spotting Harry.

Harry rolled his eyes.

"Barney was just telling me how they flew here from Michigan today. Harry, I had no idea you had friends in Michigan," Lil said, disarmingly. "Michigan is such a lovely place. Did you know that I attended the University of Michigan in Ann Arbor? Great school. And the cutest little town you've ever seen."

"Lil, why don't you leave the kid alone? Let him get some sleep."

"Why, of course," she said, standing up. "I'm sorry. Did I bother you?" She directed the question to Barney, who rubbed his eyes and merely smiled.

"Well, we actually live in New York City, not Michigan," Barney started to correct Lil.

Lil clasped her palms together. "New York. How thrilling. Now that's a place with a lot of hustle and bustle. So you went to Michigan from New York and now you're in Phoenix."

"Actually, we went to Michigan via Toledo, Ohio."

Lil turned and looked at Harry. "A journey of a lifetime," she said with dead seriousness. "That's a lot of travel for young people."

Barney smiled. "We were fine. We're very capable."

"I'm sure," Lil cooed.

"Lil," Harry interrupted, reaching for Lil's elbow, "how about we let Barney get some rest?"

"Oh, of course," Lil said, backing out of the room. "I'm sorry. But it was lovely meeting you. I hope we get a chance to talk again," Lil continued as Harry pulled her along.

"You're a pistol," Harry said as they headed back to the kitchen. "What was that all about?"

Lil looked surprised by the question. "What do you mean?"

"You know what I'm talking about," Harry challenged her. "What were you doing exploring?"

Lil offered an indignant expression. "Why, Harry Aldon ... you really are an ass."

Harry took a breath. "Lil, that might be true, and God knows I have my flaws, but what makes you think you have the right to show up at ten at night with your sad little bottle of red and then go searching through my house?"

Lil's combative demeanor faded. "Harry, maybe I was wrong. Maybe I like you more than I know. Maybe," and her eyes locked on his, "I'm insecure about us."

Harry's eyes bulged. "Lil, there is no 'us,'" he said, palms high in the air. "There never was." He leaned against the kitchen counter.

"Now, Harry," Lil pressed, "you know that isn't true. We have something very special. I get that you're a writer. You keep all your feelings bottled up."

She tilted her head as she spoke, and Harry wondered if that was her way of filtering out reality. Smiling, cajoling, and flattering.

"You never even told me about Edward. What was I to think?" she pouted.

Ah, Harry thought. *There it is. There's the reason for all this nonsense. She's jealous.*

"Lil, I don't owe you any explanations. In fact," he said scratching his head, "weren't you the one who said we're not in a relationship."

"And what does that have to do with Edward?" she asked, seemingly surprised by the turn in the conversation.

"You're jealous of Edward," Harry announced with certainty.

"Edward?" Lil backed up. "Why would I be jealous of Edward? What are you talking about? Isn't he your editor?"

Harry paled. "Yes."

"Then what the hell are you talking about?" she said in a sharp tone that he'd not heard before. "I was angry that you didn't introduce me when he came to visit. He might have enjoyed meeting me. But you keep blocking me out of your life."

"Lil, I have company," Harry said impatiently as he escorted her to the door. "This conversation will have to wait for tomorrow," he said as he ushered her out, wine bottle and all.

◆

Harry shook his head as he slipped into bed, Beetle resting contentedly at his side. There was a world of misunderstanding and confusion between him and Lil. Why, he wondered, had he ever allowed her into his bed? He'd done her a terrible disservice. Neither she nor Edward would ever truly own him. Those days were over. He was too old for this *relationship thing*. If there was one thing Harry was certain of, relationships were too confusing and messy. Not his style. He'd so much preferred being alone. Quietly working out the lives of his characters on paper. Away from the raw emotions and energy that seemed to surround real people and their desires and wants.

You're not immune, Harry.

The voice was Richard's.

You don't need to be alone. You should be with someone.

Harry sat up in the dark. He hadn't anticipated the voice. He turned on the light on the side table and pulled out a crossword puzzle from the drawer. Beetle nuzzled ever closer, releasing a yawn as he dropped his head back onto the covers.

You don't have many years left. Do you want those years to be spent alone?

Harry looked up. "I'm not alone," he said softly, "I have Beetle."

He glanced down at the sleeping dog.

Make a choice, Harry. Choose Lil or Edward. But choose someone.

"Why?" Harry said. "Why do I have to?"

Then you've chosen loneliness. You've chosen yourself.

◆

The next morning at breakfast, sitting with Barney and Harry, a bowl of half-eaten oatmeal in front of her, Rikki blurted out, "So you two were gay together."

Harry choked on his coffee as Barney let out a howl.

"Did you tell her?" Harry asked Barney as coffee ran down the corner of his mouth. He wiped his mouth with a napkin.

Barney shook his head and shrugged his shoulders. "Evelyn had said you guys were friends. As for you two being together—that wasn't so clear. All that *code talk*. But then, she figured it out. I just told her that she was right."

Harry used his tongue to dislodge a seed from a rear molar, a byproduct of the toasted sesame seed bagel that sat before him. "So, now you know."

"Oh, my God," Rikki said leaning forward. "That's big news. How did my mother deal with it?"

Harry exhaled. "Now, that's an odd question. Don't you think you should be asking how your Uncle Richard dealt with it? After all, your mother had her own life. Richard's being gay had very little to do with her. What should it matter?"

Rikki sat back in her chair. "So, I'm asking the wrong question?" she said in a small voice.

"Yeah, I'd say," Harry lectured. "You know, you don't just wake up, jump out of bed, and leap for joy that you're gay. There's this painful period of adjustment."

"But why?" Rikki asked.

"Does it have to be?" Barney wanted to know.

Harry was beside himself. "Don't you two know *anything*?" he said, exasperated. "Being gay is being different. No one wants to be different."

"But it's everywhere," Barney pointed out. "Rosie O'Donnell, Ellen DeGeneres, and even Mr. Sulu from *Star Trek*. And *Will & Grace*. Come on!"

Harry nodded.

"And we have a teacher at school—Mr. Rosenfeld. He's gay," added Barney.

"Well, we don't actually know that for a fact," Rikki pointed out. "He's never told us."

Barney arched his brow. "He's gay!"

"Yes, I think he is," Rikki agreed.

Harry shifted his gaze from Rikki to Barney and back. "Well, okay. Maybe today it's more acceptable. Granted. But back then, not so much. It was a big deal. A true act of courage to be who you were. To live your life out and proud."

Barney scratched his head. "Now it's just kind of cool."

Rikki agreed. "I don't think it defines you as a human being."

Harry dropped his face in his hands. "I can see this just might be harder than I thought."

◆

"Rock Hudson had just died," Harry explained. "It was a big deal. If Rock Hudson could be gay, well ..."

"Who's that?" Barney asked.

Harry shook his head. "Seriously?"

"Yeah," Rikki added.

"Oh, my God." Harry placed his hands on top of his head. "Seriously? You don't know who Rock Hudson was?"

Both kids offered blank stares.

"He was a major Hollywood movie star. *Giant. Magnificent Obsession. Pillow Talk.*"

Still no response.

"*McMillan and Wife? Dynasty?*"

Blank stares.

Harry continued. "It was the 1980s."

"We're only fifteen," Rikki finally said. "How are we supposed to know that?"

"Don't they teach you anything in school about AIDS?"

Rikki laughed. "Are you serious?"

"Yes," Harry stammered. "There's a whole history of how Reagan ignored the epidemic. Of a brilliant and brave group of men and women who fought the system and came together to make a death sentence into a chronic illness. And there's an entire generation that's been wiped out from the disease."

Rikki chimed in, "Like Uncle Richard."

"Yes," Harry said.

"A lot of others died?" Barney asked.

"Okay," Harry said. "I think we need to do a little education here. If you want to know about your family, we're going to have to get you two educated."

◆

Together, Harry and Rita had sat in the fourth floor waiting lounge at Beth Israel Medical Center in Manhattan. Rita stared into the distance as Harry waited for her to speak. Richard was back in the hospital and Harry thought it was time that Rita knew the score. In the four years since he and Richard had lived together, Rita hadn't been part of their lives. A call twice a year, usually made by Richard, seemed to be the limit of the relationship.

Harry shifted awkwardly in his chair. The entire experience with Richard had been a roller-coaster ride. From the moment they'd connected, Harry's world had been turned upside down. He'd always been a solitary soul, but Richard loved people. And so they went clubbing and to parties ... lots of parties. Harry had never met anyone quite like Richard. Someone who was so comfortable in his own skin. "Don't let the bastards get you down," he'd tell Harry. "Love yourself."

Harry found value in those words. He discovered his own courage as he watched his lover negotiate the world with confidence and energy. Where Harry had been afraid, Richard was fearless. Dinner together at a romantic restaurant on a Saturday night had once been unbearable for Harry. *Surely everyone will know.* But Richard didn't care. He saw no reason to cower or hide, going so far as to kiss Harry on the lips in public one night. "There," he said glancing about. "No one cares. Stop being such a homophobe."

And now, with Richard's illness raging, Harry's world centered on Beth Israel.

Rita broke her silence. "He deserves this," she said emphatically. "If he chose to be gay, then he deserves to die."

Harry was stunned. "That's outrageous."

"Well, that's how I feel," Rita said stoically.

Harry could feel his blood pressure rise. "Then you can't see him," he calmly said.

Rita shifted in her chair to face Harry. "Don't tell me what I can and can't do. I'll do exactly as I please."

Harry stood. "Let's go." He signaled for her to stand up. "Time to leave."

Rita's mouth hung open.

"Come on, now," he said, pulling her up by the arm. "You're leaving."

"I'm not going anywhere with you!" Rita snapped.

"Oh, yes you are," Harry said as he forcefully pulled her along the hallway and to the elevator. "You're leaving, right now."

◆

"Tell me about Rita. What did she do?"

Harry didn't know if he should say anything about Rita, but Rikki pressed.

Harry bit his lower lip. He didn't want to go through it all again. It had been so many years. What good could come of it now? Rita was who she was—and who she'd always been. Why share such awful stories? And then a thought flashed in Harry's mind. *Maybe it was more than the family could handle? Maybe Rita simply wasn't strong enough.* Like a thunderbolt, Harry's entire view shifted. He'd spent years vested in a vision of Richard's family as selfish in the face of tragedy, never considering that they were actually incompetent.

Rikki waited.

Barney sat back and locked eyes with Harry.

The young, serious faces before him yearned for the details about Rita.

As Harry gazed into their innocent eyes, he realized that the story of Richard's death had become a private construct that had defined his life. He'd embedded the tragedy and allowed it to shape his future. It was an intense moment of clarity. And as he held that fleeting truth in his grasp, he understood that this was his chance to heal. His moment to grow from pain. Something that he hadn't allowed himself to do. It was as if he'd waited for Rikki and Barney to be born and grow up, to come and find him, so that he might come to terms with the life events that had traumatized him so many years earlier.

He weighed his words as if spiritually imbued with a power not of his own mind but of a higher energy. "Rita proved," he began, "to be who she always was. Only more so. In the face of Richard's diagnosis, she was unavailable. And now that I look back on it," and Harry took a deep breath and sighed, "instead of being angry at her, I am grateful that she wasn't there. She made the right choice for Richard and me. Not having to deal with her was the greatest gift she could have offered."

Two puzzled faces stared back at him.

"I can't explain it any more but to say, when someone doesn't have the capacity to be helpful, best that they stay away."

A tear escaped Rikki's eye. "And your own family?" Rikki asked.

"I never told them."

"That's terrible," Barney said.

"What did Uncle Richard say?"

Harry arched his brows. "We didn't talk about it."

"Ever?" Barney asked, frowning.

Harry tilted his head. He thought for a moment. "No. We never did."

"He must have known how Rita was," Rikki concluded.

Harry looked at her, aware that Rikki was speaking a truth he'd just finally considered. "Yes, of course. Why would he be surprised? He knew who she was. He knew what to expect of them."

"Them?" Barney asked. "I thought we were just talking about Rita."

Harry's face paled. He'd say no more.

◆

Harry had tried one last time. As he dialed Elle's number, he searched for something new to say. Something that might be more persuasive. "Elle, he wants to see you. It would mean so much," Harry pressed. "Please say you'll come."

"I'm sorry, Harry. I want to, but I can't."

"But Elle ..."

The resistance on the other end was palpable. "I can't, Harry. Please stop calling and asking me to. I'm happy to speak to him by phone. I'm just not going to risk getting sick."

"Elle, *I'm* not sick. And we've been intimate," Harry declared.

"But you might be," Elle answered. "I just can't take that chance."

Harry sighed. It was hopeless. "So, you're going to allow your brother to die without seeing him. How can you do that?"

"Harry, don't make me out to be an evil person. I'm not. I love Richard. I've called him every day since he's been in the hospital. But there's nothing more I can do for him now. He's got *you*, Harry." Her voice was clear and determined. "He has you. You're there. And I know how much he loves you. He doesn't really need anyone else."

Harry closed his eyes. "Elle, that simply isn't true."

"Oh, Harry. I do want to be there. But I just can't risk it. I'm pregnant. I have a new life to protect. You can't expect me to come."

Harry nodded, the anger building inside with such a fury that he wondered how he could stop from exploding. "I do expect you to be here. That's exactly what I expect," he said sharply. "You can't catch it from breathing the air in his room."

"Oh, Harry, please stop asking me."

But Harry persisted. "Elle, don't do this. It's unforgiveable."

"I know, Harry," she whispered. "I know."

Harry clenched a fist. "Elle, I think it's a damn shame that you've shown yourself to be so selfish," he snarled, as he hung up the phone with a resounding bang.

14

Harry poured a shot glass of whiskey and took a swig. The sharp heat of the liquor on his throat cleared his mind and cut though the confusion of the last few hours. He stepped out onto the patio, Beetle on his heels.

It was a bright, moonlit night. He waited and listened, but there was no inner voice. Only the sound of crickets and a dog barking somewhere off in the distance.

Beetle whined. Harry lifted the terrier into his arms and awkwardly settled into a lounge chair. He glanced up and admired the clear night sky. Beetle, sitting on Harry's lap, was on full alert.

Harry stroked Beetle's back until the animal settled in and relaxed. There was a new pain in his left hand. An ache in his thumb. He rubbed the sore digit, noticing for the first time that he had old-man hands. The skin, once taut, now seemed loose. What had been strong and powerful had somehow changed. When did this happen? Why had he not noticed it before?

Afraid to live and yet growing older every day, he thought, resigned to the reality of his circumstances. *As if by keeping myself apart from the world, I could avoid the pain of being alive.*

How sad it now all seemed. His living alone in Phoenix. His refusal to commit to either Edward or Lil. He remembered Richard's words: *By not making a decision, you've made a decision.* He grasped the irony. He'd avoided emotional entanglements, protected himself, and yet, on the patio with Beetle sitting contentedly on his lap, he was still afraid.

The day after Richard had died, he'd promised himself to become active in the AIDS movement. He'd been angry then. Frustrated that a virus could disrupt a life and take away the man he loved. It had all seemed so unfair. *I wanted to reach out,* Harry remembered. *After he was gone, I wanted to.*

But the reality of grief had interceded. An awful depression had set in, so dark and murky, it frightened him. And so he couldn't. Not after all the months of caring for Richard. He'd been worn down physically and emotionally and was simply unable to cope with anything to do with illness or death.

An owl hooted in the distance, the call so lonely and sad that it brought Harry to tears.

I've done nothing with my life. I should have... He closed his eyes and wondered if perhaps the real truth was that he simply wasn't strong. *Richard had all the strength. He was brave. He'd have stood up for what was right. Had the situation been reversed, he'd have been fighting for a cure.*

Instead, Harry gave way to more-confident voices. Gay men who had faced the terror of AIDS and held their ground. Those who pressed for research, legal protection, and dignity, all the while burying loved ones as Harry receded into a writer's fantasy world. Nothing was real but what he was able to create. And now, on the patio in the cool night air, Harry realized that he'd failed Richard by not being more. He'd failed himself by not even trying.

"I should have done better," he said as he massaged Beetle's neck, hoping to hear Richard's voice. But there was no response. Only the sound of Beetle's breathing, persistent and struggling as he started to wheeze.

Harry placed his hand under the terrier, gently massaging his tummy. "There you go, boy, take it easy," he said soothingly. "You're okay."

◆

Elle checked her watch. "Honey, please, we've got to get a move on. I need to get to the airport. I can't miss that flight. Your Uncle Bill will kill me."

It was an early September morning as Rikki slipped on her shoes. Elle's job at Jacobson's had come to an end, and even though she had refused to move back to New York, Bill Allington had asked her to once again join Haney & Lewis. "You can telecommute," Bill had said. "And Detroit isn't so far from New York City. You can hop a plane and be in the city by noon."

Rikki laughed. "He'd never kill you," she protested at the mere mention of such a violent act. "He thinks you're wonderful."

Her mother stood in the hall outside Rikki's bedroom door, a brown leather workbag on her shoulder and a black roller bag at her side. "Yes," she agreed. "He does. But then he has great taste."

"When will you be back?" Rikki asked, gathering up the school-books on her desk.

Elle had one hand on her hip as she watched her daughter. "I told you twice already. Tuesday night."

Rikki remembered; she'd just wanted to hear her mother say it one more time.

"Now, when you come home from school, go straight over to Evelyn's," Elle called out as she headed down the stairs, the roller bag banging injudiciously against the steps as she struggled to lift it in the air.

"Yes," Rikki answered, following close behind. She knew the drill. Dinner with Evelyn and then she'd spend the night. Perhaps Evelyn might even take her to the movies. Rikki had so wanted to see Mariah Carey in *Glitter*. Elle had said no, but Evelyn was such a soft touch, Rikki thought she might be able to get Evelyn to go.

"She's doing us a really big favor," Elle warned her daughter as Rikki followed her out to the car. "And no to *Glitter*."

Rikki gasped. "Of course not," she feigned surprise. "It's Monday. A school night. I'll have homework."

Elle placed her luggage in the trunk. "That's right. So, don't you give Evelyn any trouble," she said, walking around to the driver's side.

Rikki smiled as she got into the passenger seat. "Mom, Evelyn loves spending time with me. It's no bother."

Elle laughed at her daughter's assertion. "That she does," she said as she fastened her seat belt before checking Rikki's. "Why, I'll never know," she said jokingly as she backed the car down the driveway.

◆

Rikki awoke in a sweat. She kicked off the covers before realizing she wasn't in her bed, back in Queens, and Rita wasn't down the hall.

She was in Phoenix. She was at Harry's house.

She sat up. The faintest bit of light shone through the curtains from the outside streetlight. The room felt too warm, almost claustrophobic. Not quite awake, she moved in a daze, reaching for the lamp on the side table, missing her target, and knocking it over. The sudden crash startled her. In an instant, a memory flashed. The sound of a crash. Voices screaming. She could hear it all. It was as if she were there.

"Are you okay?" a voice called from the shadows of the room.

Rikki gasped. "Mom, is that you?" she cried.

"Rikki, wake up," the voice demanded.

When Rikki opened her eyes, Barney was by her side, in only a pair of white briefs. The lights in the room were on. The lamp hadn't fallen at all. It sat perfectly straight on the side table.

"Are you okay?" he asked as he ran a cool palm across Rikki's wet brow. "You've just had a bad dream. That's all."

Rikki nodded, as if Barney's explanation made perfect sense.

The smell of his musk caught in her throat. She hadn't ever seen him without his shirt on. His skin seemed to glisten as he eyed her with concern, a bit of hair falling into his eyes.

"Would you like a glass of water?"

"No." She was slow to answer, still lost in a state between dreaming and waking. "I'm fine, really."

"Okay, then. Lie back," he instructed her.

Rikki did as she was told as Barney pulled up the cotton blanket. "Now, try to get some sleep. If you need me, I'm just next door."

"Wait," Rikki called out as he started to go. "Don't leave." A strip of brown fuzz lined his belly. She wondered how it might feel to stroke it.

"Are you sure?" he asked, head tilted to the side, one brow raised.

"Yes," she said with a growing certainty. "Stay with me."

Rikki wet her lips and adjusted the pillow beneath her head as Barney slid down next to her. "What was the dream about?" he asked, leaning on one elbow as he looked at her. She spotted a patch of dark hair under his arm.

"I don't know," she said, hoping to get him to move closer to her. "I don't really care anymore." Her heart was rapidly beating as the blood coursed through her body.

"But it had to be something," he said as he took her hand.

She gazed into his eyes. "Barney, thank you for coming here with me."

He smiled an impish smile. She sensed his desire. "I really should go back to my room," he said, unconvincingly, leaning in closer for a kiss. She lifted her head, and as their lips touched their noses awkwardly collided.

"Oww," Barney said as he rubbed the tip of his nose with his fingertips.

She blushed, deeply embarrassed.

"I've never done this," Barney admitted, as he came closer again, leaning in to smell her hair, his body against hers.

"Me neither," she whispered, feeling foolish, certain that he already knew that.

"But," he said, as a hardness pressed against her thigh, "I can't think of anyone I'd rather be with."

She closed her eyes as she pulled him closer, her hand now exploring his manhood, his tongue buried in her mouth.

◆

Harry pulled the bedspread back with one hand as he gently placed Beetle down. "You're getting heavy," Harry said as he massaged his right arm, sore after carrying Beetle in from the outside.

The terrier stumbled over to the middle of the bed, releasing a small cry as he lowered himself, resting his head on his paws.

"There you go," Harry said sweetly. "You look nice and comfortable."

As Harry brushed his teeth, he thought about the day. The surprise of the two teens showing up at his door. The familiar expression on Rikki's face, which so reminded Harry of Richard's. The questions the teens had posed … and his awkward answers. He wondered why he was still so uncomfortable in his own skin. Perhaps that's why he wrote mystery novels. Maybe the genre lent itself to escaping the facts of his own life.

Surely a man of my age should be past all this, he thought as he gargled. *Life should be easier at this point.* And yet, his confusion over the past, his sexuality, Lil and Edward, all seemed to be critical to his very identity. As if, without the confusion, he'd cease to exist. Cease to be Harry.

He sighed as he slipped under the covers. Beetle remained in the center of the bed, facing the master bath, his legs stretched backward. "Come over here, boy," Harry instructed, gently patting a spot next to him.

But Beetle didn't move.

"Beetle," Harry repeated, "Beetle?" he said louder, sitting up to touch the terrier's paw as Beetle rolled on his side and began to pant. "*Beetle!*" Harry cried out as he leapt over the covers and came around to kneel at the foot of the bed. Beetle's eyes, glassy, unfocused, the whites exposed, signaled distress as the tiny chest heaved valiantly. Harry caressed Beetle's back, hoping his touch might calm the terrier. "I'm here," he softly said, "right here," as Beetle continued to pant, a paw quivering, as urine pooled on the blanket. Each moment an hour, until Beetle's breathing finally settled back to a steady rhythm.

"Oh God, Beetle," Harry said, as he lifted the terrier, now fully alert, and placed him on the floor. "You scared the crap out of me."

Harry pulled the blanket back to inspect the sheets. The urine had soaked through. With a sigh, he stripped the bed, carrying the blanket and sheets down the hall where he loaded the washer.

You better get that dog to the vet. It was Richard's voice.

"I know," Harry said, as he added detergent and set the temperature to hot. With a click of the dial, the washing machine started.

Don't wait for the morning. Get him to the Emergency Clinic now.

Harry rushed back to the bedroom. Beetle was curled up in his crate. All was calm.

Perhaps there's nothing more to do, Harry thought as he sat down next to the crate. Leaning against the wall, wearing only his briefs, Harry took a deep breath. He could feel the tension in his chest on the exhale. *Whatever that was, he seems okay now. He'll definitely need a bath, but I should probably let him rest. Time enough for Newbar in the morning. I'm sure he'll take him first thing.*

Harry stretched a hand out and gently touched Beetle's head. The little dog opened its eyes. Harry could feel himself begin to relax. "You are my life," Harry whispered as Beetle lifted his head, inviting Harry's touch. Harry leaned sideways and slipped two fingers beneath Beetle's chin and scratched. "What am I going to do if something happens to you? You're my best buddy," Harry said as tears gathered. "I don't think I could stand it, Beetle."

◆

When Harry awoke, he was next to Beetle's crate. He'd fallen asleep, knees pulled into his chest, head resting forward. He craned his neck to see the clock. It was nearly midnight. He licked his lips and blinked, acutely aware that his body, unaccustomed to sleeping in such a bent position, had grown stiff. He looked over at the crate. Beetle remained in a curl. Harry smiled. He was glad that he hadn't rushed to the emergency vet.

Harry struggled to his feet. Hands on his hips, he swiveled back and forth, blinking hard as he pondered his unmade bed. *No need for sheets or a blanket,* he thought as he grabbed a bathrobe out of the closet and slipped it on.

As he sat down on the bed, he once again looked over at Beetle. The terrier seemed at peace. Harry smiled. "I'm so lucky," he thought as his eyes settled on Beetle's chest in anticipation of the familiar rise and fall. But there was no movement. No movement at all as Harry waited and stared, his breath growing shallow as he was overcome by fear.

◆

Edward's voice rang out. "I'm so sorry, Harry."

Harry had called Edward first, too distraught to do much else. Tears streamed down his face as he sat on the floor of his bedroom, Beetle next to him on a bath towel. "I let him die," Harry sobbed. "He was in distress and I should have rushed him to the emergency vet. How could I be so stupid?"

"Oh, Harry," Edward sighed. "You're too hard on yourself. That little dog loved you and you gave him a wonderful life. But Harry, he was old and he was sick. You know that. You took such wonderful care of him. And wasn't he lucky to have died in his own home? I'm certain that was *the best* ending, for Beetle's sake."

Harry had no idea how to get past the next few moments, let alone consider the actions required for the next day. "I'm lost ..." he mumbled between gasps. "I don't think I can stand it, Edward. My beautiful Beetle is gone."

"My dearest Harry." There was a gentleness in Edward's voice, a kindness that Harry had never paid much attention to. "I know this is hard. But you're not alone."

"I am," Harry cried, stroking Beetle as if his touch might revive the terrier. "Totally."

"I'm here, Harry," Edward assured him.

Harry realized that Edward too had been the other constant in his life. The editor, the friend, the lover. The touchstone that Harry could always count on. Now, he wondered why he'd kept Edward at a distance.

"But you're not *here*," Harry answered, barely able to get the words out.

"Not now … but I can be there tomorrow."

"You'd come all the way back?" Harry sobbed.

"Certainly," Edward said. "I think you just might need me. Do you, Harry? Do you need me?"

Harry stopped crying. "I do," he answered, his heart breaking as he looked down at Beetle's silent form. "I need you more than you could ever know."

◆

Rita groused as she worked her way down the aisle to seat 21F, her bag periodically catching in an armrest as she struggled to move forward. She'd awakened at 3:00 a.m. to catch the 6:25 flight out of Kennedy International, arriving in Phoenix at 9:15 in the morning with the time change. *Dear God,* she thought, eying the traveling public. *All these people packed together in a sardine can. And look how they're dressed.* She passed a young woman seated next to a toddler. The woman's red top was cut so low, Rita was certain the entire plane was being treated to a titty show.

It's worse than taking a bus, Rita thought, as she slid into the window seat, tightly tucked beside two black men. The older one in the middle seat, who appeared to be in his fifties and was wearing a blue cardigan sweater, nodded and smiled. "Traveling alone?" he asked in a warm tone.

"Yes," Rita answered, searching through her purse for a tissue. Perhaps if she pretended to be sick, he might leave her be.

"I'm taking my son back to Tempe."

Rita nodded, not wanting to continue the conversation.

"He's a star athlete at ASU."

Again she nodded, directing her attention out the window just as, down on the tarmac, a young man in an orange vest approached the side of the plane.

"Who is that?" she asked, concern in her voice, forgetting her lack of interest in conversation.

The man leaned forward to get a better view. "Just an airport worker. Probably someone who needs to check the cargo hold."

"Oh, God," Rita said aloud. "If I didn't have to fly, I never would."

The man chuckled. "I know what you mean. But there's no other way. If you want to get to Phoenix from New York, you really have to fly."

Rita felt a mild sweat breaking on her brow. "I don't know..." she said, without thinking about the consequences.

"Well, you're perfectly safe," the man said. "Junior and I are right here. And Junior plays defensive end. Trust me, with my boy around, you never need fear."

"But ever since 2001 ..." and her voice trailed off. She'd promised herself not to think about it.

"9/11?" the man asked.

"Yes," Rita revealed, her voice sounding like that of a little girl. "I've been frightened."

"Oh," the man answered sympathetically. "And you haven't flown since then?"

"No," she admitted. "But now, I guess I have no choice."

A flight attendant announced that the doors were secured for take-off.

Rita sighed. "It's now or never," she said to the stranger as she leaned back and tried to relax.

◆

Harry sat outside the vet's office in his car and waited for the staff to arrive for the start of the morning shift. He'd been up most of the night, unable to sleep. Edward had recommended a warm bath, but Harry hadn't followed the advice. He was too upset to sit in a warm tub, bombarded by the same thought over and over. *I should have taken him to the emergency vet. Why didn't I?*

Michelle, a veterinary technician, took Beetle's wrapped form from the backseat. "Please be careful with him," Harry implored as the bundle was carried off.

Dr. Newbar came outside and offered his condolences. "How are you holding up?" he asked as Harry got out of the car to meet him.

"Not well, but I'm managing," Harry muttered. "I don't really have a choice."

"You were a good doggy dad," Newbar said. "Beetle had a great life because of you. You took really terrific care of him."

"But last night…" Harry was unable to continue. Instead, he looked down, reliving Beetle's last moments. The wild-eyed stare, the quivering paw.

"Harry, you know Beetle had congestive heart failure. And I told you that his enlarged heart might actually tear. We had discussed all that."

Harry nodded. "It's just so hard, isn't it? How do *you* manage through this?" he asked Newbar.

"It's just how life is. None of us is here forever. When it's our time, we just hope that we go easily and quickly, like Beetle. He was a special little guy."

Harry shook Newbar's hand. "I really should thank you for everything that you've done for Beetle."

"Well," Newbar said. "That's my job."

"But you're really a kind of hero."

Newbar smiled. "And so are you, Harry. So are you."

Harry was unable to stop himself from putting his arms around Newbar and pulling him in for a tight hug.

◆

"I just got here," Edward told Harry as he raced to the cab stand, cell phone held tightly to his ear. "The flight was on time. Thank God."

"I just dropped Beetle off at the vet," Harry replied. "I'm afraid I scared Dr. Newbar. The way I hugged him, the poor man probably thought I was in love with him."

Edward sighed. "Oh, Harry. I'm so sorry."

"Should I come get you?"

"No need," Edward said, as he leaned forward and asked the cabbie to take him to the Biltmore. "I'm on my way now…I should be there in fifteen minutes."

"Okay," Harry answered. "Well, you'll be there well before me. Don't ring the bell. The kids may still be sleeping. Use the spare key. You know where I hide it."

"Kids?"

"Oh, yeah," Harry answered. "I'll tell you about that later. I have two kids staying with me."

"Tell me now," Edward insisted.

◆

Rita waited at the carousel for her luggage. The flight had terrified her. Every bump, every rumble had set her heart thumping loudly in her chest. *I'm such a silly woman,* she thought as she caught sight of the man who'd occupied the next seat. He stood at the other end of the carousel beside his son. He waved and she couldn't help but smile. He'd been so very kind throughout the trip. Explaining aerodynamics and how planes managed to stay in the air. Offering to purchase a cocktail for her, which, of course, due to the early-morning hour, she'd immediately refused. Even holding her hand when the plane hit turbulence. It hadn't been until that moment that she realized that Colby Johnson was a very attractive man. That was the first time, with her palm pressed against his, that she noticed the warmth in his eyes, the tenderness of his smile.

"You're going to be just fine," he'd assured her. "I always used to hold my wife's hand when we flew. She wasn't much different from you. A nervous little thing," he intoned. "It was hard losing her to cancer. Hard when a man can't do anything but stand around and watch the only girl he ever loved slowly disappear."

He'd shared himself so easily, so freely, it had made Rita blush. She admired his honesty.

"I discovered a long time ago that being alone isn't the same as being lonely. There are some people who wanted me to remarry right away," he acknowledged. "I don't mind admitting that there were more women floating around my door than I was prepared to see."

Rita found herself laughing, only too keenly aware of how aggressive some women can be in the presence of a widower. "Well, what did you *do*?" she asked, genuinely interested in hearing more.

"I locked the barn door," he joked, smiling broadly to reveal a gorgeous set of white teeth. "What else could I do? I had a son to raise." He looked over at his boy, who was wearing ear buds and listening to music while reading an issue of *Sports Illustrated*. "These kids today ... He hardly even knows I'm around anymore," Colby admitted. "I might as well be back in Long Island, for all that Jake knows."

Rita thought about Rikki. "I'm raising my granddaughter," she admitted.

"Well, good for you," Colby answered. "That's a noble thing to do."

"I'm afraid I'm not doing such a good job. You see, I'm flying to Phoenix to get her to come home."

"She's run away?"

"Not exactly. It's hard to explain."

"You know, sometimes, even with our best effort, we fail," Colby offered.

"I guess," Rita admitted. "But I haven't given it my best effort. If I had, I wouldn't be on this plane. You see," she said softly, "I've never been a good parent. And I'm afraid that hasn't made me a better grandparent."

"It's never too late."

"I suppose," Rita answered. "I suppose."

◆

Edward ran his hand over the top of the doorframe until he came upon the spare key. He let himself in, immediately aware of the silence. There was no Beetle to greet him. No high-pitched barking that might scare away an intruder. Putting his suitcase down in the hall, he dropped his overcoat onto a living room chair and headed to the kitchen to make a pot of coffee.

It'll be a long day, he thought. *I need some caffeine.* As he scooped coffee into the brewing basket, the doorbell rang. He looked at his watch. Ten o'clock. *Who the hell can that be?*

Lil stood in the doorway, wearing a form-fitting black yoga outfit, her hair pulled back in a ponytail. Edward thought she looked like a little girl instead of a mature woman. She eyed Edward suspiciously. "He's gay, isn't he?" she said.

Edward stared at her, uncertain what to say.

"Are you two having a fling?" Her eyes grilled him.

"I don't think I'm the one to answer those questions," he said hoping to sidestep the issue.

"Can we please just cut through the crap?" she balked. "I know about life. I'm a grown-up girl and I get it. It's that *down-low thing*, I suppose. I watch Oprah. So are you two an item?"

He didn't answer her.

"Well, clearly you can't be," she said, talking herself through the answer. "After all, you live in New York City. How committed can he be to you if you don't even live here?"

Edward sighed. What she said was true.

"But he'll never really be happy with me," she said, searching Edward's eyes as if he might know the truth. "Am I wrong about that?"

Edward glanced down. He had no idea.

"I just wish he'd been upfront in the beginning. Oh, I could manage knowing we'd just be friends. God knows he wouldn't be the first man with whom a relationship transitioned into a friendship. Some women get sensitive about their men sleeping around," she said almost matter-of-factly. "But I'm a realist. I like Harry. I really like him. It doesn't have to be exclusive. It could just be friendly. I'd be grateful for 'friendly,'" she said, shifting her weight back a step.

"I'm alone," she admitted, a hand touching her heart. "I've always thought that something better was bound to come along. So I waited. And as other women bury their second husbands, I'm still searching."

Edward took pity on her. "Would you like to come in?" he offered, standing aside. "I just put a fresh pot of coffee on."

◆

"Where the hell are you?" Edward asked when Harry answered his cell phone.

"I thought I was done, but I had to fill out some paperwork, pick out a box for the cremains, and pay for it all."

"Well, you've got a surprise visitor."

"Who?"

"An athletic little blonde who you've been sleeping with?"

"Lil?" Harry choked and coughed. "I've put her off."

"Maybe so … but have you told her the truth?"

Harry bit his lip. "You know how I am. I'm not good with strong women."

"Apparently, you're better than you think," Edward answered.

"Don't be ridiculous," Harry bleated. "Can you get her out of there?"

"No, Harry," Edward declined. "She's upset about Beetle, and besides, I'm not about to do your dirty work. I happen to like her."

"What?"

"That's right. And I feel bad for her … the way you've treated her."

"Trust me," Harry confided, "she's manhandled me more than I've manhandled her."

"Poor baby," Edward answered sarcastically, completely unsympathetic to Harry's dilemma.

◆

"Are those kids still asleep?" Harry asked as Edward met him at the door.

"I haven't heard a peep. Are you sure they're even here? Maybe they got up early and went for a hike?"

Harry shook his head. "This is their first time in Phoenix. They wouldn't know where the trails are."

"What's there to know?" Edward said, looking out onto the front patio. "You just walk out the door."

Lil's voice called out from the kitchen. "Is that you, Harry?"

The voice sent chills through Harry's body. "You couldn't get rid of her? I'm not in the mood for this. It's been a hard morning. You told her about Beetle!"

"I did."

"And she's still here? How can she be so insensitive?"

Edward eyed Harry. "I can't imagine where she might have learned that."

"Not from me," Harry said angrily. "I'm just a sex toy."

Edward pulled back and laughed. "You'd better get hold of yourself. You're beginning to lose touch with reality."

Lil emerged from the kitchen, a cup of coffee in hand. "So, you're afraid to face me."

"Lil," Harry stammered, "of course not." He hung back from the threshold.

"Harry, I'm so sorry about Beetle. Really. And maybe this isn't the best time—but why don't you be a man? I'm not going to dissolve right in front of your eyes. I haven't gotten this far in life by not facing the truth. You don't find me attractive? I'm not the right style for you? You'd like someone taller? With a larger bust? A brunette, perhaps?"

Harry looked over at Edward, who was staring at Lil. He had an astonished expression on his face.

"You think you can do better," Lil finally blurted out in an angry tone.

"Do you see what I have to put up with?" Harry said to Edward. "She doesn't get it. Didn't you tell her?"

Edward rolled his eyes.

"Tell me what?" Lil insisted on knowing. "Tell me what, Harry Aldon?"

"That I'm," and Harry swallowed hard, "bisexual." And as the word left his mouth he felt a sudden relief to have gotten it out. "I'm bisexual, Lil. That's the answer."

"Barely," Edward mouthed.

"I heard that," Harry snapped. "I don't know whether I'm a 4 or a 7 on that ridiculous Kinsey scale. But I know I'm not a 1 or a 10."

"Oh, Harry," Edward said, disappointment in his voice. "You're not the first gay man to ever fall in love with a woman. Ask the men who've fallen for Liza Minnelli. She's had her share."

"Don't be ridiculous," Harry answered. "Those men *were gay*."

"And, darling," Edward intoned, "that's *exactly* my point."

"But wait," Lil interjected. "There was no denying the chemistry between us."

"Oh, Lil," Harry moaned as a cab pulled into Harry's driveway.

"Who the hell is this?" Lil asked, eyeing the cab. "Another playmate?"

Harry strained his neck to see. "I have no idea. I'm not expecting anyone."

"Yes," Lil cracked. "You're just a victim of circumstances."

◆

Harry watched as an older, red-headed woman, stepped out of the cab. "Who on earth is that?" he said to no one in particular.

Standing at his open threshold, Lil and Edward just inside, Harry on the outside, he waited as the woman approached. "Can I help you?" he asked, unnerved by how complicated this was all becoming.

"Harry?" She eyed him suspiciously, a winter coat in her arms. "I'd have thought you would have remembered me?"

"Yes …" Harry replied politely, until he suddenly recognized the face. "Holy crap. Not you!"

"You have my granddaughter," the woman announced to

the threesome in a regal tone. "I'm Rita Goldenbaum. Rikki's grandmother."

Harry stood back on his heels. "Richard's mother," he said in a tone of shock.

Rita held her head high. "Yes. Elle and Richard were my children."

"Holy crap," Harry said. "After all these years, you dare to show your face here."

"I have cause," she reminded him. "You have my minor grand-daughter in your home. So, before you start a war on your doorstep, I'd suggest you invite me in. Otherwise, I'll call the police and tell them a deviant has kidnapped my underage granddaughter. A sexual pervert of the lowest order. *A homosexual.*"

◆

"Well, aren't *you* a touch of frostbite?" Edward said sarcastically, as Rita pressed her way through the door. "Harry is not a pedophile."

"Lord knows," Lil backed Edward up. "He wouldn't have the time or the energy for it."

Harry glowered at the two. "Well, thank you," he said to Edward and Lil. "I appreciate the support."

"Where is my granddaughter?" Rita interjected as she looked about the front hall.

Harry stepped inside. "She's in the guest room, apparently still sleeping."

"I want to see her now," Rita instructed. "Right now."

Harry led her down the hallway. "She's staying in my guest room. Right over here." He gently knocked on the door.

"Out of my way," Rita said as she pushed him aside and opened the door. She let out a howling scream.

Harry rushed to the door as Lil and Edward, just a few steps away, came up from behind to peek inside.

"Good morning, Rita," Rikki said as she gathered the white blanket about her bare chest.

"What are you doing?" Rita shouted, as Barney slipped under the covers.

"This is Barney. He's a good friend."

Barney stuck his head out of the blanket and smiled. His dimples practically lit up the room.

"So I see," said Rita, full of bluster. "So I see."

15

"This is outrageous," Rita ranted, pacing back and forth in Harry's foyer as Lil, Edward, and Harry listened. "And you're the one to blame for this," she said wagging a finger in Harry's face. "This is all your fault."

"*My* fault?" Harry could hardly believe the nerve of Rita. Showing up at his house uninvited and expecting him to take the blame for what was clearly *her problem*. "Listen, lady," he shouted, voice at full pitch, "I just met them yesterday. They had separate rooms. I made that clear. It's not my job to lock them in. Perhaps you should have done a better job of keeping Rikki at home. She tells me that she's been traveling with Barney all week. One week! And where the hell were you? Did you call the police? Did you do anything?"

Rita's complexion went ashen. "I didn't know ..." she stammered. "How could I? She was supposed to be visiting Toledo with a friend."

Harry wasn't about to let it go. "Did you ever speak to the parents of the *friend*? Did you even check in with them anytime during the week?"

"Now, why would I do that? I trust my granddaughter," Rita quickly blurted out.

Harry gave her a long hard look. "Yes. And so did I."

Rita took a breath. "Oh, God," she said, staring off into the distance, seemingly taking responsibility. "What have I done? What is happening?"

"Why don't you sit down?" Lil recommended. "Let's all sit down," she said, looking at Harry and Edward as if asking for permission.

"Come on, honey," she said to Rita. "There's some coffee in the kitchen."

Harry ran a tongue across his bottom teeth as he and Edward followed the women into the kitchen. *I need to get all these people the hell out of my house,* he thought, as he longed for peace and quiet. *This is why I live alone. All this drama.*

"Harry, get us a cup of coffee," Lil suggested, nodding in Rita's direction as she sat down next to her at the table.

Harry started to obey, moving to the cabinet to grab a mug, not sure why he had to be the one waiting on the old battle-axe, before Edward intercepted him. "I've got this," he offered. Harry mouthed a silent *thank you.*

"Harry, don't you think you should introduce us?" Lil recommended, as Edward poured from the pot.

Harry looked at the three people in his kitchen. A feeling of sheer nausea gripped him. His worlds had collided; his thirties spent with Richard; his on-again, off-again dalliance with Edward; his indiscretion with Lil. He felt exposed, humiliated, wishing he could just evaporate.

"Well," Lil nudged him along as he stood with his mouth agape.

"I really don't know where to begin," Harry said, gaining his composure. "Rikki and Barney, the two we just met in the guest room, arrived yesterday morning on my doorstep. Two teenagers on their own. Completely out of the blue. And Rikki wanted to know all about her family. Her dead Uncle Richard. Her dead mother. And even about *you,*" he said, looking at Rita. "Don't you ever talk to that girl?"

"Of course I do," Rita defended herself.

"Well then, maybe you should think about *what you're not saying.* She seems to have an awful lot of questions."

Rita pursed her lips. Harry was reminded of a photo he had seen of Sitting Bull in a history book when he was a kid.

"And this is Lil. You two have already met," he said to Edward. "She lives a few doors down. Bossy little thing. In fact, I can't ever seem to get through to her. Whenever I try, she plows right over me. Lil,"

Harry asked, "when was the last time that you listened to what anyone was saying to you? I know you hear the words... but do you get the meaning?"

Lil burst forth with a loud "Harry! That isn't very nice."

"And this young man serving us coffee today is Edward. I'm afraid I've done him a great disservice. While Edward has been my editor for many years, I've pretty much kept him at bay. I think he might actually be in love with me, but I wasn't sure how I felt about him until last night. You see, I'm a big dope," and Harry took a deep breath. "Last night, my beloved Beetle died, and as he lay limp in my arms, I realized how very much I needed Edward. Not as my editor, though God knows my books haven't been selling like they should, but as a real partner. Someone in my life."

Edward smiled warmly as Harry reached out and grabbed his hand.

Rita gasped. "Disgusting."

"Rita," Harry answered, "the only thing disgusting in this room right now is you."

◆

"So, what's the plan?" Lil asked Rita.

"I'm taking my granddaughter out of here as soon as she's dressed."

"And you think this is the end of it?" Harry asked.

"I don't know what you mean," Rita answered indignantly.

Lil glanced at Harry and then back to Rita. "Do you think your granddaughter will just go home with you right now?"

"Don't bother." Harry directed his words to Lil. "There's no point in trying to reason with her. She clearly hasn't learned a thing. She's doing the same thing to Rikki that she did to her son and daughter."

A new voice entered the mix. A younger voice. Unbeknownst to the adults, who were immersed in their own conversation, Rikki had entered the room with Barney in tow. "What did she do to my mother and uncle?"

Harry bit his lip as he turned to see the two teenagers.

"Go on," Rikki goaded him. "I want to know. You have to tell me."

"Actually," Edward chimed in, addressing Harry, "I'd like to hear this, too. Maybe it might explain why you're so damn hard to reach at times."

Harry leaned against the kitchen counter, bracing himself. "She shuts people out. If they don't behave exactly as she wants, she closes everything down. She shut Richard out because he was gay. She was too proud to have a gay son. Too scared what people might think of her."

"That isn't true," Rita insisted. "That isn't true!"

"Then why did you reject him?"

Rita gasped, "I couldn't deal with him. I never could. He thought he was superior. Smarter than me. And he was," she said, pleading as she made her case to the group in the kitchen. "And then, when he told me he was gay, it was like I'd finally found something to justify my feelings. A reason to not like him. I was glad. For all his superior behavior…I was glad. You see, I didn't like him. Is that a terrible thing to admit? I didn't like my own child," Rita cried, between large gulps of air. "And then when he got sick, I couldn't be there. I couldn't," she sobbed, bending over till her head touched the table. "I was scared. So scared. And it was too late to do anything. I'd been such a terrible mother."

Rikki came up to Rita. She placed a hand on her grandmother's shoulder. There was silence as all eyes focused on Rita as she composed herself, slowly sitting up once again, straight in the seat, a hand reaching up to cover Rikki's hand.

"And Elle. You told Elle not to visit," Harry reminded her.

Rita lifted a fist that held a crumpled napkin. "I never told my daughter what to do."

"But you made it impossible for her, didn't you? She loved Richard, but you didn't want them to be close. You got in the middle of their relationship."

"No," Rita insisted. "Never."

"Then why didn't Elle go to the hospital? Why did Richard die without his sister by his side? Why did I go through all of that alone? Only Richard and me?"

Edward's expression shifted. He appeared visibly moved. "Oh, God, Harry. You were all alone?"

Rita defended herself. "She was scared. It was 1989. No one knew what the hell was going on and she'd just found out she was pregnant. She didn't want to risk catching AIDS. How could she risk her life? The life of a baby growing inside of her? It wasn't fair to ask her to see him. If he hadn't been gay, it would never have happened," Rita screeched. "It was his fault. He was the one to blame. Don't you see? It was *all Richard's fault.*"

Rikki pulled away from her grandmother. "His fault?"

"Yes," Rita pleaded. "What's wrong with you people?" she asked as she looked about the room. "I wasn't the one who made him sick. I wasn't the one who made him into a homosexual."

Harry glared at her. Lil held a hand over her mouth in seeming disbelief. Edward looked away. Barney crossed his arms as he joined Harry, leaning against the kitchen counter.

"Well, I didn't," Rita continued. "It's always the mother, isn't it? We're always the one to blame. Where the hell was his father?"

"Seymour was dead," Harry interjected. "The man died years ago. And besides, no one's blaming you."

"Yes, they are. Everyone is blaming me," she gasped. "*I'm* blaming me," she finally admitted, shoulders stooped, a look of total defeat on her face.

"Is that why you erased him from our lives?" Rikki asked. "Is that why there are no pictures of him?"

Rita offered no answer. Just a blank stare.

"And my mother. What happened to my mother?"

Harry held his hands in the air, sensing the need for privacy between Rikki and Rita. "Okay, the show's over for today," he said as he ushered Lil and Edward out of the room, leaving Barney. "We don't all need to hear this. Let's leave them be."

◆

Rita looked over at Barney. "Does he really need to be here?"

"Yes," Rikki answered as she looked over her shoulder and smiled back at him. "I want him to hear this."

Rita struggled to find the words to begin. "This is very difficult for me," she started, tears welling in her eyes. "I know what you must think of me. I'm hard. Very hard. But life's made me that way. I wasn't always like this. I was once gentle, like you," she said to her grand-daughter, as she looked into Rikki's trusting eyes. "Just like you. But that was so long ago."

"So, tell me," Rikki said. "Tell me why you've kept so much from me."

"Because none of it is very nice to tell," Rita admitted. "When I was a girl, I loved *Sleeping Beauty. Cinderella.* Stories with happy endings. I was too naive for my own good."

Rikki nodded. "I can't quite imagine you as a young girl."

"Oh, I was," Rita assured her, a softness in her eyes. "I was. And as I grew up, I learned a lot." The expression on Rita's face hardened. "Things were not exactly as I imagined. And then I got married. Had a family. More disappointment. But I always loved your mother. She meant the world to me. And no matter what happens, you need to know that the day your mother died, my world stopped. It was as if God was punishing me. Maybe because I was so mean to your uncle." She nodded. "And I was," she said, accepting responsibility. "But to take away Elle, that was too much. Too cruel," she said.

"But I still don't know what happened," Rikki said. "How did she die?"

◆

Lil and Harry faced each other in the hallway, Edward by Harry's side. "Lil, I'm so very sorry about all this," Harry said. "I should have been clearer."

Lil gazed up at Harry as if seeing him truly for the first time. "Well, I shouldn't have pushed so hard. I always do. Pushing seems to be my way."

"Maybe if I wasn't such an idiot, you'd have known to stop."

"Oh, Harry, don't be so hard on yourself," Lil said. "It wasn't like you were my perfect match. Far from it. And you weren't that terrific in bed. Believe me," she said, smiling over at Edward, "I've had better. I guess I just missed having someone around. And since you were around," she said, glancing back at Harry, "I decided to pick on *you*."

"So, then you'll be all right?" Harry asked.

Lil's eyes flashed. "Be all right? This bisexual thing really threw me off my game. I just didn't understand what the hell was going on. Now that I know, well, Harry, maybe we can be friends," she said giving his shoulder a hard push. "There are plenty of old goats like you hanging around waiting for a gorgeous gal like me."

Harry offered a disbelieving look. "You're still hurt, aren't you?"

"Well, I am," Lil admitted. "No girl likes to be rejected. And certainly not when she's competing with a man. But at least," she said, smiling again at Harry, "I wasn't in love with you. And Edward is kind of sweet." This elicited a smile from Edward. "I just hope," she said, directing her comment to Edward, "that you're here to stay. If not, I might come knocking on Harry's door again. It gets lonely at night, if you know what I mean."

Edward laughed. "Well, I think I'll be able to work remotely from here. Of course, I'll need to wrap some things up in New York."

Lil smiled. "Well, then, I'll see you around," she said as she turned and walked out the door.

"She's nice," Edward said.

◆

Rita sighed. "You still don't remember, do you?"

"No," Rikki admitted. "Every now and then I have a flash of a memory, an inkling. But I'm not sure. It's not very clear."

Rita bristled. "I never wanted you to know what happened. Those doctors all told me I was wrong. That slowly the memories would flood back. But I said, '*Why should she be hurt? Why should she have to suffer? Isn't there enough pain to go around without her having to suffer?*'"

"I need to know," Rikki quietly said. "You can't protect me forever."

"I tried," Rita admitted. "I did everything in my power to stop the memories. First, I went to Michigan. You were in the hospital so I stayed at the house. Evelyn was with me all the time. And then, I thought about taking you home. I knew we had to leave Michigan. I couldn't risk it. I had to take you back to Queens. And I didn't want you struggling with all those memories. So I took your mother's paintings down—put them all in storage. It nearly killed me—but I did it. You don't remember the day I took you out of the hospital, do you?"

Rikki didn't.

"The doctors said it was too soon, but I didn't care. And when Evelyn tried to contact us, I told her 'no.'" Rita jabbed the air with her finger. "'*You can't see my baby. I don't want anything hurting her ever again.*'"

"But I was in school. I got well."

"Yes, slowly. It was the beginning of the New Year and I enrolled you in school. You still couldn't quite remember anything about your mother, but otherwise you seemed fine. You were talking again. Reacting to your surroundings. And I thought the routine was good for you. You'd finally come out of that terrible stupor. And then you came back to yourself. No worse for wear. Really. No one would have ever known you'd been in a psychiatric hospital. No one. You seemed perfectly normal."

"But I had no memory of my mother. I still don't."

"Yes, which is why I put that picture in your room. The one from high school. It was your mother when she was a young girl. When our lives were perfect. Before"—Rita hesitated—"before the world started to catch up to her. When she was still safe."

◆

"You were with Evelyn that morning," Rita started. "You should have been in school, but Evelyn had let you stay home."

"*Glitter,*" Rikki remembered. "I'd begged her to take me to see the movie. She was horribly embarrassed."

"She should have been," Rita emphasized. "Imagine, listening to a girl of eleven. That Evelyn is so irresponsible."

Evelyn's voice played in Rikki's head. *Your mother's going to kill me. First, you talk me into taking you to see that horrible movie and now I've allowed you to skip school. I'm going to tell your mother that I was afraid you were getting a cold.*

"Yes, I do remember," Rikki said. "I do." She closed her eyes and could see Evelyn standing against the kitchen counter, a cup of coffee in her hand. Rikki heard herself speak. "But we're having so much fun. It's like being best girlfriends."

"Don't you just love it?" Evelyn said in a silky tone. "Having this time together with you is so wonderful. I swear, Rikki Goldenbaum. I am going to steal you away. Your mother will never know what happened."

It was all playing back in Rikki's head. She could hear Evelyn. She could hear herself. She was remembering.

Evelyn turned on the small television that sat on the kitchen counter. "Now, my darling, what would you like for breakfast? We have raisin bran, oatmeal, and for you, I bought a box of Fruit Loops."

The television screen slowly came into focus as Evelyn retrieved a bowl from the cabinet and filled it with the Fruit Loops. On the television screen, there was a building on fire. Smoke rose from the structure as Evelyn poured milk into Rikki's cereal bowl.

"Evelyn, look." Rikki pointed at the screen. "What's going on?"

The milk overflowed as Evelyn turned to the television. "Oh, my God," she said, as she put the carton down and adjusted the volume. "What in the world is happening?"

Rikki got up from the table to get a closer view.

Evelyn put an arm about Rikki's shoulder just as a plane suddenly appeared, crashing into the adjacent building, sending a fireball into the air. Evelyn screamed as she pulled Rikki closer.

"*A second plane has just flown into the Twin Towers,*" came the voice of the CNN announcer.

Evelyn clutched her throat. "Oh, my God!"

Rikki stepped back, fear spreading through her entire body. "Is that New York City?"

"Yes," Evelyn answered as Rikki watched the image of two buildings smoking and burning.

"What's going on?" Rikki shouted.

"I don't know," Evelyn answered. "I don't know."

◆

"I was with Evelyn that morning." Rikki said again, but now as a statement of fact.

"Yes," Rita acknowledged. "Your mother was working in Manhattan. You were staying with Evelyn."

"And then my mother called," Rikki said as if in a daze. "She called me."

"You were the only one on her mind."

Rikki listened. She could hear the static on the other end of the line. "I remember now," she told Rita. "I remember," she repeated as she looked into her grandmother's frightened eyes. "I remember," Rikki said quietly.

◆

"Rikki, darling, sweetheart? This is Mommy." Elle gasped for breath.

"Is she all right?" Evelyn asked Rikki, as she hovered nearby.

"Mommy, where are you?"

Elle looked up. "I'm in an office building in Manhattan, darling."

"Mommy..."

"I don't want you to worry, baby. I'm okay. I'm going to get out of here. Do you hear me? I'm going to be home with you soon."

"But Mommy, we can see the fire," Rikki cried as CNN repeatedly played the image of the second plane hitting the twin towers. "Mommy, you've got to come home!" she cried.

"I know, baby," Elle wheezed. "I will. I just wanted to hear your voice. And tell you how very much I love you."

"Mommy …" Rikki was wracked by tears as Evelyn took the phone, pulling Rikki closer, as Rikki pressed her ear to the shared receiver.

"Elle, are you okay? What's happening?"

"I don't know. I just got here when the first plane hit. I should have left then, but I had this meeting, and everyone thought it was an accident in the South Tower. I wanted to leave, but instead, like a fool, I watched in horror at what was going on across the way, and then …" Elle took a deep breath, "there was another plane. It hit below. Somewhere below. The explosion threw me to the floor. I've hurt my arm."

"Oh, my God, Elle."

"Evelyn, I'm not sure I'm going to get out of here," Elle barely whispered.

Rikki screamed.

"You will, Elle. I'm sure of it."

"I don't know," Elle admitted. "Put Rikki back on. I have to hear her voice."

"Mommy, I love you!" Rikki cried.

"I love you too, baby. Now, make sure you mind Evelyn. Listen to her."

"I will, Mommy, but please come home."

"I will, darling … I will," Elle said with certainty.

And then there was a deep rumbling, followed by an explosion. The line went dead. Rikki screamed, "Mommy! Mommy!" as she and Evelyn watched on CNN as the North Tower of the World Trade Center imploded with astonishing speed.

◆

"By the time I got to Michigan, you'd been hospitalized. You'd stopped speaking. Shock. You completely shut down," Rita said, as she took her granddaughter's hands in hers. "I made up my mind. I'd already lost two children. I was not about to lose another."

Harry stood by the open door. Rita looked up, noticing his presence. "I may not have been much good as a mother, but I was going to make damn sure that my granddaughter survived. I owed that much to her mother. And, in a way, to Richard, too. You see, you're his namesake, and I had so much making up to do. So much," Rita repeated, shaking her head. "I'd been a selfish, foolish woman. I know that now. My first thought had always been about myself," she admitted. "You were my chance to make it all right."

Rikki withdrew her hands. "Then why didn't you help me? Why didn't you talk to me?"

Rita looked at Harry as she answered. "Because some people are unable to change their nature. And my nature is to run from things that are unpleasant. I don't like to see what I don't want to know."

Harry nodded.

"But I promise, from now on, I'll change. You may need to help me," Rita said as Rikki moved in for a hug. "Now, as for you, young man …" Rita turned her attention to Barney. "How did you happen to find yourself in my granddaughter's bed?"

Harry interjected. "I'd like to hear that explanation."

Barney shifted nervously. "Nothing really happened," he swore, hand in the air. "We just fell asleep."

Rikki pulled away from Rita.

"Nothing happened?" Rita asked.

"I was too scared," Rikki admitted, blushing.

Harry exhaled.

"Are you sure?" Rita probed one more time, glancing at Barney and then back to Rikki. Both heads nodded affirmatively.

"Nothing," Barney repeated.

"Well, good," Rita said. "Thank God for small wonders."

◆

Harry gently knocked on the guestroom door. "Rikki, are you ready?"

"Yes," Rikki said, as she appeared in the doorway, her face glowing. Her thick brown hair, freshly washed, was pulled away from her face, revealing brown eyes that seemed to sparkle.

"You look wonderful," Harry said, amazed at the transformation. "Lighter, easier."

"A shower and a change of clothes will do that," Rikki answered as she turned to lift her knapsack off the bed. Her roller bag stood nearby.

"Can we talk for a moment?" Harry asked, nodding for Rikki to take a seat.

"Sure," she said, as she sat down on the edge of the bed.

"Barney and Rita are helping Edward load the car," Harry started as he searched for exactly the right words. "Your flight leaves in two hours."

"Yes, I know," Rikki answered as her eyes focused on him. "I'm so sorry about Beetle."

Harry nodded.

"Is there something you want to tell me?" she asked, her tone serious. "Something else I should know?"

Harry rubbed his forehead. "I'm afraid I'm just not very good at this," he admitted, as he studied the worried expression on the teen's face. "It would be so much easier for me to write this down. Easier, if you were a character in a novel. Then I'd be able to tell you anything."

She cocked her head. "This sounds serious."

Harry's eyes glistened. "We have something very important in common," he said. "I loved your uncle very much. And, had Richard lived, you would have been my niece. We'd have been family."

Rikki bit her lip. "I've thought about that."

Harry rubbed his nose with his thumb. "Do you think that there's any way you might consider … I mean could we … somehow … only if you wanted to … stay connected? Remain friends?"

Rikki broke into a smile. It was Richard's smile. "Why, of course," she said with delight as she stood up and offered Harry a hug. "I was hoping that we might."

"Good," Harry said.

Edward's voice carried from down the hallway "Come on, Harry. Let's get a move on. I've got the bags in the car."

"We're coming," Harry hollered back. "Just another second." He took Rikki's hands in his as he admired her lovely face. "It would really mean a lot to me," he said, giving her hands a gentle shake.

"Lord," Edward sighed, as he stood in the doorway. "Harry, you are the slowest person I've ever met."

"Yes," Harry said, putting an arm about Rikki's shoulder and pulling her in for a final hug. "It's taken me a lifetime to find Rikki, and now that I have, I won't be letting her go."

◆

Rikki waved to Edward as the car pulled away from the curb. Rita, seated next to her, had directed Barney to sit up front with Harry. "A little distance might do you two some good," she said as Barney followed her command.

Rikki leaned her head against the passenger window as the car made its way out of the Arizona Biltmore, turning onto 24th street and passing a jogger. *My poor mother*, Rikki thought as Macy's in the Biltmore Fashion Park came into view. Now the living, breathing, essence of Elle seemed forever tied to the horrible circumstance of her death.

Rita reached over and gently squeezed Rikki's hand. Rikki wondered if her grandmother had read her mind. Were these the same thoughts that had troubled Rita? Was this the pain her grandmother had wanted to shield her from?

As the car merged onto AZ-51, Rikki's thoughts drifted to Harry and her uncle. She didn't understand why her mother had not gone to the hospital or why Rita had so many issues with her son. That all seemed too complicated and overwhelming for her to think about. For now, she'd found a connection to Richard through Harry. Perhaps that was good enough.

"Hey, check this out," Barney yelled over the roar of engines, stretching his neck to catch a better view as an airplane passed overhead, coming in low for a landing at Phoenix Sky Harbor. "Wow."

"Wow, indeed," Rita said sarcastically. "Stop distracting the driver," she scolded Barney.

"I'm fine," Harry assured her as the shadow of the jet passed over the car.

In the momentary shifting of the light, Elle's face flashed. Rikki had tripped and gashed her knee. They were together in the bathroom back in the Michigan house. Rikki, propped up on the toilet seat, Elle leaning down dabbing at the wound with ointment before applying a Band-Aid. "There's my brave girl" Elle said as she examined her handy work. "Now you're ready to face the world," Elle's voice so sweet, so tender, Rikki couldn't help but smile at the memory.

"She'll always be with you," Rita suddenly said.

Rikki glanced over at her grandmother.

There was a tear in Rita's eye. "Trust me. I know."

Rikki nodded. Despite the pain, she'd found Elle, met Harry, and reconnected with Evelyn. And her feelings for Barney had blossomed. She took a deep breath. It had been a journey worth taking. A journey she was certain never to forget.

Did You Enjoy Reading *After the Fall*?

Then please:

1. Rate the novel on a retail site like Amazon.com

2. Join Brad Graber's email list at **bradgraber.com** and receive his blog: *There, I Said it!*

3. Consider giving it as a gift to friends and family

4. Recommend the book to your local book club

5. Mention you loved the book on your social media platform. Use the hashtag *#AftertheFall*

6. Write a review on your blog

7. Follow Brad Graber on social media: Twitter **@Jefbra1** and **Like** Brad Graber's Facebook page

And most importantly—don't give away the ending!

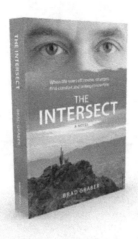

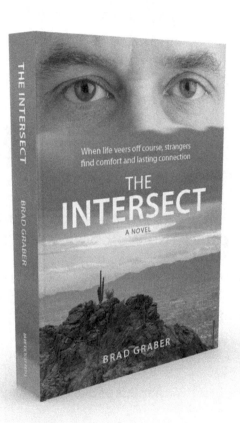

When life veers off course, strangers
find comfort and lasting connection

THE
INTERSECT

A NOVEL

BRAD GRABER

1

US Airways Flight #610 took a sharp bounce, jostling Dave Greenway in his seat. It was the 6:00 a.m. flight out of San Francisco to Phoenix. The scent of freshly brewed coffee wafted through the first-class cabin as he planted his size tens firmly on the floor beneath him, hoping against hope, to stabilize the Airbus 320.

It didn't work.

The plane took another nasty hop.

As Dave struggled to hold his cup steady, coffee splashed everywhere. "Dammit, I knew that was going to happen," he muttered, his hand soaked as he downed the last of the liquid.

Again, the plane bucked hard.

A woman nearby let out a muffled cry. Everyone else fell dead silent. An elderly gentleman emerged from the first-class restroom, zipper down, a surprised look on his face, the front of his khakis wet. As he stumbled to his seat, the unlatched door swung freely. A stewardess jumped up to secure it, balancing herself precariously with one hand on the cockpit door.

Perfect, Dave thought, turning a ghostly white. He pulled his seat belt tighter. *We leave earthquake country and die in a plane crash.*

Seated beside him, his partner Charlie nudged him with an elbow. "It's just a little turbulence," he said confidently. "There's nothing to worry about. Hey, check this out." He held up an old issue of *People* that he'd lifted from the airplane magazine rack. Ryan Reynolds offered a seductive stare.

"Very nice," Dave said dryly, still unnerved by the plane's erratic motion. He searched Charlie's angular face for any sign of tension. "How can you be so calm?"

"Thermal inversion," Charlie said, as he returned to perusing the magazine. "It happens over the desert. If you're scared, just look down at your sweater."

For the big travel day, Dave had worn his favorite black pullover, purchased on a whim at a Greg Norman sale. It contrasted nicely with the silver coursing through his mostly dark hair which he wore conservatively parted on the side. The cotton/poly blend with a zippered collar at the neck, sported the signature shark logo encircled by Norman's motto—*Attack Life*—an attitude Dave admired. Dave loved the primary colors of the shark logo and wondered if it was the designer's nod to the rainbow flag.

The plane jumped side-to-side. Dave gripped the armrests.

"There's no point freaking out," Charlie said, still reading, oblivious to the motion, the dark-grey wispy curls atop his head indifferent to Dave's need for order. "Think of it like riding a roller-coaster. Go with the flow. Tensing up only creates sore muscles."

Dave tried to relax. If Charlie was so blasé, there couldn't be any real danger. After all, Charlie had logged hundreds of thousands of air miles. "I take paradise and put up a parking lot," he'd told Dave when they'd met some twenty years earlier at a Human Rights Campaign Fund Dinner. Dave had returned a blank stare as Charlie, tall, tanned, and dapper in a black tux, explained that he worked with developers on site locations for new stores. Since then, Dave had watched Charlie ricochet around the country, providing market research to support trade area development for retailers, investment banks, and anyone who needed predictive sales modeling.

Charlie closed the *People* magazine. He looked over at Dave. "March is really a great time to move to Phoenix. The weather's ideal. And I can finally say goodbye to all those flight delays at SFO. *No more morning fog.*" He practically sang the last few words.

The motion of the plane calmed as Dave assumed Charlie's joyous mood. "No more jumbo mortgage on that tiny Mill Valley house we once called home."

Charlie's hazel green eyes lit up. "Good riddance to those break-the-bank California taxes."

"Adieu to the rain that arrives in November and stays until April. And a fond farewell to those outrageous gasoline prices."

Charlie smiled. "We're going to save a shitload of money."

"We will," Dave agreed as the plane unexpectedly lost altitude. Dave's gut pressed hard against the seat belt. A second later, his bottom reunited with the cushion, and the mood turned serious. "Beware the Ides of March," he mumbled.

"What the hell does that mean?" Charlie asked, perplexed by the ominous reference.

Dave had no trouble explaining. He'd already given it considerable thought. "Gay people flock to San Francisco. Everyone wants to live in the Bay Area. And here we're leaving. And tomorrow, March 15th of all days, I start my new job."

Charlie sought a positive spin. "With scientists predicting *the next big one*, we'd have been crazy to stay. If our home had been destroyed in an earthquake, we'd have still been on the hook to pay off that huge mortgage."

"True," Dave said, impressed by Charlie's ability to turn the argument. "An earthquake is a terrific strategy to minimize overcrowding in the Bay Area," Dave laughed. "But moving to Arizona ... *a red state?*"

"How do you think red states turn blue?" Charlie's eyes twinkled. "Pioneers like us. One day we'll look back and say, remember when Arizona was red?"

Dave relented. "I guess that's one way to look at it."

"Sure. And there's a large gay community in Phoenix." Charlie reached down and retrieved his black leather briefcase. Unzipping the front pocket, he pulled out a full-color *Phoenix Homes* magazine. "You have to check out these properties," he said thumbing through the pages. "I've already hooked up with a realtor to show us around."

"Show *you* around," Dave corrected. "I'll be in the office tomorrow.

Physician practices need to be managed. From now on, my life will be one long operations meeting, physicians in the morning, physicians at night."

"Well, you took the lead in getting us settled in the Bay Area when we left Michigan. Now it's my turn. God knows I'll have plenty of time. With credit frozen, consumer spending down … retail's in such a deep slump. Last Christmas was a real bust. I don't think 2010 will be much better. I should have plenty of time to get us set up. There's not much business on my plate at the moment."

Dave felt bad for Charlie. He'd worked so hard to build a successful business. "Well, Obama really pulled us back from the brink," Dave said, still uncertain that the worst of it was over.

"With so many Americans out of work, it's more like a depression than a recession," Charlie observed glumly. "But we should look on the bright side. With such high employment … you have a new job. That's freaking amazing."

"It feels really out of step," Dave agreed, still ambivalent about his good fortune. "Kind of unsettling."

"You're nuts. You should be ecstatic."

"I'm too on edge. I have all these crazy thoughts running through my head," Dave admitted, a nervous tingling shooting through his body.

Charlie gave Dave his full attention. "Tell me. I want to hear."

"It's ridiculous," Dave admitted, blushing. "It's too silly."

"Tell me," Charlie insisted. "I want to know."

Dave relented. He hoped Charlie would be understanding. "Okay. Take my car. It's black with a black interior."

"And?" Charlie asked, stifling a laugh.

Dave continued. "It gets brutally hot in Phoenix during the summer. Black retains the heat."

Charlie offered a huge smile. "You're kidding, right? You know you can't get incinerated driving to work." His voice dripped with sarcasm. "There's such a thing as air conditioning. And if it's a real problem, you'll trade that car in for a white one. Problem solved. What else?"

Dave hesitated.

"What else, what else?" Charlie probed, eager to hear the next concern.

Dave took a deep breath. "You know I'm susceptible to nosebleeds. It's dry in Arizona. I read on the Internet that it's the nosebleed capital of the world."

Charlie gave Dave a sidelong glance. "Now you're making that one up."

"I read it," Dave insisted.

"Your body will adjust," Charlie promised. "You'll be fine. So that's what's worrying you? Here I thought you had concerns about the job."

"I should have kept it to myself. Real men never share," Dave sharply remarked.

Charlie placed a hand on Dave's thigh and gave it a gentle squeeze. "Real men who love each other do. Why not look on the bright side? We'll have domestic partner benefits. For the first time, I can get health insurance through you. No more HMO. Hello, Blue Cross Blue Shield."

"Yeah, that is pretty progressive," Dave agreed, "And of all places… Arizona."

"That's what happens when you stop working for Catholic organizations."

"True."

"And the roof won't leak. It barely ever rains in Phoenix. And… get ready… here it comes… we can buy a *new house*. We could never afford that in the Bay Area."

Dave perked up. Images of Sub-Zeros, marble countertops, pebble-tech pools, and flagstone patios danced in his head. "A new house… wouldn't that be something?"

"We can do whatever we want," Charlie answered, once again opening the *People* magazine and flipping through the pages.

Dave looked over Charlie's shoulder. "My God," he said, pointing at a photo of Gilles Marini. "He looks a bit like you when you were young. You had the same five o'clock shadow and all that jet-black hair."

"I was hot," Charlie agreed. "But if I worked out like you," Charlie rubbed his tummy, "I'd probably drop these last ten pounds."

"Hey, I'm at the gym to manage stress," Dave emphasized, explaining his obsessive need to work out.

Charlie shot him a doubtful look. "Maybe you should try Xanax."

"No drugs," Dave pushed back. "I don't need them," he said, defending himself against what he felt were Charlie's hurtful accusations.

"Dave, there's no shame in medication."

Dave gave Charlie a piercing look. The conversation was over.

Charlie regrouped. "Well, I'm glad we took the first flight out. The sun will be coming up soon. We'll have all day to settle in, unpack, and go grocery shopping."

Dave shifted, stretching his arms overhead to ease the tightness in his lower back. "I hope we like living in Phoenix."

"We'll love it. And if it's any consolation, I'm proud of you. Not many men in their fifties would have the courage to take a new job. It's says a lot about you."

"That I'm an idiot," Dave said tongue-in-cheek, as he twisted about his finger the black onyx ring Charlie had given him years earlier.

Charlie shook his head. "No, you have faith in the future," he countered as the plane suddenly shook violently, the thrust so sharp, it caught both men off guard. Dave grabbed Charlie's hand as the yellow oxygen masks dropped, dangling just above their heads.

"Oh my God," Charlie said, his voice dead serious.

"It's just a little thermal inversion," Dave snapped as he slipped the plastic mask over his head, all the while trying to remember to breathe normally.

* * *

Daisy Ellen Lee was a fixture in her Biltmore Greens neighborhood. Spry and energetic, she attributed her vigor to the Phoenix climate. While others complained about the intense summer heat, Daisy likened herself to the mighty saguaro, the desert cactus that dotted the Arizona landscape. During the summer months the saguaro stood tall, defying the searing desert sun. Come the monsoon season, the prickly succulent miraculously budded, yielding an array of bright white flowers. Daisy admired the saguaro's resilience. If the saguaro was a survivor, then so was she.

Each morning, Daisy walked the gated community, part ambassador, part drill sergeant, undertaking the morning inspection of the grounds. She was barely five foot two, even with her blond bouffant teased to a fluffy fullness. Final Net held it perfectly in place. From a distance, in her green lululemon yoga attire, she resembled a yellow poppy on the march.

The exclusive neighborhood of Biltmore Greens abutted the grounds of the Arizona Biltmore Hotel, a five-star resort opened in 1929 and visited by United States presidents, the Hollywood elite, and foreign and national dignitaries. Designed in the architectural style of Frank Lloyd Wright, the Arizona Biltmore, and the developments that encircled the property were a much-desired address in Phoenix.

"Well, good Sunday morning. You're certainly up early," called out Sheila, who worked the midnight shift on the security gate. Her bright red hair was pulled tightly back from her moon-shaped face into a neatly knotted bun that rested at the back of her head just above the neck. The severity of her hairstyle matched her uniform of blue polyester pants and jacket, interrupted by a white cotton button-down shirt.

"I couldn't sleep," Daisy admitted, eyeing the broken concrete block on the base of the little gatehouse.

"Is anything wrong?" Sheila asked.

"When are they fixing that?" Daisy pointed at the offending block. She'd complained about it at the last Homeowner's Association meeting.

"Next Tuesday. I received the notice yesterday."

"Oh, that's good." Daisy gently nudged a loose stone back with her foot into the small rock garden that decorated the side of the gatehouse. "And how's your mother feeling? Is her back any better?"

"She's much better," Sheila answered.

"Oh, I'm so glad," Daisy said, checking the chalkboard on the side of the gatehouse. She didn't expect to see her name on the list of residents who had packages waiting to be picked up, but checking the board was as much a habit as retrieving the mail. She laughed at her own foolishness.

"And how are you feeling this morning?" Sheila asked.

"I awoke with such an unusual burst of energy," Daisy recalled. "So eager to greet all the flowers and shrubs and say hello to my four-legged friends. Silly, isn't it?"

Daisy adored the dogs of the Biltmore. Unlike Sheila, who knew every resident by name and house number, Daisy knew the neighbors through their dogs.

"And who have you seen so far?"

"I saw Jasmine go by with her two Dads. And Millie on her way to Starbucks at Fashion Mall with her folks."

"Lovely," Sheila said as the eastern sky started to brighten. "The sun will be up any minute. It's almost time for the shift change. Bert should be here soon."

Daisy repeated the weather forecast from the morning news. "It's going to be eighty-five with lots of sunshine."

A gentle breeze stirred the smell of orange blossoms. Both women inhaled and sighed.

"Spring is in the air," Daisy wistfully acknowledged. "Ah, another year older come May."

"I just hope when I'm seventy-five," Sheila said, "I look as good as you."

Daisy was pleased to see the admiration in the younger woman's eyes. "Yoga," Daisy declared. "Stretching is the best medicine. I'm going this afternoon to a hot yoga class."

"They have hot yoga for seniors?" Sheila asked in disbelief.

Daisy frowned. "It's not a seniors class," she said. "Why would I be in a seniors class?" It irked her that anyone would make such an assumption.

"Oh," Sheila said, seemingly unaware of her faux pas. "But aren't you uncomfortable ... can you keep up?"

"Absolutely. And I love young people. All tatted, like walking canvasses. You can learn a lot about them based on their artwork."

Sheila giggled.

Daisy bent down to retie a lace. "When you're young, there's so much to occupy your time. Jobs and school ... oh these young people come and go ... in such a rush to get to the *next place*. I'm practically standing still watching as life passes by. It can be a bit lonely."

Sheila looked astonished. "You ... lonely? I don't believe it. You always seem so active. Going to all those meetings for the Democratic Party. And the Breast Cancer Walks. And gathering signatures on the latest petition drive. My goodness. I don't know where you get the energy."

"Well, I do try to stay engaged and mentally sharp. Oh, but I get lonely. I've lost so many friends over the years. I almost hate to read the obituaries. And those poor souls who wind up in nursing homes ... that's the worst. I guess life's a crapshoot. You never know how it's going to end."

Unnerved by the conversation's sudden change in tone, Daisy decided to move on.

"Well, dear ... it was wonderful seeing you ... you have yourself a glorious day," she said sweetly, waving goodbye.

* * *

Charlie stood with Dave at the luggage carousel at Sky Harbor Airport. He placed his right foot on top of the of conveyor belt, staking out his territory as the other passengers crowded about.

"I can't believe the oxygen mask dropped," Dave said. He shook his head as if reimagining the entire fiasco. "That scared the shit out of me."

"Me too," Charlie admitted. "In all my years of flying, that's never happened."

Dave slipped out of his pullover. The change in climate from the Bay Area to Phoenix was already noticeable. "That last hard bounce must have tripped open the compartment."

"Did you see the look on the stewardess's face?" Charlie laughed, remembering the woman's frantic expression. "I thought she'd have a cow."

"Well, to her credit, she jumped right up and tried to close it."

"But you'd already put on the mask." Charlie roared with laughter, capturing the attention of nearby travelers. "Prepared to go down with the plane," he said, index finger in the air.

"Hey, there's nothing wrong with my reflexes," Dave defended himself, now standing behind Charlie. "In a real emergency, I'd have been breathing. You'd have been starved for oxygen."

"Small consolation. In a real emergency, I'd rather not know what's happening."

"Is that why you didn't put on the mask?"

"I couldn't," Charlie admitted. "My heart stopped."

They both laughed, grateful for the release of nervous energy on what was otherwise a stressful day.

"Well, it's all behind us now." Charlie placed his hands on his hips and gently twisted. "Damn those airplane seats." He spied the electronic board. "It's only 9:15. We did okay on time."

"I hope that flight wasn't a bad omen."

"Oh Dave, knock it off. Nothing good comes from a negative attitude. You know, you always *find what you're looking for*. Stop putting out negative vibes. Phoenix is a terrific place. There's culture, it's young and hip. Lots of bars and restaurants . . . we're going to love it."

Dave hated when Charlie lost his patience. "God, you sound like the freaking Chamber of Commerce."

"You've got to look on the bright side," Charlie lectured.

Dave nodded. "The bright side."

Charlie continued. "You've worked hard. We deserve this. In a month, you'll be comfortable in the new job. In three months, you'll feel like you've lived in Phoenix your whole life. Just give yourself time to adjust."

"I know," Dave answered. "I have to go easy."

"You do that," Charlie said as the luggage carousel came to life, "and I'll grab the bags."

* * *

Daisy pulled up to the Biltmore Greens gate in her red Honda Fit. She rolled down her window and greeted Bert who worked the morning shift.

"Bert, it's so good to see you. How are you feeling?"

Bert stepped out of the little gatehouse. "Much better, Ms. Lee. It's kind of you to ask. The doctor told me it was just a touch of sciatica."

"Oh, I'm so glad you're better," Daisy gushed. "I hear that's very painful. "

"Yes, it most certainly is," Bert answered, rubbing the affected leg.

"Well, it's wonderful to see you back."

"Thank you." Bert blushed. "Where are you heading this morning?"

Daisy's voice perked up. "Sprouts. They're having a big sale on pineapples. They're usually $3.99. Today, they're 99 cents," she whispered in a conspiring voice.

"That *does* sound like quite a sale."

"Would you like me to bring you back one?" Daisy offered.

"Frankly, Ms. Lee, pineapple makes me gassy. I think I'm better off sticking to protein bars."

Daisy had never had a protein bar. She wondered if she'd like it. "Is there anything you might need while I'm out?"

"You're too kind. Please don't bother about me. I'm just fine," Bert replied.

"Well, I better get going then. I'd hate to get caught in noontime traffic when church lets out."

"You have a few hours for that," Bert chuckled, checking his watch. "It's only ten o'clock now. "There's not a lot of traffic on a Sunday."

"But there's nothing worse than driving when the roads are crowded," Daisy confided. "People tailgate, honk their horn, wave wildly at me. I can see them in the rearview mirror. It's so distracting."

"Maybe you're driving too slowly?"

"Oh no, I'm a terrific driver," Daisy said indignantly. "I'm just cautious. My only problem is finding my car in the parking lot."

Bert frowned. "I had an aunt who got lost in a shopping mall. It was quite an ordeal for the family. She was diagnosed with early onset dementia."

"Oh dear, that's terrible. But it's not my memory that's the problem. It's the other cars. They dwarf my little Fit. Last week, my car was parked between a Ford Super Duty and a Chevy Silverado. My Fit looked like a clown car at the circus."

Bert chuckled. "That can certainly be a problem."

"Well, it was lovely seeing you, Bert. I better get on with the day."

"Enjoy the morning," Bert called.

Daisy stepped on the gas pedal and without yielding at the stop sign, brazenly pulled into the intersection, busy thinking about the best way to select a pineapple, by smell or by the ease in which leaves at the crown release. It was too late for her to stop when she finally became aware of the Allied Van Line truck, thanks to the driver leaning down hard on his horn. The squeal of metallic brakes was unmistakable.

* * *

"What do you think?" Dave asked Charlie as they looked about the furnished rental. The relocation company had arranged for the turnkey apartment with its faded beige carpet, old oak furniture, and white walls sporadically decorated with cheaply framed posters of desert landscapes. Dave thought it horribly ugly.

"It'll have to do," Charlie answered, "though I wish we'd talked before you agreed to this particular apartment."

"Why?" Dave asked. "They assured me every apartment is exactly the same. There's a second bedroom for your office. When they connect the Internet, you'll be all set to work. And it's close to shopping and the freeway. Besides, it's only temporary until you find us a house."

"Yes, but we face west." Charlie tapped on the window that looked out onto the community pool below. "That means intense afternoon sun. And with these cheap, single pane windows, it'll get nice and toasty."

"Oh geez, Charlie, I didn't even think about that." Dave was suddenly aware that the room was already on the warm side. He'd have to find the thermostat and turn on the air.

"Well, it's okay. We're here now." Charlie waved a hand, the sign that he was ready to make the best of it.

"How bad can it get?" Dave wondered, setting the thermostat at sixty-eight, upset that he hadn't asked for Charlie's input before he made the final arrangements.

"May is when the heat really ratchets up to triple digits."

There was a violent rumble above as the air conditioning unit situated on the roof jerked into action. A musty odor filled the room.

"Well that settles it," Dave announced. "We're going to have to be in a new house by May."

"Two months isn't a lot of time to find a place," Charlie warned, flopping down on the tan sofa. The expression on Charlie's face warned Dave that the cushions were hard. Charlie poked at the fake potted fern on the oak coffee table. "Are they kidding with this?" He held up the green plant by one of its floppy plastic leafs. "This thing weighs nothing."

"How hard can it be to find a place?" Dave called out as he opened the cabinets in the tiny galley kitchen, finding the glassware and dishes. "We're sitting on cash from our sale in California. We should be able to find a terrific house." He ran a finger over the white linoleum countertop. They'd need to purchase cleaning supplies. "Remember the homes you showed me in that real estate magazine?"

"Too far from your office," Charlie said, bending the plastic leaf on the fake cactus back and forth.

"But they're all new subdivisions," Dave remembered. Some of the houses appeared palatial.

"That's Chandler and Ahwatukee," Charlie answered, shaking the coffee table to determine which leg was loose.

"Awaa ... what?"

"Never mind. The Phoenix metropolitan area is huge. We'll need to find something closer to your office so that you don't spend your drive time in bumper-to-bumper traffic."

"Well, you'll find something." Dave was certain. "I have faith in you." He began loading the cheap ceramic dishes directly from the cabinet into the dishwasher. "When you're done over there," he said to Charlie, who was still playing with the coffee table, "how about stripping the bed? I think we better wash everything before we sleep on it."

Charlie checked his watch. "Okay, it's ten after ten now. I say we spend an hour or so working on this place, unpacking, and then head off to lunch."

Dave nodded. "You got a deal."

* * *

Daisy's forehead rested on a deployed airbag. She felt slightly nauseous from the adrenaline coursing through her body. The truck had slowed, and still, the Honda Fit had taken a hit to the passenger side. Daisy's body had jerked hard against the driver's side door before coming to rest. She'd heard a crack, like stepping on a branch in the forest. The sound had seemed to come from deep within her own body.

"Ma'am, are you okay? Please tell me you're okay." A man with a deep, gruff voice pleaded as he removed his Arizona Diamondbacks ballcap to reveal beads of sweat pouring from his brow. "I'll never forgive myself if you're dead."

"I'm not dead," Daisy finally confessed as she lifted her head, face flushed. "I'll be fine." She looked at the expression on the poor man's face and took pity on him. "I'm just a little stunned."

"Thank God," the man said, wiping his brow with the back of his hand. "You really should pay closer attention," he now scolded her. "When was the last time someone gave you a driving test? Jesus. You gave me the scare of a lifetime."

"Ms. Lee, are you okay?" Bert called, running up to the site of the collision, cell phone in hand, the 911 operator still on the line.

"She's fine," the truck driver answered, eyeing the damage to the car. "She's absolutely fine."

"Now you stay still," Bert advised. "The ambulance should be here any minute."

Daisy could hear the approach of emergency sirens. "Oh Bert," she softly said, "I don't need an ambulance." But when she tried to move, there was a gnawing pain in her left hip. She winced as the ache intensified.

"Now please, Ms. Lee. Don't move," Bert instructed as the first EMT approached. "I'm here with you. Don't you worry."

Daisy felt flush. "Oh Bert" were the last words she managed before everything went black.

* * *

Phoenix's well-trained EMTs surrounded the vehicle as Daisy came to. On a scale of one to ten, the pain was fifteen. Daisy cried out in agony as she was lifted from the car and placed on a stretcher. Any movement was sheer torture. The sharp, stabbing sensation in her left hip ruled every breath.

The ambulance ride was a blur.

At the hospital, a young emergency room physician, with blond wavy hair and an angelic smile, provided morphine. Daisy sighed as the drug, injected directly into her IV, immediately took effect. "Thank you," she said, her heart full of gratitude as the pain finally receded.

"While you rest," the doctor quietly advised, "we're going to schedule that hip for surgery."

"Oh dear," was all Daisy could muster. *Surgery is such serious business*, she thought, focusing her attention on the doctor's mouth, watching and waiting for his lips to once again move.

The doctor scanned Daisy's chart as he engaged her in light conversation "The paramedics said you were lucky. Your age … the nature of the accident … you could have been seriously hurt."

His comment rubbed her the wrong way. Adrenaline surged through her small frame and perhaps due to the morphine, she spoke sharply before thinking. "This isn't serious enough?"

The doctor pulled up a chair and sat beside her bed. "Ms. Lee, your broken hip was not a result of an auto accident," the doctor explained. "We see this all the time. A woman who presents as perfectly healthy suddenly falls to the ground. She thinks she's tripped. She hasn't. It's osteoporosis. The disease generates weak bones and in women of a certain age, fragile hips. You broke that hip in a seated position. It was primed to break."

Daisy could hardly believe her ears. She'd heard of osteoporosis, but she'd always thought such a condition was evidenced by poor posture. She hadn't realized that someone who stood perfectly straight could experience the effects in places other than the spine.

"It could have happened in the supermarket or in the privacy of your bathroom. You were lucky. There were people around. Have you spoken with your primary care physician about osteoporosis?" His warm blue eyes pressed her for an answer.

She folded her hands in her lap, fingers intertwined, like a schoolgirl, politely waiting for the teacher to reveal the day's lesson. "No," Daisy admitted. "I don't have a primary care doctor."

The young physician was unable to hide his surprise. His response was quick and abrupt. "And why is that?"

Daisy hesitated. She wondered if it might be rude to share her theory about doctors with a doctor. She'd always been a confident woman, and yet here, in this antiseptic environment, with everyone dressed in white coats and green scrubs, clearly knowledgeable about things she only guessed at, she reconsidered her opinions.

The young physician awaited her response.

She cleared her throat and lifted her chin slightly, believing a regal posture lent authority to her words. "I think doctors overmedicate seniors. For every complaint, they write a prescription. I don't believe in drugs. I don't think they're good for you. I think they bring on confusion in people my age." She paused and took a deep breath before continuing. "There's nothing in my medicine cabinet besides lipstick and face powder," she proudly boasted. "I've been healthy all my life. Why would I pay a doctor to search for problems where none exist?"

The doctor glared at her. She cringed. She'd angered him.

"Do you realize the risk you're taking? Osteoporosis is a serious condition that should be managed. And at your age, you need a family physician. I hope you've at least had an annual flu shot."

Daisy blushed. She'd passed on flu shots. What was the point? She never got sick.

The young doctor shook his head. He returned to the discussion at hand. "The orthopedic surgeon will stop by later. A counselor will also come by and make sure your paperwork is in order, including emergency contacts."

"Emergency contacts?" Daisy repeated.

"Ms. Lee, you're having surgery. It's a serious matter. We need to know who to talk with in case there's a problem."

"Oh my," Daisy fretted. "I really don't have anyone. My family is back east and we've lost touch."

"No children?"

"No," Daisy confirmed.

"Friends. You have friends?"

"Well, I did, but …" and Daisy stammered unable to complete the sentence. She was suddenly very tired.

The doctor bit his lower lip. Daisy wondered if he'd encountered her situation before. An older person admitted to the ER with no available next of kin. How many other seemingly alert, independent seniors found themselves alone during a health crisis?

He stood up. "Okay then. We'll have a social worker stop by. Don't worry about it," he said, leaning over and squeezing her hand.

It was a kind gesture. Daisy appreciated the change in his manner. If only she could remember his name. He must have told her, but then it seemed rude to ask again. Instead, she accepted his warmth and was grateful. Whatever his name, at least there was a heart behind that tough clinical exterior.

* * *

"Isn't this nice?" Charlie said, taking a deep breath and enjoying the fresh air. "We're sitting outside and eating lunch. The sun is shining, the sky is blue. It's not too warm. You can even see Camelback Mountain from here. It's Shangri-La."

The hour in the apartment had made Dave tense; now Charlie was trying to get him to relax, but it was difficult.

Dave nodded grudgingly. "It *is* wonderful."

"And after we eat and go to the grocery store, maybe we'll take a nap." Charlie lifted an eyebrow provocatively.

"We'll see," Dave answered. He looked down at the brunch menu. "Do you know what you're having? What looks good?"

"I think *I do*," Charlie said, his voice throaty. He leaned forward and winked.

"Okay, okay, I get it, Mr. Subtle," Dave answered. "How about we order before we make plans for the rest of the day?"

"Sex will relax you," Charlie coaxed.

"Don't feel like it," Dave said. "Not when I'm upset."

Charlie placed his menu on the table. "A little backrub and you'll be fine."

But Dave was not to be persuaded. "It's best to leave me alone when I'm in a mood."

Charlie said nothing.

"Did you hear me?" Dave asked.

"Okay … okay … I hear you," Charlie acknowledged. "Just trying to help."

A tow truck passed by. A red Honda Fit was hoisted high in the air, the passenger side punched in. Charlie nodded in the truck's direction. "Check that out. Someone's really having a bad day." Dave turned to see the damaged vehicle. "See … we have everything going for us," Charlie continued. "You've got a new job. We're healthy. The weather is terrific. We're so lucky."

Dave nodded, hesitantly.

"We have a great life," Charlie continued.

Dave had to agree.

"You should be more mindful of that," Charlie counseled. "And appreciative, instead of getting yourself all worked up and stressed out. A wrecked car … that's a problem."

Dave's appetite improved. "Okay, I'm going to get the Greek salad with chicken," he said, more positively. "That sounds good. And an order of hummus. We can split it."

"Okay." Charlie brightened. He waited for Dave to put his menu down before signaling for the waitress.

"And maybe I'll have a Diet Coke," Dave added.

"How about just water?" Charlie suggested. "We're in the desert. You should be drinking plenty of water," he said, knowing from experience that carbonation and sex didn't mix.

"Okay," Dave acquiesced.

Charlie assumed a Cheshire smile as the waitress approached. *Putty in my hands*, he thought. *He's just putty in my hands.*

2

....

When Daisy awoke, she had no idea whether it was day or night. A bright white curtain created a makeshift space that separated her from the rest of the world. Beside her, an electronic monitor seemed to repeatedly hum, *hello there hello there hello there.*

She felt small, fragile, and very alone.

She inhaled and exhaled in a series of slow, deep breaths. She'd learned in yoga about the importance of the breath to ease anxiety, but now, she was unable to achieve any sense of calm. She was too scared about what might happen next.

Tears came to her eyes as her mind drifted back to the day when she'd begun her journey to this place in the desert.

It was August 12, 1952.

She was eighteen years old, standing on the platform at Grand Central Station in an inexpensive blue traveling suit and matching navy beret, white gloves, and holding a straw purse, all purchased from Gimbel's bargain basement. She'd wanted to go to California but could barely afford the fare to Phoenix. With both parents long gone, she was on her own. Still, it had been a heart-wrenching decision to leave New York City. She adored her older brother Jacob, but her sister-in-law Rose had made it clear that Daisy had to leave.

How different my life would have been if I hadn't . . .

The thought stopped midstream. Buried pain was best left in the past. And yet she couldn't resist a final memory. The beautiful eyes searching her face; tiny hands peeking out from a blue blanket; the smell of talcum powder on his warm, little body.

She held her breath as she remembered.

When Daisy arrived in Phoenix, America was in the midst of a post-war industrial boom. Jobs were plentiful. Phoenix was a sleepy town of mostly one-story buildings. Outside the city perimeter, it was still cowboy country—sunburned men with hats and chaps, horses, corrals, and trails across the desert. Daisy landed her first job as a barmaid at the San Carlos Hotel. For most women of her generation, marriage came before work, and yet marriage eluded her. Men came and went, none staying too long. Daisy adjusted. She bore her disappointments quietly. Life taught her that nothing was guaranteed. If she wanted to survive, she'd have to learn to take care of herself. She'd have to be strong. It had been a hard lesson.

A nurse appeared from behind the curtain.

"Ms. Lee, we're just about ready. How are you doing?"

Daisy was too upset to answer and tried, instead, to smile. The young woman stroked Daisy's arm as she checked the IV, then slipped a pair of socks on her feet. The pain from her hip was gone. The nurse pushed aside the curtain and maneuvered the gurney down a short hallway and into a room with a bright white light. A drug was administered as she was instructed to count backward from ten. Somewhere between nine and eight Daisy found a peaceful freedom from thought ... a total immersion into the unconscious.

* * *

Dave stifled a yawn. He'd arrived at 7:30 a.m. for his first day on the new job. After grabbing a glazed donut and a cup of coffee, he found an aisle seat in the crowded auditorium where new hires from across the regional market were going through a communal orientation. At the front of the room, there was a large screen. Projected in large white letters against a dark-blue background ... *The Mission of Bremer Health*. On the stage, a young woman in her late twenties, a manager in human resources, repeatedly checked her watch as Dave took the first bite of his donut. *Dear God,* he thought, savoring the sugary goodness. *When was the last time I had a donut?* He licked his lips and sipped the coffee; the combination, pure pleasure.

As the other new hires settled into their seats, Dave spotted Phyllis, his boss's secretary, entering the front of the auditorium through a side door marked *Exit.* It had been weeks since they'd last seen each other at his final interview. She scanned the auditorium, eyeglasses perched atop her luxurious blond mane, wearing a blue knit dress that seemed a bit too tight for her curvaceous figure. Phyllis appeared stressed as she looked about. Dave wondered what could possibly be wrong. He stifled a second yawn as Phyllis slipped on her eyeglasses, squinted, and then nodded in his direction. She hurried over. "Mr. Greenway?" she asked, kneeling next to his chair.

"Yes," he answered, suddenly aware she wasn't quite sure. Up close, he could see the dark circles gathered under her lovely eyes. He guessed she was in her late thirties.

"I'm so sorry," she said, "but it's been crazy around here. I just processed four job offers last week for new executives. I'm having trouble keeping the names and faces straight."

Dave smiled. That seemed like a lot of new positions. He hoped Bremer was expanding. More jobs, more opportunity.

"Mr. Allman wants you to join the executive team meeting," she said. "You'd better bring your things along. These meetings can run long."

Dave grabbed his briefcase and followed Phyllis out of the auditorium, struggling to keep up as she rushed down the hallway toward the executive boardroom.

"Every Monday morning the executive team meets," she called back to him, miraculously balancing the shifting weight of her ample backside on a pair of six-inch black heels. "The meeting will always be on your calendar for 8:00 a.m. and Mr. Allman expects everyone to be prompt." She touched the knob to the boardroom and then stepped back, nodding to Dave to open the door and go inside.

All eyes turned as Dave entered. He was motioned to a chair at the end of a large conference table. Daniel Allman, Chief Operating Officer of Bremer Health, sat at the head. Daniel made the brief introduction. "Ladies and Gentleman, this is Dave Greenway, our newest vice president."

Heads bobbed and turned. Dave recognized a few of the faces from the organizational chart which had arrived with his relocation packet. The seats at the conference table were filled by hospital CEOs and their medical and nursing leadership. Lesser executives, directors and managers, sat in chairs scattered about the room. Dave had never seen so much high-priced talent gathered in one place for a weekly meeting. He'd researched the market and knew many of the executives had journeyed for hours to be in attendance.

Daniel returned the group's focus to the agenda. As Daniel spoke about financial targets, Dave remembered the first time they'd met. He'd been impressed by Daniel's sheer size. He stood six foot four with the build of a retired basketball player who had filled out after a few years off the court. His huge mitts clasped Dave's hand with an energy that had caught Dave totally off guard.

"I'll be frank," Daniel had said, "I need your expertise to help run this place. Sometimes, I think I'm surrounded by idiots. Right now the corporate office is all over my tail. But I don't give a rat's ass about them. Only the Chairman of the Board has the power to hire and fire me. The corporate office is just so much background noise."

Dave had been charmed by Daniel. He appreciated his honesty. He appreciated his informal manner. But now, Dave wondered how Daniel ran his empire, as he refocused back on the meeting.

"I'm going to ask again," Daniel said, glancing about the room, "who shared this month's financials with the corporate office?"

The tension in the room was palpable as Dave coyly looked about, trying to put faces together with the photos and bios he'd been given. He'd have to know the players if he expected to hit the floor running.

Craig De Coy was the first to speak.

Dave recognized Craig from his brush cut. He was a first-time CEO who had held lesser positions in small, rural, community hospitals.

Craig leaned forward, breaking the line of straight-backed executives who had turned to face Daniel. "Corporate tells us to send the information directly to them. What else can we do?"

"You call me," Daniel said sharply. "I've told you that I'll handle all communications with corporate."

"But they leave us no option," Craig insisted. "They expect immediate turnaround."

"That's ridiculous," Daniel said, his voice booming. "How many times are we going to have this conversation? How many times do I have to repeat myself?"

Daniel looked about as if he actually expected someone to answer the question. There was total silence.

He continued. "If the people in this room are unable to put off corporate, maybe you shouldn't be in the C-suite."

"That's not fair," Craig responded, his face bright red, sounding like a third-grader objecting to a homework assignment.

Daniel scanned the room. His dark eyes defying anyone to speak. "Who else doesn't think it's fair?"

Barely a breath was taken.

"It appears you're alone in that opinion, Craig. Perhaps if you ran your operation as well as you answer to corporate, you'd have hit your budget targets this month."

Craig clenched his jaw. The muscles in his cheeks visibly flexed. Dave wondered how long Craig planned to stay in his job. His future with the company seemed bleak.

Daniel's tone shifted. "How do you think I feel when corporate asks me to explain financials I haven't yet seen? All they want to do is catch me off-guard. Make me sweat." He was now playing the martyr. "Those people don't know how to run a business. They're bean counters. I'm the one holding this ship together. So remember, the next time the corporate office calls, it's the regional office that pays your salary. You do what I tell you," he insisted. "I hired you, and by God, I'll fire you! Is everybody clear on that?"

Dave couldn't believe his ears. Is this how the company conducted its meetings? Like an over-the-top Telemundo drama?

Daniel next held up a packet of handouts. Colored pie charts graphed each hospital's performance according to Medicare's quality standards. Green indicated success; yellow, the need for improvement. Nearly every page was dominated by red.

Daniel focused on Craig. "Your hospital's performance is especially dismal," he bristled.

Craig glanced at his chief nursing officer. A middle-aged, attractive brunette, nervously recounted the steps that the hospital was taking to turn the subpar performance. Dave watched Daniel's face as he listened to the woman. It was quiet, impassive. After three minutes had passed, Daniel suddenly pounded the conference table with a closed fist. The force was so great, that the modem at the center leapt from its position. "Bullshit," Daniel shouted. "This is all bullshit."

The poor woman sat slack-jawed, unable to continue.

Daniel stood up. He held the offending data above his head and glared about the room, like an angry giant reaching for the heavens. "I've had it with these excuses, people. Get ready to change jobs because I won't tolerate this kind of performance."

Executives shifted nervously in their chairs as Daniel headed to the door. Before leaving, he slammed the offending packet into the waste can with such force, that it crashed loudly onto its side and rolled over. The sound, a veritable bomb going off, reverberated throughout the room.

After Daniel's exit, the people in the room gathered up their belongings. Empty pads slid into cases, and unused pens dropped into satchels. One-by-one they rose. Defeated children.

Dave's heart sank. *Bullying to achieve results. What have I done? This isn't the work environment I signed up for.*

"Buck up," Charlie said later that evening. "It was probably a once-in-a-blue-moon meeting. Executives don't behave like that."

"I don't know," Dave said. "There was so much negative energy."

"Dave, you're exaggerating."

"I wish I was. I just hope he doesn't go off on me."

"He won't," Charlie insisted. "You're the fair-haired child. He paid a lot of money to recruit you."

"Something tells me he takes no prisoners," Dave worried. "This guy doesn't play well with others."

⚔ ⚔ ⚔

While Daisy's surgeon described the operation as a success, she wasn't quite so sure. The total hip replacement had left her in severe pain, and for the first time in Daisy's life, she welcomed medication. Lots of medication. So much medication, she lost the ability to stay in the moment. One day blended into the next. People came in and out of her hospital room. If strangers introduced themselves, Daisy was too groggy to remember who they were or why they were there.

The nurses insisted Daisy get up and walk. That was the first rule following surgery. She tried. But despite the objections of the nursing staff, the pain from the incision and the dizziness from all the medication forced her back to bed. She wanted to rest. She had to rest.

But resting in a hospital is impossible.

Daisy lingered the maximum number of days allowed by Medicare before a young woman in a white coat visited. She told Daisy arrangements had been made to transfer her to a rehabilitation facility. Daisy couldn't remember the details of the conversation, how the decision was made, or who actually made it, but there was no turning back. The young woman toting the documents had made that very clear. They needed to free up the bed.

Luis, a nurse's aide, showed up the next morning.

A large Hispanic man with a sweet disposition, Luis helped Daisy to sit up. "Pardon me," he said, slipping his huge hands under Daisy's armpits, before pulling her close. She could smell his Paco Rabanne. He gently lifted her, and in one smooth motion, shifted her into the wheelchair he'd placed bedside.

The soreness in her hip was a potent clarifier of the day's activities.

It effectively cut through the confusion of the pain medication. She was once again alert to her surroundings.

Luis glided the wheelchair down the hallway, past the nurse's station, to the elevators flanked by floor-to-ceiling mirrors. Daisy couldn't imagine why anyone would install mirrors in a hospital. She caught sight of her reflection. She flinched. She had no makeup on. Her bouffant hairdo looked like a deflated balloon. She'd planned to have her ash-blond color touched up before the accident, but had missed the appointment. Dark grey roots created a two-tone effect.

I look like a psychiatric patient who just had electroshock therapy, she thought sadly.

The elevator doors opened. It was midday and the car was crowded. Strangers stared at her. She took a deep breath and resigned herself to the situation. She didn't look her best and there was absolutely nothing she could do about it. She was at the mercy of her left hip.

A young man with shaggy brown hair wearing a *Jesus Loves Me* tee shirt smiled politely and stepped to the side of the elevator. Luis turned the wheelchair around and pulled Daisy in backward. There was just enough room.

Daisy faced the front of the car. In the reflection of the metallic doors, she could see a girl of six or seven standing nearby, cradling a stuffed floppy-eared white bunny in her arms, sneaking furtive glances at a bald spot on the side of Daisy's head. The child's eyes searched Daisy's crown like an explorer traveling through uncharted waters. Daisy closed her eyes to block the little girl out.

When the elevator doors opened onto the lobby, a stiff breeze blew up from the shaft. The gust caught Daisy by surprise. She struggled to keep the front of the flimsy green hospital gown closed but her fingers were like hardened rubber. The two tiny strings, barely knotted in a bow, unraveled. As the wheelchair advanced, the gown slipped hopelessly out of Daisy's grasp and caught in the mechanism of the wheel. Kindly strangers turned away. Others stared as she fumbled and tugged on the trapped gown, bare breasts exposed.

Daisy blushed crimson.

Luis pulled the chair backward in an effort to release the gown as he reached over Daisy's head to stop the elevator door from bouncing back and forth against the wheelchair. The first bounce had created a high-pitched beeping which had alerted security. Daisy was soon surrounded by uniformed guards.

Luis successfully freed the gown, but the damage had been done. The child who stood at Daisy's side had witnessed the entire debacle. The mother tugged roughly on the little girl's hand before she finally left the elevator.

What had taken less than three minutes to unfold felt as if it had happened in slow motion.

Daisy boldly returned the gaze of those in the lobby who'd been too shocked to look away. She nodded politely, as if it had all been planned. She pretended she was enjoying a ride in an Audi convertible on a warm Phoenix day. And though nothing could have been further from the truth, for that moment, Daisy shifted reality.

"Daisy Ellen Lee?" asked the driver, an African-American man whose bent posture and graying hair hinted he was well past retirement age. He took the paperwork from Luis and quickly compared it to his own documents. "Yup, that's you," the man answered with a warm smile. "You just sit tight and relax."

The wheelchair was rolled onto the van's electronic hoist. In moments, Daisy was lifted like so much cargo. "There you go," the driver said, unlocking the safety and pushing the wheelchair into place, his brown eyes projecting pure kindness and consideration. With a quick snap, he locked the chair. "Now that wasn't so bad."

The hospital disappeared in the distance. Daisy thought, *Thank God, I'll never see those people again* as she tightened her grip on the hospital gown, reliving the experience.

"I'll have you at The Village in no time," the driver called back.

Along the interior walls of the van were large glossy photographs of active seniors. A fashionably dressed woman, silver hair cut in a short perky bob, gaily held a glass of red wine, smiling as if ready to make a toast; a handsome gentleman in a bright green Tommy Hilfiger golf shirt and white shorts was on the greens, club in hand, preparing to putt; an older woman emerged from a hot tub, cap adorned in brightly colored flowers, her smile beaming. The Village promised to offer more than rehabilitation. It professed to be a lifestyle community.

Daisy thought, *The Village… now that's a lovely name.*

* * *

Jack Lee broke into a big grin as his 2007 white Ford Escape passed Anthem on Interstate 17 heading south. He'd spotted the olive green marker. *Phoenix—33 miles.* They'd traveled three days, stopping overnight in St. Louis and Amarillo, some two thousand miles across country from Detroit. Enid, his wife, fast asleep in the passenger seat, was gently snoring. She'd drifted off somewhere south of Flagstaff, leaving Jack alone to thrill at the majesty of the red rocks of Sedona.

Growing up in New York, Jack had often heard about Arizona from his father Jacob who had boasted of having a sister, an aunt Jack had never met, who'd settled in the Phoenix area. Cowboys. Desert. Wide open spaces. Jack fondly remembered his father expressing an interest in visiting, though he never did get west of the Mississippi. Together, they watched *Wagon Train, Bonanza,* and *Have Gun—Will Travel.* Jack could never seem to get enough of the Westerns. And then, in 1985, Jack made his first trip to Phoenix to attend a conference at the Arizona Biltmore. The memory of the beautiful property and the surrounding homes had stayed with him. *I'm going to live here someday,* he thought.

It was a promise he'd been determined to keep.

"Hey, sleepyhead," he said, gently nudging his wife's shoulder, "you've got to see this. The scenery is amazing."

Enid, a petite woman of delicate features, who wore her dark auburn hair in a severe mannish cut, opened her eyes. "My God, it's so bright," she said, shielding her face with her hand. "Someone dim the lights."

"You're just tired. It's been a long trip. But I promise, you're going to love it."

"You didn't tell me you could go blind from the sun." She pulled down the car visor.

"We'll get you a pair of dark shades. Heck, we'll be like movie stars and tint the car windows. *'Who's that?' everyone will ask. 'Enid and Jack Lee. They're new here.'*"

Enid shifted in her seat. "Are you being funny, Jack?" she said with a withering glance.

"Come on. This is the beginning of a new life. Arizona. Yee ha!"

"Jack," she admonished him, checking her hair in the visor mirror, "you're acting like John Wayne is going to show up atop a stagecoach with guns blazing. Phoenix is a sophisticated city. Last night when you drifted off, I read *Fodor's*. The days of the Wild West are over," she announced with certainty.

"Ah, but nature is everywhere. Just look around. You can see it in the cacti and the desert landscapes. So beautiful. This is a dream come true for me." His voice was barely able to contain his excitement.

Enid sighed. "I don't know why I let you talk me into this. Why not Florida? What was wrong with Boca Raton? I have family there."

"Enid, this is an adventure." Jack sidestepped the perilous trap of commenting on Enid's family. "We can still vacation in Boca."

Enid nodded, seemingly appeased.

Jack caught sight of an eagle soaring overhead. His heart skipped a beat. *Besides*, he thought about Florida, *if I wanted to live in a damp swamp, I'd have moved to the bayous of Louisiana.*

* * *

Jack Lee couldn't wait to get out of Michigan. After thirty years teaching high school history in Detroit, he was terrified that his pension might be affected by the trials and tribulations of Michigan's financial woes. The auto industry was on its knees, with the city of Detroit struggling to find bottom. Sick of listening to the daily drumbeat of financial mismanagement, he and Enid had agreed to sell their historic Indian Village home after the fourth break-in in two years. Each time, they'd been lucky. Neither of them had been home. The following week Jack was on a plane to Phoenix where he made an offer on a two-bedroom townhouse in The Biltmore Terraces; a great property with views of the golf course.

"It's so small, Jack," Enid complained when she reviewed the property online.

Jack was not about to be second-guessed. "We're awfully lucky to have picked up a Biltmore property at such a great price. And this is the time in life when we can do with a little less. Besides, that house perfectly fits our budget."

Another reason Jack had pressed for Arizona was its reasonable cost of living. Too young for social security, he'd seen the value of Enid's trust setup by her father, tumble. Over the years, it had generated enough income to keep Enid in the style she craved. But with the uncertainty of the times, and the bottoming of the stock market, the value of the portfolio was at an all-time low. They'd have to watch their spending.

"It won't be long now," Jack said as the car headed down Missouri Avenue toward 24th Street. "Look at those hedges."

A high wall of greenery enshrined the one-square-mile Biltmore property that included the hotel and surrounding property.

"Oh my God," Enid gasped, her mood suddenly brightening. "You didn't tell me it was so private and lush. It's as lovely as the Boca Raton Hotel and Country Club."

They crossed 24th Street and entered the Biltmore. Enid sat up straight and adjusted her blouse. Jack smiled as she checked her face in the mirror.

"Where's my lipstick?" She searched her bag. "Jack, you didn't tell me it was so exclusive. I should have worn something nicer."

Enid's eyes popped as the car crossed the 18-hole golf course before passing the many mansions that lined Thunderbird Drive. Jack was thrilled that she was so excited. *I knew she'd love it. She just needed to experience it.* A quick right, and the car stopped at the gate of the Biltmore Terraces.

"Hello," Jack said to the redhead who popped her head out of the window to greet him. "We're the Lees. We're new. You should be expecting us."

The woman checked the roster. "Lee, Lee. Oh yes. Here you are. Well, welcome. I'm Sheila. I'm filling in today, but anything you need, be sure to ask."

"So you're new too," Jack said exuberantly.

Enid nudged him with her elbow. It was her cue for him to stop talking to strangers.

"Not exactly," Sheila explained. "I work full-time at Biltmore Greens. I'm just helping out today." She handed Jack a manila envelope. "Inside is a parking pass and a decal for your window. Make sure you place the sticker on the inside driver's side. It allows you access to all the Biltmore neighborhoods."

"Thank you," Jack beamed. "Tell me, is it always this beautiful here?"

"Absolutely," Sheila smiled.

"This is just a dream come true. A dream come true," he said.

Enid's elbow poked him again.

"I know this is an odd question," Sheila suddenly asked, "but are you folks related to Daisy Ellen Lee?

Jack was astonished. "My father had a sister Daisy who moved to Phoenix. I was just thinking about her."

"There must be a million women named *Daisy* in the world," Enid offered. Her tone left no doubt that she was eager to get past the gate.

"But you did say Daisy Ellen?" Jack clarified with Sheila. "How many *Daisy Ellens* can there be?"

"A quarter of a million," Enid snapped. "At least as many as there are Jack Allen Lees."

"She's a lovely woman," Sheila went on. "Now my brother's daughter, my niece Alison, is the spitting image of me as a girl. Every time I look at her, it's like looking in a mirror. You know, Mr. Lee? The more I look at you, the more I think you and Ms. Lee are just like two peas in a pod. You have the same eyes. It's quite unnerving."

"I wonder if she's my aunt," Jack said to Enid, before turning back to Sheila. "Now that would be quite a coincidence. Tell me, which is Daisy's house? I'd love to meet her."

Sheila's expression shifted. "Oh, I'm sorry," she said, a worried look crossing her face. "Perhaps I shouldn't have said anything. I'm not allowed to provide personal information about the residents. But I'll tell you what. Why don't you give me a note with your name and phone number, and I'll make sure Ms. Lee gets it."

"Fine," Jack agreed. "Whatever works." He waited for Sheila to open the gate. "Imagine that," he said, turning to Enid, "I may have an aunt who lives in the Biltmore. A long-lost aunt. Who'd have guessed?"

* * *

Dear Ms. Lee,

My name is Jack. My wife and I have recently moved to Phoenix. I wonder if we are related. My parents were Jacob and Rose. They're gone now, but I remember my Dad telling me about a sister who lived in Phoenix. Is it possible you're my aunt? If so, we'd love to meet you. Please ask Sheila to share with us your phone number. Or, if you'd like to call us directly, I've enclosed my phone number on the back of this note with our address.

Fondly, Jack Lee

* * *

Later that day, Sheila visited Daisy at The Village. She offered a friendly hello to a gentleman sitting in the lobby before realizing he was babbling to himself. She averted her eyes as she passed the white-haired seniors, dressed in their bedclothes, who lined the hallways slumped over in their wheelchairs, fast asleep. The closer she got to the wing where Daisy was housed, the stronger the smell of urine.

She gagged.

Arriving at Daisy's closed door, she knocked. "Ms. Lee," she called out. "Ms. Lee, are you there?"

There was no response.

She knocked again, this time louder, cracking open the door and peeking inside. The room was dark. It was midafternoon and the Venetian blinds were tightly drawn.

Perhaps this is the wrong room, she thought, rechecking the name on the door. No, she was in the right place.

She entered, slowly approaching Daisy's bedside.

Daisy stirred. A weak voice pleaded, "Nurse, I need to go to the bathroom. Please help me."

"Ms. Lee, it's me, Sheila."

Daisy struggled to focus. "Sheila, where did you come from?"

"I've been concerned about you," Sheila said in a sudden pang of guilt. Why hadn't she made it her business to visit sooner? "How are you?" she asked, helping Daisy to sit up.

"Not well, I'm afraid. I've developed an infection and I have a fever."

Sheila's heart sank.

"They're giving me antibiotics."

"That sounds like the right course."

"I don't know." Daisy shook her head. "I'm so tired . . . and I have terrible cramps. What time is it?"

Sheila looked at the wall clock. "It's three."

"How long have I been here?" Daisy asked.

Sheila had no clue.

"How about we open these blinds?" she suggested, tugging on the little white cord. Light flooded the room. "There, that's better," she said, turning back to Daisy. "It's such a lovely day . . ." she began, as her breath caught in her throat. Seeing Daisy in the bright light, she struggled to suppress her shock. Daisy's face looked haggard. The gentle lines which had once graced her friendly eyes and mouth had deepened severely from sudden weight loss. Her skin was white and pasty, a far cry from Daisy's normal rosy complexion. Daisy was no longer the vital, energetic person Sheila knew. She'd become a withered old woman,

"I wish I felt better," Daisy said, adjusting herself in the bed. "But it is so good of you to visit. How kind."

Sheila leaned against the windowsill, unwilling to commit to a seat. The smell of disinfectant permeated the air. She maintained a pleasant, outward demeanor, all the while knowing that something horrible had happened.

"Bert sends his regards," she said in a chipper voice. "We both came to the hospital to visit but you were really out of it. I'm not sure you even knew we were there."

"I don't remember," Daisy confirmed. "Morphine is an amazing drug."

And then Daisy pulled back the top cover of her bedding. Her feet were blueish-red and swollen. Sheila diverted her eyes, fighting the urge to flee. Instead, she retrieved Jack's note from her purse.

"Well, you'll never guess who I met," she bravely said, holding up the note from Jack which after all had been the reason for her visit. "It was the strangest thing . . ." and as she started to tell the story, a young African-American woman sporting a close-cropped Afro appeared in the doorway.

"Honey," the aide called to Daisy, "have you been ringing for me?"

"Oh yes," Daisy answered, relief in her voice. "I have to go to the bathroom."

Sheila, grateful for the interruption, placed the unopened note on the bedside table. "Well, I better be going," she said, concerned her presence might cause Daisy embarrassment. "I need to get home," she lied, eager to escape. "I just wanted to be sure and bring this note."

Mission accomplished, Sheila was out of the room before the aide lowered the bars on Daisy's bed. She moved quickly down the hallway, past those who seemed frozen in time. *Is this what becomes of us?* Sheila thought, rushing to her car. *I'd rather die than wind up in a place like that.*

* * *

"I'm home," Dave called from the open door, his key still buried in the lock.

He was exasperated. He'd hoped to leave the office early, but cornered at five o'clock, he'd fidgeted his way through an impromptu meeting with Daniel that lasted nearly two hours.

Doesn't he have a wife and a home to go to?

He chalked it up to Daniel's endless need to micromanage.

Charlie stood in the galley kitchen, separated from the living room by an eat-in counter. A small dinette table was within steps. "The roast's in the oven, warming." Charlie came around the counter. "Let me give you a hand with that key. You have to jiggle it."

Dave and Charlie switched positions.

Dave dropped his workbag by the door and headed to the kitchen. "It smells good," he said, spotting the mail on the counter. He looked through the stack.

Charlie twisted and turned, eventually loosening Dave's key before dropping it on the counter. "Hey you," he said approaching Dave from behind. With his arms about Dave's waist, he pulled him in for a hug.

Dave turned, and they kissed. He relaxed into it. It felt damn good. "Sorry about being so late," he apologized. "It's impossible to get out of that building at a reasonable hour. I think this might be the way of life at Bremer."

"I'm just glad you're here. Time to relax."

Dave loosened his tie as Charlie pulled out the roast and placed it on top of the stove.

"So how'd it go today? Any better?" Charlie asked, lifting the roast out of the pan with a large fork to settle it on the carving board.

"Any better than what? The same people, the same meetings, the same Daniel. He has all these questions about the financial performance of the business, which is surprising considering he signed all these terrible contracts. Every lousy deal has his fingerprints on it. And he's so damn angry. He's just a very hostile guy."

Dave spotted an oversized card in the middle of the stack of mail. He opened it. A photograph of two Golden Labs, eyes bright, tongues dangling, smiling the way only Golden Labs seemed to do, stared back at him.

"Well, I have a surprise for you." Charlie pointed at the dining room table, carving knife in hand.

There, sitting on Dave's plate, was a box wrapped with a red bow.

"Oh no," Dave moaned, realizing the card he held had been sent by friends in California. "It's our anniversary..."

Charlie smiled. "You make it sound like a terrible thing."

"But I didn't get you anything," Dave said mournfully. "All those early morning meetings and late nights, I kept thinking, *I have to get Charlie a gift.* But I kept running out of time. And then I forgot."

Charlie leaned forward on the counter. "Don't worry about it. You'll take me to dinner this weekend. No big deal."

"Oh Charlie, that isn't right. I wanted you to have something special."

"I *do* have something special." Charlie wiped his hands with a dish towel before pulling Dave into his arms. "I have you. And now, I have Phoenix. Dave, I love it here. This is the best decision we've ever made."

Dave was sorry to hear Charlie say that.

Charlie returned to the galley kitchen. "I couldn't imagine us living anywhere else. I mean, can you believe this weather? In April? It's amazing."

Dave fingered the ribbon on the gift. "I've been thinking this move was a mistake," he said, his voice low, nearly imperceptible. Uncertain Charlie had heard him, he blurted out, "I really can't stand working at Bremer."

Charlie, his back turned to Dave, opened the refrigerator, though he seemed to hear every word. "You just need time to adjust. You'll see. We'll buy a great house, make new friends, and get a dog. We'll have a wonderful life."

"Charlie, I don't know." Dave was heartsick. It had been a long time since he and Charlie had been so far apart on an issue.

Charlie dressed the salad. "You've always been slow to adjust to change. Every new job has been a crisis. Given time, things will smooth over. You'll see. It'll all work out. It's just bumpy in the beginning."

Dave sighed. "I wish I was as optimistic as you."

"Well, you never *have* been," Charlie said. "That word isn't in your vocabulary. You're a worrier."

"But this time it's different," Dave confessed, a hand resting on what remained of the unopened mail, eyes pleading for Charlie to understand. "This is really bad."

"You're upset," Charlie acknowledged. "You've had a hard day. Why don't you go ahead and open your gift."

Dave tore at the paper. *How*, he thought, *can I possibly make Charlie understand?*

The gift was a box of See's Chocolates. Mixed Nuts and Chews. Dave's favorite.

"Well, open the card," Charlie demanded.

Dave opened the envelope. Two tickets to Tennessee Williams's *The Glass Menagerie* at Arizona Theatre Company slid out. "That's nice," Dave said quietly, his words more polite than heartfelt. Upset, he needed to be alone. "I think I'll change before dinner."

Charlie, oblivious to Dave's mood, trailed after him to the bedroom, talking about the small events of the day. The neighbor he'd met in the supermarket. The noise the kids made after school as they played in the pool, screeching with delight. The dog he'd seen from the small terrace off the kitchen as it walked by with its owner in tow. And then, about the afternoon activities househunting.

"Ronaldo and I checked out a few more houses," Charlie said, as Dave dropped his tie on the bed.

"What'd you think?"

"Honestly, not much."

"Why?" Dave asked, removing his white dress shirt and handing it to Charlie, who in turn, stuffed it into a blue, dry-cleaners bag.

"I didn't really like the neighborhood."

"Then why look there?" Dave wondered. "Just tell Ronaldo the neighborhoods you're interested in." Dave stepped over to the en-suite sink in his briefs and washed his face.

Charlie picked up Dave's slacks, folded them, and slipped them onto a wooden hanger. He hung up the tie on the metal rack inside the closet. He placed the black Cole Haan loafers on the appropriate shelf. "Well, that's the problem," he said, emerging from the closet. "I really don't know the neighborhoods. So, we've been checking out North Central and a lot of houses closer to your office. I know you're concerned about the drive."

"The traffic can be tough," Dave admitted, drying his face with a towel, "but I don't want to live too close to the office. I already spend too much time there."

"Physically and mentally," Charlie added.

"So nothing yet?" Dave stepped into a pair of grey Nike shorts.

"Oh, I've seen nice houses, but they aren't for us."

"Too bad," Dave said, slipping on a dark blue tee shirt sporting the logo of the San Francisco Police Department.

"I thought you were afraid to wear that thing." Charlie had bought the tee shirt at a fundraiser during a Bay Area street fair.

"As long as we're staying in, it's okay. Remember when that woman ran up to me in the city and said she needed my help?" Dave smiled at the memory, suddenly longing to be back in the Bay Area.

"How could I forget?" Charlie let out a chuckle before returning to the subject at hand. "Maybe I'll have better luck tomorrow. We have appointments to see five houses in Scottsdale. We'll see how that goes."

＊ ＊ ＊

Delirious from a blood-borne infection, Daisy was admitted to an intensive care unit in the middle of the night. The nurse's aide who coordinated the transfer spotted the note lying on Daisy's bedside table. Glancing at the contents, she handed it to the lead EMT. "Mac, this might come in handy." Mac, a stocky guy sporting a crewcut who had played defensive end in high school, shoved the note in his pocket.

That morning at Denny's, after finishing breakfast, Mac pulled the note out when he reached for his wallet to settle the check. "Crap," he said, reading the note. "I've got to get this back to that old lady." But with his shift over, he had no desire to return to the hospital. Instead, he opted to do the next best thing. He pulled out his cell phone.

"Hello, is this Jack Lee?" Mac asked.

"Speaking."

"I'm afraid I have some bad news for you."

* * *

"Oh my God," Jack said, hanging up the phone. He'd been outside planting miniature cacti when his cell phone rang. "She's in the hospital," he told Enid who was stretched out on a lounge chair sipping lemonade.

"Who?" Enid asked, sitting up with alarm. She wore a white outfit; white top and white shorts; a large straw gardening hat rested in her lap.

"Daisy," Jack answered. He examined her face for any sense of recognition. "The woman we thought might be my aunt."

"Oh," Enid said, seemingly relieved, "is that all." She relaxed back into the lounger. Though she'd told Jack she'd help with the planting, after opening the first bag of fertilizer, the smell had put her off.

"She's ill," Jack said, his voice tinged with annoyance. "Here we have a chance to get to know her, and now it gets complicated."

But Enid still didn't seem to care. "That's too bad Jack," she said, checking her manicure. "Jack, we really should have hired someone to do the gardening. It's such a messy job."

Jack wiped the sweat from his forehead. He hated when Enid changed the subject in mid-discussion. Irritated, he ignored her behavior. "Do you think we should go visit her?"

Enid offered a perplexed look. "I don't see why. We don't know her. This seems to be a private matter. What does she have to do with us?"

Jack arched a brow. "I don't know exactly, but if she's my father's sister, I should do something."

"Oh no." Enid waved her hands in the air. "We're not taking on the care of an old woman, someone we've never even met. Forget it."

"Then again, she might not be my aunt," Jack said, his face registering a modicum of relief. "That certainly is possible."

"That's right," Enid agreed. "She probably isn't."

"It would be too much of a coincidence, don't you think?" Jack caught sight of an eagle soaring in the distance. The graceful majesty of the bird reminded him of his Dad's love for everything Southwest. "No ... I'm going over to the hospital," he reconsidered. "I better just go."

Enid sneered. "And what do you think that'll prove?"

"I don't know," Jack said. "It just feels like the right thing to do."

Enid pressed her lips together. "Okay, but if you're going ... I'm going with you. Give me a few minutes to change my clothes. You're too soft-hearted for your own good, Jack Lee. Much too soft-hearted."

* * *

Daisy's eyes felt like hot coals. She'd tossed and turned, confused, uncertain where she was. She'd tried to remove the IV from her wrist when the ICU nurse entered the cubicle to check Daisy's vitals. Daisy struggled, certain the woman wearing a facemask had come to kill her. But by nine o'clock in the morning, her fever had broken. Exhausted, she napped on and off.

She was awakened by a gentle touch to her arm. A nurse hovered nearby. "Good afternoon, sweetie. Are you awake?" Her voice was like honey. "Do you remember me?"

Daisy smiled, hoping that was enough recognition.

"I need you to tell me your name and birth date, if you can."

"I'm Daisy Lee," she managed to get out. She then provided her birthdate.

"Good, very good." The nurse smiled and patted her shoulder. "I have a few more questions for you. There's a gentleman here who says he might be your nephew. Do you have a nephew?"

"I don't have any children," Daisy answered, shaking her head from side-to-side, eyes closed.

"No, dear," the nurse tried again. "A nephew. A man named Jack Allen Lee?"

Daisy drifted off.

The nurse touched her arm. Daisy opened her eyes. "Can you tell me the name of your brother?" she asked.

"Jacob," Daisy replied weakly. "Jacob. Is he here?" she asked somewhat confused, her eyes searching about.

"His son is," the nurse answered.

"Oh." Daisy nodded off again.

"Ms. Lee," the nurse gently called as she stroked Daisy's hair. "Do you know a Jack Allen Lee?"

Daisy's head cleared for a moment. "Yes," she nodded, eyes wide open.

"Is he your nephew?"

"Jack," she murmured. She smiled broadly.

The nurse adjusted Daisy's head on the pillow. "There you go, dear. Now you rest."

* * *

Jack took a seat in the cramped medical director's office. The desk was a mess. Freebies from pharmaceutical companies, blank pads and pens embossed with names like Merck and Pfizer were mixed in with scattered pink and yellow papers, and a variety of tiny mechanical windup cars and robots. A white coffee mug with red *We Love You Grandpa* lettering, still a quarter full with black coffee, rested on an open copy of the latest edition of the *New England Journal of Medicine*. Jack wondered how anyone could work in such surroundings. Enid had gone to the restroom. He glanced repeatedly out the open door to the hallway, hoping to catch a glimpse of her as she walked by.

Dr. Mueller, a balding man in his late sixties with fine white hair and a large bulbous nose, shifted a stack of medical records from his chair to the floor near his feet so that he might sit down. "Excuse the mess," he apologized. "I'm the chairman of the hospital's quality committee. I have to review these cases before our next meeting on Friday morning."

Jack nodded in sympathy as if he understood. "My wife should be here any moment," he said, shifting the conversation as he continued to look toward the door. "I'd prefer if we waited for her before we begin. I'm not very good with all of this."

Mueller looked at his watch. "Well, I don't have much time. If it's okay with you ..."

"Over here," Jack called, spotting Enid.

She stopped midstep. While Jack wore an old pair of jeans with a cotton shirt of bold, red and blue stripes, Enid had dressed for the occasion in a sophisticated olive green dress and white sandals, full makeup and gold jewelry.

Enid took a seat.

"We've spoken to your aunt," Mueller started.

Jack's tone revealed his excitement. "So we *are related*?"

"Ms. Lee confirmed her brother's name was indeed Jacob. And she did recognize your name."

"Really," Jack said enthusiastically. "Are there any other family members? Children?"

Mueller shook his head. "We have no next of kin."

"She never married?"

"We don't know her full history. We just know she's currently single." Mueller's face was stoic.

"When might we be able to talk with her?" Jack asked.

"Her condition is very serious. These superbugs are hard to knock out. She's barely holding her own, though I'm happy to say her fever has come down and she's no longer delirious. We should know more in a few days."

"Oh," was all that Jack could manage.

Mueller lifted the coffee mug, tilted it, looked inside, and then returned it to the desk. "You understand that you have no legal rights to make any healthcare decisions on her behalf."

"Of course not," Jack answered, surprised at the turn of the discussion. "We just wanted to know if she was indeed my aunt."

Afterward, as he and Enid waited for the elevator, Jack was deep in thought. Stepping into the elevator, he couldn't help but acknowledge the obvious, "It's really crazy. I never met my father's sister, and now I have the opportunity, but she may not survive. It's the damnedest thing."

Enid, who'd been quiet and pensive, brightened. "You're probably her only living relative, Jack. If she dies, there could be an inheritance."

Jack was aghast. Leave it to Enid to be focused on money.

"Jack, you might inherit her estate. We could trade up to a bigger Biltmore property. A home in Taliverde. Those homes are one-of-a-kind." There was a gleam in Enid's eye. "This could be quite a windfall."

"Taliverde is well beyond our means," Jack countered, annoyed by Enid's suggestion. "The monthly association dues alone are more than we can afford."

"Daisy's house must be worth some money. I wonder how she had the means to settle in the Biltmore. She must have a sizeable nest egg."

"Enid, I don't think we should be counting her money. After all, we're strangers. For all I know she's living on Social Security."

"Jack, that's ridiculous. No one in the Biltmore is living on Social Security."

"You don't think so?"

"Tomorrow, I'm going to find a lawyer who can advise us."

"I'm not comfortable with this," Jack admitted as they walked through the hospital lobby. "I feel like a vulture."

"Someone has to help her," Enid argued. "She's all alone. She may need us to make medical decisions. We might need a power of attorney. We have a lot to do."

"It's all happening too fast," Jack said, as they crossed the parking lot toward their car.

"And tomorrow, we're going to ask Sheila for the key to Daisy's house. I want to see her place."

"She's not going to give us the key," Jack insisted.

"Oh yes she will," Enid assured him. "You just leave that discussion to me. I'll get those keys and we'll see that house. Mark my words."

Jack had no doubt. Enid could be a dog with a bone, especially when money was involved. As Jack backed out of the spot, his cell phone rang. He fumbled for it in his pocket. "Yes," he said, listening carefully to the other party on the line. "Okay, we're coming back."

"Who was that?" Enid asked.

"The hospital. She's gone into convulsions."

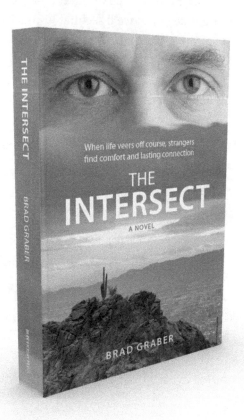

The Intersect is available in paperback or e-book on Amazon.com and through all fine retailers.